SHADOW CITY

THE SHADOW HOUSE CHRONICLES, BOOK 2

A. R. SILVERBERRY

TREE TUNNEL PRESS

SHADOW CITY, © 2025 by Peter Allan Adler, writing as A. R. Silverberry. All rights reserved. Printed in the United States of America. No part of this book may be used or reproduced in any manner whatsoever, or stored in a retrieval system, or transmitted in any form or by any means, electronic, mechanical, photocopying, or otherwise, without written permission from the publisher, except in the case of brief quotations embodied in critical articles and reviews. For additional information or permissions, contact Tree Tunnel Press, P.O. Box 733, Capitola, CA 95010

Cover Design © 2025 Jamie Noble Frier

Print Edition ISBN - 13: 978-1-7375173-4-4

 Formatted with Vellum

CONTENTS

ONE

Diary of the Damned ...

I'm writing this with charred sticks. My mind's not often clear. When it is, I'll try to scrawl a few notes on this battered notebook I found.

I'm lost.

The start ...

My friends faded. I'll never forget the look on their faces. Maybe they won't forget mine either. How often do you see your friend get her guts sucked out?

I didn't understand what was happening to me. I still don't. I wish it were a nightmare. Then I would wake up.

My mouth moved, my lips forming words. No sound came out. I was on the brink. I knew it was over. I would fade. And my short pathetic life would end with a pop, the last bubble before soda goes flat.

That's not what happened. It would've been better if it had, or so it seemed, and would continue to seem for a long time. As my friends grew faint, the room with them, another place faded in, like the dissolve to a new scene in a holo-vid. I found myself standing on a block of concrete. I quickly took on solid form. As soon as I did, I lost my balance. The block was jutting out at an acute angle.

I squatted, clawed the edge to keep from falling, then scrambled down and looked around. The sky was a flat gray and overcast. Smoke hung in low patches and assaulted my lungs. Great, I'd been sent to my own personal hell. I could plan on wheezing and hacking from now to eternity.

Were my sins so terrible that I deserved this? I couldn't help but do a quick review of the highlights. Okay, I slept with a few boys. No big deal. Lots of girls did. AND MADE IT OUT OF THE FRICKIN' HOUSE. So that wasn't it. I sassed my father. I pestered my brother. I cheated on an algebra final.

No offense to the cosmic Tally Keeper, but none of that deserves this. So yeah, I was completely unrepentant. Not much motivation to change my tune with the situation before me. It's not like St. Peter came down and offered me one more chance to be good. Believe me, if he had, I would have bent his ear. This was a raw deal, no matter which way you looked at it.

How bad soon became apparent. But first, I took in the rest of my surroundings. Fallen buildings stretched as far as I could see. The entire city seemed to have been leveled by a bomb. All was rubble, jagged, barren. Not another soul was seen anywhere. I was consumed with emptiness and loneliness unlike any I'd known, and believe me, I endured plenty in my family. If it hadn't been for a friend or two, I would've either gone mad or checked out long ago.

One look at this city and the thought of ending it all wasn't far from my mind.

There were other matters to attend to first. Sad to say, the first thing to cross my mind was what I would eat. A diet of mortar and ash won't take you far. I climbed off what appeared to be the remains of a wall and stepped onto a street littered with scree. Part of me wanted to call out, "Hello, anyone home?" But aside from the desolate silence that hung over the place, which suggested that I might *be* the sole occupant of this corner of hell, it didn't seem prudent to announce my arrival until I'd checked it out.

I wandered from street to street, peering into the skeletal remains of buildings. I found nothing of use, no clothes, no shoes, no blankets. No food or water. Nothing grew. You don't know how much you miss green until you're in a world without a single plant.

I was half an inch from collapsing to the ground and crying, but I told myself, *Get up, girl. No sense whining. You're not dead yet. But you will be if you don't find something to eat.*

My stomach started rumbling, confirming I wasn't dead. Unless endless starvation was part of my punishment in the afterlife. I heard that was one definition of hell. Piles of food. No way of eating it. *Send me there,* I thought. At least I can look at it. I can hope. I can try to find a way to get some of it in me. Kick over the table. Crawl on my hands and knees and eat it off the floor. Desperate times, desperate measures, right?

So I kept exploring, stopping every once in a while in dread when a handful of explosions rattled the city. They sounded like they came from underground. Most of them were far away, but not so far that they didn't rain down showers of dust from the surrounding ruins. One blast was so close it sent me ducking for cover—or I would've been buried—and it sent up smoke from somewhere nearby. Not a lot of it, not much more than already hung over the place, permeating everything, including my clothes. Enough to get me coughing.

That's when shit hit the proverbial fan. A stampede of feet came toward me, muffled at first, then louder. Don't ask me how I knew, but it didn't sound friendly. Perhaps it was the grunts and howls that accompanied it. Whatever it was, it didn't sound particularly human.

I dashed to a tumble of blocks on one side of the street and crawled beneath them. From my hiding place, I saw them rush like a wave down the street. Almost as a group, they loosed an inhuman cry of lust, hunger, and rage.

Problem was, they were human. Or at least what remained of them was. They ran on two legs. Their clothing was tattered, as if they'd been shipwrecked on a desert island for a decade. They wielded rakes, shovels, pitchforks, clubs, sticks, doorknobs, seemingly anything they could use as weapons. But it was their eyes that got to me. Red and fierce as a mad dog's.

Halfway up the street, they stopped cold. The one in the lead, a big fellow with long grizzled hair and beard, tipped his head to one side, listening. Turning in my direction, he sniffed. His eyes flared. His tongue protruded from his mouth, preternaturally long and dripping foam.

It seemed impossible that he could smell me. Men aren't dogs. Not where I grew up. Maybe they were here. I held my breath, fighting the urge to cough.

He took a step toward me. As if on cue, the rest of the mob turned too, following his lead, sniffing, their eyes crimson saucers. They were looking in my direction, but not exactly where I was. Yet. They approached, surveying the wreckage above and to both sides of me.

I didn't know what they would do if they found me, but

as they say, the natives didn't seem friendly. I guessed that the offer of a spare bed and a hot meal wasn't in their plans. Well, maybe the hot meal was, only I had the dreadful feeling I was the main course. Maybe it was their half-starved bodies that tipped me off. From the look of things, they might not bother cooking me.

That tickle in my throat had grown past annoying. It was singing to me, crooning like a lover to be scratched. My mouth was dry, but I built up a mouth of spit and swallowed, hoping it would coat my throat. And then it just burst out of me. I hacked two, three times.

Maybe there is a god somewhere. At that moment, two things happened. First, one of the underground explosions shook the ground. This one was pretty near and fairly loud.

Second, a man appeared at the end of the street. He stood on a fallen slab of concrete, much as I had when I got here. He started to lose his balance, but he righted himself with the grace of a gymnast. Even in that desperate situation, I paused to admire his frame, which was packed with muscle, lean and hard. He was turned away from me, but I would know that body anywhere. I'd spent countless classes contemplating—dreaming—okay, drooling over it from several seats behind throughout high school. It had to be him, and instead of being elated, I was filled with sadness.

If I was right, if that was him, it meant only one thing. The House had taken him too.

TWO

New Earth, 12:45 p.m. ...

The crowd spread across the plaza in a turbulent sea of protest signs. A few had surged up the front steps of Grafton's courthouse, where they were tossed to the fringes. Reporters and news cameras, staking out territory near the entrance, had been there before sunrise. They would not be denied the biggest story to hit New Earth in decades. Maybe ever.

Everyone focused on the white sedan parked before the steps. Johari Hightower, the occupant at the rear passenger window, wished he could slip from the car, melt into the crowd, and hightail it to a deserted alley, not to evade the trial—the trial would be a relief, had been looming over him for two weeks—but to stay anonymous, out of view. His natural place was in the shadows.

Beside him, his attorney, Cody Gilbert, scrutinized the crowd. "We can enter the back way."

Johari shook his head. "I can't duck who I've become any more than I can duck my past."

Cody laid a freckled hand on his shoulder. "Then let's secure your future."

Easy to say. Johari tore his eyes from the throng and searched Cody's freckled face for some sign of how he really thought this would go. Uncertainty flickered in his powder-blue eyes. Fair enough. That summed up Johari's best guess, too. His chances were about as good as a roll of the dice.

A lump pushed into his throat. He knew there were going to be protesters. But he never expected anything so huge. Living on the edges of society hadn't prepared him for the spotlight.

The protestors were staked out in two groups like opposing armies, waving placards and slogans. On one side, the signs said:

FREE JOHARI HIGHTOWER!
THE HOUSE REDEEMED HIM!
DROP ALL CHARGES!

On the other side, they said:

KEEP OUR CHILDREN SAFE!
NO MERCY FOR CONVICTED CRIMINALS
STAMP OUT EVIL

And more to the point:

BANISH HIM

Those against him outnumbered those for him. Johari suspected that many of the latter were friends of the few friends he had. The rest had gotten caught up in the drama and injustice of his plight.

A policeman opened the sedan door. A blast of heat rushed in, canceling the coolness of the car's air conditioner. The officer placed his hand on Johari's head, protecting it as Johari stepped from the car. Cameras clicked. Microphones thrust at his face. A dozen reporters crowded in, shouting questions.

"What are your chances today?"

"Will you beat Phillip March?"

"Did you cheat your way out?"

"They say you had a key? Any comment?"

"How has the House changed you?"

Clamor rose from the crowd. Both sides pressed in, trying to get a look at him—the man condemned to Banishment, the fugitive from justice. The man who'd defied the Supreme Council, entered the House, and survived.

The side opposing him began chanting. "Banish him! Banish him!"

His supporters countered with, "Justice for Johari. Free. Free. Free him now!"

Cody held his hand up to the reporters. "My client won't be answering questions until after the trial."

A reporter cried out, "Will you seek a pardon or argue for a reduced sentence?"

Hot wind blew across the square, scattering leaflets on the pavement. Cody wiped perspiration from his brow. "My client is innocent. We expect all charges to be dropped. If you'll excuse us, ladies and gentlemen, we have a trial to win."

Officers flanked Johari and began escorting him up the steps, Cody tailing them. The heavy doors of the federal courthouse loomed above.

On the pro-Banishment side, a woman's voice rose like a fire-and-brimstone minister's above the other protesters. "Allow not those with blackened hearts to walk among us, for they contain the seeds of doom." She waved aloft the *Little White Book of Sparra Givvens* and shook it, as if it contained holy water and she was conducting an exorcism. Her other hand clutched the tiny palm of a girl, no older than three, who stood frozen like a frightened doe, her thumb jammed desperately in her mouth. Why her mother had brought her was unfathomable.

Eyes burning zealously, the woman pointed the book at him. "Send him to hell!"

Others took up the cry. The crowd pressed in. Like a storm-filled dam, it broke past the police line and flooded the steps. The little girl was ripped from her mother's hand. She tumbled down two steps. The crowd surged, threatening to stampede over her. Johari tore away from the officers escorting him and leaped up the steps. He wrapped his arms around the girl, shielding her with his body.

"Oh my god," the mother screamed. "Stop him!"

"He's killing her!" a man shouted.

The crowd swirled around them. Johari tucked his chin and held the child tight. From his vantage point, he could see only the shoes and ankles of the mob, charging like spooked cattle. The little girl took her thumb from her mouth and clutched with both hands onto his collar. Blows rained down, knocking the wind from his lungs. They were beating him with protest signs and the wooden handles. Hot agony spread across his back, and then he was struck on the head, his muscles went loose, and the world spun in dizzy circles.

Cody was shouting, "Get them off him!"

A police officer bellowed through a bullhorn for the

crowd to step back. Johari was lifted by his armpits. He swayed on rubbery legs, woozy but still clutching the girl protectively. She was taken from his hands and given to the mother.

"You see what he did?" she cried. "He's an animal. *An animal!*"

The crowd roared, or perhaps the roaring was in his ears. The rest was a blur as he was jostled and carried up the steps. The only clear sensation was of something warm and salty trickling down the side of his face and into his mouth.

THREE

Johari's temple throbbed, but at 1:40 p.m. he walked into the courtroom with his head held high, grateful he wasn't shackled like he'd been in his first trial. This time, they'd injected trackers into his bloodstream. If he tried to escape, they would find him inside thirty minutes.

People were crammed into rows of benches. A single line could divide them—those behind the defense table supported Johari; those behind the prosecution wanted immediate Banishment. You could tell from the way each side looked at him. Eyes filled with sympathy. Eyes filled with malice.

Did Banishment mean execution? Or were you sent to an off-world penal colony where you slaved out the rest of your days? No one would say, or if they could, they weren't risking breaching the shroud of secrecy that hung over New Earth. Johari guessed only the Supreme Council knew the truth. When he was sentenced to Banishment seventeen days ago, they'd doomed him to be "extinguished from this world." The phrase still buzzed in his brain and curdled what little breakfast he'd been able to hold down.

Two guards ushered him down a long aisle to the defense table. Spectators craned their necks to get a look at the boy who'd defied the Supreme Council and survived the House.

Johari ignored them and focused on the stage where the next hours would decide his fate. Ten feet long, five feet high, rearing with its dark-stained wood from a sea of cold marble tiles, the Supreme Council's bench was an imposing fortress. It seated five, with the central chair raised above the others. Along the courtroom walls, columns rose to a domed ceiling ringed with tinted clearstory windows. Light filtering down seemed bleak, as if it came from a different sun than the one blazing outside.

Cody wasn't there yet. He'd been pulled into a last-minute conference with the prosecution about Johari's beating outside. But Johari's friend, Dannie, was seated behind him, their rows separated by a wooden banister. She'd left her short-cropped hair alone—there wasn't much she could do with it—but a light summer dress left her boyish shoulders bare, revealing a new tattoo of teardrops. It looked like she'd done it herself. Knowing her, she probably had.

"Did that hurt?" he asked.

"It was worth it." From the jut of her jaw to her wiry muscles, everything about Dannie challenged the world: Just *try* messing with me. She could back it up too, despite her compact size. Eyes alight, now she softened as she drank in his dark gray suit. She caught his navy-blue tie with slender fingers made for picking locks and tugged him toward her. "Aren't you a sight for sore eyes?" She winced when her gaze fell on the small bandage just above his hairline. "What happened?"

She started to climb over the banister, but the guard stopped her with a shake of his head.

"A little mishap," Johari replied. "I'm okay."

"I'll kiss it and make it better." Her eyes bored into his.

"That won't go over well with Greta."

"I won't tell if you don't." She nodded toward the empty chair to Johari's right. "Where is she? If I were your girl-friend, I'd already be here."

"She's coming." But disquiet stirred within him. He could think of no reason why she *wasn't* already here. Back in an anteroom where Johari had changed his shirt and suit —the original torn and bloody from the mob—Cody had looked like a lost puppy as he'd riffled through his satchel for his glasses, asking repeatedly where she was.

He entered the courtroom now, sat at the defense table, and eyed the empty chair between him and Johari.

"She'll be along," Johari said, but his voice sounded hollow. He nodded toward the table opposite them. Neither Phillip March, lead council for the prosecution, or his assistants, had arrived. "How did it go with March?"

"He argued for a delay." Cody glanced at his watch. "He's playing with us."

Tension tightened Johari's throat. "I don't want this hanging over me."

"It won't. We're going forward with it."

The back doors swung open and a murmur ran through the crowd. Phillip March and two assistants entered, carrying armfuls of files. When they arrived at their table, they dropped them with a resounding thud.

With eyes as predatory as an eagle's, March glanced at his watch, at the spectators, and finally over to Cody. He didn't bother to look at Johari. He'd already done that, coming to the jail the night Johari had turned himself in. For an eternity, it seemed, March had stood in a shadow of the corridor outside the cell.

Johari had extended his hand through the bars. "No hard feelings."

March had only glared, as though he could make Johari evaporate with his eyes.

The crowd rustled as Greta entered, her jaw firm, her steps resolute. Her hair, usually falling in carefree waves of honey, was pulled back in a no-nonsense ponytail. She was sinuous in a tweed business skirt and jacket. Johari's heart seemed to stop, as it often did when he saw her.

In one arm, she cradled an armful of thick law books with hundreds of Post-its sticking out like little wings. A briefcase clutched in one determined hand was swinging like it might go flying. When she arrived at the defense table, she dropped everything with a louder bang than March's files had and stared at him like she'd thrown down a gauntlet. He gazed back, unruffled.

She turned to Johari. The intensity on her face melted away, replaced by tenderness. He reached up and brushed gently near her eyes, puffy from lack of sleep but still flashing like blue mountain lakes.

"You were up all night," he said.

"You're more important than sleep." She touched his bandage lightly, and damn if the wound underneath didn't hurt a little less. "I saw it on the news. Are you okay?"

"Ready to swim with sharks." He grinned, trying to show confidence. His insides were a bundle of knots.

She sat, opened the briefcase, and removed an outline, typed notes, and a copy of Givvens's *Little White Book*— also marked with Post-its. Afterward, she hung Cody's glasses around his neck with a necklace she clipped to the temple tips. "You'll always know where they are."

Greta turned and regarded Dannie.

"The difference between you and me?" Dannie said. "I didn't leave him alone. He found a friend when he walked in here."

Greta extended her hand. "Hello, Dannie. Thanks for coming."

Dannie stared back sullenly and refused Greta's hand.

A bailiff entered through a side door and rang a bell. When the courtroom grew quiet, he cried out, "All rise for the Supreme Council of New Earth, the Honorable Sparra Givvens presiding. May their wisdom reign."

Johari stood. Every vein in his body seemed to throb. A dull roar sounded in his ears. This was it. No place to run, no place to hide. In a few hours, his life would either open before him or get snuffed out.

The Supreme Council appeared, disappeared, and reappeared on their bench, as if a strobe light flashed, controlling whether they were in or out of the room. The flicker-phasing stopped, and they stood before the courtroom, their skin like ash, their prosthetic eyes like liquid gold, swiveling and shutter-clicking about the room.

Tall and painfully gaunt, dressed in Puritan-black, Sparra Givvens stood in the middle. His prosthetic eyes protruded, rolling in their sockets with short, jerky motions; the pupils enlarging, contracting, and blinking as they scanned the spectators.

Dannie breathed in Johari's ear. "Sick. Creepy sick."

It was. No one knew where they came from, or how, only that they did. It was just another of the mysteries hanging over New Earth.

Givvens sat, beat his gavel once, and read in a hollow

tone, "Appeal of Case 255798, State versus Hightower. Proceed with opening arguments."

Cody rose, taking up the outline he and Greta had prepared. "Your Honors, a little over two weeks ago, the Supreme Council found my client guilty of stealing a ten-million-dollar antigrav sports car and sentenced him to Banishment. New evidence exonerates him of that crime. First, a witness will testify that the car was loaned. Second, Brice Bernhard purposely set up Mr. Hightower for a crime that was never committed."

A murmur rippled through the courtroom. And well it should. Brice Bernhard was the son of New Earth's richest man.

"Third," Cody continued, "Brice Bernhard kept this witness from testifying. Fourth, and most compelling, my client entered and survived the House." He put his hand piously over his heart. "The House is the bedrock of New Earth. We send our sons and daughters within its walls, testing them with a terrible ordeal. Most never return. But a few, the precious few, come back to us." Cody picked up the volume of Sparra Givvens's *Little White Book*, and read, "'For the House purifies; the House redeems.'" He turned the page. "And, 'Only the worthy return.'" Cody pointed to Johari. "According to every principle our world is built on, nothing he did before entering the House matters more than a hill of beans. I'm confident you will reverse your decision and free him."

Phillip March rose, his jaw thrust out, his black eyes piercing. "Your Honors, defense council's appeal stretches credibility. Their witness is suspect. So is the defendant's claim he escaped the House. He has already rocked the peace of society, as witnessed by the violence outside the courthouse. Such evil must be excised. I am confident when you hear all the evidence, your original decision will stand, and this ... this ..." His forefinger stabbed twice toward Johari. "Will be eliminated from New Earth."

"Call your first witness," Givvens said.

Cody called for Greta.

March had remained standing. "Objection. Ms. Orngold is assisting defense council."

Greta took up one of the heavy books she'd brought, opened it to one of the Post-its, and handed it to Cody. He said, "In Collins versus Daniel, the Supreme Council ruled that 'no one who can shed light on the truth can be excluded from testifying.'"

Givvens phased out and back into the room. "Overruled. Call your witness."

As she took the stand, Greta drilled March with her eyes. If he showed any reaction, it was a slight tightening of his lips.

"The night of September fourteenth, were you at a party at Brice Bernhard's house?" Cody asked her, after she had been sworn in.

"Yes."

"Did you meet the defendant, Johari Hightower, there?"

"Yes."

"Did you know him before the party?"

"I'd never seen him before."

"Did you leave the party with him in the Bernhard's Spider?"

"Yes."

"That's an expensive car. How did it happen?"

"Brice Bernhard's friend, Randy Evans, gave us the key. He told us Brice wanted Johari to give it a spin."

"Did you believe him?"

"I wasn't sure at first. But Randy pointed out that Brice was generous, which is true. In the first grade, he gave us all expensive toys for his birthday. Every year was the same, and lots of times in between."

"What happened next?"

"We sailed off in the car, believing we could keep it until nine the next morning. We stayed up all night. Johari dropped me off at home and left to return the car."

"And left to return the car." Cody looked meaningfully at Sparra Givvens, and then continued, "Did you see the defendant after that?"

"No, not for two weeks, not until the day I entered the House."

"Why not?"

Greta's voice went cold. "I was grounded, pretty much locked in my room without phone or internet. Friends couldn't visit."

"You had no idea the defendant had been arrested?"

Greta looked directly at Givvens. "None. If I had, I would've testified at his trial."

"Right after you entered the House, what happened?" Cody asked.

"Johari rushed past the escort and joined us."

"Did he say why?"

"Not at first. It seemed crazy. No one enters the House unless they're scheduled. I thought he'd come to protect me."

"When did you find out the truth?"

"After we lost Calista ..." Greta choked back tears.

Cody poured water from a pitcher, the ice cubes clinking in the hushed courtroom, and handed her the glass. "Take your time."

Greta drank, her knuckles hardening around the glass.

"After we lost Calista, Brice confessed he'd set up Johari and bribed my mother to keep me locked up."

The courtroom exploded. Givvens rapped his gavel like he was hammering a nail.

March shot to his feet. "Objection. Hearsay."

Cody struck the top of his head in disbelief. "Your Honor, the witness is reporting what she heard, not what someone told her was said."

"Sustained." When the room was quiet, Givvens brandished his gavel at the spectators. "Another outburst like that and I'll clear the courtroom."

For a few ticks, Cody stared at Givvens, dumbstruck. His hand trembling, he began flipping through his notes distractedly, like he wasn't seeing them. At last, he paused and tapped an entry. "With the court's indulgence, we would like to question the witness about Mr. Hightower's interaction with others in the House. We'll keep it to that."

Johari held his breath. The House was a secret rite, casting a shadow of doom over all eighteen-year-olds. No one talked about what happened inside beyond one simple fact: people go in; most don't come out.

Givvens stiffened, then leaned forward sternly. "Tread lightly, counselor."

Cody nodded. "How did Mr. Hightower conduct himself in the House?" he asked Greta.

"We were stuck in the attic," she replied. "He came back to show us how he got out."

"He. Came. Back. He'd gotten out of the attic, could've searched for a way out of the House, but he returned to help his friends. Isn't that about the size of it?"

Greta's eyes shone. "Yes."

"Anything else?"

"He tried to save Calista ..." Tears pooled in Greta's

eyes. She fought them back and drained her glass. "Brice too, even after he confessed to setting Johari up. I fell unconscious for much of the rest of the ordeal. Johari refused to leave me, was there when I came to, with one hour left to get out."

"Instead of saving his own skin ..." Cody gave Givvens another sideways glance. "He stayed by your side, nursed you as best he could. No further questions."

March approached the witness stand and studied Greta. "Isn't it true that your memory for what happened in the House is hazy?"

Greta picked up her water glass and turned it in her hands before taking a sip. "It's like a dream, Mr. March. The details fade; the important parts remain. I'll never forget what I've told the court under oath. It'll stay with me till I die."

"Do you love the defendant?" he asked.

She looked at Johari as if no one else was in the room. "With all my heart."

"I can see that. You'd do anything for him?"

"Yes."

"How about lie?"

Greta hesitated. March had set a trap. Admitting she would lie undermined her credibility as a witness.

"Would you lie to save his life?" he persisted.

Greta fixed her eyes on March. "No."

"You say the defendant was in the House. Did it change him?"

Another trap. "He was beautiful before going in; he's beautiful now."

"In other words, no, he didn't change."

"You're wrong." She looked directly at Givvens. "Seeing Calista and Brice die would change anybody."

Givvens's mechanical eyes rested on her, the first time they'd been still since he'd arrived. Johari was struck by how cold those orbs were, with no more warmth than camera lenses.

March paced before her. "Isn't it a fact, Ms. Orngold, that the defendant didn't enter the House at all—"

"No—"

"That he met you when you came out and made it look like he'd been inside."

"No—"

March paused, hovering before her like a hawk about to dive. "Isn't it a fact that the defendant had an illegal key he used to get the two of you out?"

Greta smiled at him. "Make up your mind, Mr. March, was he in the House or not?"

"Answer the question."

"No, he did not have a key."

"Did you, Brice Bernhard, or Calista Morra have a key?"

Greta, Cody, and Johari had talked about this. For now, they would not reveal Brice had brought an illegal key into the House, otherwise there was no way of proving Johari hadn't entered with it or taken it from Brice. That hadn't stopped the DOTHs, Givvens's elite core of goons, from ransacking Johari's studio looking for one.

For the second time, Greta lied—the first about not lying to save his life. "No."

That's my girl, Johari thought.

Greta stepped down and March called his first witness, Dr. Donna Pressler. A woman in her forties with a slight frame, thin lips, and sagging eyelids took the stand. Her hair was like coarse straw, and from the dark roots, appeared dyed.

"Dr. Pressler, what is your specialty?" March asked.

"I'm a forensic psychologist." She spoke in clipped tones and looked comfortable perched beside the Supreme Council, like she'd been there before.

"What is that exactly?"

"I study psychological profiles, make predictions about future behavior and risk to society."

"Have you studied the defendant's case?"

She nodded toward the files stacked on March's table. "I examined his complete history, including the notes of his caseworkers, therapists, and psychological examinations done triennially from age three."

"What did you find?"

"He suffers from sociopathic deviancy."

"Is that remediable?"

"In the defendant's case, no."

"Explain."

"As we develop, we learn morals, to distinguish right from wrong, to trust. In mild cases and with a lot of therapy, an individual can overcome their difficulties. In the defendant's case ..." Pressler's eyes took in the mountainous files on the prosecution's table. "He's too far gone. His personality is like Swiss cheese. The holes are too big. They can never be filled."

"What makes you certain?"

"A thorough knowledge of his past. I've summarized salient points in a holo-video."

Cody shot to his feet. "Objection. Mr. Hightower's past has no bearing on his case."

March spread his hands. "With the court's indulgence, we will show the defendant is beyond remediation."

Givvens nodded, his robotic eyes lingering on the spectators. "I'll allow it."

Johari's blood started to steam. Depending on how far back they went, he knew what he'd see: a one-sided portrayal of his life, gleaned from notes and reports stuffed in his case file and recreated using computer simulation. What else could it be but biased?

The courtroom dimmed ...

FOUR

March pressed a button on a holo-vid projector, standard at prosecution and defense tables. A three-dimensional image of the psychologist appeared on the marble floor. "Johari Hightower, placed in an orphanage and made a ward of the court at age three, demonstrated violent behavior from day one."

Tense, Johari leaned forward and held his breath. His earliest memories were from age six. This time in his life was blank to him, though sometimes, behind a locked door in his mind, he sensed a deep and terrible ache.

"He could never establish an attachment, let alone a loving bond, with his caretakers." The narrator dissolved. Several quick-cut scenes followed—a three-year-old Johari burrowing under a blanket or pulling down clothes in a closet and burying himself beneath them. A kindly woman was attempting to coax him out.

The scene changed, showing a grimy young Johari, his black curls grown wild and matted into a rat's nest. A stout woman was trying to wrestle him into a bathtub. He wriggled away and threw a bar of soap at her. Scene cut to two men restraining Johari, while the woman took an electric clipper to his head and he snarled like a rabid dog. He tore his hand free and raked his nails down her arm, leaving bloody tracks.

"To calm him, and for his own safety, all stimulation needed to be removed." The vid showed him being carried, kicking and squalling, to a closet, where a montage depicted him pounding on the door and yelling for hours.

"Providing food, clothing, shelter, and basic medical care was a challenge." Johari was shown biting a nurse trying to give him a shot.

"He refused food during the day." Little Johari sat on the floor in a dark empty kitchen, wrappers and crumbs scattered about him, the contents of a smashed ketchup bottle dripping down the wall. He pushed aside shards of glass, dipped his fingers in a red puddle, and ate.

Every eye in the courtroom seemed to be on him. Greta laid her hand on his arm and stroked it. The spot where her fingers lay was the only warmth he felt. The rest of him had turned cold. Memories started coming, slow at first, like fuzzy snapshots, and then in a flood, with startling clarity.

Baths in water and ice cubes. Getting strapped to a cot and injected with "medicine" that made him nauseous and the world spin. The time he'd been shoved into a refrigerator.

The darkened basement was the worst. He'd screamed and screamed and screamed. Not from anger, from fear. Every shadow held a monster with ferocious teeth and razor-sharp talons. Weren't the short whip-like tails, the skittering scratching sounds and beady eyes proof? Didn't the little red wounds on his arms and legs demonstrate they feasted on him?

He would take any of these punishments if he could

just be with Paul, his older brother. Their visits were denied on the grounds that Johari was too difficult to handle when he returned. That didn't stop him, as the vid showed: age seven or eight now, he broke windows, stole keys, and ran through the streets, sometimes barefoot and in his pajamas, only to be found the next morning curled up on Paul's doorstep. Why wouldn't he? Paul was the only person to play with Johari, to turn a smiling face his way.

To love him.

The rest of the vid was a blur to him. And then it was over.

He hugged himself, shivering. Silent tears traced down his cheeks and the courtroom seemed hazy ...

Cody was standing by the witness stand, cross-examining Dr. Pressler.

"You testified that you'd studied Mr. Hightower's complete history."

Pressler steepled her fingers and tapped them. "That's correct."

"What was Mr. Hightower like before age three?"

Pressler dusted the lapel of her jacket. "I didn't review that."

"Why not?"

"It wasn't necessary."

"Isn't it because the information is sealed, along with the fate of his parents?"

Sparra Givvens leaned forward. The parchment-thin skin around his eyes hardened. "Careful, counselor, you're on delicate ground."

"I'll rephrase. Mr. Hightower's brain could have been just fine before the age of three, isn't that right?"

"Not in my opinion."

"Come now, *doctor,* wouldn't the separation from loving parents and a loving brother, wouldn't the cold and callous handling of orphanage staff cause behaviors like you've shown?"

Pressler shook her head. "Your client's responses were out of proportion to the circumstances."

Greta scribbled madly, then waved a note to catch Cody's eye.

He studied it a moment, then asked, "Didn't those behaviors go away when Mr. Hightower was with his brother? That he never had one incident when he visited his brother, showed no violence toward people or property where his brother lived."

"That's true, but temporary lulls prove nothing. Mr. Gilbert, year after year, caretakers and foster parents repeatedly described him as ..." She looked directly at Johari. "An *animal.*"

"Move to strike," Cody said. "Witness quotes lay opinion, not scientific evidence."

"Overruled." Givvens flicker-phased out and back into the room. "Move it along, counselor."

Cody's jaw pulsed with tension. He took a deep breath before continuing. "Did you examine Mr. Hightower?" he asked Dr. Pressler.

"It wasn't necessary."

"So, you only know what he was like before, from the accounts of others, not now?"

She raised a finger like she was a teacher correcting an errant student. "His prior assessments have high validity and reliability. From them, we can make accurate predictions of future behavior."

"Do those tests take into account the House?"

Her eyes flicked back and forth uncertainly. "No."

"Well, can the House fill in those holes in the cheese?"

Sparra Givvens's eyes stopped roaming the courtroom and fixed on her.

She paled. "I've never had the opportunity to measure that."

"Is it possible?"

"Yes ... of course." She gave a nervous little laugh. "Bless our House."

"Bless our House, indeed. Only the worthy return, isn't that right?"

"Yes ..."

"And they come back to live peaceful, prosperous lives. Isn't that right?"

"Yes."

Greta scrawled another note and fanned the air with it to get Cody's attention.

He hurried over, retrieved the note, and smiled. "Doctor, can a sociopathic deviant show empathy, compassion, and altruism?"

The witness folded her hands. "Absolutely not."

Cody turned to Givvens. "We would like to recall this witness in a few minutes. First, we'd like to show a video of our own."

March jumped to his feet. "Objection. We haven't had an opportunity to review this evidence."

Cody smiled. "What's good for the goose is good for the gander, Your Honor. We didn't get to review the prosecution's little demonstration, either. Besides, everyone on New Earth has seen ours by now." He looked directly at Givvens. "Except you."

Givvens pondered a moment. "I'll allow it."

Dr. Pressler stayed on the stand. The lights dimmed.

Sitting on the edge of the defense table, Cody pressed the button on the holo-vid projector at his table. To the left of the witness stand, the courthouse steps, filled with chanting protesters, reporters, and flashing cameras, appeared. A sedan pulled up. A policeman opened the back door. Assisted by the officer, Johari stepped out, his disobedient curls tossing in the wind. The camera zoomed in on his face. Something soulful, almost savage, burned in his eyes. He started up the steps and the camera zoomed out. Above the clamor, a woman was screaming. She shook Sparra Givvens's *Little White Book* in one hand and held the tiny palm of a girl in the other.

The crowd pressed in. The child was torn from her mother's hand. She tumbled down the steps. The crowd surged. The camera angle swung, catching the sky, the trees, the peak of the courthouse carved with mythological figures. Then it came down. The little girl was about to go under a stampede. Johari broke from his escorts and was up the steps in a flash. He cradled the girl in his arms and made a shield of his body. A moment later, blows rained down on him. He held on, protecting her. The camera zoomed in on her face. She nestled into the crook of his neck, while a two-inch wide wooden sign handle landed on his temple. Blood flooded into his eyes.

The video ended. The lights came on. The spectators sat in stunned silence.

Cody took a slow breath, rose, and strode to the witness stand. "In your expert opinion, Dr. Pressler, did Mr. Hightower demonstrate compassion, empathy, and altruism?"

Pressler hesitated, glanced at March. "I could hardly say based on one sample."

"What I saw, *doctor*, is a bunch of people standing around, doing nothing, while a little girl was about to get trampled. Not one police officer came to her aid. Not one reporter put down his camera to assist her. Heck, I'm ashamed of myself for not doing something. Only this man —" He pointed at Johari. "Only this man protected her. Did you see that doctor, and wasn't that the biggest demonstration of empathy and altruism you can imagine, allowing himself to be beaten to save a child?"

Her shoulders sagged. "Yes, I would say it was."

The trial came to a swift conclusion. March's closing arguments recapped what he'd said earlier. Though Johari was bundled in a woolen suit, frost had settled over him, chilling him as though he was still cowering in a cold basement. He hugged himself for warmth, as he had most of the trial.

March pointed at him. "See him there, arms crossed in defiance, slouching and sullen. That is not the picture of a man redeemed. That is a blight that must be removed. For the safety of our families, there is only one response: Banishment."

By this time, the Supreme Council was flashing erratically.

Cody stood. "Your Honors," he said, "I'll be brief. Don't let the prosecution's crusade against an innocent man sway you. You've seen the evidence; the *world* has seen the evidence. We're confident you will move quickly, dismiss all charges, and free our client."

The Supreme Council phased from the room. In less than five minutes, they returned. The spectators buzzed.

Sparra Givvens quieted them with his gavel. "The defendant will rise."

Johari stood. He seemed to be floating, his feet lost somewhere far below him. How many more minutes would he see the blue of the sky, the green of the trees? How many more minutes would he taste the sweetness of air in his lungs, or feel Greta's lips pressing softly on his? Everything came into sharp focus, all of it precious: the light from the clearstory windows, the rustle of spectators and journalists, the faint smell of polish on his shoes, the whirl of his thoughts.

FIVE

Givvens's eyes ceased to meander about the courtroom and locked on Johari. Greta found Johari's hand and gripped it, her fingers hot and sweaty. Outside, a marching band struck up a lively number in the park across from the courthouse.

Givvens's voice seemed to come from the end of a tunnel. "Bless our House, for it redeems. Johari Hightower, this court finds you innocent of all charges—"

The courtroom exploded. The rest of what he said was drowned out. He struck his gavel, his eyes shutter-clicked once, twice, and he phased from the room, the rest of the Supreme Council flickering away with him.

A mob surrounded Johari, Cody throwing his arms around him and shaking his hand and wiping away tears and then hugging him again. Dannie squeezed her way through the crowd. She said to Greta, "Hope you don't mind," and jumped onto Johari. Her legs wound around his waist; her arms wrapped about his neck. He squeezed her tight and swung her back and forth. When she climbed down at last, she said to Greta, "Treat him right, or I'll steal him from you."

Greta smiled. "Count on it."

Her father was next, pumping Johari's hand, telling him he was proud of him and to come 'round, they would shoot some golf.

The crowd parted and Philip March faced Johari, his dark eyes fixed on him.

Johari held out his hand. "No hard feelings."

March left Johari's hand hanging awkwardly in the air. "This isn't over," March said. "Not by a long shot."

"Now just one minute," Cody protested. "I won't have you threatening my client."

March ignored him. "One slip and I'm all over you. There won't be any escape, no House to save you." Without waiting for a response, he turned and shouldered his way through the crowd.

"Don't worry about him," Cody soothed. "He can't touch you now."

Johari looked after March, disquiet stirring in him. He shook it off. The years of terror were behind him. The *House* was behind him. He'd jumped right over it. And he'd gotten the stamp of approval from the Supreme Council, hadn't he?

It was a strange place to be in. He hadn't thought about what he might do if he survived the ordeal. Life was wide open, full of possibilities. Greta's dad had offered him a job running errands at his newsroom. He would probably take that until he could sort out his hopes and dreams, now that he could allow himself to have them.

One thing he knew, one hope, one dream, was beside him. He could smell her perfume, that intoxicating mix of soap and what was just Greta. He turned, and her eyes, a limitless blue, pulled him in. But there was tension tugging the edges that he didn't understand.

He needed to pull her aside, see what it was all about. But the press surrounded them both, calling out questions. He answered a few and suddenly his knees felt like rubber.

Cody steadied him with one hand and held up the other. "That's all, people. Mr. Hightower will release a statement, all in good time."

Grumbling, the journalists turned away. Dannie elbowed him to get his attention. She nodded toward Greta, who was peeling away from the crowd and walking out of the courtroom with her father.

"She isn't going to the party?" Dannie asked.

"She'll be there," he replied. "Her father must be giving her a lift."

Dannie stepped closer. "Darn, I was hoping to get you all to myself."

He turned to her. She gazed up at him, her smile wry, her eyes inviting. The dress softened the tough street punk lurking underneath.

Johari squeezed her shoulders with his hands. "I haven't had a chance to thank you. For all you did."

"I'll take a kiss."

"Don't push it."

"Can I get a lift to Cody's?"

A quick shot from a doctor to flush the trackers from his bloodstream, and off they went to the party. Cody drove. Johari and Dannie piled into the backseat. She leaned against him, her head resting on his shoulder. She smelled of cigarettes mingled with deodorant.

"This isn't encouragement," he said.

"I'm not an idiot," she replied. "I know where things stand." But she nuzzled in deeper.

Twilight was setting in when they reached Cody's house, a sprawling, upper-middle-class ranch home. It had the comfort of overstuffed furniture, well used. The shag carpet was flattened with miles of traffic, but everything was neat and orderly except Cody's study, which was a towering fortress of papers and files. That had to be the one place his wife couldn't penetrate.

She was a small and cheerfully plump woman who bustled about the hors d'oeuvre table, removing plastic wrap from bowls of olives, celery sticks, chips, salsa, hummus, crackers, and fish sticks. The long necks of soda bottles protruded from a nearby ice bucket. What would they have done with it all if he'd been Banished?

Dannie went outside to smoke. People began arriving. A few of them Johari had seen around. Most of them he didn't know. He talked to his landlady, Dandelion Jones, a short woman with graying hair who fawned over him while he kept an eye out for Greta. She hadn't arrived yet and should have been here by now. Something tightened in the pit of his stomach.

Cody's wife whisked Dandelion away to see the garden, leaving him alone on the edge of things. He sucked a pimento from an olive and then popped the olive in his mouth. It left a sour taste. Someone put on jazz. It was soft, so people could talk, but it had a good beat, the kind that makes you want to dance. He looked again for Greta. The whirlwind that had enveloped the two of them for the last weeks had kept them from really being together. He thought about the kiss they'd exchanged in the inky-black pool when they'd escaped the House. It was the first and last intimacy between them. When she got here, he would hold her close and dance, their steps almost imperceptible so they could feel each other's heart.

Calista's mom entered the room and threaded her way past knots of people until she stood before Johari. Head to toe, she was an older Calista—except for the pencil-dot mole on her daughter's right cheek. They had the same petite nose, pouting lip, and small, almost fragile, fingers. Her hair was a shade darker than a sunburned field. She appeared haggard, her eyes bloodshot and circled with dark rings.

"How're you holding up?" Johari asked.

"I'm not."

"I'd like to visit, if that's okay." It seemed a strange thing to ask. He'd only known Calista a few hours inside the House.

"That would be fine." She looked around at nothing in particular, distracted.

"Greta will be here soon."

She turned back to him, tears welling. "I need to go. I just came to congratulate you, to thank you for everything you did to try to save—" She made a little choking sound, waved her hand once, twice, but couldn't bring herself to say Calista's name.

Johari watched her depart, broken and lost. His jaw tightened, stemming a surge of anger. He'd left the House, but had anything really changed? New Earth was still New Earth. Every day, teens passed through those rotten doors, never to return.

Greta entered, glanced at him, and began mingling. Most of the young people were probably her friends, people she'd rallied to attend the trial. He wove through the crowd, trying to get to her. Each time he neared, she moved on, strangely stiff. Beneath the mechanical smiles and greetings she gave, she seemed stony, and her golden skin was unusually pallid.

After circling the room to reach her, he found himself back near the hors d'oeuvre table. The smell of cigarette smoke on clothing announced that Dannie had slipped up beside him.

"Trouble in paradise?" she asked, nodding toward Greta.

"Saying hi to friends."

"Yeah, right. If you were my guy, I'd be right here. Hey, I *am* right here."

She had a point. He searched through the last few days. Had he said something wrong, something that hurt Greta's feelings? Zip came to mind.

Greta flicked another glance at him, took a breath, and started across the room to him.

"Damn," Dannie said under her breath, "dropped an earring. I should never wear them; they're allergic to me." She disappeared behind a sofa, searching.

The next moment, Greta was in front of him.

He held out his arms. "Wanna dance."

She shook her head. "We need to talk."

The finality in her tone sent a shiver through him. Was this their breakup moment? It couldn't be. They'd hardly been together. "You're spooking me."

She touched his arm, her fingers making little strokes meant to comfort him, but didn't. "I don't mean to."

"Then what?" he asked.

She looked around and pointed to the Gilberts' veranda, where several huge plant pots overflowed with ferns. "Out there."

He followed her through double doors into the evening air. The night was warm, and he caught the scent of damp soil and roses. Despite feeling she might be ending what had hardly begun, an urge came over him to sweep her into his arms, to lose his fingers in the wealth of curls tumbling to her shoulders, to find her lips. Her somber face squashed the impulse.

She looked up at him with a blend of determination and fear. "We have to go back."

He went blank. Back where? The courthouse?

"Into the House," she said.

A chill ran through him. When he spoke, his voice was husky. "Why?"

"You know why."

He studied her. She had her two feet planted on the ground as well as anyone he'd ever met. But this was insane. She searched his eyes; hers filled with pain and hope.

And then it hit him. Calista. She wanted to go back for Calista.

"That's crazy," he said.

"What if it's not? What if when they disappear from the House they go somewhere? You've heard the rumors. Everyone has."

"That doesn't mean it happens." *The House could recycle people's body parts for food, for all we know.* He kept the thought to himself. She didn't need that image rolling around her brain.

The track on the stereo changed to something upbeat. The trumpeter launched into a wild improvisation, the notes running like fire. The faint aroma of cigarette smoke mixed with the perfume of the Gilberts' roses.

Greta clutched his wrist with one hand. "Help me, Johari. You're the only one who can."

"I'm the only one who can't," he said dryly. "You heard March. One screwup, and he's all over me."

"It's not illegal to enter the House."

"Trust me, if I go in, March will dig up a law. He's itching to."

"Leave that to Cody. We've got to bring Calista back. And Brice."

"You're kidding. After what he did to me, you're still loyal to him?" The world had suddenly gone topsy-turvy. One thing Johari knew for certain when he was in the House: she loved him. Did the real world change that? Old ideas surged through him, carried on a flood of resentment. Out here in the real world, he wasn't good enough for her. He was the delinquent, the troublemaker, the kid with the terrible rep, the rap sheet five miles long. Nice girls didn't marry bad boys. They hitched up with even-tempered accountants or doctors who wouldn't rattle the nerves of spinster aunts. They married rich guys like Brice, who took them to yacht parties attended by movie stars and gave them a ring with a diamond the size of a boulder.

Fire flared in her eyes. "I made a vow that all of us would make it out. I can't slip into an easy life, knowing they're out there somewhere—" She stifled a sob. "Who knows what's happening to them."

"It's too dangerous. We barely made it out."

"You could do it . . . You did it twice. That much I remember."

He remembered it too, that he had gone in at age ten and watched the House take his brother in the most brutal way. Further proof this was crazy. If you were to bet on someone making it out, it was his brother Paul.

Dannie rose from behind one of the huge plant pots and stepped beside Johari. "And you're supposed to love him?" She sneered.

Greta didn't take her eyes off Johari. "I do love him, with all my heart."

"You're asking him to put his neck in a noose. That isn't love."

Johari put his hand on Dannie's shoulder to send her back inside. "This isn't your business."

She shrugged away. "It's a free country. I'd think you'd appreciate someone covering your back." She stared daggers at Greta. "*She* isn't."

Greta winced, gave Johari a last, pleading look. "Please, you're the only one ..." she said, and stepped swiftly from the veranda.

Johari slumped against the stucco fence separating the veranda from the garden, feeling like the wind had been knocked out of him. An hour ago, he was flying high. He'd defeated Phillip March, gotten past Sparra Givvens, made it out of the House with the only girl he would ever want. And for the first time, he had a life, or the possibility of one.

Before, his past followed him wherever he went, spoiling everything he touched, blocking his future. Who could think of the future with the House looming over you? Now he had a chance to make something of himself. A job, going back to school, getting a high school diploma. Whatever it was, didn't matter, because now he could start to dream. What kind of job, what kind of life? Wasn't even sketchy. It was all up in the air. The only clear thing was that Greta was in it. He never thought about having kids, but if she wanted them, it wasn't a far leap. With Greta, anything was possible. Except now she was receding from him like a boat, sailing toward the edge where the world drops off.

Dazed, he saw himself sleepwalk through leaving, giving his thanks to the Gilberts, promising to call them in the morning, arranging a ride for Dannie—though she looked up at him hopefully and offered to go home with him —and then Dandelion was driving him through town. A few cars cruised by. Grafton seemed like a shell, almost empty because of the House, a lonely place where storefront signs blinked for nobody.

What were his choices, really? Risk it all for a mad adventure with Greta, or play it safe ... for what? A life as empty as the buildings and homes around him?

Dandelion parked at the curb, and then Johari was up in his small room—a converted utility shed on the rooftop—sitting hunched on his bed. A billboard across the street flashed a new message through his window and splattered bleak rays onto his wall: One House, One Family, Life for All! The urge came over him to fetch the baseball bat from his closet and put it to good use on the LED lights of the sign. But Phillip March's words reverberated in his mind, "One slip and I'm all over you. There won't be any escape, no House to save you."

He had to walk the straight and narrow. Greta's idea wasn't just suicide. It was impossible. For him. He didn't have an inch of wiggle room.

The only thing he could do was give her time. She loved him. She said so. He couldn't believe their bond could be broken so easily. She'd come around, drop the idea, and they'd move on, make plans together.

Even as he drifted off into sleep—not a sound sleep but a kind of gray ghostly twilight where he saw himself lying on the bed—he thought, *But she won't. She won't let it go.*

He thought he must be dreaming ... Figures wearing ski masks rose on both sides of the bed. The next instant, rough hands jarred him awake, duct tape was plastered over his mouth, stifling his scream, and he was shackled. Someone jabbed a hypodermic into his arm, and the world faded.

SIX

Diary of the Damned ...

I'm back, as back as I get. I'm not sure why I write this, except maybe it helps me hold on to a piece of myself.

Where was I? Oh yeah, the athletic guy on the concrete slab ...

Whoever he was, he found his balance and took in the situation like a seasoned soldier. He turned toward the mob. The light in the City is dim, but there was enough of it to see his face. Horrible burns left the skin raw and red, the mouth twisted, one eye almost closed.

It was him, his beautiful face twisted into a gargoyle. What did the House do to make him like this? If I was back there and had a torch, I would set it all in flames. For the monster who did this to him. To me. To everyone who was ever sent here. For all I knew, the madmen racing up the street toward him were once people who'd had cherished dreams like I had, people the House had taken and reduced to snarling animals.

He looked around, saw a metal cable hanging from a

fallen beam, and tore it out. He dashed to the end of the street and turned the corner, the mob on his heels.

I scrambled out of hiding. With as much stealth and speed as I could, I followed. The City isn't huge, but it's a maze. I didn't want to lose him. We'd be stronger together, and from the condition of his face, he needed me.

It wasn't hard to track the mob, which clambered ahead like a pack of hyenas. As I turned one corner, I saw that the walls and beams of a collapsed skyscraper blocked his escape at the end of the street. He leaped onto a fallen pillar, planted his feet, and faced the mob.

He swung his cable, whipping it so I heard it hissing clear from the other end of the street, where I peeked around a corner.

"Come on, you sons of bitches!" he yelled. "Let's do this!"

The lead man plowed ahead, storming up a pile of rubble like it was stairs. My beloved—dare I call him that?—nailed him with the cable, which struck the side of his head with a loud crack. The man crumpled and rolled down to the street. The crowd paused, uncertain.

My angel took a step forward. "Anyone else?" he taunted.

No one was game. They hauled away their fallen comrade and took off the other way. I ducked out of sight until they were gone. When I came out of hiding, he was seated on the column, his head in his hands.

I'd made only a few steps when his head whipped up and we locked eyes.

He grinned, a big twisted grin, and ran toward me, sweeping me in his arms. He crushed me to him. His body was hard, powerful, enveloping, and for a little while, too brief for me, I felt safe.

"I thought you were dead," he cried.

I still wasn't completely sure we weren't. "If I were, a hug like that would revive me. Don't let me go."

He didn't, and we just hung on to each other. He was gentle, tender, actually. I was stunned. The big guy had feelings for me. I couldn't say if they were love feelings, but there was real affection, and I'm guessing this might've been one of the few times he'd allowed something genuine to show. You know, without all the grandiose I'm-the-hot-stud-ruler-of-the-teen-world fall-at-my-feet stuff.

He seemed reluctant to break the embrace. I was too, and not just because the strength in his body made me feel safe. When we pulled away, I wouldn't be able to avoid looking at his face. I had a strong intuition he didn't know his condition. Why would he? As soon as he'd gotten here, he'd been attacked. I'd found him with his head in his hands, but that could've been despondence, knowing he was no longer in the House. That he'd become separated from our group. That he'd come to a place with savage dog people. That the life he knew was over. No fancy parties. No sexy cars. No luxury yachts. No harem of girls going gooey-eyed over him.

"You feel good," he murmured, his nose buried in my hair.

I melted. God, if you exist, you're horrible and cruel. Why couldn't you let this happen six months ago? Why now, when there's no possibility for a life for either of us?

I knew what was coming, what would happen when our bodies parted. The dread of it stabbed me. I wanted to hang on forever. The thrill of holding him had passed. I clutched now to delay the inevitable.

He drew back slowly, bent his head for a kiss. I felt him

tremble a little, like he was nervous. His fingers brushed beneath my chin, tilting it up. Our eyes met.

I'm not sure what he saw in them. Horror? Pity?

Whatever it was, he pulled back. "What?"

"It's nothing," I said, trying to hold the moment, to bring it back. It fluttered away like a startled bird.

"Don't lie to me. Not you."

My mind raced, searching for something to say. None of it was good. The truth seemed best. I touched his cheek. "You don't remember?"

He jerked back. His hands went to his face, feeling his swollen nose, his twisted lips, his half-closed eye. He whirled left, right, hunting, hunting—for what? He lurched across the street, kicked through smaller rubble until he found a piece of shiny metal.

By then, I was beside him. He lifted the shard, holding it out like a mirror, and stared. A wail rose, a lion with its leg shorn off or finding its mate cruelly slaughtered. And my own heart ripped from my chest.

SEVEN

Johari awoke to a throbbing headache. His hands were no longer shackled. The duct tape was gone. The soreness around his mouth and chin confirmed they had taken no care in ripping the tape off. He lay on a cot in an orange jumpsuit. The six-by-eight cell was dark, the walls concrete. Little light came through the small barred window at the door. Water dripped incessantly nearby.

He rose, swayed on his feet, and leaned against a cold damp wall until he regained his balance. Whatever they'd shot him with was wreaking havoc with his head, like someone working a jackhammer in there.

After a couple of deep breaths, he braved crossing to the door. No surprise to find it locked. He'd been incarcerated enough to know he was in some kind of prison, though this one was older and danker than any he'd seen.

He peered through the bars. Opposite him was a windowless door, painted dark gray. Bare bulbs suspended from the ceiling weakly illuminated a corridor.

He listened. Music played far away, perhaps in an inner office. He banged on the door. "Hey! Where am I?"

A metal door sliding open then crashing closed confirmed this was a prison. Footsteps approached. A tall man came into view, wearing a prison-guard cap. The metal badge pinned above the brim glinted.

"We'll have quiet here," the man said when he stood in front of Johari's window. He turned to go.

"Wait, where am I? Why am I here?"

"You know why."

"I don't. I was kidnapped and brought here. You must have seen them."

The man looked down at him. His eyelids sagged and he looked depressed. "I came on an hour ago. You were already here." He grinned mirthlessly, displaying tobacco-stained teeth that were black at the edges. "You won't be here much longer."

"Why? Where will I go?"

The man turned and nodded meaningfully at the gray door opposite them. An icy hand closed over Johari's throat.

"What's in there?" But he already knew. It was the how and why that baffled him.

The man raised a finger. "If I were you, I'd start preparing."

Johari gripped the bars. "I demand to see my attorney."

"You're way past that now," the man scoffed. "Prepare for what's due to you. Where you'll go, if you go anywhere, I can't say, but you're a banner as sure as there's a Supreme Council who sentenced you." He stepped away, started to go.

"But I was exonerated. You must have heard about me. I'm Johari Hightower. I'm all over the news."

The guard was already moving down the corridor. "Sure you are. And I'm Santa Claus." He cackled, the laugh melding into a phlegmy cough.

Johari banged on the door. "This is a mistake! I'm innocent!"

The man was back in front of the door in a trice. He put his hands on his hips, his fingers closing over a wide belt carrying key clips, walkie-talkie, club, pepper spray, and Taser. "It's going to be peaceful in that cell. Are we clear?"

Johari glared back. "How do you live with yourself?"

The guard displayed those teeth again. "Just doing my job."

Johari glanced at the gray door. "When?"

"Four a.m. You want a last meal? I'll order it for you."

Johari shook his head. Whatever they'd drugged him with was lingering and left him queasy.

"Most people order everything under the sun," the man mused. "Fried chicken, pizza, apple pie à la mode. You like rare steak? I can get you a juicy steak."

"Just a phone call. I need to talk to my attorney, Cody Gilbert."

"Not allowed. Let me know if you change your mind about food."

"What time is it?"

The guard glanced at his watch. "One fifty."

As the guard's footsteps faded, Johari slumped on the cot.

Two hours and ten minutes to live. It seemed impossible, like he'd stepped into a nightmare, and for one horrible moment he wondered if he was still in the House, that he and Greta had never really gotten out, that the trial and everything else that had happened was all part of a House-induced hallucination, and now he was hurtling on a train bound for oblivion.

As fast as it came, the thought passed. Something hot

welled up inside him, and it seemed he was about to burst at the seams. He sprang from the cot and began pacing. If the walls had been padded, he would've punched them, but one blow on that concrete and his hand would be a bloody broken mess.

This couldn't be happening. How do you go from being at the top of the world, beating Phillip March and having a whole life ahead of you, to this? It stank of something rotten. But why should he be surprised? When had things ever gone his way?

A thousand questions flooded his mind. Why was he kidnapped? Who wanted to get rid of him? And why? No good answer came.

The door across the hall loomed. It seemed to draw him like a magnet. Two hours and ten minutes. No, now it was two hours. Maybe less. He'd long had the idea that everyone is given a certain amount of sand, each grain a moment in his or her life. When the last grain falls, life is snuffed out. Johari's sand was streaming through the hourglass, and there was nothing he could do to stem the tide.

He began to shake. A film of cold sweat coated him. In a minute, his T-shirt clung to his skin. He forced himself to pace, trying to focus.

The only hope was escape.

He examined the cell carefully, patting the walls for weakness. They were as solid as granite. The ceiling was out of reach, even standing on the cot. The door was made from a single slab of wood. He could see the width in the frame of the window. It was two inches thick and reinforced with metal plates. The window was too small to crawl through. He tested the bars anyway. If he could work one of the bars loose, he could use it as a weapon. He wasn't going down without a fight. The bars didn't budge. It didn't matter. Prisons were equipped with riot gear. The simplest thing was to tackle him with a mattress. He'd seen it done in juvie. The kid was pinned in three seconds and then airplaned to a timeout room, where he was strapped down and injected with a heavy sedative.

In Johari's case, they would just carry him across the hall and through that door.

How was it done? Were you strapped to a chair? Injected? Gassed? Was Banishment just a polite way of saying you were executed, a nicer way of putting it so feathers weren't ruffled?

He broke into another sweat, his stomach twisting and turning. All he could think about was this was the end. No sunshine, no music, no walks in the forest . . .

Tears welled in his eyes. No Greta ...

What would she think? Would she even know what happened to him? Probably not. The men who kidnapped him were not in goon uniforms. The whole thing happened in secret. She would think he ran out on her. That he didn't care.

He sank onto the cot. Escape out of the question, he came to a resolution: his last bit of time in this world would be spent thinking about Greta, that he'd gotten to love her. He pictured her hair, golden as honey. He thought of the mole at the base of her neck, and how their first night together he had an almost irresistible urge to kiss it. He thought of their time in the House. Most of that was a blur now, but he remembered that she'd stood by him, refused to leave even when it meant she might be killed. He had done the same for her, though the House threw every imaginable terror at them.

He lay back, hands tucked behind his head, and

contemplated that a moment of love like that made for a good life, no matter how short.

He was tired, but his brain was buzzing too much to sleep. He'd sleep for an eternity soon enough.

Then it occurred to him … one slim chance. Order that last meal, keep the fork, use it as a weapon. He could also ask for paper and something to write with. A last statement seemed reasonable. Maybe he could get a message to Cody and Greta, so they knew what happened to him. If he wasn't allowed to keep the fork, maybe he could use the pen as a weapon. He had no desire to kill anyone, but he didn't want to die, either. If he plunged the pen into someone's eye …

He banged on the door. The guard returned, wrote his order for a last meal on a clipboard—a coke and a cheeseburger—but refused the request for pen and paper.

"Why?" Johari asked.

"Orders." The man's eyes were puffy, suggesting Johari had awakened him. He had an easy job. Few people were Banished. Why not kick your feet up on a desk and catch a few winks?

"Is that typical?"

"No, but them's the orders and I follow them."

"Just doing your job." Johari allowed an edge of sarcasm into his voice, but not enough for the guard to be sure.

"Just doing my job."

"Who wrote the order?"

"It's official, that's all you need to know. I think we're done here. I better call in that food, or you'll be bolting it down just before meeting your maker."

"How much time?"

The guard checked his watch. "An hour and twenty-five minutes."

"Rush that food."

The guard glanced at his clipboard. "You sure you don't want more?"

Johari didn't. Gripping the bars until his knuckles were white, he watched the guard depart. Then he pushed away and gave the cell one more inspection. There was a slide large enough to push food plates through near the bottom of the door. It was locked from the outside. He tested the joints of the cot. No give there. The metal slats holding the mattress were welded into place. He turned the cot over and tried kicking one or two of them out. None of them budged. He pondered the foam pillow. The only thing he could think of was to tear it up and throw the pieces as a distraction. That idea got abandoned fast.

He swung his arms like boxers do when they enter the ring. He stretched and then dropped to the floor and ripped off a set of pushups and sit-ups. He wanted to be loose and ready when he sprang into action.

How would it go? He'd eat the food on the cot. No one would enter at that point. They might watch him from the window, but not the whole time. Hopefully, he could pocket the fork.

What if they didn't give him a fork? That could happen. They'd probably thought of all of this beforehand, had rules and procedures in place to prevent any possibility of escape.

Okay, no fork. What else, then? They would come in, two, maybe three of them. They would shackle him, even for the short walk across the hall. Whatever he did would have to happen before he was shackled. He could think of only one thing: try to snatch something from the belt of one of the guards, pepper spray, or better yet, the Taser. Failing that, he would settle for the flashlight, which could do some serious damage.

An alarm, pulsing and echoing through the prison, cut off his thoughts. Shouting and staccato gunfire followed. As quickly as it started, the alarm stopped. Johari listened, straining to penetrate the silence that followed. He heard a few muffled orders. Then the metal door crashed open and footfalls hurried toward him.

EIGHT

An assault team rushed down the corridor, their black-green uniforms ghostly in the feeble light. More equipment than Johari could imagine was strapped, clipped, and suspended on their bodies: vest armor, ammunition, handguns, stun grenades, communicators, gas masks, and more on their packs. They wore helmets and night-vision goggles and carried high-powered rifles. As far as Johari knew, New Earth had no armies. None were needed. War had been eliminated. There were the DOTHs—Defenders of the House—an elite unit that dealt with rare criminals or young people who refused to go into the House. But they were police, not a military unit. The only conceivable explanation was that these were mercenaries, armed and hired for private missions. Why? By whom? And why were they here?

The lead man was a six-foot-four wall of muscle. He stopped at Johari's cell and pulled up the goggles. A long turtleneck collar covered his face up to his eyes, leaving him disguised. A set of keys dangled in his hand. They jangled as he applied one to the cell door.

The door swung open. The man urgently motioned him out.

Johari backed away. A lifetime of raw deals had him on high alert. "Who are you?"

"No time to explain," the man barked. "That alarm will register at the police station. We need to get you out before they arrive."

"Where to?"

"Safety."

The wariness of a guard dog reared in Johari, but whoever these guys were, whatever they wanted, they were buying him a reprieve from whatever fate was awaiting him at 4:00 a.m. in the room beyond. The man's rifle wasn't raised. With no immediate threat before him, Johari nodded. Outside the cell, the team surrounded him protectively and escorted him down the corridor. They passed the metal-bar gate that he'd heard crashing open and closed earlier. On the other side was a small office. The door was ajar. His guard was sprawled across a desk, a tipped-over whiskey bottle near his outstretched hand. The odor of alcohol filled the air.

"Dead?"

"Tranked," the team leader replied. "When the authorities come, it'll look like he was drunk and stumbled against the alarm button." He patted one of his utility pockets. "Took his only record you were here."

Passing through darkened corridors, head reeling, Johari tried to parse the significance of what the soldier said, of everything that had happened. It had been no error, no mistaken identity when he'd been snatched from his bed earlier that night. Someone wanted him dead, and secretly. Whoever that was, this team worked for someone else. Someone had gone through a lot of trouble to keep him alive. That made zero sense. Ninety-nine percent of his life, he mattered to no one. The only exceptions were Dannie, his brother, Paul, and Greta. Paul was gone, had been for years, evaporating like so many other victims in the House. Dannie and Greta cared about him enough to save him, but neither commanded these resources. Like Johari, Dannie was dirt poor, little more than a street waif. Greta was smart —winning the state science fair and perfect scores on her Academic Aptitude Test proved that—but lower middle class. Besides, neither of them knew he was here.

They exited the prison through a delivery bay, probably used for laundry and crates of food. A plain, unmarked van waited by the curb, engine running, side door open.

Johari gauged his chances. A high outer fence with curls of barbed wire across the top blocked his freedom. Two hundred yards ahead was the main gate of the prison. The guard tower was dark. The assault team probably took them out first. He doubted he could outrun his rescuers. The van would quickly run him down. Thank-you-mates-I'll-take-it-from-here not an option, he entered the van.

The team piled around him. They removed their goggles. Like the leader, they were disguised up to their eyes. The leader slammed the door shut and the van took off, wheels screaming. They whizzed past the guard tower, through the main gate, and on to a narrow highway. First opportunity, they turned onto a side street. Somewhere in the distance, Johari heard sirens fading away behind him.

"Why me?" he asked the leader.

Light from LED streetlamps flickered across the man's eyes. "You'll learn when we get there."

"Which is where, exactly?"

"I told you, safety."

"What if I say, 'Thanks, I'll take it from here.'"

The man removed an envelope from one of his pockets and handed it to Johari. "If you did, I was told to give you this."

Johari opened the envelope and glanced at the contents, neat crisp bills, wrapped with a bank band. "How much?" he asked.

"Ten thousand."

Johari whistled. "Just for playing along."

The man must have smiled; his gray eyes crinkled upward. "You need to change."

Johari was given a conservative suit, dress shirt, tie, and dress shoes to change into.

"Why the fancy duds?" he asked.

"So you blend in," the leader replied.

They took a meandering route, the van making a bewildering series of turns down unfamiliar streets lined with shrugging cypresses and homes whose windows stared back, lightless and blank.

The men kept their rifles at the ready, their heads cocked, listening for pursuit. They offered Johari a burger and a coke, but the smell made him sick; his stomach was coiled too tight to think about food. He accepted water from a canteen to ease the dryness in his throat.

He sat on the edge of his seat, pondering the situation. The money suggested he had a choice. No one was forcing him. He could leave the van right now. But he had no idea where he was, and goons were investigating an alarm this moment at a prison. If he was picked up and questioned, he'd be in a tight corner. The guard would identify him. That course surely ended in the room beyond the gray door.

If he went along with these men, he could get mixed up in something bad. He had a rep and a record. Maybe somebody thought he was a good man to do something shady.

March's words echoed in his mind. One slip and the lead prosecutor would be all over him. On the other hand, somebody had gone through a lot of expense and trouble to keep him alive. Whatever they wanted, he was more than a little curious. For reasons he couldn't explain, he was wrapped up in something big. He wanted to know, might need to know, what it was.

He sat back. That burger smelled good now. He dove into it, caring little where the juices spilled, and washed it down with coke. The night was shrouded in too much mystery to not let this play out.

They entered an area he recognized as the edge of Grafton, where several luxury hotels had been built along the shore of a man-made lake. The van pulled up at the rear entrance of the Lakeside Grande hotel and stopped.

The leader spoke into a communicator by his collar. "We're here." He leaned forward and adjusted Johari's tie. Then he opened the side door, exited, scanned in both directions, and disappeared from view, presumably to make sure all was clear from all sides. A few ticks later, he returned. After helping Johari from the van, he said, "Go inside. You'll see two men in blue pinstripe suits. Tell them, 'The pigeon's loose.' If they don't respond with, 'Time for its bath,' return here because something's wrong."

"Got it. The pigeon's loose. Time for its bath."

"Good luck."

Johari hesitated. "Thanks ... for back there."

"Just doing my job."

They shook hands. Johari expected it might be one of those crushing handshakes you feel up to your elbow for the next hour. But while it was firm, it was sincere and absent of malice.

The leader said, "Better get going."

Johari entered the hotel and found he was in a long carpeted hallway with guest rooms on both sides. At the end of the hall was a foyer with an elevator and machines for snacks, beverages, and ice. Two men dressed in blue pinstripe suits waited there. One of them held the elevator door open. Both were tall and barrel-chested, reminding Johari of henchmen from Old Earth gangster films. Not a reassuring image.

Johari said, "The pigeon's loose."

"Time for its bath," one of the men replied. He and his partner entered the elevator and gestured for Johari to follow.

Swelling near their breast pockets suggested both men were packing handguns. Every instinct told him to turn, pull the red fire alarm above the ice machine, and run for the lobby, which had to be on street level. But his rescuer's handshake lingered on his palm, and the desire to have a few questions answered nudged him into the elevator. A button was pressed for the fourth floor. The door closed. The elevator rose. An almost inaudible purr indicated they were moving. Both men were as silent as the sphinx. Expecting no answers, Johari asked no questions.

The door opened, and they exited to a similar foyer—though the machines here had microwaveable burritos and cups of soup—stepped down a long corridor, and stopped before room 444. His recent date with doom at 4:00 a.m. made him wonder if someone consciously selected this floor and this room as a symbolic reminder of a debt owed.

One of his escorts knocked on the door. A man—cut from the same cloth as the gangster henchmen, right down to the bulge beneath the breast pocket—admitted them. The lights were off, the curtains pulled. Through the darkness, Johari had the impression of a large suite. Silhouettes of a sofa and chairs suggested this was the living room. The edge of a canopy bed was visible through the entryway to a room on his right. A man sat on one of the chairs, an end table beside him, his features lost in shadow. Johari was seated in a chair facing the man and eight feet away. The escorts stood at a respectful distance, arms folded, two behind Johari, one to the side. They weren't there for his security. His throat went dry again. He wondered if he should've asked the van to pull over and let him out earlier. He looked around, gauging possible escape routes. He had none. The guards behind him blocked access to the outer corridor.

The shadowed man spoke in a honeyed baritone. "You've had quite a night, Mr. Hightower. How are you holding up?"

"Happy to be alive," Johari replied. "Hoping I stay that way."

"As do I." The man waved an arm toward a bar on their left. "Can I offer you a drink? After what you've been through, I'm guessing you'll want something strong."

"A coke. No glass. Just the can." Johari had used a soda can as a weapon on more than one occasion. Surviving a juvenile detention center will do that to you.

"A coke for Mr. Hightower, scotch on the rocks for me," the man said to one of the guards. "You must have a million questions," he said to Johari.

"A few."

"Ask. I'll answer as many as I can."

"Who are you?"

The man raised one finger and waved it like a wind-shield wiper. "One thing I know about you, Mr. Hightower, you're smart, although your grades don't reflect that fact. We're in a darkened suite. Let's leave it at that."

Johari's eyes were beginning to adjust to the dimness

of the room. He had the impression of a pug nose and cheeks and small eyes that seemed at once amused, sharp, and in control. A tall frame, thickening waist, and the suggestion of an arch half-smile added little to identify the man.

"Okay," Johari replied. "Who kidnapped me, why, and why did you save me?"

The guard brought Johari his coke on a tray and then served the scotch to the man in shadow.

"Bravo, straight and to the point." The man swirled his drink thoughtfully, the ice cubes tinkling. "There is no easy answer to your first question. Let's just say there are people who would like you gone. I don't know all their reasons."

"Phillip March?"

The man seemed to smile. "Good, you're as sharp as I hoped. Yes, I'm fairly certain March is one of them. He couldn't dispose of you legally, so he had it arranged." The man leaned forward. "But others may be involved."

"Who?"

"If I knew, I would tell you."

Johari took a sip of his coke, saddened that the tab had been pulled. It made a better weapon unopened. "How did you know they'd grabbed me?"

The man tasted his scotch. "As a businessman, Mr. Hightower, it behooves me to keep my fingers on the pulse of things."

"Like kidnappings and illegal executions, things like that."

"That and more."

"What do you want with me?"

"You're valuable to me."

Johari waited.

"I have a proposition for you." The man swirled his

drink and took another sip. "I want you to return to the House."

Johari's grip tightened on the can. Had he somehow fallen into a bizarre dream? Twice in the same night he'd been asked to return to the House, first by Greta, now by this mysterious man. As he had earlier, for a terrifying moment, he wondered if he *was* still in the House, that Greta and this man were phantoms come to knock him back to reality, to awaken him to where he really was, that perhaps he had only moments to pull out of some stupor or enchantment or he would disappear forever as Calista and Brice had. And he half expected the walls of the hotel room to roll back or dissolve, replaced by a ghastly snake pit or dungeon in which he was imprisoned.

His throat was as dry as a desert. He downed half the can. "Why?" His voice sounded far away.

"I'm a man of power and means. You've figured that out already. It's my business to know what happens, how things work. Few people know what I'm about to tell you." The man leaned forward. "Those who don't leave the House don't die. As some have speculated, they do indeed go to another place to live out their lives."

"What kind of place."

"That I don't know, but I know it exists. I've seen official documents about it. I want you to go there and bring some-body back."

"Who?"

"The scientist who created the House."

NINE

Johari wasn't sure what he expected to hear; perhaps a lost loved one or a friend, as Greta had proposed. But the inventor of the House?

He downed the rest of his coke and stared at the can. His head was swimming, and he had the urge to press the cold can against his temple. He put it on the table beside him, trying to pull his thoughts together.

"He'd be pretty old by now. How do you know he's still alive?" he asked.

"I don't."

"Let me see if I've got this right—you want me to go back into the House, but you don't know where this world is, if it even exists, and you don't know if the guy you want is still alive. And I'm guessing if I made it there, you're not sure if I can leave. That sum it up?"

There was enough light in the room to catch an impression of the man's eyes. They seemed to curl up, like he was smiling in appreciation. "To a tee."

"You said you thought I was smart," Johari said dryly.

"I do, Mr. Hightower. And I don't expect you to do it

out of the goodness of your heart, nor do I think you'll do it because I saved your life. I offer a business proposal, pure and simple. If you bring back Dr. Welty, the scientist I seek, I will pay you fifteen million dollars. That's enough to set you up for life."

And then some. Still hot, maybe hotter, Johari loosened his tie. "Can I get another coke?"

The man nodded to one of the guards, who brought Johari another can. This time, Johari put it against his brow before popping it open and taking a long swig. "I'll pass."

"I'm not done with my offer." The man took a legal-size envelope from an end table beside him and his guard brought it to Johari. Johari opened the envelope and drew out a copy of a torn document. With a chill, he saw Sky Stormrunner and Loïc Hightower typed on it. His parents! More astonishing, written at the top were the words, Classified, Sealed Under Section 502.

"How did you get this?" Johari asked. "Even my attorney couldn't get at it."

"I told you, Mr. Hightower, I'm a man of means."

And a man used to getting his way, Johari thought. "You've gone to a lot of trouble for this."

"As I said, you're not stupid. I needed to sweeten the deal."

"It's torn."

"I don't have the whole file, but I can give you the other half of what you see."

"If I bring back Dr. Welty."

"No, Mr. Hightower, if you return at all. I don't expect you to take the risk for nothing."

Johari slid the papers back into the envelope and held it up for the guard.

The man in shadow made a pushing motion in the air with his hand. "It's yours. Study it at your leisure."

Johari gazed at the envelope, considering. Questions had plagued him all his life, mysteries, puzzles, secrets, all surrounding his parents, why they disappeared, where they went. Why they left him. Somewhere deep within him was a gaping fissure. It plagued him in his dreams. It kept people at arm's length. As far back as he could remember, he'd had the idea that if he could answer those questions, about himself, about his parents, the fissure would close. "What happens if I refuse?"

"You go your way. I go mine."

Johari turned the can in his hands. He could hear it fizzing. He wondered idly how many bubbles a can of soda contained, how long before each of them popped. "Sorry, can't do it."

"I understand. No one has a pretty idea of the House. Few people make it out. It seems like suicide to risk it twice."

"This would be my third time."

"That I didn't know."

"No one does except Greta Orngold. I went in when I was ten, to be with my brother, Paul."

That smile touched those eyes again. "You see, you really are the man for the job. You made it out, even as a boy."

He'd made it out. He was clueless how he'd done it the first time ... The second time, with Greta, the parts he remembered had been dark and filled with terror. "Sorry, it doesn't change anything."

"Perhaps this will." The man gave a second envelope to his guard, who passed it to Johari. "Don't open it now. I'll leave you to consider my offer. This suite is yours. Enjoy it.

If you decide to decline, there's ten thousand dollars in there, for your trouble. I ask that you keep this meeting a secret." He glanced meaningfully toward the guards, as if to say, *Blabbing would be unwise*. "If, on the other hand, you take my offer, I will have a car waiting to pick you up at 8:15 a.m. tomorrow." The man rose. "Now if you'd be so kind as to step into the next room ..."

Johari went into the bedroom and sat on the corner of the bed. The guards were wiping down the bar, presumably to remove fingerprints. As the architect of this night passed into view, Johari was able to discern that the man wore gloves. At the door, he said, "Good night, Mr. Hightower. See you in the morning." A triangle of light from the hallway penetrated the room and then narrowed to nothing as the door closed.

Johari jumped to his feet, found a wall switch that turned on the bedroom lamps, and then another that controlled the living room lights. He thought of rushing to the door, to see if he could catch a look at his host, but the whole interaction had been so polite, so respectful, it seemed wrong to not honor the man's privacy. Besides, all Johari would see is the man's back, and he was certain the guards would be blocking that view.

He stepped to the phone pad and tapped for the front desk, leaving the screen on audio only. His recent brush with Banishment, as well as shadow man's desire to remain incognito, made him cautious. A sleepy-sounding young woman came on the line.

Johari asked, "Who's this room checked out to?"

"Why, you, Mr. Jackson."

"How many nights do you have me down for?"

"Let me check." There was a pause. "You have it through Sunday."

Five days. In a place like this, that was ten thousand dollars, easy. "Who paid for it?"

Another pause. "You did. The credit card is under your name."

Jackson wasn't the man's name; he was too shrewd to miss a detail like that. It must be an alias he'd arranged to keep Johari off March's radar, if Johari was to believe that March was behind his kidnapping. On the other hand, who else was gunning for him? Shadow man could have arranged the kidnapping so he could also save Johari. But that seemed unlikely. He appeared supremely confident in his powers of persuasion.

Johari glanced at the unopened envelope on the table. Well, the man might be persuasive, but that didn't mean Johari had to play along. He stepped to the window, pulled open the blackout and gauzy drapes, and looked out. The lake was midnight blue and mysterious in the moonlight. On the other side of the water was the silhouette of the Ferris wheel from the Merrimaker Amusement Park.

He turned and checked out the bar. It was stocked plentifully with soda, beer, and various white wines in the fridge, a variety of reds on the shelf—all expensive, he was certain—along with gin, rum, tequila, bourbon, rye, vermouth, vodka, and a good selection of liqueurs. He popped open another coke and, skirting the table with the unopened envelope, returned to the bedroom. After the narrow mattress in his studio, the hotel's bed was a lake. He was too on edge to sleep. Adjoining the bedroom was a large Jacuzzi. He had plenty of time to try that. Hell, first thing in the morning, he would call Greta, invite her to join him in it. Even as the thought rose in his mind, he squashed it flat. She'd made her intention clear at the party. He couldn't reopen that conversation. Not now, anyway.

Back in the living room, he checked out the entertainment system. It boasted a vast library of holo-vids and some new virtual games. He would try them as soon as he could focus straight. The events of the night were still tumbling through his mind: his kidnapping, facing certain Banishment, his rescue, the improbable conversation in this room. It all seemed like a surreal nightmare. He glanced at the digital clock on one of the walnut dressers. 3:52 a.m. Eight more minutes and he would've been a goner.

The man's words came back to him: "Good night, Mr. Hightower. See you in the morning."

Johari had to hand it to him, the guy was confident. What could there possibly be in that envelope that would make him so certain? It didn't matter. The House was out of the question.

He picked up the open envelope with the torn info from his parents' file. Why had they been targeted? Why had the file been sealed? These questions and dozens of others had tormented him for years. Yet now that he held some of the answers in his hands, going down that road seemed like a rabbit hole. One without a bottom.

He pushed the chair back and went to the game console, but before he'd even started playing, he was back, staring at the second unopened envelope.

See you in the morning.

He ripped the envelope open and removed a holo-vid disk. He dimmed the lights, powered on the projector, part of the entertainment system, and popped in the vid. The next moment, Greta stood before him, ghostly, the room visible behind her.

She wore the same dress she'd worn at the trial. Had this been filmed just before?

She spoke, the same troubled expression he'd seen at the

party etched on her face, "My angel, by the time you see this, I'll be in the House. Please don't be mad. I wish we could have had more time. You must know, I'll never forget, will always treasure the moments we shared, the night in the amphitheater ..." She colored slightly. "Our kiss in the pool outside the House after we escaped it. I know you'll be hurt. If I make it out, you may never want to see me again. Try to understand, as children, Calista and I swore we would leave the House together, that we would stand together, never abandon each other. I can't live with myself if I don't try to bring her back, and I would be no good to you. She would always be on my mind, a shadow hanging over me. That wouldn't be fair to you. If I return, please don't ask me who the man is who gave you this. I promised him I wouldn't reveal his identity. Know this: I believe him when he says there's another world beyond the House; I believe him when he says the House is the way there; I believe—" She stifled a sob. "I believe him when he says it's a terrible place." Her throat tightened, but her next words weren't strangled—they were determined. "I won't leave Calista there. If I don't return, at least she won't die alone." Her eyes seemed to lock right on him. "Forgive me for with-holding all this. Never doubt, I love you with all my heart."

The image vanished, and with it, the world seemed to crumble.

TEN

The walls were falling in, the room fading to lifeless gray, its opulence no more important than the remains of a demolished building. In a kind of stupor, Johari put the vid back in the envelope and stared at it, trying to gather his thoughts, to parse what she'd said. He rose, wobbled, and began to pace. The temperature of the room seemed to have risen twenty degrees, though the air conditioner was blowing. He stepped into the bathroom, washed his face with cold water, and poured handfuls of it down the back of his neck. He gazed into the mirror. The young man staring back looked haggard, his eyes swollen and dazed.

"Greta," he murmured. "What have you done?"

He had finally turned his life around, put his past behind him. And he had Greta, the last girl anyone would match with him but who fit with him like two parts of a whole. They had it all. A bright future beckoned. She'd flushed it all down the toilet, taking him down with her.

Something reared up inside him, snarling like a cornered beast. In a red haze, he whirled and rushed into the bedroom. He ripped the comforter, blanket, and sheets from the bed. He tore at the pillows until the room was a blizzard of feathers. He hurled a fruit basket at a mirror above the bureau. The mirror cracked and a Picasso reflection looked back, half like him, half a fragmented creature, the mouth twisted in a snarl.

He wilted to the floor, soaked in sweat, shaking, shivering, his heart pounding and roaring in his ears. Her words swam in his head: *My angel ... don't be mad ... try to understand ...*

"Greta," he moaned, a wounded animal now. But she was not to be silenced.

Terrible place ... can't live with myself ... bring her back ...

Her words kept shuffling, as if there were another meaning, if only he could grasp it.

A shadow ... always on my mind ... bring her back ...

It was no longer her voice; it was his, as though his mind knew before he did what he must do.

Bring her back ... the House is the way.

ELEVEN

Diary of the Damned ...

There my beloved was, staring at his face reflected in a fragment of steel. His cry would've woken the dead. Sadly, in the City, the dead are better off dead, and if they walk the streets, they leave you alone.

The near dead, however, took his scream as a dinner call. How we survived the next hours is a testament to his strength, determination, and survival skills. I'm not flattering myself when I say that it had a lot to do with me. After seeing the condition of his face, a big part of him wanted to let go, move on from the world, which had offered so much in New Earth and left him so little here. But I was there, the one thing that made him hang on. Without him as my protector, I was dead meat.

He had a minute of self-pity. Then it seemed we were locked in hours of running, hiding, battling, fighting with anything we could lay our hands on, then running again. Rats, dogs, mobs like we had seen before, crazed and red-eyed men and women who converged on us like a pack of wolves and who just as easily tore at each other.

The rest of that first day is hazy. I know we found a hole and huddled together, whispering about what had befallen us in the House, about where we were now, about how we would survive.

The need for food and water drove us from hiding. Strangely, he adjusted quickly to the situation, as if the pampered life he'd led were a big mistake, and all along this was what he'd been made for. If you dropped him in a jungle—hundreds of miles from civilization—filled with snakes, poisonous spiders and plants, hostile savages armed to the teeth, and man-eating lions, tigers, and a host of other ferocious predators, he would be the one in a thousand who would walk out alive.

I'm certain I was more of a liability than an asset.

He doesn't hesitate to kill. The rats avoid him. They may be the smartest mammals in the City. The dogs are another story. They never stop coming after us, no matter how many of them we kill. A fallen comrade means nothing to them. They storm over the animal as if it's part of the rubble.

It seemed at times that the higher on the phylogenetic scale, the more bestial and crazed the animal. I'm glad there aren't any monkeys.

A million fears crowd my mind when he leaves to hunt. Will he come back? Will he be killed? Will he inadvertently lead our enemies back here and we're both killed? If he dies, how will I survive? If I had a watch, I would count the seconds until his return. Even now I worry he won't. He always does, and I beg him not to leave again. But we need food and water, and he says I'll be safer if I remain unseen. Somehow, it doesn't make me feel safer. I'm convinced the dogs and mobs have developed an uncanny sense of smell and detect me. It's only a matter of time before they sniff me out.

We move often, finding some new hole to set up camp. He scavenges food and water. I don't ask where he gets it or what the meat is. In a few hours of arriving here, he'd fashioned weapons.

In a few hours they were stained red.

There's no day or night here. When he comes back, we spend hours holding each other. We haven't made love. There's no reticence on my part. I don't care about his face. I know what's inside him. I've touched his soul, and it's beautiful. It may seem hard to believe. He was smug, arrogant, cold, selfish, full of himself. All that's gone. He says the House took something from him. Maybe it did. The old him I would sleep with for a fling. The new him I could love. If he'll let me.

He's too ashamed of his face to let that happen.

What was I saying about a cruel god?

I can't be sure, but I think I started feeling sick that first day. I didn't say anything. Why worry him? Three days into our ordeal, it was clear something was really wrong with me. My eyes burned. Sweats, chills, trembling, and high fevers wracked my body. At times I raved. He never said a word about it, but when I came out of one of the spells, I found I was talking nonsense.

He hovered over me, wiping sweat from my brow, covering me with a blanket he'd found, spooning broth past my reluctant lips, as I had little appetite.

He tied me down when he left to hunt, so I wouldn't wander off, delirious. The times I was clear, when he wasn't tending to me, he sat hugging his knees, brooding.

It seemed he never slept. His head cocked to the side at the slightest sound. He continually watched the shadows.

The worst part of my illness was the voices, sometimes in my head, sometimes whispering just behind me. The things they told me to do, things I wanted to do: to gnaw my own flesh. To gnaw his. I wanted to kill him, to sink my teeth in his neck until his blood spilled over both of us.

When I was clear, I told him to kill me. Better for me; better for him.

"I'll never do it," he swore, but I saw my eyes—crimson discs that showed me my future—reflected in his eyes, tender and adamant.

He tied me up all the time then, as much for my safety as his. But still, he needed to hunt. I must have chewed through my bonds. The rest is a blur. I stumbled and wandered through the City, I don't know how long, until I saw a face, a beautiful face, half man, half dog, he seemed, the paws of a dog hanging by his jaws, a dog's head crowning his human head, and he whispered and crooned that I was safe, that he would take care of me, that I would never want for food or water. If I joined him, I would never feel pain again.

I fell to his feet, clutching his ankles.

I'm not the same. It isn't just that the chills and fever are gone. I'm different. I remember everything about my life, growing up in Grafton, going into the House, coming to the City. None of that seems important. I serve *him*.

He calls himself Lightfighter, lord of the City. He rules over a ragtag mob of followers. The illness burns in our eyes like hot coals. Our minds are clear but not clear, like being junked-up without losing coordination. I am, anyway. I know exactly what I'm doing. I *want* to do it.

Lightfighter wears a hood made from the pelt of a dog. Paws are tied on the sides with leather thongs. The glassy-eyed dog's head sits on top like an aborigine's shrunken head. Unlike the other men in the City, who have long matted hair and beards, his face is smooth, the lines of his jaw clean, like polished marble. He holds you fixed with smoky gray eyes. The eyes of a sorcerer.

I only desire to serve him, to please him. I'm his little kitten, his toy, his child, his lover. I sit at his feet and do his bidding. He gives me to the men and some of the women as reward for good service. I go willingly, not just for pleasure but because it pleases him. When I lay with them, I feel my power. It intoxicates me. I'm a demon. A goddess. I make them weak; they make me strong.

I walk in the City now without fear. We, the dog people, *are* gods. The Lost Ones—as we call the souls who have not joined our band—shun us. Our dogs protect us from the strays that run mad through the streets. The rats fear our dogs.

Once, in an alley, straggling behind the group, I heard a whisper from the shadows. Turning, I saw a figure squatting behind a rusted trash can, a mask of rough burlap and crudely cut holes for features over his head. He called my name, his voice no more than a breath.

I walked on.

Tales grew ... A new god walks the City. He slays rats, dogs, and men. He eludes our band, scaling the walls with ropes, then showering down a rain of projectiles. He seems to melt into the ruins, to disappear from the streets. He rules the sewer, the one place we, the Dog People, dare not venture. We shun the bats that haunt the pipes and tunnels.

"Get him," Lightfighter tells us. "Or feel my wrath. The City has but one god."

We feel his wrath. Piteous cries come from the punishment room where Lightfighter metes out discipline to those who displease him.

He asks me if a masked man came with me to the City. I can't lie to Lightfighter. I speak the truth: no masked man came with me. I arrived alone. He asks if a masked man had been in the House with me. Again, I do not lie.

He strokes my hair, twining it through his fingers. He pulls it sharp, yanking back my head, and searches my eyes. With a grunt, he releases me, and I lean against his chest, purring like a cat. He has other women. I'm his favorite.

Often, with a bonfire blazing and meat roasting, I strip off my clothes. I rub fat on my skin and hair until they glisten. I dance for him, for the group, for me. I smolder. I burn. The night drenches me.

My stage is a slab of fallen concrete that once was a floor of the subway. Thirty feet above, where it broke away, is a dark balcony.

Once, I saw him squatting in the shadows there, the holes of his mask peering down at me. I was so lost I didn't care that he saw what I'd become. I reveled in it.

The House took something from me. That's why I got

sick, became lost and soulless. Even then, a part of us remains, a tiny ember that refuses to die. I do what Light-fighter wants. I'm his to command, to use or toss aside.

But I never breathe a word about the Masked One—the only one who lives forever in my heart—or the location of his hideouts. I would throw myself off one of the ruins first.

TWELVE

At 8:00 a.m., pumped with coffee, fortified with a three-egg omelet, and dressed in jeans, polo shirt, and sneakers that fit him to a T (found in the closet and no doubt courtesy of his mysterious host), Johari stepped to the front desk, where a young woman in a crisp suit typed at the hotel computer. Her shiny name tag said JANET COLLINS, YOUR CONCIERGE WITH A SMILE!

"Hi, Janet. Is there a hotel safe?" he asked.

"Yes, sir." She looked about his age. She wasn't smiling.

He handed her the two envelopes, one containing the file on his parents, the other Greta's holo-vid. He'd sealed both with tape from the gift shop—where he'd also bought a Good Times chocolate bar for later—and wrote "Mr. Jackson, Room 444" on the outside.

"Put these in the safe. If I don't return for them by checkout, send them here." He handed her a piece of paper with his attorney's name and number on it. "If they aren't here when I return, or Mr. Gilbert doesn't get them, I'll sue this hotel for ... Let's just say I'll be your new boss."

"Don't worry, Mr. Jackson. We'll take care of it."

She gave him a form to sign indicating the hotel was holding two envelopes.

"I had an accident," he said. He put five hundred dollars on the desk. "That should cover any damages."

She stared at him. "You look like that guy ... The one on trial."

Johari laughed. "I've heard that. Can you imagine his life? Must be a living hell."

She laughed uncomfortably. "He made it out of the House. That says something."

"No big deal, right? We did it."

She shook her head, her face paling. "I go in two months."

"You'll make it."

Her voice quivered. "My brother and sister didn't." She plastered on her concierge's smile. "They said they'll hold my job for me. In a year I could be an assistant manager."

He reached out and gave her hand a reassuring squeeze. "Then I'll come back next year. I expect to see Janet Collins in charge."

He exited the hotel and leaned against the wall near the entrance. One of the valets lifted a woman's luggage from the trunk of her car, helped her into the lobby, and then drove off to park it. The sun glittered on the lake and promised a hot day. A few people were already jogging and riding bikes on the boardwalk. A light breeze bore the scents of roasted peanuts, hot dogs, and popcorn from the amusement park. The roller coasters weren't running yet. One of the cars, left stranded when they'd turned it off, was perched on the edge of a precipice, about to make the plunge.

He had four days left in room 444. If he and Greta made it out, they could stay here. But he wouldn't bring her.

It would make him think of assault teams, masked henchmen, and the gray door where one disappeared into oblivion.

The valet returned. He was little more than a kid. Johari wondered if, like Janet with a smile, the guy was waiting for his crack at the House.

Johari asked him for the time. It was eight thirteen. Two minutes later, a stretch limo pulled up and stopped. The windows were tinted almost black, preventing him from seeing inside. A chauffeur got out, went around to the passenger side, opened the middle of three passenger doors, and raised a gloved hand to Johari. Johari entered the limo. The door was closed. He faced the back seat, but a partition was up, and all he could see beyond the smoky glass was a man's silhouette.

The silky baritone of his recent patron came over the intercom. "I hope you were able to sleep, Mr. Hightower."

"Not a wink," he replied. "I was too busy destroying the room."

"That's too bad." Whether this was a reference to sleep or the room wasn't clear until the man said, "You'll need your wits about you in the hours ahead."

"Don't worry, I paid for the damage."

"I'm not the least worried. I have complete confidence in you."

"Why's that?"

"I've read your psych reports. That's why I selected you."

They left the parking lot and pulled onto a road that ran along the lake. Johari strained to see something he might recognize of the man, but the glass was impenetrable. "How about Greta? Did you read up on her too?"

"Greta came to me."

The car atop the roller coaster started moving, blinding Johari for a moment as its metal frame flashed in the sun. It didn't go crashing down the track, as he imagined, but was brought down slowly by the operator. Coffee and peppers from the omelet he'd eaten earlier bubbled up and scalded the back of his throat.

"You wonder why she didn't speak of her intentions sooner," the man continued. "She wasn't holding back on you. She was protecting you."

It was unnerving that the man put his finger on what Johari was feeling. But there were limits to the guy's power; Johari wasn't reassured. For now, there were bigger fish to fry. If this guy had read up on Johari, what else did he know? Maybe something that would help him get Greta out safely.

"Why do you want the scientist?" Johari asked.

The man picked up a coffee cup, waved away steam to cool it, and took a sip. "I'm a businessman. It suits my plans."

"What else can you tell me about the House?"

"Survive it, Mr. Hightower. Don't let the House take you, or you won't be able to return."

"How do I do that?"

"There's an exit to the other world, the world of the scientist, just like there's an exit to this one."

"Any hints where?"

"I wish I knew. You'll have twenty-four hours to find it and return here."

"Or the House takes me, and I'm a permanent citizen in hell." Johari could make little of the man's facial expressions. A blink or crinkling around the eyes might reveal a lot. All he had to go on was the man's voice, which was rich, confident, and in control. Breaking the glass flashed through his mind. That was no longer Johari's style. And fruitless. Anyone who commanded a secret army had the limo equipped with bulletproof glass.

They pulled onto a highway. As they left Grafton, they passed a vandalized billboard facing inbound traffic.

"Your work?" asked the man behind the glass, without a glance back at the sign. He knew it was there. Johari wasn't surprised.

"Maybe."

But it *had* been him, a protest after seeing a young man get dragged from his home. The whole incident was as clear in his mind as if it happened yesterday. As soon as he'd seen the goon cars, he'd known what was going down. Two of them came tearing down the street, lights flashing. He'd melted behind a tree to watch. Goons don't like witnesses, but he could see more than a few upstanding citizens peeking from behind curtains.

The DOTH streamed from their cars. Three circled to the back of the house. Three strolled up the walkway to the front door. An old Saint Bernard lolling on the porch lifted a sleepy eye and allowed one of them to pat his head. An officer pushed the doorbell, which rang like church chimes. A man and a woman opened the door.

They didn't look scared; they looked abashed, apologetic. It didn't take half a brain to tell they were the parents and probably the ones who called the goons, who were welcomed into the house like dear relatives.

The door shut behind them. The dog settled his head on a forepaw and went back to sleep. All was quiet except the whoosh of cars a few blocks away on Harte Boulevard. Then a youth cried out a piteous *no!* Furniture crashed. He started yelling, swearing, desperation rising in his cries. They dragged him kicking and screaming onto the porch.

The only loving one in that house was the Saint Bernard. He scrambled onto shaky, arthritic legs, bared his fangs, and lunged at one of the goons. He was rewarded for his loyalty with a Taser to his head that sent him crashing to the ground. Despite his discombobulated nervous system, he still tried to rise and snap at the legs of his enemies.

Galvanized, red with rage at the sight of the Tasered dog, the kid pulled an arm loose and slugged one of the officers. Two shakes later, he was on the ground getting clubbed senseless. As he was carried to one of the squad cars, blood streaming from his temple, his mother and father stood in the doorway, clutching their hands, calling out encouraging pieces of parental advice: be brave, you'll do fine, make us proud. And the icing on the cake: we love you, son.

Johari didn't know the kid. Didn't need to know him to feel for him. This was the reward for refusing to enter the House: goons ripping you from your home.

It burned. Johari had to get it out, launch it somewhere. But he had to do it in a way that wouldn't make him a banner.

He'd slung his daypack over his shoulder and wove through side streets so no one spotted him and placed him in the area. He came to the edge of town where the highway stretches across empty fields to distant mountains, and a lone billboard—a rare one that wasn't plasma—greets departing drivers. Beaming parents, their hands on the shoulders of a smiling girl and boy, filled the sign. Above them was written:

BLESS OUR HOUSE, GIVER OF PEACE!

Johari wasn't an artist. He didn't leave tag-murals on the

sides of buildings or freeways. In New Earth, almost no one did. But he did keep spray paint handy for special occasions. Checking first to see that no one approached, he pulled down the metal ladder, which complained like a sick cow, and climbed to the scaffold below the sign. While he shook the can, he pondered the slogan.

Then inspiration struck. He erased the right leg of the *H* and the left leg below the crossbar, using a color that blended with the background, and stood back to admire his handiwork.

The sign now read:

BLESS OUR LOUSE, GIVER OF PEACE!

Seemed fitting. A louse is a wingless, parasitic insect that feeds off mammals and birds.

Now, in the black-windowed limo, driving past the sign, Johari was gratified to see his handiwork still there.

The rest of the trip passed in silence, until they pulled off the highway and drove down a country road. They exited a stand of eucalyptus. Strawberry fields stretched away on both sides, untended and left to grow wild. The car stopped beside a platform where tearful families usually said goodbye to their children, which now stood empty.

His host said, "No one is scheduled to enter the House today."

Johari wasn't surprised. Grafton was a small town, and the House had decimated the population. The government appeal for having large families notwithstanding, New Earth was careening toward extinction. And most of the population was skipping and laughing to the brink like children following the Pied Piper.

"No one except Greta," he replied bitterly. "Tell me she hasn't already entered."

"She wouldn't tell me her plan, for obvious reasons. If I told you, you would try to stop her from entering. All I know is that she's already in there."

The rage he'd felt in the hotel surged up again, but he contained it. It wouldn't help Greta if he lost it now. "Then she has even less time than me."

A panel slid open below the window separating them. An envelope was passed through and the panel closed.

The man said, "That's information you'll need to find the scientist."

Johari opened the envelope, which contained a brief dossier and a photograph of a bespectacled man in his forties or early fifties. He also found a business card with no name or address, only a phone number. He scanned the dossier. It revealed little and what one would expect: an eminent scientist with degrees in neuroscience and physics. Johari tossed it aside. He didn't want to be weighed down inside the House. But he pocketed the photo—of course, the man would be much older now—and the business card.

"Call that number if you get out. The money I promised you is in an escrow account."

Johari looked hard at the silhouette across from him. "I'm not doing this for the money; I'm doing it for Greta."

"I know. Better get going."

Johari started to get out, but paused. "I'm also a judge of character. You used Greta to get to me. If anything happens to her and I make it out, I'm coming after you."

The man's laughter bubbled with contempt. But when he spoke, his voice was as calm and congenial as it had been last night and contained no malice. "Good luck, Mr. Hightower."

Johari stepped from the car and faced the House. It was as he remembered, a three-story A-frame, the paint all but peeled off, wooden walls, weathered and sun bleached a mottled gray. Ornamental scrollwork adorned the gables. The woodwork was especially complex on the upper gable, with the shape of a hand raised in warning at the center of the triangle, as he'd seen before. But who knew? The thing was abstract, and perhaps he was only seeing what his mind conjured.

He followed the brick path toward the front door and passed the oil-black pond he and Greta had exited from not many weeks before. He paused to retrieve a key from beneath a rock, took the six broad steps onto the porch, and stepped to the front door, the floorboards creaking beneath his feet. Far away, so far he could not be certain he heard it, a seagull cried.

He unlocked the door. It swung open.

The House began to moan.

THIRTEEN

His impulse was to rush in. What if the moan was Greta's? But this was the House. One thing he remembered from before, everything kept shifting. Nothing could be trusted.

He shut the door and stopped. A striking symbol was carved on the center of the door: eight jigsaw pieces scattered about a star. Some of the pieces appeared to fit together, though what they formed was anyone's guess. To Johari's mind, the star was pulling the fragments in.

He gave a quick try at the door. The knob wouldn't turn, even though he hadn't locked it. Like his last time here, there was no easy way out of the House. For the last hours, he tried to recall how he'd escaped before, to no avail.

Turning away, he scanned the entryway. It seemed familiar: a blue rug running up the center, steps going upstairs on his left, a parlor and living room on his right, an entryway dead ahead. The House moaned again, but at the end, the sound seemed to twist up in the cry of a small child. It gave him the shivers, made him think of dark basements at night and profound loneliness.

He shook the feeling off and treaded quietly forward,

taking in details. The rug seemed off. Hadn't it been burgundy? The scrollwork on the wainscoting seemed different too. Just what the pattern had been teased at the edge of his mind. This one used the symbol on the door in a repeating pattern. That scrollwork had been important before, but why now eluded him.

He went through the entryway and stepped into a dining room. He passed a polished teak table and gave a quick try at the door to a side porch. It wouldn't budge. Whatever exit led to the other world—or out of the House— wouldn't be so obvious. But he had to try.

He passed into a pantry and from there the kitchen, where he saw Greta. She was standing by an old-fashioned gas stove, her back to him, humming. Even now, with the feeling the House was breathing down on them like a sleeping beast, his heart leaped at the sight of her. You could throw rags on her and she would look fantastic; now her plain jeans and T-shirt only emphasized that she moved with the poise and grace of a dancer.

He pulled himself together, was about to enter the kitchen, when she sang softly, "Red as the red of a red-winged blackbird, oh red as the red of a red-winged blackbird."

The melody had a haunting lilt to it, like an old ballade he'd once heard. It sent unsettling ripples through him.

The song apparently finished, he stepped forward. "I'm pissed."

She gasped and dropped an old-fashioned percolator coffeepot she was about to put on the fire. It landed on its side, some of the water hissing over the flame, the rest pouring on the floor. She whirled, her eyes narrowed, grabbed the coffeepot, and brandished it like a weapon. "Is that you or a phantom?"

"Me, last time I checked, but you better use that pot. I'm about ready to strangle you."

"You're not supposed to be here."

"Happy to see you too."

Her eyes blazed. "Not here. Dannie was right. If I loved you, I wouldn't think of pulling you into this. It's too much to ask."

He stepped toward her, snatched one of two dishtowels hanging on the oven handle, and began mopping up the mess of wet coffee grounds on the stovetop. She grabbed the other towel and began wiping the brown streams pouring down the oven door and spreading on the floor. Finished above, he squatted to work on the floor too.

"I've got this," she said.

"I don't think so. It's running all over the place."

"I can handle it."

"You can't."

Their hands collided. She left hers there, warm beside his. He was about to wrap his fingers around hers when she rose abruptly, stalked to the sink, and began wringing out the towel. When it was twisted tight, she threw it into the sink and turned on him. "I have a right to do this."

He joined her and wrung liquid from his towel. "Would have been nice if you'd told me yourself, instead of some guy with thugs in a dark hotel room."

"He wasn't supposed to tell you so soon."

Johari's laugh was cutting. "And you trusted him?"

She returned to the stove, started to wipe the top, kept wiping even though the porcelain gleamed. Her silence hurt more than anything she could say.

"Greta, he used you as bait to get to me."

She looked up at him, shocked. "What are you talking about?"

"So I would come after you."

"I don't understand."

He led her to a small kitchen table covered with a freshly pressed tablecloth with a yellow flower pattern and made her sit at one of the two chairs. He took the other and glanced around. The door to the basement at the far end of the kitchen and the passage at the right leading to the mudroom were as he remembered them.

"Let's start with you," he said. "Why did he seek you out?"

"He didn't. I went to him." Her hands were trembling, and he found himself softening.

"You know him?"

"Not well."

"Who is he?"

"I can't tell you."

"Even to me? After all we've been through?"

Her eyes flared. "Don't push me. I gave my word."

"Okay, okay." He drummed his fingers on the table, feeling time breathing down on him.

"Why did you go to him?"

"To see if the rumors I'd heard about another world were true. I hoped he could tell me how to get there."

"And he told you the way to get there was through the House."

"Yes."

"And you believe him?"

"He has no reason to lie to me. I'm helping him too."

"How?"

"I can't tell you. I promised." She picked up a saltshaker beside a peppermill and a jar of preserves and began turning it in her fingers.

Frustration mounted inside him, but he pulled on the reins. "Did he say anything about a Dr. Welty?"

She shook her head. "Who is he?"

"The scientist who invented the House." He took the photo out and placed it before her.

Her face darkened, and her hand tightened on the salt-shaker. She put it down with a rap, barely glancing at the photo. "It makes no difference."

He rose and held out his hand. "It's a fool's mission. We should leave while he can. We did it before."

She took his hand between both of hers and squeezed it. But she didn't rise. "Not without Calista."

He sat again, studying her. Her gaze was far away, her face hard to read. He searched for a last argument, something that would make her abandon this idea.

"The House has taken lots of people. I'm guessing some of them were your friends. Why are you throwing your life away for Calista?" It was harsh, but he had to say it.

"Would you come for me if I was wounded and lost and trapped in the deepest pit? Would you do that for me?"

"You know I would."

"That's what I'm doing for Calista. We had a bond. It's hard to talk about." She stood and turned away. "I was making coffee. Want some? You look like you haven't slept."

"I haven't."

"That's bad." She stepped to the stove, retrieved the coffeepot, and began washing it in the sink. "We can't let the House take us."

"He told me. How long have you been here?"

She glanced at her watch. "An hour."

He breathed a sigh of relief. "You weren't exactly rushing around looking for the exit."

She filled the percolator with water and spooned coffee

from a can into the top. "I wasn't. Do you remember much about the last time we were here?"

"Bits and scraps."

"Me too. It's faded, like a dream." She put the pot on the burner and turned on the flame.

"More like a nightmare. You took notes, didn't you? Last time you were here?"

"They got wet while we were in the pool. Most of it's unreadable."

The pot began hissing and vibrating and the first rush of water knocked at the glass top. She reached for two mugs hanging from hooks and her T-shirt rode up, revealing her hips, waist, and the golden skin of her back. It was going to be hard to stay angry at her.

"What was your plan?" he asked, pocketing the photo.

"To wait here."

"That makes no sense. We have to find the exit, and you've only got twenty-three hours."

She turned the fire down on the coffee, the steam filling the kitchen with an aroma that made him feel nostalgic, though why, he couldn't say. He'd only heard about percolators and was surprised Greta knew how to even use one. But then, everything about Greta was surprising.

"What do you remember?" she asked.

"Getting trapped on the second floor and in the attic."

"Exactly. We can't waste time getting stuck. What I remember is the House shifting and changing." She turned the fire off and poured the coffee.

"So we wait for it to come to us."

"We wait. How do cookies sound?"

"Sounds good. I bet this damn house never had anyone ignore it."

"That's the plan. Look in that cupboard. See if you can find flour."

He stepped to the cupboard, opened it, pushed aside boxes and jars of staples from a bygone era, and found a tipped-over sack of flour. The bag was torn and some of it had spilled onto the shelf. Something moved inside the bag. A rat thrust its head out of the flour. Then something strange happened. Superimposed over the whiskered muzzle was a man's face, the skin as black as night, the hair and beard frizzy, white, and untamed. He took a deep breath and blew. Flour jetted onto Johari's hair and into his nose. He fell backward. Powder filled the room, as if the kitchen no longer had a roof and it was snowing. There were flashes of light, little sparks of bright color. He seemed to be falling in slow motion.

Then everything went dark.

FOURTEEN

Johari could watch her forever. In a field dotted with yellow and violet wildflowers, holding her white summer dress out, Greta swayed to music only she could hear. Smiling, she drew Johari toward her with eyes like luminous lakes, with lips, soft and inviting. Only inches away now, wind fluttered her curls against his cheek, and they transformed into butterflies ... in the way things do in dreams.

He tried to dive back into the warmth and desire of the moment, but he was floating up, up, and the dream evaporated.

His head was a dead weight, the rest of him numb. He had a ripping hangover and thought that it must have been a hell of a party. He tried to remember where it had been, but couldn't.

He shivered. His eyes, gummy with sleep, opened halfway. He struggled to hold them open so he could see the fireflies swirling and dancing on the wind, as cool and light as a moth's wings on his skin. Gradually, all came into focus, and he realized it was snow.

A face loomed in front of him, the skin like rawhide.

Wine-colored scars were cut deep into it, as if someone had carved runes there. The lid hung at half-mast over the right eye, which fixed on Johari with the sharpness of a knife.

Johari's hands were pulled behind his back. Cords bit into his wrists. He yanked at his bonds, unable to move. The man dragged him to a stump and tied him there, then riffled through his pockets. His wallet was torn open and the bills tossed aside. Loose change was tested on the man's front teeth and slipped into a leather pouch around his neck. He sniffed at the Good Times chocolate bar and tossed it aside.

Through eddies of snow, the man moved on to Greta, a dozen feet away. He bound her to a fallen tree and searched her. Johari wrenched at the cords. His head pounded, a sledgehammer battering inside his skull.

Greta and the man faded as snow turned the world to white confusion.

Small fingers pulled and tugged at his wrists. A boy's face hovered before him. Johari fell onto his side into the snow. A fur skin was thrown over him.

The cry of a hawk, shrill and insistent, roused him. He sat up, pulling cobwebs from his mind. Greta was still pinioned to the tree, sleeping beneath a blanket. The boy sat cross-legged in the snow, regarding him placidly. He was wrapped in a bearskin cloak. Snow frosted his hair. A single braid hung down to his chest; a white feather fastened at the top fluttered like a wing. His skin was an earthy red ochre.

His jaw was set, his eyes determined, his bearing poised, though he appeared no older than nine.

The boy rose. "Can you walk?" His voice was as sweet as a flute. "We need to go."

Johari stood. The world spun for a long moment, but he regained his equilibrium. He gathered the wallet, bills, and candy bar, which had been laid at his feet, and returned them to his pocket, along with a few coins—fallen from his billfold, half buried in the snow—the scarred man had missed.

"Where?" Johari asked.

"Away from here."

They were on a bluff. A white hawk circled above them; a forest spread out below. Beyond, partially shrouded in clouds, a mountain reared up, girdled with snow.

A million questions ran through Johari's mind. Greta came first. He crossed over to her and nudged her awake. She reached for him. Her lips started to curl in a smile, but froze as she took in the boy and their surroundings.

She stood and brushed off snow. "I saw you," she said to the boy. "And a terrible man too. I thought it was a dream."

"He'll be back." The boy headed toward a cluster of pines at the edge of the bluff, beckoning them to follow.

Greta looked questioningly to Johari.

"He untied us," Johari said. "Let's see where this leads."

She gazed about her a moment and nodded. They had little choice. The vast landscape offered nothing but solitude. She pocketed her wallet and a picture of Calista, which had been retrieved, as Johari's things had been, and placed neatly by her feet. Both of their watches were gone.

They followed a narrow trail, the boy's moccasined feet treading soundlessly ahead.

"What happened?" Greta whispered to Johari.

"I'm not sure," he replied.

"But we're still in the House, right?"

He honestly didn't know, but he recalled shifting land-scapes they'd encountered in the House before. "Probably."

"Who was that man? Why did he tie us up?"

Johari pointed to the boy. "Maybe he can tell us."

But the boy turned, brought one finger to his lips, and hissed, "Do you want to bring Muloch!"

The name conjured images of a monster. "Who's that?" Johari asked.

"The man with the scars. *Hurry*."

They kept to narrow paths, cutting through the ivy-carpeted forest, always heading toward the mountain.

Several times, Johari felt the urge to pull Greta aside, to beg her to stop and look for a way out while they could. But there was no apparent exit in all the vastness. Even if they found one, the way Greta had looked at Calista's picture, the way her eyes grew misty, convinced him she wasn't leaving without her friend.

Still, Johari wanted more information. "Where are you taking us?"

"To my master, the Enchanter."

That didn't make Johari feel any better, and tension spread up his shoulder and into his neck.

At last, the boy stopped before an ivy-cloaked boulder. He looked around, peering deep into the snow-laden foliage about him, and then poured water on his fingers from a skin tied about his waist. His fingertip barely grazing the leaves, he drew a crescent moon with an eye inside the crescent.

"Quick," he said. "Before it dries." He stepped into the ivy. It shimmered like a woodland pool, then he was gone. A moment later, his head and shoulders stuck out from the leaves and he waved for them to follow.

Johari felt a tingle as he and Greta passed through the ivy and the boulder. On the other side was a ring of fir trees with a tent in the middle. A gypsy wagon—with walls, a roof, and two shuttered windows on the side—stood near the tent, and an untethered horse browsed on clover that cast an emerald mantle over the clearing. Warm sunlight flashed on a big brass bell she wore around her neck. Beyond, more boulders encircled the trees, effectively hiding the place. Despite all the snow outside, none of it lay here.

The boy raised the tent flap and held it for them as they ducked inside. An old man sat on a mat in the center. His skin was as black as obsidian, his body frail. His hair and beard were frizzy, white, and untamed. Gold-rimmed teeth were just visible beyond half-open lips, and drool, oozing from a corner of his mouth, traced a line down his chin. His eyes were vacant. But what caught Johari's attention was the man's face: it was the one he'd seen in the kitchen amid the blowing particles of flour.

"What's wrong with him?" Greta asked.

The boy dabbed away the saliva tenderly with the edge of his cloak. "Muloch stole his shells."

Greta glanced at Johari, her brow wrinkled with confusion. "Why?"

"He wants my master's power." The boy fetched a clay jug from one corner and knelt before the old man. With a piece of flannel soaked with water from the jug, he squeezed drops into the man's mouth, making the gold rimming his incisors shine.

"Why did he tie us up and take our things?" Johari asked.

"He'll steal anything he thinks has value."

"Did he bring us here?"

"No, my master did."

Johari glanced at the old man, whose blank stare and bony frame suggested he hadn't been capable of much for some time. "Why?"

"To help you."

"With what?"

The boy seemed about to answer, but the old man, who had remained motionless up to this point, stirred. With a great effort, he raised his head and fixed his eyes on Greta.

He spoke one word: "Calista."

Then he fell back and began bucking and jerking and frothing from his mouth.

FIFTEEN

All three rushed to the old man.

"Give him room," Greta cried.

But the boy insisted on holding the man's hands. A minute later, the shaking stopped. The boy blotted away saliva that had collected like sea-foam on the man's beard. He looped both of his arms securely around one of the man's arms and began lifting him back to a seated position, a testimony to how frail his master was, not to the boy's strength.

Greta moved in to help. "We should leave him on his side."

"He wants to be up," the boy replied.

Greta stared at him, incredulous. "How do you know?"

"He tells me what he wants. Like where to find you when Muloch tied you up."

"You hear him in your mind?"

"And my dreams. He's never far away."

Greta sank to her knees, feeling the man's pulse and looking a little stunned.

Johari knelt beside her. "Can your master show us the way to Calista?"

The boy arranged the man's hands, one above the other, palms up, and placed a wooden bowl on top. "Yes, but not like this."

Greta looked doubtfully at the old man.

"You think he's ready to die." A half-amused smile quirked the boy's lips. "He's as old as the mountains. Muloch would have to steal all his magic to kill him. Even then, he probably couldn't. But he's ill—" He choked back a sob. "Terribly ill."

"You want our help," Johari said. "To cure him."

The boy nodded. From a pedestal near the tent wall, he fetched a wooden staff, jagged as lightning and weathered to a dark brown. He placed it before the old man. "He needs the shells Muloch stole."

Greta stood. "We'll do it. Where do we find him?"

A chill went through Johari. He rose and took Greta aside. "Let's think this through," he whispered.

"It's a clear path, what we were hoping for."

"Not so clear to me." He waved his arm, encompassing the boy, the tent, and the old man. "If this is the House, and I'm pretty sure it is, we can't trust it."

"Not everything was bad before. There was a woman who guided us."

He remembered. She was robed and not quite human. "Right to where we lost Calista."

"She led me, and I made it out."

"Barely. Greta, he's sending us to the man who tied us up. That guy would stick a knife in you with less thought than he would a steak."

She studied him. "You have a better plan?"

He didn't. She knew it and turned away.

"How do we find Muloch?" she asked.

The boy's eyes lit up. "My master will guide you through me." From a shelf filled with small colored jars, he selected one that was indigo and emptied the contents, which looked like dried flower petals, into a small pot. He placed the pot over a fireless hearth, but a moment later, he tapped the pot with the Enchanter's staff and the water began to steam. A few minutes later, it was simmering, and a pleasant aroma filled the tent. The boy let the brew steep, then he poured the liquid into a cup. With one hand, he propped up the old man's head. With the other, he brought the drink to the man's mouth. To Johari's surprise, the lips parted, and the boy dribbled in some of the tea. After putting the cup aside, he eased the Enchanter back.

A ruddy light seemed to flare around the Enchanter's heart, so faint and brief, Johari wasn't sure he saw it. He looked to Greta, but she gave no sign she had noticed anything unusual.

"Are you ready?" the boy asked.

Greta nodded.

The Enchanter's eyes opened. He rose from the bed and stood with a great effort, swaying. Johari and Greta rushed in to support him.

"This will be too much for him," she cried.

The boy took the old man's hands. "Watch."

The old man's eyes rolled back so that only the whites showed. His lids fluttered. The boy's body jolted. A moment later, his eyes rolled back too.

"Help him to the wagon," he said.

With the boy backing out of the tent, and Johari and Greta on each of the man's arms, they led him to the wagon.

Outside, eyelids fluttering, seemingly blind, yet able to navigate as though he could see, the boy called to the horse,

"Hist, Millie!" She trotted over to him like a pet. Strangely, her bell didn't ring. Perhaps the clapper had been wrapped so it didn't strike the sound bow, alerting Muloch to their presence.

"Do you know how to hitch a wagon?" the boy asked Johari.

Johari did, the one bright spot of his bouts in juvie was a summer laboring on a horse ranch. The horses had a calming effect on him, and he loved anything that needed to be done for them, from currying to pitching hay.

"Just don't say ..." The boy whispered in Johari's ear, "Pretty Millie."

"Why not?"

"We've been trying to train her to turn right." In front of her, the boy backed five feet away and held up his hand. "Pretty Millie." Abruptly, Millie turned left and sat.

The boy looked grief-stricken. "See?" he said. "You wouldn't want her to do that on a mountain trail."

"No, that would be pretty bad."

While Johari hitched the horse, Greta helped the boy take the old man up the stairs and into the wagon. Johari lent them a hand sliding the stairs beneath the wagon. Then the three of them climbed onto the driver's seat. With the Enchanter's staff across his knees and a flick of the reins, the boy steered them through the rock-and-ivy wall. Soon they were bouncing along across the forest floor. At a turbulent stream, he stopped and climbed down from the wagon. With only the whites of his eyes showing, he waded in and guided the horse across, drawing an anxious breath from Greta. And when the way followed a narrow ribbon along a cliff wall, she cried, "Wait! You'll go off the edge!"

"Shhh," he hissed. "Do you want to warn Muloch?"

"I'm sorry," she murmured.

"The Enchanter guides my steps," he said more gently now. "He flies above us."

Johari had seen through the trees glimpses of the white hawk, soaring in the blue. Now it wheeled above and sent out a cry.

They plunged back into woodland alive with birdsong. At last, they stopped in a thick stand of pines. Sunlight slanted through the branches. A light wind bore the scent of smoke.

The boy raised his head and sniffed. "He was close. Now he's gone." He urged Millie forward. His eyelids no longer fluttered, the whites no longer showed, and he scanned their surroundings with those round deer-brown eyes of his.

A few minutes later, they found a campsite. Boot and hoof prints and a few horse droppings littered a clearing striped with patches of snow. Dirt had been kicked on the fire. The wood still smoldered; a half-eaten meat bone had been tossed among the ashes.

The boy circled the campsite, sniffing, examining a broken jug, stew flung near the fire, and a crude target carved into one of the trees. A tight circle of notches clustered in the center.

Head cocked, he looked skyward to the hawk, breeze stirring his feather. "He's gone to the village," he said, turning back to them. "I can take you there."

They exited the trees. The boy pulled on the reins, and Millie stopped; a hundred-eighty-degree view of a valley lay before them. A road snaked through verdant pastures and farmland until it came upon a small village nestled at the knees of a mountain.

"Is that where we're headed?" Greta asked.

The boy nodded. "There's a tavern at the far end. He'll be there, drinking."

She signaled forward like a soldier. "Lead on."

As the wagon bounced along, Johari studied the distant buildings with growing disquiet. It wasn't just the prospect of facing Muloch—though after seeing the scars on the tree, surely made by knife throws, that was bad enough. It was the way this was playing out, so different from the last time they were in the House. Then, he'd had a feeling of being restricted. And of constant danger. Now he wondered if they were being led astray.

The boy brought the wagon to a stop at a crossroads. A scattering of trees and rocks, some of them quite large, bordered the road here and a short way down toward the village.

"We need to walk the rest of the way," he said.

The sun prickled the back of Johari's neck. He swatted away a fly. "That'll take too long."

"No choice. Everyone knows the Enchanter's wagon."

"Won't they know you too?"

The boy slipped inside the wagon. He returned with a hat pulled low. "Let's hope this works."

Johari liked none of it, but there seemed little choice. They climbed off the wagon, and the boy whispered in Millie's ear. The horse bobbed its head twice and trotted off across a pasture, the wagon bouncing behind her. "She'll be there when we need her," the boy said.

Dust blossomed at their feet as they tramped on. The butterflies floating about the wildflowers, the lazy motion of the grass, and the hillsides sleepy with sheep did little to calm the ever-tightening knot in Johari's stomach. The rugged landscape, Muloch, the Enchanter, and everything else here were projections. Solid projections. The House had a way to do that—though Johari couldn't begin to fathom how—and the House was dangerous.

Half a mile down, when the boy ran ahead to pluck berries by the side of the road, Johari grabbed the chance to talk to Greta.

"The clock's ticking," he said.

"I know." She marched doggedly on.

"He's led us all over the mountain. We're no closer to finding Calista."

"We don't have a choice."

"We do. Look for the exit. Get out while we can."

Her face hardened. "If you think I'll do that, you don't know me."

He turned on her. "Don't we matter?"

Something fierce lit her eyes. "What good is us, if I'm all wrong?"

"What does that even mean?"

"I can't explain it." She stalked on.

"Try."

"I don't want to drag you into this. You should go. Look for the exit. You're better off with Dannie."

What the hell was she saying? Did she love him or not? His face went hot. "If you think I'll leave you to the House, then you don't know *me*."

She stopped, looked down, and studied her feet. When she spoke, her voice was little more than a whisper, a hoarse rasp the wind snatched and flung away. "Don't ask me to say more, please."

He reached for her and enfolded her in his arms. She

stayed a few heartbeats, as if balancing on a point, then fell away, her eyes misted.

He caught up with her, and they trod on in silence. He sifted through what she'd said, through all they'd been through, trying to make sense of it. It didn't take a genius to figure out why. Hadn't it always been that way? Who'd ever stayed? Not one foster family. Not one counselor or parole officer. Not his parents. Not even Paul. Every single one of them had left.

A mile on, they stopped as sheep crossed to graze in a field on the other side. Then they left the meadows and pastures behind and came upon farmland. Men tilled with wooden plows pulled by oxen, and sometimes by men with wooden yokes, harnesses, and ropes that bit into their flesh. A few stopped to stare at their clothing, but a crack from a whip turned the curious back to harsh toil.

None of this looked good.

"We need a plan," Johari said. "The House can take one of us any time. That's what it does."

Greta stared fixedly ahead. "Nothing bad has happened yet."

"That's what's bothering me. Before, shit happened fast. We got trapped. We were running, from what, I can't remember, but it was out of my worst nightmares. Then Calista and Brice were taken."

She pondered that. "So something will come."

"We need a way to fight it."

"I don't remember much either, but we didn't fight. That's not how we got out."

They paused to allow a cart, loaded with large mason jars, to trundle by and up the hill.

When the cart had passed, Johari said, "All I'm saying is

don't forget—this kid? The House brought him for a reason."

"But it brought the woman too. She never hurt us." She stopped and stared at him. "She guided us."

Memories were starting to come back. How Calista had evaporated before his eyes in a cold barren place. It made him shudder.

But it wasn't all bad. He recalled a girl with pitch-black hair and savage eyes—a wild thing, no older than fifteen, dressed in crudely sewn animal skins. Feathers grew from the sides of her head and upper arms, as if a transformation was taking place, bird to human or human to bird.

When Greta had fallen unconscious, seemed a breath away from death, the girl had somehow been part of what cured her. Afterward, Greta seemed stronger, more vibrant, more truly herself. Even when they had left the House. He supposed that same determined spirit spurred her now to find her friend.

"Greta?"

She turned to him, her eyes dazzling in the sun, but touched now with vulnerability and pain he hadn't seen before. It brought out something tender in him.

"Can we start over?" he said. "I—"

She gripped his hand. "I love you too."

"Do you?"

"If you have to ask ..."

He let it stay there. She'd said it. Though it hardly seemed true, it was something to hang onto. He needed that. All of New Earth could blow up, the House with it. If he lost Greta, nothing mattered.

They walked a spell in silence. Sunlight worked magic in her hair, spinning it to gold. But her eyes, fixed like darts on the village, cooled him. Once, she hummed that same haunting ballad he'd heard in the kitchen, and then sang the last line softly to herself, "Red as the red of a red-winged blackbird."

The melody was beautiful, but it gave Johari the shivers. It reminded him of a folk song he'd sometimes listened to in the Grafton library. Unbidden, some of the verses came to him now:

> *Why are you going, my own true love,*
> *Down to the River Gray?"*
> *"To find my friend,*
> *Who tarried there,*
> *Now gone for many a day."*
>
> *"Go not, my love, 'tis a terrible place,*
> *All are lost at its shore."*
> *"Go, I must, I can't delay,*
> *To her an oath I swore."*
>
> *"The river, my love, hath but one strand,*
> *And the Gray King dwelleth there,*
> *He holds on tight*
> *To those he claims*
> *And chains them in his lair."*
>
> *"With magic he may snare them,*
> *But I am not afraid.*
> *Love for a friend is a worthy sword*
> *And sharper than his blade."*

More lyrics he couldn't recall followed, but he knew the end, which troubled him then as it did now:

"Have you been my love, to seek your friend,
Down by the River Gray?"
"I tarried there, to seek my friend,
Gone now many a day.

"For the love of a friend,
I fought a king,
Who pierced me in the heart,
Now lay me down and lay me deep
Where the blackbirds trill and sing."

Though the sun was warm, Johari hugged himself and glanced at the old and gnarled olive trees and the unplowed fields, as if the Gray King would spring from one of the trunks or out of the soil and spirit Greta away to the underworld.

He shook off the feeling and refocused. "I get it," he said after they'd walked on awhile. "You're mourning."

She stared straight ahead. They passed a man and woman carrying baskets of figs and grapes toward a low hut. At last, her voice strained and barely audible, she said, "Yes." They were almost on the edge of the village when she said, "But there's more."

He had no time to question her. The boy dropped back and stopped them. "You can't go in like that." He looked them over. "You need a disguise."

Made sense. Muloch had already seen them up in the snow. If he recognized them, he would either slip away or kill them. Killing the likely choice, by the look of him. With no change of clothes or theatrical makeup available, Johari couldn't see how to avoid detection, and said as much.

"I'm going alone," he added. "I won't risk Greta in there."

The boy shook his head vehemently. "You'll need her. Don't worry. The Enchanter has a plan. Follow me."

He led them behind the enormous trunk of a pepper tree, Johari following reluctantly. The trunk hid them from anyone looking from the road or the village. To Johari's surprise, Millie was there.

"I thought you didn't want her around," he said.

The boy grinned, a bright note in his usually solemn manner. "I didn't want her seen. She took a shortcut. No place for us."

He went inside the wagon and brought out a sack, from which he pulled two tunics and two pairs of sandals. "Quick, change inside," he said, handing a set to Johari, "before someone sees you. The farmers behind us won't say anything. Neither will their slaves. But someone from the village might."

Inside the wagon, the Enchanter lay on a straw pallet, motionless except for the fluttering of his lids, his eyes still rolled back in his head. Johari found a large trunk stowed in the front. Two cabinets of flasks and vials were attached to the inside of the shutters, so remedies and elixirs could be sold from the outside when the windows and shutters were thrown open. A narrow straw mattress lined one side, presumably for cold or rainy days when camping beneath the stars was not an option. Sweat permeated the air, but also pungent herbs and minerals needed for the Enchanter's potions.

Johari changed quickly and exited the wagon, feeling foolish in the tunic, which ran halfway down his thighs.

Greta grinned from ear to ear, the first thaw in her mood all day.

"One word and this mission is over," he said.

She burst out laughing. "I didn't say anything."

"Ease off him." The boy beamed. "Till you see what we've got for you."

She frowned. "Tell me."

She bent down and he whispered in her ear.

Her eyes widened. "Impossible."

"Possible," he replied.

"How?"

He opened the wagon window and selected from the array of potions a copper flask and a small leather pouch. He poured the contents of the flask into an earthenware cup. The liquid was as dark and blue as a sapphire. A pungent aroma like a mixture of fennel and wintergreen filled the air. He took a pinch of powder from the pouch, sprinkled it into the liquid, and swirled it around. Fumes rose but quickly dissipated.

He handed her the cup. "Drink."

"Greta—" Johari warned.

"It's okay," she replied. "If he was going to hurt us, he would have done it long ago."

The boy handed her a tunic and sandals, which she carried into the wagon along with the potion. They saw her close the window from the inside. A few minutes later, the wagon door opened, and a young man climbed down the steps. His hair was light brown. The shadow of a beard and mustache clung to his face.

Johari folded his arms. "Nice trick. Where's Greta?"

The boy's eyes twinkled. "You're looking at her."

SIXTEEN

While preparing for his second trial before the Supreme Council, Johari had spent a good deal of time memorizing every inch of Greta's body. He knew it better than his own. Countless afternoons, when they'd plowed through files, reports, and depositions, he longed to get lost in the thick waves of gold that tumbled to her shoulders, to explore the down on her arms with lingering fingertips, to press his lips to hers.

This man, little more than a boy with bony sticks protruding from his tunic, was not Greta, though there was a mild resemblance. Somebody must have hopped into the wagon, perhaps one of the farmers, while Millie meandered through the countryside.

When the young man spoke, he sounded like someone whose voice had just begun to drop. "It's me."

Johari folded his arms. "No."

"We kissed in the dark pool outside the House. I never wanted to leave your arms, though my father was frantic for my safety."

"The House might know that."

"But not that we danced all night in a forest amphitheater and watched the sun rise over the lake, and later you wiped syrup from my cheek at breakfast."

He looked at her in wonder, seeing now the tiny mole, just where it should be. "How?"

The boy glanced toward the village, his face solemn again. "Never mind, we've got to get going. She won't look like that forever. An hour, and she'll be back to normal."

"What do we do?" Greta asked.

"Muloch's haunt is at the far end of the village, a tavern called The Hatchet. Be bold. Stake your territory. But don't intrude on his space."

"How do we do that?" Johari asked.

The boy handed him the Enchanter's staff. "Drive this into the floor between you and him. He won't touch you."

Johari examined the staff, which had a thick end. "It's not sharp enough to pierce wood." He tried pressing it into the boy's hands.

The lad pushed it back. "It will."

"What's to stop him from carving us up with his knife?"

The boy nodded toward the staff. "He knows who that belongs to. Tell him you stole it from the Enchanter. That'll get his attention. You might have to improvise, say how you did it."

The more Johari heard, the weaker the plan sounded. "He'll just take the staff. That'll weaken the Enchanter more."

The boy's eyes, large and wise beyond his years, regarded Johari patiently. "He's shrewd. It took a dangerous man to get the shells. He'll be cautious with those who took the staff."

"Then what?"

"Get him drunk." The boy grinned. "I mean piss drunk,

so he passes out. You'll have to drink with him. Keep the rounds coming."

Johari shook his head. "I only slept a few hours. I'll pass out before he does."

The boy selected another flask from the shelf. "Not if you drink this. It takes the fire from firewater."

Johari eyed the vial. "Okay, then what?"

"Search him. He's got to have the shells on him somewhere."

Johari stared at him. "Stick my hand in front of a viper and hope he's asleep."

"We need them." The boy choked back a sob. "To make my master strong."

Greta put a reassuring hand on his arm. "We'll get them. What do they look like?"

"They'll be in a pouch beneath his tunic. Six long brown and white shells."

Johari chinned toward the wagon. "Give us something from there. To knock him out."

The boy shook his head. "Too risky. Muloch misses nothing. He'll see you slip it in his drink."

"Where will you be?"

"Outside, getting our escape ready."

The boy turned to watch a girl, no older than eight, walking toward the village with an empty basket. Her head was bowed in submission, but she seemed to feel his eyes on her and glanced his way. He waved her over. She looked around nervously, checking to see if anyone noticed. Satisfied no one had, she crossed the road.

When she stood before him, she looked up, wide-eyed. "Is it you?"

He smiled down at her. "Yes."

"Is he with you?"

"He sees you through my eyes, speaks through my mouth."

"Will I find good fortune?"

"Yes."

She frowned. "It hasn't been. I'm lashed once a week—sometimes more."

He laid his hand on her head. "Your fortune is assured. You will be sold three weeks hence. The man who buys you will die, but his son will free you, and in a few years you will marry him."

She gazed at him, hopefully. "Seal it."

Sorrowfully, the boy put his hand over his heart. "I'm out of shells just now. But if you're on the north edge of the village in an hour, I'll toss you one."

"Promise?"

"Promise."

The girl walked off humming, head held high.

"She recognized you," Greta said.

"Children know the Enchanter's boy." He looked after the girl wistfully. "Some of them, anyway."

"I could've given her my coins," Johari said.

The boy shook his head. "You'll need those to pay for drinks. A moment ..." He scurried into the wagon and returned with two weather-beaten cloaks. "Put these on."

Reluctantly, Johari pulled the cloak over his shoulders. The rough wool of it was itchy and smelled gamey. On Greta, though, it matched her homespun garb.

The boy surveyed them with satisfaction. "You'll fit right in."

Johari shook his head. "He'll recognize me. Change me like you did Greta."

"There's no more of what I gave her. Keep your hood pulled to your eyes and hope for the best."

He gave Greta a dagger, telling her not to hesitate to use it. She and Johari swallowed the firewater cure, a potion as thick as molasses and sour enough to make him shake. In five minutes, they'd walked the length of the village and stopped before the door to a long rectangular building made of stones. A sign swinging in the wind above the entrance bore a picture of a hatchet with bright red drops on the blade.

"Whether you get the shells or not, exit the back way," the boy said.

"I'm beginning to like you," Johari said. "You gave that girl a future."

"Not me. The Enchanter. I hope he does that for you." The boy shoved them toward the door. "Get going. Don't lose the staff. My master's attached to it."

They opened a heavy oak door and passed from bright sunshine into gloom. They stood a minute to let their eyes adjust. Even then, most of the interior, a great hall, was in shadow. The only light came from a fireplace at the far end. The glow from the flames penetrated a dozen feet and then quickly faded. But there was enough illumination to see men clustered around tables—men as rough as if they'd been hewn from granite. Knots of them gambled, tossing clay dice. Others slammed down tankards and roared with laughter. Several whispered in the corners with hats pulled low. The air was rank and suffocating.

Johari and Greta began threading their way through the mob. Servants, all female, many hardly more than girls, carried trays piled high with bread, wine, cheese, and figs. They wore long tunics, gathered at the hip, open at the side.

A man built like a boulder pulled one of the girls onto his lap and began pawing her. She stared off, far from her body, numb as an opium addict.

Greta hissed in Johari's ear. "I'm going to plant this dagger in his back."

"You know you can't," Johari replied.

"I know." But Greta started toward the man, her hand tightening on the hilt of the dagger.

Johari gripped her arm. "Look around. We can't fight them all."

Greta glanced about the room, her mouth twisted in a snarl. Half a dozen girls were similarly occupied. She let go of the dagger and followed Johari through the crowd, but not before growling, "I could slice them up."

A window halfway along the wall was covered with a dirty woolen blanket. Johari pulled it aside and peeked out. The road between houses was deserted save for a tumbleweed rolling in the dust.

Yelling erupted, turning him back to the room. He gripped the staff, hidden beneath his cloak, his heart pumping. Two tables away, a giant of a man reared up like a bear. His chair crashed to the floor. He overturned his table and pulled out a knife. The man across from him, a skinny weasel with an icy sneer, drew his own blade from an over-the-shoulder scabbard and rose, all in one easy motion. Onlookers rippled away from the duo, clearing space, allowing the combatants to circle and feint. With the speed of a coil spring, Weasel flicked his weapon. The next moment, the giant crashed to the floor, his eyes saucers, the knife lodged in his heart.

As quickly as the fight erupted, servants cleared away the fallen man, swabbed up the blood, and returned the table and chairs to their former spots. New customers settled there, heedless of the still damp stain at their feet.

Greta scanned the crowd with the vigilance of a hawk. "What have we stepped into?"

"A den of thieves," Johari replied.

"More like a hornet's nest."

They pressed on until they reached the far end of the hall. A horseshoe of tables faced the fireplace. Behind a tattered and stained blanket, a frame of sunlight revealed the rear exit. On the opposite side of the room, just out of the firelight, a man sat with his back to the wall. His black hat was pulled low, but the powerful shoulders, the leather jaw, and the claret line etched on his cheek marked him. Muloch. His chin hung toward his chest, as though he slept, but Johari had the sensation that he missed nothing in the room and had already spotted them.

They wandered to the fire, warmed their hands, then made their way toward him. Two empty chairs before him made a nook around a table cut from a tree trunk. They stopped beside the chairs.

Muloch spoke, the growl of a wolf. "They're taken."

Johari swept his cloak aside, revealing the Enchanter's staff. "I know." He sat to the man's right, Greta to the left, her dagger just visible. Muloch inclined his head, taking in the staff. No reaction crossed his face, though perhaps the color of his runelike scars deepened.

Johari signaled a servant. "What've you got that's stronger than that water you call wine?" he asked her gruffly.

She glanced apprehensively at the man sitting with them. She whispered into Johari's ear. "Tsipouro, but it's illegal."

"Don't quibble," he snarled. "Bring a bottle."

She looked around. Everyone was focused on an arm-wrestling match two tables away. "It'll cost."

Johari drew two coins from his pocket and banged them on the table. In New Earth, they wouldn't buy a candy bar.

Her eyes grew round. She swept them up in a flash.

"And bring cups for my friends," Johari said.

Muloch remained as motionless as the sphinx. His hands, massive rocks resting on his thighs, seemed capable of crushing stone to powder.

The servant brought a porcelain bottle and three cups. Johari filled the cups, pushed one to Muloch, and raised his to toast. "The Devil's due!"

He tossed down his drink. It burned like a ten-alarm fire and his eyes flooded. A sip left Greta gasping and coughing.

Johari laughed and clapped her on the back. "He's new to it."

Greta's eyes shot daggers. "I can put you under the table any day."

"The day I'm in my grave."

Johari refilled his cup. He extended the bottle, until it hovered over Muloch's cup, still full.

"Drink, my friend," Johari said. "There's plenty, and I'm in a generous mood."

Muloch leaned toward Johari, a wolf stretching. "How did you come by that staff?"

"Took it. Right under the owner's nose."

"How?" Muloch's eyes fixed on Johari. The near-dead one seemed to probe.

Johari waved toward Muloch's cup. "I hate drinking alone. Join me, and I'll tell the tale."

Muloch tipped his head, considering. He ran his finger over notches on his sword belt. Eight were visible. Whether more continued around the back, Johari couldn't say, but they reminded him of the tallies gunslingers made to mark kills.

Muloch raised his cup and made slow circles with it, swirling the liquor. He drank, his gaze never leaving Johari.

When he put down the cup, his eyes were dry, as if the drink were nothing more than milk. "Tell it."

Johari refilled Muloch's cup, then patted the staff. "Two tales. You say which is true."

Muloch gave a slight nod. "On with it."

"Every man has his weakness. The boy is the Enchanter's. He roams the forest for magic roots and herbs and brings them back to his master with a snared rabbit or squirrel for their meal. I spied out his haunts, set my traps, and caught him easy enough." Johari downed another cup and wiped his lips on his sleeve. "The rest was easy. I ransomed him for the staff."

Muloch remained stone-faced, but a little warmth had crept into his good eye, and he tipped another cup. "He wouldn't believe you had the little weasel."

Johari shrugged. "The weasel's braid and feather persuaded him."

Muloch's nostrils flared, an animal sniffing blood. Johari poured. They both drank.

"Go on." Muloch's speech showed no sign of the firewater.

"Tale two. The Enchanter is old, but he's a man. A girl lives in a village not far from here, a dancer who could mesmerize a snake. There are pretty girls and beautiful girls, and there's this girl, a gift from the gods to enchant mortal men. She keeps men at arm's length, playing with them. If the whim strikes her, she lures them in and breaks their hearts like eggs, leaving them raw and bleeding inside."

Muloch gazed upward, as though she were floating before him, casting her spell. He drank another cup.

"Even goddesses need money," Johari continued. "For a few coins, she went into his tent and danced before him. I waited a few minutes. When I was certain she had him in a trance, I crept in, took the staff, and knocked him out with it. That's the truth, the gods strike me dead."

"And the girl?" Muloch asked. "She didn't snare you?"

"I lit out of there. If I'd stayed, she would've sucked away my future."

Johari glanced at Greta, who eyed him coldly.

She took two gulps of her drink, which turned her eyes red. "Both stories are lies." She leaned forward, the firelight catching her whisper of beard and singeing the edges gold. "What I heard is that the girl had a soft spot for him, would die for him." She hooked a thumb toward Johari. "When she heard her love craved that staff, she waited for the Enchanter to bathe at a stream. When he was naked—"

A smile cracked Muloch's face. "Wrinkled sack of bones, he was." He reached for the drink and drained it in a gulp. Johari replenished the cup.

"Like a prune, but easy to hit with a poisoned dart. It didn't kill him—his power is too great—but he fell unconscious, and she grabbed the staff. That's what happened, from the lips of the girl herself."

Muloch's face split into a wide grin. "You made an enemy."

"Tell me about it," Johari said. "He's been on my tail for a week. I laid a trap for his wagon in the hills. He's probably still digging out of the snow."

Muloch laughed, drank, laughed, drank. They ordered a second bottle. It went on like that. They plied him with tsipouro and stories, without any sign his tongue was thickening. Then without warning, his eyes rolled up and his head dropped back to the wall and struck it with a thud.

Johari leaned forward, hesitated, then gave the wolf a shake. When he got no response, he passed the Enchanter's staff to Greta and she handed him her knife. He tore open Muloch's soiled, wine-stained tunic, baring his chest. A pouch was tied just below his sternum. Johari sliced through the leather cords and snatched the pouch.

Haunting music, like the jingle of hundreds of bells, floated in from the street.

Muloch's hand shot up.

SEVENTEEN

That enormous hand locked onto Johari's wrist. Pain shot up his arm. Muloch's eyes flared open and fixed on Greta. Her beard and mustache were dissolving, leaving moth-eaten patches.

A moment more and Johari's bones would be crushed. With a surge, he plunged his knife into Muloch's biceps. Muloch roared. His face twisted in agony. But he didn't let go.

Greta swung the staff, smashing it into Muloch's head with a loud crack. He stumbled back, and then Johari and Greta were running, pushing through the crowd of onlookers, a bloodthirsty howl coming from behind.

Johari reached the blanket hanging at the exit and risked a peek behind. Muloch was rushing toward them, overturning tables and chairs, sending customers scattering, the knife still sprouting from his arm, the sleeve drenched with a widening circle of blood. Two more steps and they were through the door and out into blinding light.

The music was louder and all around, pulsing. Johari sensed movement and soft jostling bodies and bleating. His eyes adjusted. They were caught in a sea of sheep being herded down the road, small bells around their necks jingling like wind chimes, the pulsing at once soothing and unsettling. All at once, the sound stopped, as if someone had pressed a mute button.

Johari had no time to reflect on the significance of that. The boy waved and shouted to them from the driver's seat of the wagon, parked on the other side of the road, the girl he'd promised a coin to sitting beside him. Two horses, tied to one wheel, tugged at their tethers and stamped and pawed the ground nervously. Johari and Greta dodged around the sheep, the greater number of the herd still coming up the road. When they reached the boy, they untied the horses and leaped on.

The boy flicked his whip. "Ride!"

Muloch burst from the tavern and stormed toward them. He yanked out the knife, brandishing it in a bloody arc. But now the sheep were a chaos of churning bodies, hemming him in.

Johari spurred his horse. It reared with a squeal and then careened up a side street, following Greta and the boy.

Their horses sent up flurries of dust as they zigzagged through alleys and backstreets, until Johari could see the main road just outside of town. The boy pulled up behind the last houses.

"Why are we stopping?" Johari cried.

"Muloch's a deadly tracker," the boy replied. "We've got to throw him off. Get off those horses and help me."

He whispered something to the girl. She nodded and ran off in the direction of the village.

"Tie those horses to Millie," he said. "Then help me with the Enchanter." He dashed up the wagon steps.

They joined him in a blink. The Enchanter was resting

against a pillow. His eyes were red, his breathing labored. He coughed, deep and raspy, but managed a smile.

Greta clasped her hands and gave them a grateful shake. "He's doing better!"

"Because the shells are close," the boy replied. "Put them here." He laid his hand on the man's heart.

Johari placed the pouch he'd taken from Muloch on the old man's black and withered chest. The Enchanter put his hands, one over the other, on top of the shells. This time there was no mistaking the phosphorescent glow at his breast, as though he were not a man at all but a being composed entirely of light.

As quickly as it flared, the moment passed. He expelled air sharply, as if releasing something, and tottered to his feet. "Help me outside," he said, his voice like an old rattle.

Greta shook her head. "You're still weak. We'll drive you in the wagon."

The Enchanter pointed a bony finger back in the direction of the tavern. "That man will skin us alive if he finds us. I like to keep mine on me body."

From a peg, he plucked a stained, beat-up old hat, with little pewter moon tokens hanging from the brim, and put it on. With the boy's help, he threw his bowl and a small selection of vials and pouches into a rucksack. His steps were shaky, but with Greta on one side and Johari on the other, they got him down the steps. He spoke strange words into Millie's ear. She whinnied, nodded twice, then started trotting down the main road away from the village, the other two horses following her.

He watched wistfully as they disappeared around a bend.

"You'll lose your wagon and all your potions," Greta said.

"Aye, he be burning it if he finds it." The Enchanter patted his rucksack. "I've got what we need here." His eyes grew moist. He turned away and began leading them across a field above the village.

"You left things behind," Greta said. "Irreplaceable things."

"Millie some clever girl. If she give 'em the slip, she'll come back to me."

They entered an olive grove. With the boy bringing up the rear, the Enchanter led, taking a course parallel to the village. With each passing minute, there was more spring to his step.

Greta slowed to where Johari was following behind, the shadows of the trees darkening her brow. "What you said back there, did you mean it?"

"What?" he asked.

"Your story."

"It was just a story."

"I don't think so."

"Did you mean what you said?" Heat rose to his head. He wondered if the Enchanter's potion was wearing off and the alcohol was seeping into his brain. He wondered if the lack of sleep was getting to him. He wondered most of all what the hell was eating her.

"Every word. What you said, it hurt. Don't do it again." She stalked off.

The Enchanter dropped back and walked with Johari. "You know, I watch you good from the sky, from me boy's eyes."

"So I hear."

"You got some problem with trust." Stronger, his voice now was earthy and rich, like a cello, and he spoke with a musical lilt that was winning.

"I've been burned."

"So you burnum others, 'specially one you love. Makes big sense."

"Why are we going this way?"

"Uh-uh, change subject. Good choice, me child. Let me tell you a story. In me youth, I lived in a village. It wasn't much, but the people make a life growing figs and barleys and throwing pots, and these brought good price at the spring fair in the nearest town, or would have if bandits didn't swoop down to rob 'em clean and set the place on fire. Ten long years this go, driving 'em into debt and despair. One day, a clever boy thought to build a tower with a bell on it at each corner of the village and posting guard there. When the bandits came with flaming brands, the guards rang the bell, alerting the peoples. While the men fought the brigands, the women filled buckets of water."

"Your point?"

"That's you, ringing the bell. Only there's no fire, no bandits. Just pretty girl who loves you."

The grove ended a dozen yards ahead. Greta stopped, waiting for them to catch up.

"She has a funny way of showing it," Johari said.

The Enchanter gave him a sidelong glance. "Maybe she's had her share of bandits too."

Maybe she had. People looked at Greta and saw someone who had everything: intelligence, beauty, a radiance from the inside as bright as the sun. But what did he really know about her? Her mother had been cold and selfish, and Greta wasn't speaking to her. And what lay buried and hidden underneath? Was she really that different from him? Was it marauding bandits in their past that drew them to each other?

When they'd caught up, she turned to him, making no effort to hide the sting in her eyes.

"We should be the last to hurt each other," he said.

"We should," she replied stiffly.

As they left the shelter of the trees, he took her hand. It hung limp and clammy in his and was not at all encouraging.

"What's the plan?" she asked the Enchanter.

"Find me little friend," he replied.

"The girl? Then what?"

"Pray Millie leads Muloch on some merry chase."

"I made an enemy," Johari said.

"I didn't tell you to stab him."

"He was about to break my wrist."

They found the girl hiding behind the pepper tree where they'd first met her.

The Enchanter squatted before her, matching her eye level.

"I thought you'd leave and forget me," she said, gazing at him with wonder.

"Never, me sweet." He took out a shell that flashed in the sunlight and gave it to her. "Keep that hidden. Never spend it."

She nodded, her eyes grown as large as the shell. He plucked another from the bag and held it up. "Find a farmer with a loaded wagon and bring 'em here. Pay 'em with this." He gave her a coin and she ran off to the village.

"You gave her hope," Greta said.

The Enchanter looked after the girl thoughtfully. "I gave her magic. We all need a little to get around the world."

While they waited, Johari thought about those pulsing sheep bells. It had to mean something. This journey through the House was playing out differently than before, but there were also similarities. Like the way settings shifted and changed. Perhaps those pulsing bells were an instance of another similarity. Similar but in a different form.

What pulses? he wondered.

Then it hit him. They marked time, the same way a tolling bell had marked each passing hour on his last journey in the House. Today, if he traced it back, the hawk's insistent cry when he wakened in the snow was the first instance. He was fairly certain it had shrilled ten times, suggesting an hour had passed since he'd entered the House. He was fairly certain the sheep bells had pulsed eleven times before going silent. Other markers of time would come, sparrows trilling in bushes, Millie's bell—perhaps that's why it hadn't rung yet—and the like. He would watch for them.

A farmer came trundling toward them on a wagon brimming with baskets of grapes. The Enchanter huddled with the farmer. A minute later the baskets were removed, and Johari and Greta lay down in the wagon. Canvas was tossed over them. The baskets were arranged on top. The Enchanter and the boy would be fine riding with the farmer, insisting they would see a plume of pursuing dust long before they would see Muloch, and more cryptically, that Muloch had no power over the Enchanter.

Johari didn't argue. He wanted, needed time with Greta.

When the wheels started rolling, he said, "Greta—"

She put her finger to his lips. "Hush. Just hold me."

He folded her in his arms. Her body seemed to melt into his, all the curves of her fitting all the curves of him. He found her lips, and while the wagon bumped up the trail, and the aroma of grapes, ripe and luscious, wafted around them, he lost himself in her softness.

Johari stretched stiffness from his body as he watched the farmer roll away. He turned back to Greta, the boy, and the Enchanter, standing near the hub of the crossroads. Sunlight reflected off the scattering of large rocks like they were glass, suggesting they were composed of copious quantities of fool's gold.

"Why stop here?" Johari asked.

The Enchanter took off his rucksack and let it drop. "Still the suspicious one. Have me boy and I let you down yet?"

The jury was out on that. Johari squinted at the road. Rising dust marked where the farmer had turned a corner. The road followed a winding course back to the village, but on a beeline to the village he saw a smudge, rising off the plain. The day had grown hot. Perhaps it was only heat waves. "You didn't answer my question."

The Enchanter removed his shell pouch and bowl from his rucksack. "We need to leave here."

"We just got here. That's what I'm talking about. You're leading us in circles."

"Not here, *here*." He waved an arm, indicating the fields, hills, and forest-clad mountains. "The crossroads be the way to the hermit."

"You're supposed to take us to Calista."

"Yes, yes, but we must go to the hermit, Korounos, first. We need his lamp."

Johari and Greta locked eyes. She seemed just as mystified.

"Why?" Johari asked him.

"I can't send you to your friend without it."

"You need to tell me more than that."

"It's a gift, a magic as boundless as me shells and staff." The old man's eyes glowed. "A thing of beauty and power. The blaze of the sun and the mystery of the moon in one precious drop."

"All that."

The Enchanter frowned. "Laugh all you want, child. You won't laugh when it's in your hands." He took a vial from his rucksack and pulled out his rattle. He put the bowl at the hub of the crossroads. "Sit here, facing each other."

He poured pink liquid from the vial into the bowl, a scent like honeysuckle filling the air. Next, he took up the rattle and flicked his fingers. A puff of powder streamed from his fingertips and onto the rattle. Calling out a strange word, he gave the rattle a snap.

Johari and Greta sat facing each other, but he was beginning to have serious doubts. One thing for certain: the House was dangerous. It had taken Brice, Calista, and countless others. He and Greta had barely survived the last time. His brush with Muloch aside, they'd been strolling around this permutation of the House for hours. Nothing bad had happened. That was off. Way off. It almost seemed as if the House was trying to lull them, ripen them for the taking.

The Enchanter pulled the boy aside. "Go, child. To the hut."

The boy's face pinched into a prune. "I can help."

"Too dangerous." The moon tokens on the Enchanter's hat swung as he shook his head. "I don't want you anywhere near that man."

"I can distract him. Keep him away."

"No, he will go for you to get to me."

The boy started to object, but the Enchanter leaned over and spoke in his ear. The boy nodded, turned, and trotted up the road as obediently as Millie had left the village.

The Enchanter watched him until his bobbing white feather disappeared around a bend. Then he sat cross-legged beside his rucksack, his eyes rolled back into his head, the lids started fluttering, and a low, pulsing vibration came from his throat.

Greta whispered, "What's he doing?"

"Wasting our time."

"I don't think so."

"Then what? Greta, the clock's ticking. You have less time than I have."

She laid her fingers on his arm. "Give him a little longer."

Her fingers were cool, her touch electrifying. Any other time, he could lose himself contemplating her earnest, shimmering eyes. But their immediate plight pressed in on him.

For the better part of a quarter hour, the Enchanter sat, eyelids fluttering, while the sun swung to its zenith and blazed down like a wrathful god. Somewhere, songbirds trilled in a pulsing rhythm and suddenly went silent, surely marking another hour had passed.

Johari helped Greta up and then surveyed the road. Dust from the farmer had receded, but the smudge of dust that had been near the village had grown. It was still a way off but drawing toward them.

"Something's coming," Johari said. "We should move on."

"Leave him?"

He hooked a thumb toward the dirt cloud. "Before that gets here."

"Where would we go?"

"Anywhere but here. We're overdue, Greta. The House is going to throw something at us."

She gazed at the plume. It was coming at a good clip, but Johari couldn't see inside it.

"It already has," Greta said. "We're stuck here, just like we were on the second floor and the attic."

"We had places to run to, other rooms with thick doors." He looked at the roads, the fields, the barren hills. "We're sitting ducks here."

"Whatever that is, it can find us up the road." She nodded toward the Enchanter, who still sat, eyelids fluttering, a low growl coming from his throat. "He's our only chance."

Johari studied the dust cloud. He could distinguish two of them now, a larger one in front and a smaller one trailing a short distance behind. "We've got to go. Soon."

She nodded. "Okay, but not yet. Maybe he'll come through."

Johari scanned the countryside. He had no confidence the nearby rocks, as large as they were, would hide them, nor would the scattering of trees. He reckoned the speed of the plumes. If he and Greta cut across the fields, they'd be quickly run down. Same with going up the road.

A film of sweat shone on the Enchanter's brow. His humming increased in volume. Maybe he was part of the trap, bait to lure them in. But Johari searched inside himself and decided he trusted the man. He went over and gave him a shake. The Enchanter's eyes flared.

Johari pointed to the rapidly approaching plume. "We've got company."

The Enchanter made a shade of his hand, taking in the dust clouds. "Not good."

"We should leave."

"Muloch couldn't know we're here," Greta said. "He would follow Millie and the road."

"Quiet, child. I need to concentrate."

"But what are you doing?" she asked, her voicing rising with tension.

The Enchanter gazed at her levelly. "Figuring how to do it."

"You don't know?"

"I'm almost there."

Now Greta searched the fields and the road bending up the hill as if she would bolt in one direction or the other at any moment.

"I'm your only hope," he said, and resumed his eyelid-fluttering trance.

The white hawk flew down from the hills and circled high above him, once, twice, three times, then took off toward the dust clouds. When it was over them, it began tracing circle eights. Growling from the Enchanter's throat stopped. He cocked an ear, listening. A moment later, he broke from the trance. "No ..."

"What's wrong?" Greta asked.

He rose stiffly and went to the edge of the road, facing the plumes. He waved his arms, as if shooing something away. "Turn, turn you blasted mutt."

"What is it?"

He ignored her, gave his rattle a ferocious snap. Flames shot out the end. "Quick," he shouted. "Sit beside the bowl. Face each other."

"We don't have time," Johari cried, pointing to the billowing dust. "That's bad. You know it is."

The Enchanter shook his head. "You're at a crossroads, me friend. There's no escape."

What the hell was he talking about? Of course they were at a crossroads. And in all this rocky countryside, something was coming for them, swift as an arrow. Greta was white, seemed to be teetering, an impala about to bolt.

Then it struck him. They *were* at a crossroads. In all kinds of ways. They'd left their childhood behind, crossed the threshold, and now life stood before them, a vague unknown. Greta was at the juncture between love for him and loyalty for her friend. Johari was at a similar juncture with his job, career, his future on New Earth—hadn't someone tried to Banish him?—and his love for Greta. This step in the journey was clear. Follow Greta no matter where she went. After that, everything was up for grabs.

Johari pulled Greta to the hub of the crossroads and tugged her down with him, where they sat cross-legged. The Enchanter snatched up the bowl.

"Drink," he commanded. "Quickly."

They drank, holding the bowl for each other. It tasted like an aperitif, warm, sweet, haunting, mysterious.

"Hold this. Keep it between you. Don't let it go." He gave them the blazing rattle.

He took up the pouch of shells, poured them in his hand, and threw them skyward. They flashed in the sun, seemed to hang a moment, and then began falling, far more than had been tossed up, an endless supply, a gentle rain of them. When they touched Johari and Greta, they dissolved like snowflakes.

Through the golden haze shimmering around them, Johari saw the twin clouds looming. A whinny rang out. Millie burst through the dust and rushed to the Enchanter, foam flying from her mouth, the wagon bouncing behind her.

The Enchanter threw his arms around her neck. "You sweet stupid mutt, you brought Muloch!"

They had minutes. Maybe seconds. Muloch must have been in the smaller cloud, following on a single horse while Millie towed the wagon, the other two horses following like loyal dogs. Johari gripped the bowl, readying to leap up and brandish it when Muloch showed.

The Enchanter snatched up his staff and began dancing and chanting around Johari and Greta, the shells still falling all around them. The next thing Johari knew, they were spinning, as if the crossroads had become a giant merry-go-round. The world blurred. Johari had glimpses of landscape, which shifted from the rocky countryside they'd marched in all morning, to alpine snowcapped mountains, to jungle, to oasis, to plain. Islands, beaches, swamps, cities, and tundra whizzed by. Then back to the rocky hills.

Muloch burst on the scene. He leaped from his horse, pulling a bow from his saddle as he went.

The Enchanter swung the staff. As if in slow motion, Johari saw the arc of it falling toward Greta. He cried out, tried to block the blow, but it struck Greta on the forehead. She fell toward Johari. One hand still holding the bowl, he tried to catch her with his other hand.

Beyond the falling shells, Muloch stood poised, an arrow notched in his bow, the string pulled back for a shot. The Enchanter still capered and sang. His whole body, not just his heart, radiated now, incandescent and bright.

And he swung the staff at Johari's head.

EIGHTEEN

Kaleidoscopic images whizzed by—trees and mountains, lakes and islands, swamps, tundra, and plains. Sometimes the Enchanter was there—he seemed to be laughing—and Millie, munching on straw. Yet always there was Greta. She reached for Johari, appeared to be falling into a dark tunnel. Panic seized him. He would lose her, never see her again.

He landed with a jolt. All went black ...

Presently, the world came into focus. He sat on a low hill, with Greta on the other side of the bowl. The Enchanter stopped dancing and collapsed to the ground. Still hitched to the wagon, Millie munched on a few withered blades, struggling to grow between the seams of a rock. Muloch was nowhere in sight.

Beyond the hill, an unforgiving landscape of hardened lava stretched in a vast plain, ending at snowy peaks in the distance. No grass, trees, or plants of any kind dotted the terrain, only great rents and cracks in the surface, from which smoke and steam billowed. A hot wind carried an occasional bellow, cry, or moan, such as a beast might make. The sound gave Johari the shivers.

To his left, a dirt road cut across the hill and led to a mountain pass so narrow it appeared as if an Olympian ax had cloven it, leaving sheer cliffs on either side. Dense fog blocked the view beyond. More strange sounds—like wailing and the stampede of elephants—came from that direction, though it seemed farther away.

Johari rose and helped Greta up.

"Now what?" he asked the Enchanter.

Legs splayed, the Enchanter made no move to stand. "I'm spent, child. Be so good as to bring me that skin, hanging from the wagon."

He looked more than spent. His sagging head, his cracked lips, his limbs, trembling and little more than pipe cleaners, made him look almost as sick as he'd been before regaining his shells.

He took a long draught from the skin Johari handed him and sat with his eyes closed, gulping in air.

Greta surveyed the plain. "This place gives me a bad feeling."

The Enchanter opened his eyes and followed her gaze. "Well it should."

"How do we get Korounos's Lamp?" Johari asked.

"Not we. You."

"I'm not leaving Greta."

"You have to."

"Why?"

"You each have a trial."

The sun raged on the top of Johari's head. He mopped away sweat and wished he had a hat. "Reason being?"

"The place where be your friend, it be very hard to return from. You get through this, perhaps you can. Besides, you be the only one who can get the Lamp."

"You know that how?"

"Just do. For one thing, you be a proven thief." He winked. "Very nice work with Muloch."

Johari folded his arms. The groans and screams coming from the plain filled him with dread. This wasn't a place he wanted to leave Greta. She looked at him, her brow knit with worry.

"Another thing," the Enchanter continued, "you be the only one Korounos won't kill like an ant. Him see you as a kindred spirit. Besides ..." He pointed a bony finger at Greta. "She got something else to do."

"What?" Johari demanded. He checked his watch, only to remember Muloch took it.

"Make it be safe for you."

"How?"

"The Elders guard the pass." The Enchanter nodded to his left, then pointed across the plain to the tallest peak rising toward dark clouds. "She be going to that mountain and quiet one of 'em. She be our best chance of getting through to 'em. Otherwise, you no get through alive."

"Why's she our best chance?"

The Enchanter looked amused. "Child, have you not followed her here?"

There *was* something about Greta. Sometimes Johari felt a force inside her as unstoppable as a gale. That power had increased since her first journey in the House.

"I don't like it," he replied. "Why can't we go with her, make sure she's safe?"

"I no big man with the Elders right now, only inflame 'em. You wait here. Slip through the pass when all be quiet."

Greta gazed at the distant peak. Rumbling, deeper than thunder, came from that direction, as if someone struck a drum of unthinkable size. "I'll do it."

Johari went cold inside. But the Enchanter's plan made

sense. They had two tasks, one to make the way safe, the other to get the Lamp. He couldn't be in two places at once. If only he could divide into two and go with her.

But there was still a problem.

"The peak's a long way off," he said. "It would take days."

Sunlight flashed on the Enchanter's gold-rimmed teeth. "Friends help."

A low growl from behind made Johari turn. The bird-girl from their first encounter with the House, who'd helped Greta when she'd fallen unconscious, sat astride a giant, almost black leopard, crouching on a boulder that seemed to have materialized from nowhere.

The leopard sprang. In a bound, it was beside Greta. Johari's heart leaped to his mouth. The next instant, the leopard sat at Greta's feet like a loyal dog. Bird-girl dismounted, squatted beside the cat, and scratched behind its ears. A strip of rawhide tied around her waist served as a belt, from which a leather pouch dangled. Feathers growing from her face and along her arms had lengthened, but her body, barely covered by animal skins, was still sinewy and stained with something like diluted tar.

Greta had frozen, but now her shoulders relaxed. She reached down tentatively and patted the cat's head. It responded with a purr like a bass fiddle.

"How does this help?" she asked. "It'll still take too long."

The Enchanter picked up his bowl and rattle and put them in his sack. "That cat be some ride—gobbles leagues beneath her paws."

Greta looked down at the leopard, which was the size of a full-grown tiger, in wonder.

With time ticking and all arguments in, Greta took

Johari's head between her hands and kissed him. He devoured her lips, soothing the pent-up ache and uncertainty over their relationship but none of his anxiety about what lay ahead of her.

"Bring back the Lamp," she breathed in his ear. Before he could reply, she pulled away and mounted the leopard. She held a hand out to the girl. "Are you coming?"

The girl shook her head. She pointed to the distant mountain, as if to say, *Go!* The peak was lost now in ominous thunderheads.

Closing his rucksack, the Enchanter said, "Look for someone bearing a terrible burden, child. Ease his pain and the others be soothed." He pointed to the terrible rips in the earth. "Avoid those. If you be sucked in ..."

Greta nodded. "We're lost. How will I know when to return?"

"Look for a fire, bright as the sun. I'll light it when Johari brings back the Lamp."

She mounted the leopard and held tight to the scruff of its neck. In a single bound, the cat flew from the hill to the plain. On it leaped, not going seven leagues like the boots of fairy tales but covering enormous stretches of ground, nonetheless. Thick steam erupted from the vents as she passed near them, obscuring large portions of the plain. The earth shook, suggesting giants stampeded and raged behind the mist. The moans and cries increased, and soon terrible bellows rose up.

Johari whirled on the Enchanter. "They'll tear her to pieces!"

The Enchanter held out his hands to placate, but a force, gentle but firm, also emanated from them, holding Johari back like a repelling magnet.

"You don't understand," the Enchanter said. "Listen!

They be deaf, blind, and wounded beyond belief. That be why they rage. Trust her ride. It will avoid them."

The fury of the Elders intensified, urging Johari to run after her. He could see her, almost a speck now, bursting from fog, leaping a hundred, two hundred feet with each bound.

The Enchanter touched Johari's arm softly, restraining him with that same force. "No, child. It be death for you."

Johari slumped. Yet never taking his eyes from the plain, he soon began pacing. He could no longer see Greta but marked her path as fresh angry blasts exploded from the fissures and shot like columns skyward.

Waves of terror rushed on him, exhorting him to dash after her. But her words rang in his mind—

Bring back the Lamp!

She risked her life for a friend. She demanded he do the same, not in a reckless quest across the plain, but beyond the veil of fog guarding the pass, where screams and howls rose in rage.

He looked to Bird-girl for some sign of Greta's progress. She was a part of Greta. The one couldn't exist without the other. She had shown strength and tenderness when Greta was stricken with venom. Now her eyes were fixed on the mountain, her face taut with tension.

With nothing to do but wait, he sat, but soon was up again, beating a path across the hilltop as quakes shook the earth and pillars of steam knifed the sky and the Elders railed in piteous cries, as if the leopard galloped on an open wound.

"It's been too long," he exclaimed. "I have to go after her."

"She be almost at the mountain." The Enchanter pointed. "See! The geysers shoot up."

He was right. The vents nearer to them were now calm, but those closest to the mountain vented steam skyward.

"Then it's safe for me to go to her."

"You'll never get the Lamp then. She'll have risked her life for nothing."

Johari's heart was ready to burst. With no other outlet, he treaded random loops across the hilltop, his eyes riveted to the plain. The sun seemed to have doubled in size, sending torrents of sweat down his back. Blistering wind shook Millie's bell, once, twice, and fell silent. He knew what it meant as readily as if it had been a ticking clock. Later, during another spell of anxious striding, it rang three times. The scuff of his shoes, the rasp of his breath, the pounding of his heart seemed too loud, and then he realized the stampede had ceased and the Elders were silent.

Stunned, he stopped.

The Enchanter latched onto his arm and began pushing him toward the pass. "Go, while they be quiet!"

"But Greta—"

"She be fine. Go!"

They were almost at the threshold. The fog bank loomed.

"What do I do?"

The Enchanter rolled his eyes toward the pass. "Convince a god he give you his power."

NINETEEN

Rather than feel annoyed, Johari laughed. It came to him that part of what helped them in the House before was to improvise, go with what it presented to them, as they had with Muloch. The House was dangerous, but it also presented guides. Despite his initial mistrust, the Enchanter and his boy seemed like positive forces, just as Bird-girl was for Greta.

Still, he was certain his task was every bit as dangerous as Greta's, and a shiver of trepidation ran through his bones as he eyed the pass.

"How do I do that?" Johari asked. "Get him to give me his power."

"I wish I knew, child." The Enchanter nodded toward Korounos's world. "No peoples come back from that place."

"Then how do you know he's got the Lamp?"

"He does." The Enchanter stroked his chin. "When I be a child, my father tell me tales about Korounos. There be only one path. Follow it to the seashore. Find his hut. If he be away, if you see the Lamp, grab it. Do not linger."

"Anything else?"

"Do not forget why you be there."

Forget! With Greta waiting for the Enchanter's fire? Johari wasn't going to relax until they were together again.

He passed into the fog. He sensed rather than saw towering walls on either side, but the path was visible a few feet ahead, and he walked on smooth stone as quietly as he could. The Elders were out there. Though they only whimpered occasionally now, he didn't want to reignite them.

He found the fog bewildering. Without their moans, he would have lost all sense of time. At last, he no longer heard them, and the fog brightened, indicating he was through the pass. Little by little, the soup thinned. He passed through a last finger of it and halted. Before him stretched a land as desolate as the one he'd left. No fissures ripped the earth, belching steam. This place was barren and rocky, the air cold and damp. Far ahead, the trail disappeared into mist. On either side, mountains bled into an overcast sky, gray and oppressive.

When he estimated he'd walked a good hour, the mist seemed no closer. He continued on. He thought of Greta. For the first time since they'd met, the shape of her face, the color of her hair and eyes seemed less clear, as if he saw her in a dream, and the dream distorted her features. Then he stopped, and with a terrible ache in his heart, he closed his eyes and didn't open them again until he held her in his mind, smiling, dancing, swaying as she had the night they'd met.

He pressed on. There were moments when her quest to the mountain eluded him, as if someone were drawing out the threads of his memory, one by one. There were moments when his own task receded, blurring like an out-of-focus photo, and he had to reach to pull it back.

The Enchanter's words came back to him: *Do not forget why you be there.*

Panic seized him. How could he forget so quickly? He clenched his fist and resolved to hold tight to his memory.

Greta ...

The Lamp ...

Greta ...

Greta ...

With every word she grew clearer, until he wondered how he could ever have lost her.

How long have I been walking?

Sometimes it seemed like an eternity. If not for a seagull wheeling above, he was utterly alone.

He was almost upon the mist now. Seagulls circled and squawked. Sighing—slow, deep, and rhythmic—reached his ears. He stepped into the mist. Closer now, the sighing turned to throbbing, the throbbing to the crash and roar of waves. They came into view, giant rollers, foaming and exploding on rocks along the shore, filling the air with briny fragrance.

Through the mist, a hut came into view, perched on a cliff overlooking the sea. The boards were weathered and as gray as fish scales. No smoke billowed from the chimney; no light burned in the windows. But the path leading to the front door was well trod, which made him wary.

He knocked at the door. No one answered. He lifted a board latching the door and opened it. The inside was dim, but enough light came through to reveal a single room with a stone hearth in one corner; a table, the planks crudely cut; and a wooden chair. Finding no one inside, he entered. The smell of fish filled the air. A fisherman's net hung from hooks on one wall. A thick woolen raincoat and hat hung on the opposite wall beside a coil of rope. He saw no lamp.

Back outside, he scanned the shoreline, the cliffs, and down where the sea pounded the rocks. No one strode toward or away from the hut.

The hut had appeared clean, the scent of fish fresh. Korounos would be back soon. What then? Johari couldn't exactly ask for the Lamp. If it wasn't with Korounos, it could be hidden anywhere. He could spend years combing the rocks and cliffs and never find it. The foolishness of coming here gripped him. How long would Greta wait?

The answer was clear. Not very long. They had half a day to find Calista and get the hell out of the here.

A cold breeze pushed him back inside. He looked for food in three baskets along one wall, half hoping he'd find the Lamp in one of them. All were empty.

He squatted and stacked driftwood on the hearth and a few shavings of tinder. He found flint and steel in a nearby tool chest. After two awkward attempts, he got a spark and lit a fire. Then he sat, waiting. Time slipped away. He glanced out the window. Something seemed off. He'd been here several hours. Light from the windows should have deepened as day melted toward dusk. Perhaps it was a trick of the overcast sky and the mist, both diffusing the light. Several times he stepped outside and stared at the sun, cold and pale behind the clouds. It hadn't moved.

That was reassuring. If time was frozen here, he wouldn't hold up ...

Greta ...

The Lamp ...

Greta ...

But he sensed time—he sensed it tugging on his memory. He returned to the hut, sat, and pondered how to handle Korounos when he returned. Nothing occurred to him. It would have been nice if a helpmate had accompanied him, like the leopard Greta rode.

Bird-girl and the leopard were Greta's power. He felt them coursing inside her. What did it mean that he came here alone? Was there no power he could summon? He had his wits, street smarts that helped him survive the lonely years of his childhood. Time to use it.

He snatched up a piece of driftwood, lit it, and stalked outside where he scoured the rocky terrain and the shoreline for sign of Korounos. He peered at the churning water, searching for a boat. Torch in hand, he climbed down to the beach, a rubble of stones that made him fling out his arms like a tightrope walker as he crossed it. He wedged his torch between rocks and began collecting driftwood. When he had a mountain of it, he threw on the torch and watched as flames, blue and lavender from the salt-soaked wood, blazed into a bonfire.

Back in the hut, he sat and waited, hoping he'd rung the equivalent of a doorbell. He was just beginning to think Korounos had deserted this place—who would choose to stay?—when the door opened.

A man ducked inside and paused. Sagging brows and lids left his eyes in shadow, but Johari felt them on him.

The man said, "You have come." He stepped to the table carrying a fisherman's net and pail, taking no more mind of Johari than he would the floor or the ceiling. He was gaunt, but his massive frame suggested once powerful muscles. His hands were gnarled roots, his face as rough and scored as the rocks outside, and just as ancient, as if he'd been hewn from the same stone, weathered by the same wind, rain, and waves.

He hung his net on the wall, removed his coat and hat, shook away a fine spray of drops, and hung both beside the net. Thick, grizzled hair fell to his shoulders, and he gave that a shake. He stirred the fire and added a log. From the pail, he removed two fish and put them on the table. All his motions were unhurried.

Johari searched for something to say, but the remoteness of the man, his complete indifference to Johari, left him stupefied.

The man took a burlap bundle from the tool chest and unwrapped a long knife. He tested the edge.

"You don't belong here." With one hand wrapped in burlap and jammed into the fish's mouth, he made a slice near the pectoral fin.

Johari was still wondering at the man's words on entering the hut. "You expected me?"

The man cut through the length of the fish, splitting the tail. "Are you a god?"

"No," Johari replied.

The man trimmed the fillets, lifting away the bones, and dropped the bits into an iron pot. "You came for the Lamp."

"Yes."

With the knife, the man pointed toward the door. "Leave. While you can."

Johari stirred uncomfortably in his seat. "I can't do that. Are you Korounos? Do you speak for him?"

The man grunted. Whether this was yes or no or had nothing to do with the question was unclear. He gazed off, deep in thought. "Korounos ... I haven't heard that name since time began."

Johari took that as confirmation. "If I don't take the Lamp, someone will disappear. Someone I love."

Dried kelp hung from the one of the hooks. Korounos plucked eight broad leaves and wrapped the fillets in it. These were covered with four layers of fresh kelp from his pail. After filling his pot with water from an earthenware jug, he carried the pot and fillets to the hearth.

He said, "Then you're lost."

"Not while I breathe. Five minutes with her and you'd love her too."

Korounos pushed aside the larger logs, exposing glowing chips. He buried the fillets beneath the embers, put the pot on top, and surrounded it with flaming wood. "Now we wait."

Johari rose. "This is your chair."

Ignoring him, Korounos took up a dry net, sat against the wall, and began mending it.

Johari wilted into the chair. "I *am* lost. I'd follow her to hell and back."

Korounos peered at Johari, studying him. His eyes were as fathomless and gray as the sea. "I love no man or woman."

"You must have once."

"Maybe ... maybe ..." The vertical lines between Korounos's brows deepened to trenches. "The sea grinds us to powder. Where's your love then?"

"I'd rather have it in a blaze than never know it."

Korounos grunted. He waved toward skins by the hearth. "Sleep. I'll awaken you when the fish is ready."

"She could be waiting for me."

"Who?"

Her face rippled before him as if seen from the depths of a dark pool. And her name, what was her name? He stared at the flames consuming the logs and held his breath.

The Lamp ...

Greta!

"My love," Johari replied.

Korounos's fingers worked at the net. The next thing Johari knew, he was swaddled in the skins, struggling to keep his eyes open. Korounos still reclined against the wall, his deep-set eyes fixed on the net.

Johari could not say he slept. He hardly felt rested.

Korounos stood above him, saying, "We eat."

A sawed-off driftwood tree trunk, serving as a stool, was now at the table, along with two bowls and spoons. Korounos unwrapped one of the fillets, cut it, and slipped pieces into the bowls with his knife. He ladled in broth from the pot.

The aroma of smoked fish filled the air. Johari's mouth watered. "Loan me the Lamp. I'll return it." He tried the fish, found it sweet, moist, and delicate. He couldn't imagine anything better.

Korounos ate slowly, his attention on the food. When he'd finished, he pushed away from the table. "Come."

They went outside and took a path along the cliff. The trail parted. They followed one leg down a series of steps formed by nature. About a quarter of the way down, they stopped at a shelf formation that looked like two giant chairs cut in the rock. They sat. Korounos fit his chair. Johari felt like a small child in his.

As if sensing Johari's discomfort, Korounos said, "You will grow into it."

"I won't be here that long."

Korounos didn't reply. By this time, Johari was used to the long gaps in their conversation. Giant breakers crashed on the rocks below, sprayed violently, and receded, leaving a boiling cauldron behind.

This was the world as it had been in the beginning: stark, rough, and primal.

"Are you lonely?" Johari asked.

"I have the birds ... the sky ... the fish ... the sea."

As if to prove his point, a seagull missing a foot landed near Korounos's shoulder. He took from his pocket a packet of seaweed containing a few bits of raw fish and fed the bird.

"I really need the Lamp," Johari said.

"If you find it, take it."

"You would let me?"

"This place seeps into your soul. You'll be back."

"You want me to live with you?"

Korounos shook his head. "You will take my place."

The chairs overlooked a cove. Warblers with yellow crowns and black bandit masks fluttered about holes in one of the cliff walls.

"I wonder what they find there," Johari said.

"High tide and waves bring food: a small crab, a bit of seaweed."

It seemed like the last place nourishment might be found.

Johari said, "I'm out of time. Tell me where it is."

"There is no time here ... only solitude."

"I believe that. Where I come from, the clock is ticking."

Korounos pondered the sea. He became so still he seemed to meld into the stone. In the same way Johari couldn't be sure he'd been asleep, now he couldn't be sure that Korounos was still there, that he hadn't become a formation of the cliff, an interesting shape and nothing more.

The waves lulled ... Nothing mattered. Peace poured in. Johari's mind floated beyond the cliffs, beyond the waves, and out beyond the sea.

No thought of the future intruded. Whatever past he

had was nothing more than a vast tapestry. Squawking crows were wheeling and tearing at the threads. Holes appeared in the picture and widened. Wind fluttered at the threads, snatching them with breezy fingers and ripping away yards and bolts of fabric.

This was wrong. He needed to return. Someone waited for him.

Arm length by arm length, like raising a heavy anchor, he hauled himself back and stood. Images flooded his mind of the House taking Greta. Desperation, dark and final, rose within him.

"Guide me to it." He waved at the ocean and the cliffs. "It could be anywhere."

Korounos sighed. The illusion he was rock melted away. "It's not something I can give. You find it or not." He began climbing the stairs.

"Don't leave," Johari cried. "Not yet."

Korounos turned. "Wait. Watch. Forget. Perhaps it will come to you."

Johari looked on with dismay as Korounos lumbered up the steps and dwindled along the cliff edge. Then he was gone.

TWENTY

The last thing Johari wanted to do was wait. An urge gripped him to leap down the stairs and comb the boulders below, even if the waves dashed him against the rocks or yanked him out to sea. Failing to find the Lamp there, he would scour the bleak landscape between mountains and sea, rock by rock, until he collapsed from hunger and exhaustion.

He pulled the reins on the impulse. He had as much chance of finding it that way as he would diving into a hayloft to find a needle.

He forced himself to wait, to watch. But he wouldn't forget. Since he'd gotten here, that was the biggest danger. If he forgot Greta, if she faded as though she'd never existed, then he was through. There was nothing left for him. No life. No future. No one to love him. No one to love.

The seagull studied him, waiting to see if he had raw fish. When Johari didn't offer any, it took off, looping for several minutes above the cove and then landing on a rock projecting from the cliff wall.

A colossal wave smashed into one of the boulders, which stood like a sentinel at the opening of the inlet. The wind brought the scent of brine and drying seaweed. Korounos was right—the stark beauty of this place seeped into you. Here you could stop struggling, let go of everything. No worries about the future, like getting hauled off in the middle of the night, like Phillip March breathing down your neck or needing to go back into the House or how Greta saw their relationship or if they even had one. This land unhooked you so profoundly you could forget there was anything but the sea. Because it all came down to one thing: the thing that ruined everything was people, and here, there weren't any.

It sounded like a good life. You fished, you collected driftwood, you mended a net or the roof. You sat on the cliff and melted into the rock. The mist washed over you. You disappeared.

You forgot ...

Absently, he watched the bandits fluttering about the cliff holes. It seemed a miracle that waves cast sufficient food for them to survive. Here, you needed little to keep you going. Every scrap was a treasure.

For the first time since he'd arrived, the clouds seemed to part and let in a ray of light, though when he looked, the sun was a dull and listless smudge, hiding in the same spot in the leaden sky.

Then it hit him. The location of the Lamp. Galvanized, he stood, his eyes fixed on the bandits. He studied the cliff wall above and below where they were feeding. Coming from below seemed the safest route.

He climbed down as far as he dared, then made his way carefully over the rocks, slick with spray, and around tide pools, teeming with barnacles, purple anemones, tiny crabs, and starfish. Breakers crashed so close that after a few minutes his clothes were soaked. Undaunted, relishing the salt air in his lungs, he scrambled on. When he was thirty feet below the holes, he began climbing. The rugged surface gave him plenty of hand- and footholds. The main danger was the wet stone. One slip and a broken back or neck was the likely result. He latched onto rocks projecting like fingers and tested the soundness of every step before moving on.

At last, breathing heavily, dripping with sweat despite the wind whipping his shirt, he came to the holes. A dozen of them pocked the cliff like tiny caves. A few yellow flowers grew around the openings. Just as Korounos had said, Johari found tiny crabs and bits of seaweed inside the lower ones. He climbed on. The bandits fluttered about him, soft as butterfly wings against his cheeks.

For some reason they reminded him of Greta. Like her, these birds were friendly and beautiful, but that black mask reminded him she had something dark and hidden, something too terrible for her to talk about.

He made for an opening that was a little larger than the others. The Lamp had to be in there. The others were too small. He was only a few feet from victory. Even as a surge of triumph swept through him, it was dashed cold. How would he climb back down holding the Lamp?

Gripping a rocky projection with one hand, he wiped away sweat with the other and risked a peek down. Directly below, a boulder reared up like an anvil, the point turned up ninety degrees. All it took was his foot sliding from its purchase or his fingers losing their grip, and he would plummet onto that. Worse, the tide was coming in. Already he felt the chill breath of the waves bearing down on him. If they were big enough to leave food here, they could easily snatch him like a chip of driftwood and sweep him out to sea. If he wasn't pulverized on the rocks first.

He shoved the thought away. Maybe there was still time to grab the Lamp, get back down, and across to the stairs. He focused instead on how to climb with the Lamp. He needed both hands free. He could only hope there was something like a handle he could tie onto.

One of the bandits hovered close and sang in his ear. He took that as a sign of encouragement. Three more footholds brought him face to face with the larger opening, roughly circular and a foot in diameter. He half expected light to stream out, but all within lay in shadow.

He tested a fingerhold. Feeling secure, he reached in with the other hand. He brushed against small things— several cool and wet, one rough—and pulled out seaweed and a sand crab. Farther in, he made out an object. It was neither the teapot shape of ancient lamps nor rectangular, like the glassed-in lamps of later centuries.

But it belonged here about as much as a car. He extended his arm. Of all the damn luck, it was too short. His fingers just grazed the Lamp. It was soft, like lambskin or suede, suggesting it was wrapped inside something. He pressed against the cliff as tight as he could. This time he snagged a bit of material and tugged. It wouldn't budge. With his longer arm, Korounos must have wedged it in good. Johari tried again, this time coming up from the bottom. He pivoted, bringing more of his side, rather than his chest, in contact with the cliff. The motion lent another inch or two of reach. He was able to grip the wrapping, give it a good yank. And got exactly nowhere. It might as well have been nailed down.

A wave crashed in his ears. Icy spray drenched him.

The tide was surging in. He had to work fast. He pivoted, crushed more material in his fingers, and gave a sharp tug. The object pulled free.

His foot slipped.

TWENTY-ONE

Johari's shoe slid from the toehold and shot into space. He let go of the object and clutched the lip of the little cave. His free foot pedaled, seeking a home, banging the cliff until he found a spot to wedge it. The hiss of the foam was fading. A glance revealed another wave building. How long did he have? Fifteen, twenty seconds?

Feeling as secure as he could on an insecure purchase, he swiveled, reached, caught the object in his fingers, pulled, and brought it to the edge of the opening. It was a tow-colored sack made from animal skin, loosely tied at the top with a leather thong. He untied it with one hand and slipped down the sack. As he did, light streamed out, so dazzling that for a moment, he was blinded. As his eyes adjusted, he saw a sphere, seven inches in diameter, and as translucent as a gemstone. Otherworldly light played inside, blues melting into greens, yellows blending into oranges, reds melding into the deepest violets, all of them shimmering like opals. A silver handle was welded to the top.

All quieted below. A peek confirmed a colossal wave bearing down on him. Three feet above, the openings, nooks, and crannies for his hands and feet gave way to smooth stone. No time to climb down, no way to climb up.

But that light, that ethereal light held him entranced, seemed to flow into him, and on a strange impulse he drew the Lamp out and held it aloft. Rays streamed out, pushing back the mist and dimness of the land, pushing back the very rock of the cliff, or rather, revealing what he hadn't seen before, what he couldn't have seen, because, he was certain, only the Lamp could reveal it: a cave, large enough to pass through.

A snap of wind heralded the wave. With one hand, he jammed the Lamp partially into its bag and down the top of his shirt. Most of the Lamp lay against his heart, the light glowing through the cotton. Then he scrambled for the cave three feet above.

Silence behind meant the wave had paused at its apex. Now it was rushing in. For a moment, he imagined it was the vengeful hand of Korounos, angry that he'd found the Lamp. Johari swung into the cave like a monkey just as the wave struck. It must have hit the cliff where he'd found the Lamp. A sheet of white shot up, covering the opening of the cave. A torrent spattered Johari like stinging bees. He scrabbled back, watching in awe as the spray shot up, up, and then plunged like an avalanche of ice.

Presently he looked out again at the sky and sea and saw to his horror another wave building, as if the earth had quaked and was sending a tsunami.

In his childhood daydreams, he might have hoped the Lamp was magic and not one drop of water could come inside. Whatever power the Lamp possessed, it didn't include force fields or invisible barriers. He was going to get trapped, flooded in here. He turned and ran, pulling the Lamp from his shirt and holding it aloft. As he went deeper into the cave, he thought he heard someone say, "Goodbye, Korounos."

It seemed a strange thing to say, a funny mistake, as if whoever had said it mistook him for someone else. Johari felt the need to correct it. "Goodbye, Korounos," he replied.

Then fainter than the brush of his shoes on the stone floor, he heard, "My net is long. You'll be back ..."

The wave struck, pouring in water. It rushed up the cave floor like surf, hissing and foaming. Johari held his breath, but it stopped near his feet and receded.

No more waves were coming. How he knew, he couldn't say, but he knew it with certainty. He turned his back on the sea and walked briskly through the cave, holding the Lamp before him. Ancient frescoes lined the walls on both sides, the paint faded and chipped, and in places, it had crumbled away. He knew he needed to return as quickly as possible to the hill and light the fire for Greta. But the frescoes were so arresting, he felt compelled to examine them more closely. One thing he knew by now about the House: nothing was accidental. These paintings were here for a reason. Maybe understanding them would help him. In one, a man robed like a prophet was leading a great mass of people through darkness. He held something bright in his hand, which provided the only illumination. In another painting, farther down the passage, the man and his followers had come to a stone fortress that reached to the sky and stretched in both directions as far as the eye could see. Dark and dreary, no plants or trees grew on their side of the barricade. On the other side, sunshine smiled down on fruit-laden orchards and abundant fields.

A border surrounded all the frescoes, a repeating pattern of jagged pieces surrounding a symbol of some kind, a star-like shape. He was certain he had seen that pattern somewhere, and it teased at the edge of his mind.

Shrugging, he hurried on. The path split several times off the main artery he was following. It narrowed and turned, and he came upon forks with more forks just visible before they bent off into darkness. He lost all sense of direction, wasn't at all certain that he hadn't circled back to an earlier point, and his jaw tightened. He guessed he was inside a labyrinth. If he didn't take the right path, he could wander forever. Or at least until the House took him.

He told himself to settle down, think it through, and he studied a fresco before him. It differed from any he'd seen and confirmed that he had, indeed, made progress. He had a hunch that if he stuck to the path with the paintings, he would find an exit.

The next fresco gave him hope. The robed man held out his light, now like a small sun. Beams streamed out. Before them, the walls of the fortress flew apart. In the next frame, his followers poured over the broken masonry to the bountiful land beyond.

Five minutes later, with a sigh of relief, Johari found an exit issuing from the boulder where Bird-girl had appeared. That he saw it and hadn't simply walked by was a testament to the Lamp. It wasn't just that it provided illumination. There was a power within its prismatic radiance, mysterious and deep. Maybe even a little frightening. He returned it reverently to its sack and tied the top.

On the highest point of the hill, Bird-girl squatted on a rock, staring intently at the mountain Greta had gone to. Nearby, wood was stacked for a fire. A flaming torch was staked close at hand.

The Enchanter was standing half a dozen feet in front

of Millie. "Pretty Millie," he called. Millie nodded, turned left, and sat.

"No, you dumb mutt, turn right, *right*."

Bird-girl sprang up and gave a cry like a hawk when she saw him.

The Enchanter's face lit up. "By all the spirits, you be here!"

Johari chuckled. "Still haven't trained Millie."

"She's hopeless."

"Where'd you get the wood?"

"Cannibalized a cabinet."

"The one you keep potions in?"

"Furniture can be replaced, not the flower called Greta." The Enchanter glanced at the leather sack in Johari's hand. "You got it?"

"Yes."

"Let me see."

"When Greta's back."

Johari grabbed the torch and threw it on the wood. A minute later, flames were leaping. But his heart sank. "It's too small. She'll never see it."

The Enchanter took a pouch from one of his pockets and opened it. "You learned nothing, child. Still, you do not trust."

He sprinkled powder from the pouch onto the fire. It looked like ordinary talc. "Stand back." The Enchanter retreated, taking Johari with him with an outstretched arm. Popping, fizzing, puffs of ugly brown smoke belched from the fire. And stopped.

Johari sagged, hope flowing out of him like air from a deflating balloon. "It's not working."

The Enchanter patted his arm. "Wait ... wait ... almost ... Now!"

Light as bright as the sun shot up in a column and seemed to touch the sky.

"Don't look at it," the Enchanter shouted. He propelled Johari away. The girl was already forward of the blaze, intent on the mountain.

"That some beacon, hey, boy!" The Enchanter laughed, slapping him on the back.

A thrill ran through Johari. This was more than a beacon. This was a torch of the gods. If anything could penetrate the clouds shrouding that mountain, this fire could. They danced and hugged each other like drought-ridden farmers in a cloudburst.

They sat near the girl, the column warming their backs. All they could do now was wait. By Millie's bell, it had taken Greta roughly two hours to make her journey and quiet the mountain Elder. It was four o'clock by the sun. She wouldn't make it back before six. Time was running down on them. Fifteen hours. Fourteen for Greta. That's all they would have to find Calista and a way out of the House.

After that, they'd be trapped forever.

TWENTY-TWO

The sun was bearing down on the horizon. The heat on Johari's back had faded. He'd been watching the fire die for the past hour. When it was down to embers, the girl looked at him with a face so riddled with sadness and grief, he felt his own heart was being torn in two.

She was linked to Greta. Did she know something?

There was no way to tell. The girl never spoke. Johari doubted she was capable of speech. But then she rose and danced, chanting with words that were strange and beautiful, and he remembered she had done that before when Greta lay unconscious and almost slipped from the world.

Chant, he thought. *Work your magic.*

The girl gyrated and sang, waving a feather at the four corners of the sky. At last, limbs trembling, skin glistening with sweat, she sat cross-legged on the rocks, panting and spent.

Johari paced, his gaze on the mountain, the fixity of his stare belying the panic rising inside him. "She should be back by now."

The Enchanter's head was sunk on one of his pink palms. "I know."

"We should build another fire."

"No more powder."

"Then we go after her."

"We raise some kind of hell if we go out there. She never get back."

"I can't just wait."

"Let the elders sleep, child, let 'em sleep."

Johari sank to the sparse earth beside the man, close enough to see little red veins in his eyes. "Did you ever lose anyone?"

The Enchanter looked away, pain wrinkling his brow. "Many."

"No, I mean—"

"You mean someone precious. Everyone be precious."

Johari looked at him, really looked at him. With every passing moment, it became harder to see him as a projection of the House, harder not to see him as a man with blood and bones, hopes and dreams like his own.

"I mean a girl," Johari said.

The Enchanter gazed at the distant peak Greta had gone to, his eyes misting. "Once ..."

"You loved her."

"She made me heart fill the sky." Her name was Celeste, he said. Outside, she was as plain as an old stump. Inside she was a flower. From the moment they met, they knew each other, knew what the other was thinking. Her smile lit up a room, lit places inside him he didn't know existed. When he was away from her, he nearly went crazy until they were together again. "That be rare, child."

Johari pondered the knowing that Celeste and the Enchanter had shared and wondered why he and Greta didn't have that. Did that mean they weren't in love? He couldn't say for sure about Greta, but he knew his own heart. Greta had opened it. If it broke, he was done. Finished. He would seal it and throw away the key.

"What happened to her?" Johari asked.

"A fight ... a stupid fight. She took a knife meant for someone else."

"I'm sorry you lost her."

"The way of the world, child. We all lose someone."

"Sometimes they just leave," Johari said bitterly. "For no good reason."

"There always be a reason. All we can do is love 'em while we have 'em and keep loving no matter what." The Enchanter gazed out over the plain, shielding his eyes from the setting sun. He leaped up suddenly. "Tomorrow be a mystery," he exclaimed. "You will hold her today!"

"What? What are you talking about?"

Moon charms jingling, the Enchanter skipped and bounced in a lively jig and pointed. "She be coming, by all the spirits, she be coming!"

Dazed, feeling the lack of sleep and the hours in the sun, Johari stumbled to his feet and squinted at the plain. All was quiet. The columns of steam belching from the fissures had died down to tendrils, curling up here and there. The Enchanter must be conjuring a mirage from heat waves. Johari would almost take a mirage, if it kindled hope.

But then the girl whooped like a hawk and danced upon the rocks, her eyes flashing and bright. Johari followed her gaze. Dust hung in a small curtain a quarter of the way from the knees of the mountain. Another popped up, perhaps a third of a mile closer to him, then another. It had to be the leopard, eating up ground, sailing over mammoth stretches of the plain.

Then Johari saw it, bursting through the dust, small but not so small that he didn't see the tiny form riding on top. "Greta!" he cried. "It's Greta!"

The Enchanter hugged him and frisked him about the hilltop and tried to dance with the girl, but she hissed at him, and he laughed and sank to his knees, happy tears running down his cheeks.

The leopard flew, a mile, two miles. It landed, and suddenly a geyser of steam burst from a vent. The earth shook, nearly knocking Johari off his feet. Another blast shot up. And another. As peaceful as the plain had been a moment ago, now every fissure seemed to be belching vapor and fumes, accompanied by the enraged screams of the Elders.

Billowing clouds streaming skyward hid the leopard's progress. Johari and the Enchanter locked on to each other's arms and held their breath.

"They'll tear her to pieces," Johari cried above the din.

"Trust her ride."

"I've got to go to her!"

"You'll never reach her." The Enchanter restrained him, grabbing both of his arms, shouting in his ear.

Johari couldn't put the words together. All he knew was that he had to get to Greta. Another moment and the giants would trample her.

"The Lamp!" the Enchanter exclaimed. More words followed, unintelligible. Then, "The Lamp!"

In a flash Johari understood. He drew the Lamp from its pouch. Light streamed out, penetrating the clouds, revealing the plain, illuminating it like night goggles. The fissures were deep violet. The columns of steam a vivid crimson. Giant shadowy forms stumbled blindly through the mist, their arms questing. Greta was leaning on the leopard's neck like a jockey, her fingers sunk in its fur.

Johari grabbed the Enchanter's arm and shook it, excitedly. "She's dodging them," he exclaimed. "She's going to make it!"

As fast as it started, it was over. The leopard bounded up the hill, tongue lolling, and knelt so Greta could dismount. She slid off the beast stiffly, tottered on shaky legs, righted, and stumbled into Johari's arms. He crushed her to him so hard he felt her heart beating—unless that was his, pounding like a giant drum.

"I thought I lost you," he said, burying his face in her hair, soft and somehow sweet, despite being oily with sweat.

"I thought I'd never see you again," she murmured. Her lips found his, holding him until it seemed their souls would meld.

The Enchanter took out his staff and plunged it in a seam between two rocks. "Children, it be time."

With his fingertip, Johari brushed her lips, dried and cracked from her ordeal. "She needs rest and water."

She pressed his hand against her cheek. "I'm okay. Give me five minutes."

That hardly seemed enough. But all that was left of the sun was a waning afterglow. If the Enchanter was going to open a way to where Calista was, now was their chance, their only chance, to find her and bring her back.

Greta drank from the skin, washed her face, and let water run in streams down her neck and back. She and Johari ate a quick meal of flatbread from the Enchanter's wagon. When she stood, her legs were steady.

The girl and the leopard stood near the boulder Johari had exited from. Greta waved farewell to them. The girl threw back her head, shrilled like a hawk, and mounted the leopard. The beast leaped toward the wall of the boulder. Johari held his breath. It seemed they would crash into the stone. But beast and girl passed through it as if it was air and disappeared.

Millie's bell rang seven times. Time breathing down their necks, the Enchanter sat Johari and Greta beside his staff. He put the Lamp between them and then poured the honey-sweet liquor into his bowl and made them sip.

"No shells, no rattle?" Johari asked when the heat of the liquid faded from his throat.

"No need," the Enchanter replied. "We have the Lamp."

"Aren't you coming?" Greta asked.

"Where you go, I cannot. Neither can the Lamp."

"But someone will take it," Johari objected.

"No one comes here," the Enchanter replied. "The Elders will not touch it. Now. Watch."

Silver and bright, a full moon had risen above the mountains. Prismatic light pulsed inside the Lamp. A ray of it streamed out and touched the moon. At first, Johari thought his vision blurred. The moon seemed to be shifting back and forth between one image and two. With every moment, that second moon became clearer, going from ghost to a darker, indigo twin of the first one.

Gazing at the two moons, the Enchanter took off his hat and pressed it to his heart. "Now, now you be going."

As if it were drinking the moon's rays, the Lamp brightened, turning Greta hazy and golden. Johari's body too seemed faint, as were the Enchanter, Millie, the plain, and the distant mountains—except a darkening veil, six feet high, four feet wide, hanging a few steps away. Through the veil, light from the Lamp shone faintly on another hilltop. Beyond, all was dim and indistinct, the shadow of a shadow.

Johari's ears roared. The feeling of being insubstantial intensified. Not just his body but also his thoughts, which seemed to be dissolving. Yet what frightened him was the world beyond that dark curtain. He wanted something that would bring light and warmth there. "Let us take the Lamp," he shouted to the Enchanter.

"You cannot." The Enchanter's voice came from a distance, like he was at the far end of a tunnel. "It will disappear, snuff out from existence."

"How will we find our way back?"

"The door will stay open. You will see the Lamp's light. But, child, you have only till morning. Then it closes forever."

A cold breath from the opening stirred Greta's hair. She called to the Enchanter. "Will you be here when we return?"

"I go to me boy," he replied, his words now a faint echo. "But never far away ... never far ..."

Greta's fingers curled around Johari's. He gave her hand a hopeful squeeze. They ran to the opening and leaped.

TWENTY-THREE

"Phillip March had a long black hair protruding from each nostril," Greta was saying.

"Like insect antennas," Johari replied.

"Like a cockroach."

"Insecticide would have helped my first trial."

"Cockroaches need something stronger."

"Like a mallet."

"You can't be too sure with pests."

The world came into focus, the way it feels coming out of anesthesia, and—crossing that strange line between conscious and unconscious—Johari realized he and Greta had been talking. They were standing on a hillside. A dark and overcast sky stretched above, as if the sun was a dim and distant object. Smoke hung ghostly over a valley. Through the murk, the shadowy outlines of a city and the silhouette of a bridge were just visible. Beyond, as far as the eye could see, stretched a wasteland as bleak as the moon. The stench of burning rubber wafted past his nose.

Perhaps it was a trick of the light: Greta's hair and

eyebrows seemed to have turned from honey to stained mahogany, but her eyes remained deep and luminous.

"You'd need a sledgehammer for Sparra Givvens," she said, then looked about her, confused. A moment later, her face cleared. "That was strange."

Johari gestured toward the city. "Not as strange as that."

Greta frowned. "Did the Enchanter miss his mark?"

"Maybe. But there's nowhere to go but down there."

She nodded, and they followed a narrow track, cracked and littered with rubble, into the outskirts of the city. The buildings were skeletons, the windows black rectangles. Only outer walls, mangled steel, and concrete beams remained standing. Row upon row of them receded into the distance like broken tombstones. A shroud of gray ash lay over everything.

"Bombed?" Greta asked.

"Whatever it was, let's hope it's over."

They came to the bridge, a narrow suspension a quarter-mile long and spanning a deep chasm. As they stepped onto it, a chill wind keened softly, and the bridge groaned.

Greta glanced apprehensively at the cables. "Will they hold?"

Johari scanned the valley for a road or another bridge leading into the city. The chasm appeared to surround the whole of it. "It better. There isn't another way in."

The bridge complained like a sick goat but held. On the other side, they found more ruins and streets littered with broken concrete and bricks. Entire city blocks were reduced to rubble. Skyscrapers were empty shells the wind moaned through. Everywhere it was dark, dreary, cold, and wet. Occasional lightning flickered above, followed by low thunder. More frequent was a deep rumble from somewhere below the city.

If the Enchanter had sent them to where Calista was, as promised, it was a bleak and forbidding place. Johari hadn't a clue where to look for her. If she hadn't already starved to death or been buried beneath the wreckage. This last thought must have been gnawing at Greta. She was as pale as chalk.

He put his hand on her shoulder. "We'll find her," he said, trying to sound more certain than he felt.

They reached a square with the remains of a fountain in the middle. Johari was just thinking the city looked deserted, that nothing here could sustain life, when he saw someone running across a third-floor walkway, the outer wall having fallen away. At that moment, one of the subterranean explosions struck. Johari and Greta were thrown sideways. They clutched onto each other. Johari managed to roll beneath her, cushioning her fall, though his shoulder screamed as he hit the pavement.

"Are you all right?" she cried.

Rattled, he rose slowly, but managed a grin. "If that's what it takes to hold you."

She fished tissue from her pocket and began blotting a nasty scrape on his arm. "When we get out of here, you can hold me forever. Johari, I saw someone right before the explosion."

The building started groaning. Without warning it roared down in an avalanche of brick and mortar. Johari and Greta ducked behind a remnant of the fountain, seeking shelter from flying debris and dust. But he kept his eye on the building and saw the man tumble with it, screaming as he went, until he was silenced beneath fallen concrete and steel. His arm protruded from the wreckage. His fingers twitched once and sagged.

They leaped up and took off toward the fallen building.

There was the barest chance they might dig him out, though what might be left of him, or if he was even alive, was too terrible to think about.

They didn't get the chance. Another sound stopped them short. It screeched like a breaking train, increasing in volume until it turned into squealing and scrabbling.

Johari grabbed Greta's hand. They ran for the nearest wall and ducked inside an open doorway to a collapsed building. The rooms inside lay in a jumble. If whatever was coming found them, they would be trapped. He peeked from the doorway, scanned the square, searching for an alternative place to hide. Another doorway was forty feet to his right.

Greta read his mind. "Should we try for it?"

The question was settled for them. The screeching reached an ugly crescendo as hundreds of rats streamed from one of the street drains near the building that had just fallen. They leaped onto the extended arm of the fallen man. The entire limb was instantly wrapped in a sleeve of writhing bodies. Rats that could not find exposed flesh scurried into the nooks and crannies between the rubble, searching for what lay beneath. Johari held his breath. If the man wasn't dead, he faced a slow, painful end. No screams came from the rubble, and Johari exhaled in relief.

He turned to scan the area behind him and plucked out a bent steel rod he could use as a weapon. Greta picked up a chunk of concrete and hefted it in her hand.

"Run for it?" she whispered.

"Not yet." He had a hunch the rats had highly tuned senses; knew there was food after the building collapsed.

A dozen rats scurried back and forth, searching for a way in through wreckage not blocked by comrades. Several of these rose on their hind legs, forepaws flexing, and sniffed the air. With a surge, they scurried back down the drain.

Seconds later, Johari heard sharp yapping. And the scratch of claws coming toward him. Then he saw them: dogs, their coats the palest white, as if dusted with chalk, the color blending them into the pavement, concrete, and ash blanketing the city. They rushed in from the far side of the square, teeth bared, mouths foaming, straining against ropes tied around their necks. Men and women holding their leashes were just as fierce and wild-eyed. Rent with holes, their mismatched clothes looked like they'd been snatched from a trash can. With rail-thin limbs and long flying hair, they could have been the crazed survivors of a death camp.

Rats feeding on the man turned and fled, but not before the dogs sprang on dozens of them. The hounds feasted, blood painting their muzzles like macabre lipstick and sprinkling down on the ashy pavement. Sated, they seized the remaining rats in their jaws and gave a quick jerk, snapping their necks. Soon, dead rodents were piling up, and the rabble began stuffing them in canvas bags.

A shrill cry rang out from the other side of the square. Another mob with dogs rushed in, as dirty, disheveled, and emaciated as the first group. But the newcomers wielded clubs, pipes, and steel rods sharpened at the tip. On their backs, a candle with a black flame had been crudely painted.

A river of rats streamed down the drain as the two groups clashed. The new dogs leaped for the throats of the vanguard, man and beast alike. A man with tiny Christmas lights braided into his hair shrieked as a Doberman sank its teeth into his neck, cutting off the scream as it tore out the man's windpipe. A woman and a girl, not much older than Greta, met the same fate. But most of the dogs yipped and howled as bone-crushing blows sent them running and limping away. The first group turned tail, fleeing the square as fast as their legs would carry them. A dozen of their party didn't make it. Shattered kneecaps, gored stomachs, split-open skulls left them dead or dying. It seemed the goal of the black candle group was to capture the dogs and kill their owners.

Greta gripped Johari's arm, and he heard her gorge rising. How she kept it down he would never know, nor how he kept his own from lurching from his stomach, which seemed to be plunging and swaying like a boat in a storm.

He watched in a daze, little believing that men and women could be reduced to this state. Yet the precariousness of his position didn't escape him. At any moment the hounds would smell him and Greta.

Soft shuffling from above and to his right made him look up. A large man crouched in the shadow of the staircase. A burlap mask, little more than a bag with holes cut for the eyes, nose, and mouth, covered his face and fell to his shoulders. He brought his finger to his lips to indicate silence and waved for them to follow up the stairs. Johari hesitated. The steps didn't seem to lead anywhere. The man could be inviting them into a trap.

"They'll smell you in a moment," the man whispered.

Johari glanced back to the square. One of the dogs lifted its nose and sniffed in Johari's direction. Its new owner clubbed it into whining submission. How long would it be before the new master understood its impatient cries? Little separated them. The master already treaded the hinterland where the beast lived.

"Hurry," the man on the stairs hissed.

Johari's mind raced. The man hadn't attacked, hadn't

alerted either group in the square. Why he would help was unknown, but there seemed little choice.

Johari locked eyes with Greta. She nodded, indicating she'd come to the same conclusion. He took her hand and followed the man up the stairs. Ten steps and they ended, the rest having fallen away.

Furious barking broke out and charged toward them.

TWENTY-FOUR

There was no going back now. In a moment, the dogs would burst past the doorway. Johari's hand tightened on the steel rod.

The man who led them leaped from the last step. He caught the edge of a strip of concrete, the narrow remains of the second floor, and hung by his fingers like a monkey. With a surge, he pulled himself up. A moment later, he cast down a rope—woven from old clothes—that must have been stashed somewhere on the landing.

Greta caught it. "It's too far up. I can't climb it."

"I'll pull you up," the man said.

Outside, someone shouted, urgent and strident. Footfalls drummed toward them. Two dogs surged through the doorway, red-eyed and slavering.

"Go," Johari yelled, and lifted Greta by her waist, while the man hauled her from his position on the second floor. She swung like a pendulum.

The scuffle of paws made Johari whirl, steel raised. The hounds rushed up the stairs, growling, fangs bared, eyes alight for the kill. The one in the lead lunged for Johari's ankle. Reluctant to kill, he brought the rod down on its head. It fell away, hopefully, unconscious. The next dog leaped over the body of its fallen comrade. Johari swung again, connecting with the mongrel's jaw. It yelped, stumbled back, toppling the dogs behind it like tenpins and rolling them back down the steps.

One of the mob streaked through the doorway, his hair wrapped in a red bandana. He also carried a steel rod. His was sharpened to a point. He leaped over the fallen dog and up the stairs, hefting the spear for a throw. Johari slid his hands down his steel and angled it, hoping he could parry his opponent's weapon before it struck. The man never got the chance. He crumpled senseless to the floor.

Johari spun. A slingshot swung in the masked man's hand. Greta stood beside him.

"Hurry!" He tossed the rope to Johari.

Johari snatched it and held tight, while the man and Greta began hauling him up.

One of the dogs streaked up the steps and snapped at air below Johari's kicking feet. Dangling, he gyrated, the room spinning below.

Two men stormed in. They looked up, locked eyes with him, and dashed up the stairs. One of them brandished a shovel, the other a club. At the top of the steps, the man wielding the shovel swung at Johari, but he was out of reach. The second man launched his club, his intent clear, to knock Johari loose and send him plummeting, where chunks of concrete waited to break his back. A sitting duck, all he could do was tuck his chin into his chest, hunch over, and pray. He twirled on the rope, his back to the oncoming club. It struck with a dull thud. His back screamed in protest. His fingers loosened for a moment. He slipped two inches down the rope and locked on it.

"Pull!" Greta shrieked. "Pull!"

More men and dogs charged into the building. They roared in frustration when they saw him out of reach. The second-floor ledge was at Johari's eye level now. One hand still on the rope, he seized the ledge. The man in the mask grasped him by the wrist and hauled him the rest of the way. Then they were running, sliding on scree, leaping over fallen blocks. They came to another staircase. This one was intact. At the top of the flight, the third floor had fallen. But a supporting beam crossed over to the opposite wall and a door. The man started across.

Johari hesitated, eyeing the broken concrete rearing up like crags and peaks below. "What if another explosion hits?"

The man shrugged. "One hit a few minutes ago and this is still standing."

He continued on. Johari and Greta followed, tightrope-walking the beam. What choice did they have? A ravenous mob awaited behind.

The door wasn't locked. They passed through it onto a bridge spanning a street and connecting to the remains of another building. Over the next minutes they scaled ledges, scurried across rooftops, and went down and up fire escapes. The screams of the men, the baying of the hounds, faded behind.

They stepped through what might once have been a posh restaurant but was now a mess of overturned tables, chairs, fire-blackened walls, and raw, hanging wires. Johari pondered the man leading them. His clothes were a grimy hodgepodge of tattered rags, but he moved like a panther, exuding raw power, his muscles honed for survival. Johari imagined that after a few years here, the man's senses had sharpened, every nerve alive and firing.

The restaurant adjoined what appeared to be the lobby of a hotel, stripped clean of furniture, paintings, glasses, mirrors, carts, chandeliers, or anything else of value. A grand piano leaned on two legs. The keys were missing. Of what use they could serve was anyone's guess.

They went down an intact stairwell and exited to a parking garage. Only the shells of cars remained. Tires, seats, windshields, and doors had been removed. From the trunk of an old car, the man removed a broken mop handle wrapped at the top in blackened rags smelling of oil. He lit the rags with matches from his pocket. Following the express ramp, they circled down three floors below ground level. The sputtering torch was the only light, a sickly yellow illuminating the man's mask and a few feet beyond. All else was hidden in layers of shadow and darkness.

Presently, they came to a section where the ceiling had collapsed. They crawled through a narrow opening between floor and ceiling. The ceiling tilted up again, and after a dozen feet, they were able to stand again near a wall. Blankets and rolled up cloth made a bed. On a small wooden crate, a cup, plate, and fork were arranged. On another crate, a twelve-inch strip of metal was laid beside a file. Nuts and bolts of various sizes were piled nearby, no doubt for the man's slingshot. A crude target in the shape of a man was painted on the wall. Chinks in the concrete wall were centered on the forehead and eye shapes, a testament to the man's accuracy. Similar holes were clustered at the hands, suggesting he didn't always want to deliver a deathblow.

Greta eyed the ceiling. "Are we safe here?"

The man stood the torch up in an old watering can. He sat on three piled up tires and began stroking the metal strip with the file. "Nowhere and no one is safe," he replied, "but this is as safe as it gets. The garage has been picked clean. No one comes down this far." Beneath the mask, his eyes glinted. "Too dark and damp."

"But will the ceiling hold?"

"It's fallen. Where else can it go?"

Greta glanced about the shelter unconvinced, as if she imagined several tons of concrete burying them. "How long have you been here?"

The man stopped filing and gazed off. "Long enough. A day, a month, a year ... It's all the same hell." He tested his blade. "I haven't seen you before."

She sat on a gallon can. "We just got here."

"The House took you?"

"No."

He wrapped electrical tape around one end of the metal, forming a handle. "You lie. There's no other way here."

"We came through the House. It didn't take us."

He put the knife down and stared at her. "No one chooses to come here."

"We did. We're looking for our friends."

"If you're telling the truth, you've made a grave mistake." He wound more tape around the handle, then held up the blade, hefting it, watching it flash in the torch-light. "What do you want with your friends?"

"To bring them home."

The man's laughter echoed off the walls, as if she had just proposed walking on the ceiling or serving every man and woman in the city filet mignon and champagne. Then he leaned forward. "What are their names?"

Johari stood behind Greta and laid his hands on her shoulder. "How about answering a few of our questions?" he asked.

The man gestured for Johari to proceed.

"Who was fighting back there?" Johari asked.

The man nodded. "The sooner you know, the longer you survive. Are you hungry, thirsty?"

Johari was. The man put jerked meat from a burlap sack onto the one plate and poured water from a gallon can into a faucet top that served for a cup.

Johari sniffed both suspiciously. "What kind of meat is this?"

The man laughed again, but this time he sounded congenial. "Not human. That's all you need to know. The water is caught rain, strained through cloth to remove ash."

The water was potable and the meat not bad, though it was tough and could have used more salt.

"There are two groups," the man began, "the mad and the near mad. If they survive their first days here, people change. It happens a few days after arriving. Often in hours. They lose a part of themselves, as if the House stripped away a vital ingredient and left them half a mind."

"They've lost all reason," Greta said. "Like a disease has attacked their brains."

"Perhaps so," the man replied. "I wouldn't know. In the worst cases, they're reduced to what you saw in the first group, mad, unorganized, and ferocious. They form brief alliances only to turn on each other." He shuddered.

"I've never seen hydrophobia in a man," Johari said. "But this doesn't seem far from it."

"I've seen things I hope you never see." The man looked at Greta. "Things you're certain to see. If you have a way out of here, you should leave."

Greta shook her head. "Not without our friends. And the second group?"

"They have a little more control, or perhaps it's because

their leader beats and scares them into a loose alliance. Whatever the truth, they work in a ragtag army, serving one man: Lightfighter."

"He's not stricken like the rest of them?" Greta asked.

"It's a thin line between madness and evil," the man replied.

Johari's mouth went dry. He poured himself another cup of water. "Which group are you in?"

"You mock me," the man said. "If I was from either group you would be dead."

"Fine, but where do you fit in?"

"Nowhere ..." The man tipped his head, as though lost in thought. "A few of us are immune," he said at last. "I don't know why. It might be better if we weren't, if we didn't see the madness and the horror. Even down here in my little hole, with my lantern extinguished, I see it before my eyes, and the nightmare invades my sleep, flashing through my dreams in a red haze."

Greta shrank into herself, curling her fingers around one sleeve. "You must be lonely ..."

The man didn't reply. His shoulders trembled. Perhaps silent tears fell beneath the mask.

Rousing from the feelings his words must have stirred in her, she stepped over to him and laid her hand on his shoulder.

"You have a kind touch," he said. "I'll help you find your friends."

"Can you?" she asked.

"What are their names?"

"Calista Morra and Brice Bernhard."

"Ah ..."

Greta waited. When he said no more, she said, "You know where they are?"

"Calista, yes." He picked up the knife and began sharpening it with the file. "The man that came with her that day is gone."

Something must have pushed into Greta's throat; her voice rose. "Gone?"

"Gone from this world."

TWENTY-FIVE

Brice had been many things: selfish, full of himself, brash. But he was also larger than life. It seemed impossible that anyone so vital and alive could be gone. Surely he would survive here. It was a harsh testament to this world that he hadn't. If a Brice could be overcome, where did that leave Johari and Greta?

"What happened?" Greta asked, her voice as thin as an old flute leaking air.

The man stared at her. "There are a hundred ways to die here. You don't want to know."

Greta paled. "And Calista? She's all right?"

"No one is all right here. You're not all right. How long before the changes come over you? Or him?" He nodded toward Johari.

"But you'll take us to her?"

"You won't like what you see."

Greta stared at him. "She's been hurt? I have to go to her."

The man rose. He tested the edge of the knife on his thumb and then held it out to Johari. "You'll use this?"

"If I have to," Johari replied.

"You'll have to." The man turned to Greta. "You'll need something."

She shook her head. "I don't think I could."

"Kill or be killed." He handed her a mop handle. A piece of metal had been sharpened, jammed into one end, and secured with a wrapping of wire to form a spear.

He took up a sword—it may have once been window flashing—and then filled a pouch hanging from his belt with the nuts and bolts piled on the crate, selecting the largest. He led them out of the collapsed section of the garage and paused near the open space between two columns.

"You need to know how to use that," he said to Greta.

She looked down at her spear as if it were a viper. "I don't want to kill anyone."

The man positioned himself a few yards in front of her. "If you work the spear well, maybe you won't have to. You'll have the advantage. Use it to keep them away. Use both hands. Don't throw; thrust, hard and fast."

He raised his sword as if he were about to rush upon her. Greta gave a half-hearted jab with the spear. The next instant he was on her, his sword at her throat. Greta blinked. Jerked back.

Returning to his former position, he shook his head, sighing heavily. "That's your idea of hard? Do you want a dog gnawing your bones tonight? Use forceful, sharp, violent thrusts. Aim for the heart. Now, try it again. Do it right, or I won't take you to your friend."

This seemed to convince Greta. The man rushed her, but she kept him at bay with a series of vigorous jabs, one dangerously close to the soft spot near his windpipe. The tip flirted with the bottom of the man's mask a moment, like she might lift it to see what lay beneath.

He pushed it aside. "Good. One more thing. If anyone gets beyond your spear point, strike with the haft."

Greta pointed to a cloth tied at the end of the spear. "What's that for?"

"Stops blood from flowing down the haft," the man replied. "You don't want to lose your grip. Are you ready?"

"No. Lead on."

"We'll avoid open spaces. You'll have the advantage where it's narrow, like alleys." He started moving toward the exit.

"Wait," Greta said. "Who are you?"

The man checked his sling and ammo before replying. "Call me Rip."

They passed through the levels of the garage like ghosts and flitted through the shadowed streets, alleys, and byways. Rip knew the ruins and took them inside, where walls concealed them. He moved with assurance and ease across jumbles of broken concrete, the way a leopard treads jungle undergrowth and is king of the trees.

Using a metal access ladder fastened to one of the walls, they climbed down an old elevator shaft. At the bottom, a few steps took them through what might have been a boiler room. Then they were outside again. Drizzle laced with ash was falling, leaving the world streaked, runny, and gray.

Once, while secreted on stairs leading below street level, they saw a battle erupt. Wielding a hoe, one man tracked another and attacked him from behind. The blade struck and the man's cries drew half a dozen people, who converged on the scene from all directions like cockroaches smelling sugar. Unlike the earlier battle Johari witnessed, there were no sides and no dogs. Everyone attacked every-one. Like ferocious and desperate beasts, they fought over the fallen, the dead or dying writhing and gasping out their last breaths.

One of them locked eyes with Johari. The man's jaw was broken, wrenched to one side at a horrible angle, and blood trickled from a corner of his mouth. He rose to his knees, began crawling toward them, teeth bared, eyes burning like a mad dog. Next to him, Johari felt Greta stiffen, readying to run. A moment later, the man's skull was crushed with a tire iron. By instinct or reflex, his nails scrabbled the asphalt—still trying to get to Johari—and went limp.

As quickly as it started, it was over. The dead or dying were carried off. The victors melted back into the shadows.

"Wait," Rip whispered.

Johari needed the time ... to fight the gorge rising in his stomach. From the sick cast to Greta's face, she needed it too.

Minutes passed, then Rip led them to a manhole, removed it soundlessly, and told them to climb down the access ladder. At the bottom, when their guide joined them, he lit a torch.

Johari nodded toward the flame. "You leave these hidden around the city?"

"Better than carrying them," Rip said. "Leaves my hands free to fight."

They were in a square space where giant pipes converged from four sides.

He led them into one of the pipes. The torch guttered and penetrated a dozen feet or so, revealing metal ribs falling away in concentric circles into darkness.

A throat leading to the belly of the city, Johari thought. "I take it people don't come down here," he said.

"Rarely," Rip replied. "The rats are too hungry."

"That doesn't sound promising."

"The rats? We've reached an understanding." What that meant was left hanging. "Bats are the problem."

Johari trudged around an oily-black puddle. "Why?"

"Disease. And they attack in swarms. More savage than what you've seen."

"Maybe we'll take our chances above."

"We can't fight the whole city. Don't worry. I know where the bats are. We'll avoid them."

They exited the pipe and entered another running perpendicular and down. Water dripped. The metal smelled rusty. Skittering feet and an occasional squeal echoed ahead and behind. They left the conduit and entered a large chamber where pipes converged. The concrete floor was cracked and crumbled, probably from the frequent explosions and earthquakes below. As they picked a path through the rubble, sulfurous fumes wafted from the crevices. Overhead, smaller ducts jutted from the walls and had broken open at the bottom, the sections connecting to the opposite wall fallen away. Out of the openings, hundreds of rats poured, until the pipes were lined with quivering, eager bodies. There was no way to go forward without passing beneath them. Johari glanced behind. A battalion of them lined the way they'd come, cutting off retreat.

"We're dead meat," he said.

"Wait here." Rip stepped forward a dozen feet. One of the rats, a monster with slate-black eyes, reared up, defiant and challenging, on the end of a pipe near where they would pass. He pulled out his sling and loaded it with a bolt. He swung it, the sling whistling, and fired. The rat dropped to the ground, its head a bloody mess. As if on cue, its comrades dropped off the pipes and converged on the fallen giant. When they were done, nothing was left, not even bones, and the ground had been licked clean. Afterward, the rats retreated to a respectable distance and allowed the humans to pass.

"That's your understanding?" Johari asked.

Rip shrugged. "Call it a sacrifice for the greater good. They eat, and they leave me alone."

Right, left, up, down they traversed the pipes. They encountered no more rat armies, though from time to time they could still be heard, claws skittering across the metal or the echo of a squeak. Johari lost his sense of where they were headed.

The pipe ended, and they followed what appeared to be an old tunnel. A draft brought more than fungal dampness. Something rank wafted from ahead. A few feet from the tunnel's end, Rip stopped them with his arm. He crept forward a few feet, torch aloft. The darkness beyond seemed to swallow the flickering light, but Johari saw hundreds of hanging shadows within shadows and sensed, rather than heard, papery rustling in the chamber beyond.

Rip backed slowly away. He didn't speak until he had guided them back to a chamber built of great blocks, resembling those used in the dungeon of an old castle.

He pointed to a tunnel opposite them. "I missed a turn. We go that way."

The papery rustling unnerved Johari. "I thought you were keeping us away from bats."

Rip turned and confronted him. "I don't make a habit of going where I'm taking you." In a strange trick of the torchlight, the face holes of the mask seemed empty, as though no one was behind the sickly yellow material.

Johari raised his palms to placate. "Lead on."

As they continued down the other tunnel, Greta said, "I thought rabies was rare in bats."

"Maybe in New Earth," Rip replied. "Here, all bets are off. These aren't like any bats you've read or heard about."

The tunnel ended. They entered another pipe, this one small and forcing them to crawl at a slope upward. They exited through a drain into a long concrete chamber, the ceiling held up on both sides by columns. The floor dropped six feet in the center, and the remains of train tracks ran down the middle. The far end was roped off. A faint glow came from beyond. Something beat, pulsed, and echoed off the walls.

Rip held a finger to his lips, then pointed toward the rope. "Your friend is with the group down there," he whispered.

Greta looked toward the glow. "She's with them?"

He nodded. "Don't let anyone spot you. Spy from near the rope. Maybe you'll see her."

They crept on cat's paws the length of the subway—so it must have been, though now, except for the faint blush and pulsing beyond, it was as dark and still as a tomb—until they stopped near the edge, beneath the rope, and peered down. Fifty feet of the structure had collapsed in one piece. On that slab, a circle of men and women gathered around a bonfire. Several of them beat with sticks on metal: a train wheel, a subway door, an oil barrel. Upon a mound above the others, a man was perched on an old easy chair, the stuffing spilling from one side. His face was lost beneath a misshapen hood.

A petite young woman danced in the ring of onlookers. Her pants hugged her hips and legs like a leotard, accentuating a slim body, which writhed and gyrated. She whipped her head left and right, sending her tawny hair flying. The play of shadows thrown by torchlight obscured her face.

Greta gripped Johari's arm. "Is that her?" she asked.

Johari studied the dancer. At five-foot three, Calista was compact, like this person. Red leather clung to her arms like a second skin and looked like it might have come from a jacket. Calista had worn one that color into the House. Had she cut it for some reason? Or had others descended on her like vultures to tear off pieces of it? From what he'd seen, the occupants of the city would as easily eat leather as wear it, as this dancer was. "Hard to tell," Johari replied.

"We have to get closer," Greta said.

Rip shook his head. "Too dangerous. Like putting your head in the jaws of a dragon."

"I need to know." Greta crawled away from the edge and stood. "How do we get down there?"

Rip exhaled sharply, his mask ballooning. "If that's her—I'm certain it is—what do you think you're going to do?"

"Let her know I'm here."

"Then what?"

"Leave with her."

He shook his head again, the small sad motions of a parent listening to a foolish child. "She won't."

Greta's eyes flashed. "She will. We have a bond. Why do you think I've risked everything to find her?"

Rip sighed. "It's your funeral. Then again, it's not. There's no one here to bury what's left of you. Follow me."

He led them to what had probably been an emergency exit on one wall of the subway. The door pushed open easily. Beyond, a short landing took them to a dark stairwell. "Down there."

Greta and Johari crossed the landing to the top of the

stairs. They turned to look back. Rip was silhouetted in the doorway.

"Aren't you coming?" she asked.

"They have no love for me down there," he replied.

"Where do we find you?"

He shrugged. "Listen to me. If Lightfighter catches you, you're finished. He has a way of sinking his tentacles into people, bending and twisting them to his will. You'll hope he does. The alternative isn't pretty."

"Thank you for all you've done," Greta said, and began stepping down the stairs.

Johari grabbed her arm, stopping her. He hated everything about this. If Rip wouldn't go down there, what chance did they have? If Calista didn't come away with them, they didn't have a clue how to navigate through the city and get back to the gate to the House. Or how to avoid armies of rats, bats, and starving mobs. "Wait," he said. "Maybe this isn't a good idea."

"What choice do we have?" she replied.

"Maybe we can get a message to her."

"Forget it," Rip said. "Even if you manage to find someone who won't try to brain you, you'll just be tipping off Lightfighter. You'll walk right into a trap."

"Then we lure her out," Johari said.

"How?" Rip replied.

Johari didn't have a clue. In Grafton, he knew the streets, the hideouts. He had a few allies he could count on, like Dannie. Here he was a bird flying in thick smoke. The only thing he knew was that he would follow Greta into hell. It looked like he'd already done that.

All arguments in, Rip wished them luck. Greta turned back to the stairs. Johari took her hand, and they stepped into a well of darkness.

Beside Greta, concealed beneath fallen rubble, the percussive beating stirred Johari's blood, vibrated in his bones, fanned up heat in the very air around him. Yet he shivered and instinctively edged toward her, as much to give her comfort as to find it himself. She edged toward him too.

A ring of onlookers urged the girl on with shakers, cans that must have gravel in them. Their eyes burned at the sinuous snaking of the dancer's arms and legs.

A woman threw a torch on a mountain of garbage and shattered lumber. It flared into a bonfire. Smoke towered up like a dark demon, the sparks hot blasts of its power.

Someone had spray painted a chain around the central stage. The links at one end of the circle ran in a line up to the hillock where the man sat above the group, his hands on his knees like a statue, impassive and impervious to the frenzy below. The only hint of emotion was the cold play of firelight on his hood.

A crescendo on the cans turned the drumming to thunder. The dancer whirled in dizzy circles. Her hair flew. Light struck her face.

Greta sucked in a breath. "No ..."

That one word—hoarsely whispered, almost pleading—clawed inside Johari with frosty fingers. Her jaw tightened, her hands curled into fists, her legs stiffened, like a cat about to spring.

He put his arm around her shoulders, ready to restrain her if needed. The back of her neck was damp and hot.

"You sure it's her?" he asked. Then he saw the mole—a pencil point on her right cheek—and the rest of Calista's face came into focus.

The drumming slowed. She dropped to all fours. With each beat, she crawled like a kitten across the concrete, lips parted, eyes latched on the hooded man. She reached the hillock. On hands and knees, she climbed the rubble and slithered onto his lap, where she curled up like a child, her cheek against his chest. He stroked her hair. Without warning, he twined his fingers into her tresses and tugged, pulling her head back. She winced but made no attempt to escape. He released her and patted the spot soothingly. She snuggled tighter against him.

Johari's mind spun. Beside everything he'd witnessed in this horror hole, this was the worst. To see someone he knew reduced to this. It could happen to him. To Greta. People didn't just lose their minds to a disease—if that's what was causing the insanity. They were turned into marionettes, to dance and grovel and ... Johari could barely think it. Kill.

He wanted to get the hell out of here, out of this ruined city with ruined people. He would welcome the House.

In only a few minutes, he'd turned into a squirrel, dashing up a tree, a gleeful dog snapping and leaping at its tail. He scolded himself for wanting to bolt. For even considering it. By rights he should rush down there like an avenging angel and whisk Calista away.

That's what friends did. That's what Greta would do. That's why she was here. And damn, he needed to do it too. Or how could he face himself in the morning (if he had another morning)?

How could he be worthy of her?

He peered into the shadows surrounding the tableau below, searching for an escape route, should they need one. Knots of men stirred like specters beyond the firelight. The occasional glint of pointed metal suggested weapons.

Greta slid closer to him. "What have I gotten us into?" she murmured.

"Just what you said. What we need to do. We'll find a way. I promise."

The next instant, cold steel pricked the base of his skull.

TWENTY-SIX

A gruff voice ordered them to back out and lay down their weapons. A spear at the back of Greta's neck convinced Johari now wasn't the time for heroics.

They wriggled out of the rubble, dropped their weapons, and stood, confronting their captors, six men brandishing makeshift spears. They wore the same patchwork of rags he'd seen earlier, wore the same haggard expression; their eyes burned with the same deranged fire. One of them turned, revealing a black candle painted on his back. With them was the turbaned man who had tried to pick Johari off the stairs. His hands were bound and he was trembling.

One of them growled, "One false move, and we'll skewer you." Though the city's questionable diet had leaned him up, even reduced to skin and bones, he possessed a massive frame and bone-crushing hands. He resembled nothing more than one of the tumbled concrete blocks, the kind of guy who pummeled people up in a back room.

To the beat of the drums, Johari, Greta, and Turban were poked and prodded across the fallen ceiling, past the ring of onlookers with bared teeth and feverish eyes, past the prickling heat of the bonfire, until they stood before the hooded man seated on the hillock.

Only half of the man's face was visible; the rest was lost in shadow beneath the hood, which was topped with the glassy-eyed head of a dog. He was clean-shaven and had perfectly formed lips, what might be called pretty, sensitive lips. But that was negated by a granite jaw, framed with dog's forepaws hanging from the sides of the hood.

"Well done, Kiel. You shall be rewarded." His voice was rich, like cream swirled into melted chocolate. And there was something familiar about it.

Still seated on his lap, Calista bit her thumbnail and eyed Johari and Greta, but gave no further reaction.

Greta reached out to her. "Calista, sweetie, it's me. We've come to take you home."

The man on the hillock held up a silencing hand. "Shh, shh, it's all right. Everything will be all right." He played with Calista's hair. "Won't it, pet?" Calista snuggled closer to him.

"You're new, frightened, lost in this strange world," he said. "But you found me. All the sad and broken wayfarers come to me at last and pay homage."

"We're here for our friend," Greta replied. "Nothing more. We'll leave and never bother you again."

"You aren't bothering me now. You are *part* of me now. You'll learn. I'm a patient, gentle teacher. I love you, as I love myself." There was something dark and forbidden in the way he said that.

While the man's eyes remained hidden, it seemed he was drinking Greta in. She must have felt it too and took an anxious step back, only to be prodded forward with a spear.

"You can't possess her," Greta said. "She belongs to herself."

"Child," the man scolded. "You're bewildered by all you've seen, the harshness, the ugliness. In me there's sanctuary; in me there's life."

"No thanks," Greta replied. "Calista? Don't you recognize me?"

The man whispered in Calista's ear. She slid off his lap and a moment later was circling Greta and Johari, tracing her finger along their arms, shoulders, and backs. She moved in so close, Johari felt the heat of her body.

"You want me," she breathed.

"Only to bring you home," he replied.

"Only?"

Greta's eyes misted. "Come with us. We have a way back."

Calista ran her finger slowly along Johari's chin and up to his lower lip. He tried to pull away. The spear at his neck dissuaded him.

"Did you know, Greta, if I hadn't pointed him out to you, I would have taken him?" Calista asked.

Greta bit her lower lip. Sweat glistened on her forehead. Her skin looked pink, like she'd stepped from a hot bath.

Calista raised her arms and began to dance around Johari, tossing her head from side to side, her hair caressing him like soft fingers. "I could take him now."

She moved on to Greta, circling, running her fingertip along Greta's back until they were face to face. She stepped close. "Or I could have you. Don't tell me you never thought about it. I know I did. All those sleepovers. Greta Orngold lying in a nightie just a few feet away."

"You know that would have made no difference to me," Greta said. "I would have loved you as a sister, just as I do now. This isn't you, sweetie. He's controlling you. Trying to get under my skin. Let us help. Get you away from here."

Calista wagged her finger. "No-o-o-o-o, you're on the far side of the moon."

She slinked back to the base of the hillock, squatted, and looked up at Dog Paws for approval.

He rose. "You understand now? No? Let me make it clear." A dark note crept into his voice. "Good behavior is rewarded. Kiel!"

The guard commended earlier stepped forward. Dog Paws gestured with his arm toward Calista. "She's yours. Take her."

Calista rose. The guard put his arm around her shoulders. She nuzzled against him as they walked away.

"You can't have forgotten!" Greta took two steps, trying to reach Calista.

One of the guards locked her arms behind her back. Though restrained, she continued to struggle. Johari whirled to aid her but found a spear at his throat.

Calista glanced back. A moment later she began wheezing and doubled over, coughing.

"You don't want to, Calista," Greta shouted. "Your asthma doesn't lie. It kicks up when you're stressed."

Confusion clouded Calista's face, but it passed quickly, and she continued away, leaning affectionately against Kiel. Greta called for her to stop. Calista rewarded her with a raised middle finger and was gone.

"You see?" Dog Paws said. "In me, no one lacks love. No one lacks safety. No one lacks protection. It's an endless craze here. You remember crazes, don't you? You went to one before going into the House. Every sense indulged. Every pleasure explored. That's what we did when we thought our lives were on the brink of being extinguished. Here, it's endless.

"But ..." He shook his head sadly. "Bad behavior ... well,

bad behavior requires an equal and opposite reaction." He crooked his finger at Turban, who stepped forward, though he looked from side to side, presumably for an escape route. The circle of onlookers tightened around him, the hot madness in their eyes intensifying. Turban's face went white, and his eyes bugged like a deer seeing the hunter before it's shot.

He was brought face to face with Dog Paws, who said, "You disappoint me. You let them escape, two defenseless, unarmed innocents. Think of what could have happened to them."

"I couldn't help it." Turban raised his bound hands, imploring. "Th-they got help. From the Masked One."

Dog Paws laid a hand on both sides of the man's head and stroked. "Shhh, shhh," he soothed. "And that's your other crime, letting our enemy slip through your fingers."

Turban seemed to melt under the leader's touch. He began to sob. "I disappointed you, Lightfighter."

"Fear not, you'll be released soon ... from fear, from pain."

"Thank you, Lightfighter."

Lightfighter opened up a small suitcase, took out a billy club, and handed it to one of the guards. "Tenderize him."

The guard took Turban's arm and escorted him away, as docile as a trained dog.

Lightfighter turned back to Johari and Greta, steepled his fingers, and studied them.

What now? Johari wondered. He hadn't expected Calista to stroll off with them. Not after what Rip told them. Despite the warning, seeing her left him deflated. She was lost to them. Unlike the frenzied souls tearing at each other on the streets outside, she wasn't insane. Just gone.

The pink in Greta's skin had spread to her eyes. She

trembled as if she'd downed ten cups of coffee. If she was heartbroken, she wasn't showing it. She glared at Light-fighter. He appeared unaware of her condemning stare. The discs of his eyes, just visible beneath the hood like pale copper coins, appeared to be fixed on Johari.

He rested his chin on one palm, pondering.

"Let us go," Johari said.

Lightfighter continued contemplating him.

"You won't give us Calista, we get it. We'll be on our way."

"Do you know me?" Lightfighter asked.

Johari peered, trying to make out the shadowed face beneath the hood. "You sound familiar."

"I know you. You've grown, but you still have those eyes, ready to burn down the world."

Cold seeped into Johari's bones, and his knees buckled.

"Let you go?" Lightfighter pulled back the hood. His head was shaved and glowed in the flickering light. "'Fraid I can't do that, brother."

TWENTY-SEVEN

Johari and Greta were taken to an empty utility closet. A guard as rangy as a greyhound bound them to a pipe, hands behind their backs. They sat side by side. The pipe was damp, frigid, rough from rust. Water for an ice rink would have frozen on the floor. They leaned against each other for warmth.

A kind of dazed numbness pervaded him. Except in his hands. The rope bit and chafed, doubly irritated by vain attempts to free himself. For the first minutes, his mind was a blank. Then a thousand feelings crowded up. He couldn't make sense of any of them.

"Are you all right?" Greta murmured.

Muffled laughter came from the direction of the fallen slab where Calista had danced.

"You knew he might be here," she said.

Someone banged one of the oil barrels a few times, but the drumming didn't start up again.

After a long pause, she said, "There's hope. We'll get him out too."

The walls seemed to be swarming in on him.

She stirred, pressing close. "You're trembling."

So was she. His wasn't from the cold.

"Paul ... To see him now after all these years," she said. "You must have had only the tiniest ember of hope he was alive."

Was this still Paul? Wasn't this just a shell of the brother he'd loved? Hadn't the real Paul shriveled up long ago from the savagery of this place? This world infected people, as readily as any disease. Failing that, it ripped away the soul and left it to wither, like a plant without soil or water. Whatever a person had been—the wonder, the beauty, the kindness, the love—evaporated like dew in a desert. Could they come back to themselves? There had been no time to ask Rip. From all signs, the answer was no.

"Talk to me," she said. "The silence is killing me."

A strange kind of silence had taken up residence in him too. It sat right on his heart.

"Are you okay?" he ventured.

"No."

"You and Calista were practically sisters."

"We *are* sisters. Having different parents is just a detail."

If Calista wouldn't respond to Greta, what chance was there that Paul had anything in his heart for Johari?

Up to now, Johari could always picture Paul and hold the memory close. That picture was shattered, and it seemed that all the buildings in the city were crashing down on him.

He pushed the feelings away as best he could. Something else had his attention. Perspiration beaded Greta's forehead. She shook like a palsy patient. Her skin appeared sunburned. It wasn't hard to figure out what was happening. She was struck with the same malady that had taken Calista and Paul.

Why had Greta succumbed so quickly, and he hadn't? He couldn't say. One thing was certain: he needed to get her out of here. Fast. If Calista could throw herself at anyone who wanted her and Paul thought he was the second coming, how would Greta change? He didn't want to find out.

"You must hate me," she murmured.

"Never."

"I dragged you here."

"You didn't. I followed you in."

"You could have stayed in Grafton. You would have mourned me, but you would have moved on, had a life. After all the hurt heaped on you, it isn't fair to not get that chance. I've robbed you."

He shook his head. "Two weeks ago, I was ready to die in the House rather than leave you. Nothing's changed. We had a few good days. Gave Phillip March a run for his money. Woke people up."

She seemed about to speak, but a heavy blow echoed outside. A man screamed. More blows followed. At first the cries were loud, filled with anguish. After several minutes, the shrieks fell to moans and ceased. The pummeling continued long past the last incoherent whimper. The pounding sounded like an old carpet getting the dust beat out of it. If he wasn't already dead, he would be soon.

Greta wept softly. It seemed she cried for him, for Calista, for the man. Maybe for the world.

When the beating stopped, they had no time to react. Paul opened the door and entered the closet. He stood before them, studying them as he had before.

The fact that this looked like Paul, even if he no longer

was Paul, rendered Johari speechless. Yet he was the first to break the silence. "What's happened to you, Paul? The brother I remember would break his own arm before he'd hurt anyone."

Paul ignored the question. "You have one option: pay homage to me."

"We'll take our chances out there."

"All roads lead to me, brother. You won't survive."

"Then we'll leave, go back to the House."

Paul shook his head, topped with the glassy-eyed dog head, which seemed to watch them like a second pair of eyes. "I looked. There's no way back. Not for myself, not for anyone."

"Then let us go," Greta said. "Because you love him. You know you do."

Paul took off his hoodie and turned so they could see his back. Every inch from the top of his neck to his waist was covered with long crimson scars. "Do you know what those are?" he asked Johari.

"From the witches?" Johari's voice sounded small, as if the years had been stripped away and he was ten again. If he had done what Paul had told him, if he hadn't followed Paul into the House, Paul would never have gone to the City with its mad dogs and ravenous rats and still more ravenous mobs and brain-warping illness. He shuddered, recalling the moment in the House when, as a boy, Paul had thrown himself on top of Johari to protect him and had been torn to shreds instead, sending him to this world.

Face to face with the mess on his brother's back, Johari forgot about the pain of his arms wrenched behind him, forgot about his wrists chafing and burning against the pipe, forgot even Greta's rasping breath beside him. The closet was suddenly huge. And he was shrinking, shrinking into his shoes.

Paul pulled his hoodie back on. Pain surged into Johari's arms and wrists, and the closet came sharply into focus.

"Any debt I owe by blood has been paid," Paul said. "Now you serve me." He turned to Greta. "Are you his girlfriend?"

Despite the desperation of their circumstances, Johari held his breath, waiting like a nervous schoolboy for her answer. Nothing had been said. All was assumed.

"Yes," she replied.

Paul squatted before her. He took her head between his hands. He leaned in. She tried to pull away, wrestled to avoid him.

"Shhh, shhh," he soothed. He bent in and forced his lips on hers. Johari pulled at his bonds, trying to yank loose. The pipe held like a concrete pillar.

When Paul pulled back, Greta spat in his face. "I'd sooner kiss a pig."

Fire flared in Paul's eyes and just as quickly was extinguished, leaving a cold black vacuum. He carefully wiped his face. And slapped her. "Share and share alike, eh, brother? She'll be fun to tame." He felt her forehead, peered at her eyes. "In a few hours, I won't have to. She'll come crawling to me."

He left the closet, shutting the door behind him.

Greta struggled at the bonds. "We've got to get out of here, while I can."

They tried rising to a kneeling position with the intention of standing and then using their legs for leverage to loosen the pipe. But they were tied not only to the pipe but to a piece of metal bolted crossways to support it. They rocked back and forth, trying to loosen the knots. A quarter-hour of that left them panting, wrists raw, and no closer to escape.

A day of that might fray the ropes enough to tear free. Greta didn't have a day. She might not have hours.

Even if they escaped, then what? How could he protect a rabid Greta? Lock her in a cage and watch her beat herself against the bars? He'd rather die.

And in the back of his mind was the question: would the disease catch him?

"If you get the chance," she said, "kill me."

"Hang on, hang on as long as you can."

———

Dim light bleeding through from the bottom of the door remained constant, making it hard to judge time. His legs cramped. Greta's breathing grew short and raspy. Sweat soaked through her T-shirt. Her lips cracked.

Neither of them spoke, though he felt there were a million things to tell her. His hopes. His dreams. All with her. In this dark place, they were snowflakes about to melt away; pale phantoms that mocked him. He held them in his heart, where they would be safe, where they would stay true and real, because the rest of the world had spun out of control.

He wondered if some tiny part of the old Calista remained, something that would compel her to find and release them.

Little chance of that. If Paul ordered her to plunge a dagger into Greta's heart, she would do it without batting an eye.

———

Water dripped. Every once in a while someone padded by outside. In the distance, people were chanting or moaning.

A new sound intruded, softly at first, like the muttering of a thousand voices. It grew in volume, fluttering like a broken-down fan or the chug of an old engine, and it swept toward them, took on the character of beating wings. Whatever it was had entered the subway. Shouts rang out. A mad stampede rushed by. People screamed—piteous, horrible screams. The running faded. The staccato flutter dimmed to nothing. All was silent except the dripping pipe and the rasp of Greta's breath. The scuff of feet approached. The door flung open, and Rip stood framed in the uncertain light.

He squatted and cut them free with a knife. Together, he and Johari helped Greta up. She swayed dizzily.

Rip felt her forehead. "You're burning up." He handed her a plastic bottle. "Drink."

She took a long swallow.

"Can you walk?" he asked.

She nodded, and he led them out of the closet. But for half a dozen bodies scattered like butchered animals, the subway was deserted. The bonfire had burned to charred logs and glowing embers. They began to cross the area where Calista had danced when a motion above made Johari look up. Paul crouched on the edge of the upper level, staring down at them.

He stood and pointed at them. "Look for me in every shadow, in darkened alleys, and beneath the ruins, for there I lurk, and the vengeance of a god shall fall upon you."

TWENTY-EIGHT

Soup bubbled in a pot. Rip took it off the flames, which threw warm shadows on the walls of his hideout.

"What the hell happened back there?" Johari asked.

"Bats." Using an old food can, Rip ladled soup into bowls: a bent hubcap and a glass jar.

"How did you get them there?"

"They go mad over dog blood."

Rip handed Johari and Greta their soup, which smelled gamey and a little sour. Johari had little appetite for it, but he ate to encourage Greta to take some in. She didn't seem worse; she didn't seem better, either. Rip didn't know how long she had. From what he'd seen, everyone's response was different.

"I hope you've given up saving Calista," he said.

Greta mopped beads of perspiration from her brow. "Not as long as I'm me."

Rip studied her for a long time. "Your best bet is returning to the House. Maybe you'll get better there."

"Not without her," Greta replied.

Rip turned to Johari. "What about you?"

Johari considered a rainbow of fat floating on his soup. "I go down with her."

"Then you're both insane. Didn't your encounter with Lightfighter teach you anything?"

"Yeah." Johari put his soup down. "He's got a Messiah complex, and he's my brother."

Rip stared at him. "Lightfighter is Paul Hightower?"

"You've heard of him?"

"Who hasn't? He was the golden boy of Grafton. Everyone loved him."

"He hasn't lost that power, it seems," Johari replied dryly.

"My advice? Stay low. Most of his followers survived. He's going to gather them and come looking for us."

"I'm sorry we dragged you into this," Greta said.

Johari pushed the soup away. "We can't stay low. We've got to find someone."

Though Rip still wore the mask, Johari felt the man's eyes on him. "Who?"

In a few words, Johari told him about his abduction, his breakout from jail, and his encounter with the man at the Lakeside Grande hotel. He left nothing out, including the sealed file on his parents and the offer of fifteen million dollars if he returned with the scientist behind the House.

"I don't care about the money," Johari concluded. "But maybe this guy can tell us how to counter what's happening to Greta. The only question is whether you know where he is, if he's still alive."

Rip stirred the fire, sending up sparks. "He's here."

"Then you'll take us to him?" Greta asked. Despite illness and the dimness of the room, her eyes shone like sapphires.

"It isn't safe," Rip replied. "Lightfighter is combing the streets for us."

"Then draw us a map," Johari said.

Rip ran his fingers along the edge of his mask. "This man in the hotel, all he wanted was the scientist?"

"Yes."

"He didn't ask you to find anyone else?"

"No."

Rip laughed mirthlessly. "You came here for Calista."

"And Brice."

"Why Brice?"

"We told you—he was with us in the House. He fought for us, for Calista," Johari replied.

"And you have no idea who this man in the hotel was?"

"No."

"Think, who has the power to command a private swat team, to copy secret files about your parents?"

Johari had considered that a million times. Problem was, he didn't know any powerful men, excluding Phillip March and Sparra Givvens, and from all appearances, they were the ones who sent him to be Banished. "Who do you think he is?"

"I don't think, I know." Rip's fingers still flirted with the bottom of the mask. "Only one man has the resources to do all that, not to mention the gumption. My father, Jack Bernhard."

TWENTY-NINE

Johari peered closely, trying to see beyond the holes to the face behind the mask, wondering how he hadn't pegged Brice from the get-go. But that mask muffled words. And perhaps the twisted muscles and damaged nerves of Brice's face distorted his speech as well, for the terrible burns Brice suffered when the House took him stood stark in Johari's mind. And bloodthirsty dogs, rats, and mobs had been a distraction from the figure padding almost silently beside him.

Johari shook his head, but he found himself smiling. "How is it that I feel like strangling and hugging you at the same time?"

"Strangle me. You'd be doing me a favor," Brice said.

Greta was staring at him. "Take off the mask."

"Allow me that dignity," he replied.

"You said you were dead."

"I might as well be."

Her eyes flashed. "Do you know how much it hurt thinking you were?"

"Forgive me for being suspicious, but your story

sounded fishy. No one comes here to bring anyone back. I figured Lightfighter sent you. He's been trying to catch me pretty much since I got here."

"I want to see your face," Greta said.

A long pause ensued. "I can't," Brice said at last. But he agreed to take them to the scientist.

The journey couldn't be accomplished solely in the sewers. When they rose to the streets, Paul's gang was on the prowl in small bands, forcing Johari, Greta, and Brice, armed as before, to flit like wraiths from shadow to shadow. No dogs were being used, presumably because growling and barking would alert the prey.

As they darted around the rubble of fallen buildings beneath a leaden sky, and with the occasional rumble of an explosion below, Johari reflected on why Greta couldn't reveal who the mystery man from the hotel was, and how she was helping him. He wanted her to bring back Brice. But she couldn't reveal his identity. That would have placed him in a precarious position. Which made sense. He commanded a paramilitary unit. He had sprung Johari from jail. He wanted to bring Dr. Welty to New Earth for reasons not likely to be embraced by Sparra Givvens and his cronies. If any of that got out, Phillip March would be all over Jack Bernhard, and not even his billions would protect him from the long arm of the Supreme Council. But he had trusted Greta, and it wasn't hard to understand why. Though she'd lied on the witness stand to save Johari, that was out of love. Greta didn't have a duplicitous bone in her body.

Now, as they made their way to the scientist, Johari had

to marvel over how fast Brice had learned the layout of the city and all the ways to travel without being seen: dodging through ruins, stealing across rooftops, rappelling down walls with makeshift ropes hidden and ready to use. Brice only shrugged when Johari said as much.

"Lots of scout badges and martial arts classes. Only the best for Jack Bernhard's son," Brice said, his tone cutting.

He took them up a wooded hill at the far end of the city, the only place where living trees still grew. Near the top, peeking out from dense cypress foliage, Johari saw a paved open circle surrounding a bronze statue of a man set on a pedestal. His cape, the map in one hand, and his gaze toward a far horizon suggested the questing spirit of an explorer. The other hand had broken off. Beyond the statue was a white circular tower, perhaps two hundred feet tall. Near the top, six large arched windows looked out in every direction. Two flights of steps led to the double doors of the entrance.

"How do you know the scientist lives there?" Johari asked.

"I'm guessing," Brice replied. "The few who've kept their marbles tell me an old man lives here. He never comes out. Never lets anyone in. People leave food, herbs, and water at his door, which he hauls up with a basket. In return, he sends down medicine and other useful supplies."

Greta said, "If he doesn't answer his door, how do we get in?"

Brice pointed to the tower. "Scale it."

"Maybe you, not me," she replied. She was panting from the climb up the hill, and several times had woven and teetered like a drunk.

Brice patted his pack. "I've got a grappling hook. When I'm up there, I'll pull you up."

Johari eyed the upper windows. "Even you can't toss a hook that high."

"A tree behind the tower will get me high enough to make the throw. I hope. Anyway, that's our only chance."

Greta leaned limply against a stump. Johari held out his hand to her. "Grip my forearm with both hands," he said. "Don't let go."

She nodded gamely and grasped him. He withdrew his arm as easily as pulling it from a pail of sand. He glanced at Brice. "She'll never hold the rope. I say we knock on the front door."

Brice shook his head. "I've tried. He won't answer. The rope is the only way. We'll tie her to it and haul her up."

Johari hated the idea, but there seemed no alternative. A trail took them past a fallen tree trunk, bleached white with age, to the back of the tower. Up a short flight of steps was a rear entrance, but if the scientist didn't respond up front, he wasn't going to back here either.

Johari's fingers tightened on the butt of the makeshift sword at his hip, which replaced the knife he'd lost at the dancers' pit. "What's to keep him from cutting your rope while you're climbing?"

Brice opened his pack and took out his hook—the bent handlebars of a bicycle attached to a coil of rope. "Nothing. We try or we watch Greta turn into an animal. If he can help her at all." With that, he began climbing a giant euca-lyptus that stood nearest to the tower. He glided from branch to branch with the speed and agility of a monkey. Three-quarters of the way up, he walked out on a stout limb like a gymnast on a balance beam and planted his feet. He gazed at one of the windows and let out slack. Holding the coil in his left hand, he swung the hook with his right. When it blurred like a propeller, he let go. The hook bounced off the wall ten feet below the window ledge and fell.

Brice hauled it back up and climbed higher. He seesawed on a flimsier branch as he whirled the hook. On releasing it, he dropped to his knees and clutched the branch, sending down a shower of leaves. His toss skittered across the window ledge, the hook clawing the surface like two deformed fingers before it fell off, plunging into foliage near the bottom of the tree.

If he didn't know we're here before, he does now, Johari thought, and the image of the rope being cut while they were climbing flashed again in his mind.

Greta shivered beside him. The rasp of her breath sent him up the tree to retrieve the hook. Brice started down to meet him.

"I'm putting you in too much danger," Greta called up to Brice.

Through the leaves, Brice peered down at them. "I asked why you came for me and Calista. You haven't asked why I'm helping you?"

Johari had wondered about that. As Rip, Brice had been a guardian angel from the start, saving them from the mob, guiding them through the sewer to Calista, and saving them from whatever horror Paul had in store. But he'd abandoned them in cold fury the last time they saw him in the House. He'd made a play for Greta, she'd rejected him, and out of jealous spite he'd had no qualms about setting up Johari for Banishment.

"Those girls in the club were sirens," Brice continued. "Even as they lured me, part of me saw you trying to stop me from crashing into the proverbial rocks, pulling me from the boiling bowl of soup, trying to revive me. You could have left. You didn't. I won't."

Johari remembered. How the House had taken Brice in a wild club packed with people in costumes. How he'd faded before their eyes.

Brice took the hook from Johari and headed back up, this time going so high he disappeared from view. Faintly, Johari heard the whistle of the rope whipping, and then he saw the hook sail up, up, and through the window, where it landed with a solid chink.

Down the tree in a flash, Brice tested his weight on the rope. It held. Then he tied Greta to it, looping it around her waist, over her shoulders, and down her back to her waist to form a harness. "Me, first, then Johari. We'll pull you up. Try to walk your way up, okay?"

She took a valiant breath and nodded. For safety, Brice took her spear, secured it at his back, and climbed. When he went through the window, Johari started up and soon joined him. Together, they began pulling Greta up. She helped as best she could, bending into an L and stepping up the wall. Two-thirds of the way, her foot slipped. Swaying like a pendulum, clutching the rope, she gazed at them glassy-eyed.

Straining against the sudden increase in weight, Johari and Brice held on, trembling at the added burden. She went limp. A few seconds later, she stirred, found her footing, and they hauled her up and through the window.

While Brice coiled his rope from the hook end, Johari untied her. A sound from behind made him turn.

An old man stood in the doorway, pointing a gun.

THIRTY

Palms forward, Johari made a pacifying gesture in the air. "We didn't come to hurt you. She's sick."

The man's tweed suit hung baggy on a lanky frame. His hair was a forest of winter-frosted trees, lending him the air of a philosopher. His cheeks were sunken, the lines framing his mouth cut deep. Black, deep, and tinged with sadness, his eyes fixed on each of them, ignoring their weapons, studying their faces.

He lowered the gun. "Follow me."

He led them down a spiral staircase, past a room neatly organized with beakers, Bunsen burners, graduated cylinders, and other chemistry equipment, and into an office. He put the gun on a desk and sat in an armchair upholstered with a faded floral design, worn from use. On shelves behind him, books rose from floor to ceiling, and books were piled in front of books. A portrait of a young woman—her gaze soft and wistful—hung on one wall near a pendulum clock.

He took a pipe from a side table and cradled it between

the arthritic stumps of his hands. "Why me?" His voice was tired, his accent British.

"You're Bertrand Welty," Johari said. Maybe he was wrong, but the man resembled the one on the photo in his pocket, albeit much older. And the lab seemed to cinch it. Behind the lab equipment in the other room, he'd also seen electronic gadgets, and along the back wall, shelves of hydroponic plants.

The man regarded Johari thoughtfully. "I haven't heard that name spoken for more years than I wish to count." He sighed. "Nothing should surprise me. I've seen too much. I knew someone would penetrate my sanctuary sooner or later." He spoke to himself more than to them. "They seem earnest; the girl kind, troubled; the wild-eyed fellow intense, but he loves her. I can see that at a glance. The man behind the mask I can't read, but he looks dangerous, armed to the teeth. But of course, he would have to be to cross the city to see me."

"We're here not just for me," Greta said. "We've got friends running mad down there."

The man put the pipe in his mouth, though it was unlit and empty. "I will help."

"Then you are Dr. Welty?" Greta asked, her voice rising with hope.

"I would rather be almost anyone else," he replied. He pointed at Greta and Johari with the end of his pipe. "There's something different about you two. The House didn't take you, else you would show the deleterious effects. How did you get here?"

"Through the House," Johari replied. "Assuming we're still not in it. Can you do something for her, then we'll tell you all about it?"

"No. You're not in it." Welty rose and nodded toward

the chairs opposite him. "Sit. I'll be but a moment." He left the room. A short time later, they heard a teakettle whistling. He returned with a tray holding a teapot, cups, and small sandwiches, and put it on his desk. "We'll let it steep."

Johari glanced at the sandwiches. The bread was nicely toasted. "What are you using for power?"

"I have solar panels on the roof and storage batteries up and down the tower."

"And the bread? You can't have any supplies left."

"A nutritious grain I grow and mill. As far as supplies, yes, scant remains, but my body desires little now. I eat every few days." He poured tea and handed a steaming cup to Greta. "This will help." She sipped it gratefully.

"Will it cure her?" Johari asked.

"It will soothe her while we talk."

"But will it cure her?"

"Relax, my young friend. She's stable for now. First, we talk."

This process was grinding along like water torture, but Johari didn't feel he could demand anything. Welty had his pace. There seemed little anyone could do to speed it up. Besides, Johari had more than a few questions for Welty about the House. What he learned might be crucial to their survival when they returned to it.

"What do you need to know?" Johari asked.

Welty pointed with his pipe to Brice. "The House brought you here. But you two ..." He indicated Greta and Johari. "... no signs of trauma. You found another way. Tell me all."

Johari ran through the tale, beginning with the first time they entered the House, the taking of Calista and Brice, his two trials before Sparra Givvens, and the bizarre events leading up to him returning to the House to join Greta. Then he turned to the adventure with the Enchanter, seeking the Lamp, and the strange time he'd spent with Korounos, ending at last with their escape from Paul Hightower.

Welty listened, his expression thoughtful, though at certain points in the account—like Calista's insides disappearing and Brice's burning in the club—the man appeared deeply shaken. Haunted.

When Johari was done, Welty folded his fingers with painful slowness and leaned his chin on them. "You must have many questions, about Earth, the House, the founding of New Earth. I will tell as much as time allows. Volumes could be written. Owing to time, I must gloss over."

He poured Greta more tea—she already appeared less flushed—then served himself, Johari, and Brice. Johari sipped. The flavor was like almonds and berries, and slightly bitter. It warmed him, though, for which he was grateful. His encounter with Paul left him chilled.

Welty wrapped his hands around the teacup, as though seeking relief for the pain in his joints. "Physicists have long known there were more than the three dimensions we see. Einstein shook things up when he added space-time. String theorists worked out elegant math to demonstrate eleven dimensions."

"M-theory," Greta said.

Welty smiled. "Yes. Unfortunately, they missed one."

Greta's brow wrinkled. "What else could there be?"

"My dear, your question is the answer. It's the product of your mind. As soon as sentient life reared up from biological soup another dimension sprang into existence. Consciousness created a twelfth dimension, and by that I mean all within our awareness, and more important, all that is unconscious, too."

"But how can mind be a dimension?" Johari asked. "It's just thoughts. I never psychically unlocked a prison cell or relocated nasty foster parents."

The scientist waved away these objections with his fingers. "It's far more subtle than that, nothing so brutal. Since the early 1900s, physicists have known that researchers themselves were impacting the outcome of subatomic experiments. Depending on how they set up their experiment with light, they got waves or particles. In your own experience, you know that changes in the world start with an idea. Whether it's a decision to stop smoking or something more dramatic, like an invention. But it doesn't stop there. In deeper levels of the mind, there are primordial images or archetypes, universal patterns that emerge as each of us develop and evolve as individuals: mother, father, healer."

"Shadow," Johari said.

"Shadow," Welty confirmed.

"But why the House?" Johari asked.

"It started as an experiment. Through advances in neuroscience, we were able to tune into an individual's unconscious. Once we had that, we were able to amplify and project it onto a mind-space continuum: the House. The implications for psychotherapy were promising. A person could quickly get to the bottom of their problems, which were played out before them. With the guidance of an experienced therapist, they could resolve their issues."

"So, the therapist would enter the House with the client," Greta said, the ragged and raspy sound in her breathing all but gone.

"Yes. The therapist was already aware of their own

shadow material—the dark, unacceptable, castoff parts of themselves—and had rejoined them with the rest of the psyche, leading to emotional growth and wholeness. No one was allowed to be a guide until they had. That way their own issues wouldn't get in the way of treatment or pose any risks, and they could focus wholly on helping the client."

"What went wrong?" Johari asked.

"The technology fell into the wrong hands."

"Sparra Givvens?"

Welty bit down on the pipe. "Yes. If only I had understood him sooner, seen his zealous involvement in the project as a warning sign, I might have stopped him. But in those days, we were all carried away with the potential of what we'd discovered, and Sparra threw himself into it with single-minded focus. I never saw how fragmented he was or how fanatic, as bad as any extremist. Too late I learned his true intention: the House as a new religion.

"He used the House as a political tool. Instead of helping people integrate their shadow, he used it to eliminate people. The world got divided into good and bad, black and white, those who had survived the House, and those who hadn't. Instead of a tool for growth, it became a tool for subjugation."

Brice's fingers played on the knife hilt jutting from his belt. "Didn't anyone try to stop him?"

Welty sighed. "We did. But he had money, power, and fear on his side. There are always people who will believe what they are told, even if it's horseshit—if you'll excuse my French—and he hoisted a steaming pile of it on an unsuspecting population, who rallied behind him. The only option I had was to sabotage my creation. Before I had a chance, he marooned me here."

"This was once a thriving city?" Greta asked.

"Never thriving. It was Givvens's first attempt at creating New Earth. But it had many of the same properties and dangers as the House. You see what happened."

In the distance, Johari heard an explosion and then another farther away. He crossed to one of the windows and gazed out at the city. Fog had rolled in. Through it, the ruins looked like an abstract painting.

"How do we survive the House?" he asked.

Welty rose and went to the bookcase. He reached for a narrow box halfway up. Returning to his seat, he opened the box, took out a tarot deck, and riffled through it. "There's your Enchanter," he said, handing Greta the Magician card, "imbued, no doubt, with something from each of you. The House was never meant to have lots of people running around in it. We quickly abandoned the idea of group therapy. Like a dream with multiple authors, everyone adds their unconscious material to the setting and characters. In other words, it becomes a big mess. And far too dangerous."

Greta peered at the card. "So the Magician is an archetype. What's his significance? Why did we bring him?"

"One of you needs a healer. Here's your Korounos." He fished out another card and handed it to them. It depicted a robed and bearded man carrying a lamp.

"Who is he?" she asked.

"The Hermit. He represents deep reflection, pulling away from the world to ponder. When he shows up in our unconscious, he may spark brilliant flashes of insight, unleash the tremendous power within us. But all the archetypes are bivalent, representing the light and dark in each of us." He tapped the card. "The safety of solitude can be seductive. If we're not careful, it can trap us."

Johari turned back to the window. Scattered across the

city, crimson flared and died in the fog like volcanic eruptions. "What about Muloch?"

"Hard to say. He may be an archetype, or he might be something else."

"What else is there?" Greta asked.

"Some of those souls who Givvens forced into the House left something behind, a sort of imprint."

"In other words, other people's shadows," Johari said.

Welty nodded.

"How do we help our friend, Calista?" Greta asked.

"A moment." Welty left the room and returned with a small carrying case. He sat, put it on his side table, and opened it. Inside were a bottle, a medicine vial, and two syringes. He held the vial up to the light, inspecting the contents. Satisfied, he cleaned the rubber top with liquid from the bottle, alcohol by the smell of it, and then filled each of the syringes. When he was done, the vial was empty.

"How does it work?" Greta asked.

"Like any psychotropic medication." Welty tapped one of the syringes, checking for air bubbles. "It restores the balance of neurotransmitters."

"Brain chemicals. Are there side effects?" Greta eyed the syringes.

"There may be a brief loss of muscle control, confusion, and loss of consciousness."

"How brief?" Johari asked.

"Ten to fifteen minutes."

Johari pointed to the syringes. "How many doses?"

"One shot." Welty turned to Greta. "Are you ready?"

Greta held up her hand. "A lot of sick people are running around down there. Can you give us more?"

Welty sighed. "This is the last of it."

She paled. "Then these two are for Calista and Paul."

Johari's mouth went dry. "Forget it. One for you, one for Calista."

Greta's eyes bored into his. "Can you really leave your brother like that?"

A helpless strangling rose into Johari's throat. He sagged into one of the chairs. "Can you make more?" he asked Welty.

"I tried," Welty replied. "I don't have the right equipment. I nursed my supply over the years, giving some to those below." He gazed at the painting of the young woman. "It kept her going."

"But you said it only takes one dose," Johari said.

Welty sighed. "She wasn't taking it for that. How do you think I've managed to live so long? Before she died, she made me promise to keep taking it."

"I'm sorry you lost her," Greta said. She dropped her chin into one hand, lost in distant thought. Then, "The madness, will it go away if I return to the House?"

"Mind you, I had no opportunity to test that theory," Welty replied. "But I believe it would for someone here a few hours, perhaps a day. Beyond that point, the illness would not remit in the House. Perhaps not even in New Earth. Someone would have to return to Old Earth."

Greta picked up the case and closed the lid. "I'll hold on. Until I reach the House."

Johari turned to Greta, sitting beside him, and gripped her shoulders. "What if you can't? I won't risk it."

Greta pressed her hands over his. Her fingers caressed, but her voice was firm: "You can't make me take it."

Johari looked to Welty for support. The scientist rose and examined the glands in Greta's neck and inspected her arms. "She has time."

"How much?" Johari asked.

"It's hard to say. An hour. Maybe two. She's fighting it. That helps."

Johari was out of arguments. "If she's close to going, what do I look for?"

"A scarlet rash on her arms and chest," Welty replied.

"Then it's decided." Greta held her hand out to him. "And you can guide us through the House."

Welty shook his head. "Every joint is on fire. I'm too old for the journey."

"Then we're killing you if we take this." She tried to hand him the syringe case, but he pressed it back to her.

"Two more doses? What good does that do? I've kept my promise. I can die knowing I've done a little good."

"You tried to do something wonderful with the House, to heal people."

Welty seemed to shrink in his chair. "It's not the legacy I hoped for. Because of me, the world cries in pain." The haunted look returned to his eyes, robbing them of the mildness and compassion evident through most of the conversation. "No, this is my punishment, to look every day upon the horror of what I created."

Johari glanced at the clock. The ticking seemed preternaturally loud. There was so much more he wanted to ask about Old Earth, New Earth, and the House. They had to get going.

But Brice spoke first. "Why am I not blind?"

Welty emerged from the troubled memories that must have been plaguing his mind, and refocused. "I don't understand."

In answer, Brice took off the mask.

THIRTY-ONE

Brice had been the catch of New Earth. Star athlete. Wealthy beyond belief. Endowed with the physique and finely chiseled features of a Greek god. And a million-dollar smile. Girls flocked to him like bees to honey.

All that changed inside the House. Many things about Johari's trial there had faded from memory. Clearly etched in his mind was what happened to Brice. How three beautiful women, projections of the House, had lured him into an alcove, tempted him with a bowl steaming with an intoxicating concoction. How Brice, under the spell of their siren song, had plunged his face into the boiling liquid.

Johari knew the burns had been bad. Now, seeing how they'd healed—or hadn't—something cold slid into the pit of his stomach. Crimson scars left Brice's lips twisted. The skin seemed to have melted, as though acid had run down his face and carved a mess of fissures. No eyebrow hair remained. One eye was partially closed.

"This is the legacy your invention left me," Brice said, his face warped further with bitterness.

Welty's eyes grew watery. He slowly raised his hands and pressed them trembling over his heart.

"Anything bad enough to ruin my face, should've cooked my eyes," Brice said. "Why didn't it?"

Welty tried to take a sip of tea, but his hand still shook, rattling the cup on the saucer. Failing to compose himself, he put it down. "Inside the House is like walking in a dream. Your mind believes what it thinks is happening, and the burns become real. But the mind is self-protective, like when it awakens you before crashing from a terrible fall in a nightmare."

"But I saw him before he disappeared," Greta said. "His eyes were like plums."

"He appeared dead to you, no? Yet here he is," Welty said. "It's what I've been telling you all along. The dimension of mind is infinite. Anything can happen."

"Can he restore his face, then? In the House maybe? Tell me he can."

"I wish with all my heart he could."

"But you said anything was possible," Greta cried.

Welty held out his hands like a helpless child. "His burns are as real as if he fell into a furnace."

Brice turned away. "Then we're done here."

"Wait," Johari said. Then to Welty, "When we return to the House, how much time will we have to get out?"

"Each of you will have the time remaining when you left," Welty replied.

"That Brice has been here weeks won't matter?"

Welty nodded. "Time will resume at the point the House took him."

"Out of the frying pan, into the fire."

"I'm afraid so. And friends ... Careful. Unfinished business has a way of following you."

The clock announced the hour with a birdcall. Welty glanced at it. "You better go while you can. Before the effects of the tea wane."

Their thank-yous and farewells were brief. Before stepping from the room, Greta turned back to him. "You're not the monster," she said. "Sparra Givvens is."

Her words left him with no smile. "The greater the saint, the longer the shadow," he replied.

They were halfway up the stairs when they heard the shot. They rushed back to the study. The gun lay on the floor below Welty's lifeless fingers.

Downstairs, someone pounded on the door loud enough to wake the dead.

THIRTY-TWO

Brice whirled and bolted up the stairs, taking them two, three at a time. Johari snatched the gun. He and Greta followed, catching up to Brice at the open area where they'd first met Welty. They looked down from a window facing the entrance. A mob of twenty to thirty bearing torches surged like a restless sea about the front door. Johari and company raced to the back window they'd climbed to. Below, a dozen shadows prowled along the path surrounding the tower. More loitered among the trees and shrubs.

"Paul's followers?" Greta asked.

Brice eyed the movements below. "Too organized to be anyone else."

"Can they scale the wall?"

"They've never been good at it. That doesn't mean they won't try."

Greta's jaw hardened. "If they do, we'll cut the rope. Can they break the doors down?"

"The landing above the back steps is too small to wield a

battering ram. The front door is another story. It's made of metal."

Johari said, "Pretty thick from the ring of it."

"Right," Brice replied. "But with enough time, they might pound it from the hinges."

"What do we do?" Greta asked.

Johari held up the gun. "We've got this."

Brice took the revolver from him, pushed the cylinder release with his thumb, and rocked it out with his other hand. He held the cylinder up and inspected it. "Empty."

"He must have more around somewhere."

Brice stared at him. "He only needed one."

True enough, but a search of the tower seemed the next step. They might find bullets or another weapon. They divided up. Brice stayed on the upper level, in case the band below the landing decided they were wall climbers.

Greta took Welty's lab. Johari searched the bedroom and bathroom. He turned up nothing useful there. But a drawer in the kitchen had a set of chef's knives. He stuck one of them in his belt and put the rest in a plastic bucket he found under the sink. Then he checked out the study. He didn't want to look at Welty. Morbid curiosity drew him there, or perhaps it was the feeling that such a great man shouldn't be left unattended.

Johari had always hated whoever created the House. It was the thing no one could dodge; the threshold all had to pass; the promise of life and a future, or death. But having spent the last thirty or forty minutes with the man, he was convinced Welty had nothing but the highest hopes for his invention and saw it as a healing balm for humanity. He must have suffered terribly knowing what the House had become, how it had been used. His penance must have been to look from his tower upon the result of what he'd created. Down to two injections of medicine, he was at the end.

He'd shot himself in the mouth. Part of his head had been blown away. Blood spread on the back of the chair like a deformed flower and had sprayed books on the shelf behind him. Quelling nausea, Johari fetched a clean towel from the kitchen and draped it over the back of the chair, covering the blood. Then he straightened Welty's head and folded his hands around the pipe. The eyes were unharmed, and he looked as if he was dozing.

"You're at peace now," Johari muttered. He turned away and searched the desk. In one of the drawers, he found a box of bullets and stuck them in his pocket. He wrapped up the sandwiches in another towel and started back to the top of the tower, the pounding on the door below urging him up the steps. Greta was already waiting at the top with Brice. She'd found much of interest—Welty's experiments, computer files, schematics, and journals—little of imme-diate use.

She'd tossed them into a small carrying case. She tried pressing it into Brice's hands. "Put it in your backpack."

Brice shook his head. "I don't want the extra weight."

"It's light. You won't even notice it. Welty's hard drive is in there. I'll study it after we leave the House; maybe we can shut it down for good."

Brice pursed his lips but stowed the carrying case in his pack. While Greta stuck one of the large kitchen knives in her belt, Brice distributed the rest at his ankle, hip, and shoulder in a way that suggested he could snap one out at a moment's notice.

He stuffed the sandwiches into his backpack. "Now you're thinking like a survivor, Hightower."

"Beats eating rats," Johari replied.

"When you're starving, you'll eat almost anything." Brice grinned mirthlessly.

"I draw the line at things needing tenderizing," Johari said, thinking of Paul's command to tenderize Turban.

Brice's jaw tightened. "Me too."

Greta hushed them. Someone was shouting below. They crossed to the window overlooking the front entrance.

Wearing the dog hood, Paul was looking up at them. He cupped his hands around his mouth like a megaphone. "You're trapped."

"And you're locked out," Johari called back.

"The door will fall eventually. Come out now and we'll make this painless."

"It's held all these years. We'll stay here."

"You'll starve."

"The scientist survived decades. Besides, your idea of food doesn't work for me."

"You're still the stubborn little shit you always were."

"Deal with it." Johari pulled away from the window and paced.

Greta stopped him with a hand on his shoulder. "He can't help it."

"I'm trying to figure out how to get out of here."

She was right, though—Paul couldn't help it, and one glance at her was a reminder of how right, and how little time they had. Welty's tea hadn't been a cure, but it had pushed the symptoms back. For a spell, the sweats and shakes had abated, and Greta had seemed almost her old self. Now perspiration dotted her forehead. How long before the telltale rash painted her neck and shoulders?

She seemed unsteady on her feet. Johari was about to ease her to the floor, so she could rest against a wall, but another voice called from below, hurrying Greta to the window.

Johari followed and looked down. Calista stood beside Paul.

She called up to them. "You're shut up like animals in a cage. Join us."

Tears welled in Greta's eyes as she gazed at what remained of her friend.

"I promise," Calista continued, "no one will hurt you."

"Run, sweetie," Greta shouted back. "Before he ruins you."

Calista scowled, was about to reply.

Paul stopped her. "We've been kind. No more. Tell that sewer rat I'll kill him first."

Brice stepped to the window, whipping his sling. "Tell me yourself, dog breath." He released the shot. It whizzed dangerously close to Paul's head. He ducked just in time and scrambled to bushes on the periphery, where he began directing the assault from out of range. A dozen or more of his men took up the bleached tree trunk Johari had seen earlier and began battering the door again.

"Don't waste your ammo," Johari said, pulling Brice away from the window.

"But it felt so good," Brice replied.

They stepped to the other side of the tower and glanced over the edge. No one was scaling the wall. Instead, a dozen armed men loitered in the trees, guarding against a descent. Going down would make anyone a sitting duck.

"How long before nightfall?" Johari asked. "Maybe we can climb down and slip past the guards when it's dark." It was a horrible plan no matter which way he looked at it. Aside from the guards below, more were marching the path around the tower, and these were crazed guards, reduced to beasts with fine-tuned senses. The worst part of the plan was that he and Brice would have to lower Greta first. She would be exposed and defenseless. And time was running out on them. The door to the House would close. Morning would trap them in the city forever.

Brice stared at him. "There's no day, no night. Only one, long, constant gray. Anyway, it's a terrible idea."

"What else can we do?" Johari replied as they both tried to ease Greta to the floor.

She struggled to remain on her feet. "No, we've got to find a way out of here."

"We've looked," Johari said.

She staggered forward, to where it was unclear. Johari and Brice caught her, kept her from falling, and helped her back to the wall.

"I'll look again," Johari said, figuring he could get Greta to rest if she thought they were doing something.

She sat, and with Brice keeping lookout, Johari went through the rooms again. In the kitchen, he found the supply of food more meager than he'd hoped. Welty seemed to have survived on air. The plants and grains wouldn't go far, wouldn't sustain the three of them long. He searched for the tea that had stalled Greta's symptoms and found no dried leaves with a similar aroma. Welty must have used a fresh herb. Of the dozens of plants growing in the lab, he couldn't be certain which was the right one.

He discovered tools in a closet: an LED lantern, a pick, several wrenches, a hammer, a crowbar, and a shovel. Potential weapons. Nothing that would help them escape.

That required wings.

He descended to the first floor. The assault on the entrance was as deafening as if he was inside a belfry with the bell ringing. The front door was holding, and no one was trying to enter through the back. There was another bedroom with an adjoining bathroom.

Returning upstairs, he stopped once again in the study. This time he avoided looking at Welty, but his eyes fell upon the Tarot card of the Magician. Strange that he hadn't noticed it before, but the drawing looked a little like him.

The sound of scratching from one of the walls turned him away. Rats. No doubt about it. The sound had kept him up plenty of nights in the orphanage and juvie.

Back above at the windows, he sat beside Greta and Brice, leaning against one of the columns between windows, where they could listen for a grappling hook. She had started trembling again; small shakes of her hands, quivering in her fingers. Occasionally, her body jerked, the way it sometimes will when falling sleep.

"Anything?" she asked.

"Zip," Johari replied.

"I'm sorry I dragged both of you into this."

"Hey," Brice said, "this is the most fun I've had in weeks."

"You must have been terribly lonely."

Brice didn't reply, confirming she was right.

They lapsed into silence. Greta's shakes came in waves. Sometimes they almost ceased only to return with more intensity. The constant gray of the sky made it difficult to judge time. Had thirty minutes passed? Forty-five? An hour?

"Did you find anything?" she asked.

Johari and Brice locked eyes. Was she losing her memory? Was that a symptom? He didn't want to ask Brice in front of her.

"Zip," Johari replied.

"We have to keep looking," she muttered. "I'm sorry I dragged you into this."

Johari bit his lip and pulled her close. "You wouldn't have without a good reason." He waited, hoping she would say something about it. The love for a friend was one thing, but Greta's fervor, her bond with Calista, was forged by something dark and terrible. She'd said as much. When she didn't reply, he said, "Maybe it would help to talk about it."

"No." She looked about her, as if awakening from a shower of ice. "Why are we sitting here? We need to find a way down to Calista."

"We looked."

She tried to get up. "We're not thinking. There's got to be a way."

"Easy. Save your strength."

She slumped back against the column, clutching her scalp. "My head's splitting open."

He pulled out one of the hypodermics. "Maybe it's time."

"No. Save it for Paul."

"I can't watch you turn into him."

"Do I have the rash?" She didn't. And pushed the needle away. "Then there's time."

Time was what they didn't have. Even if they did, what good would it do them? If somehow they could fly like birds out of here, they still had to face the House and its perils. According to Welty, the greatest of those were the dark, nameless nightmares within each of them.

What had Welty said? *The greater the saint, the longer the shadow.*

With a pang, Johari pulled Greta close. He rested his cheek against her hair. It still smelled sweet, despite sweating buckets and tromping around in sewers. *What have you buried, Greta? What's so terrible that you can't open the door?*

Ten minutes later—was it twenty?—she asked, "Find anything?"

Johari and Brice locked stares again. Brice stood, began making a series of martial arts moves, pulling a knife from the makeshift baldric behind one shoulder, slicing the blade through the air, thrusting, whirling with deadly grace.

"What are you doing?" Greta asked.

He leaped, spun, parried. "Going out with style."

Her eyes widened. "No ..."

"I'll go out the front door, distract them, while you two try escaping on the other side."

Johari shook his head. "I can't lower her down alone."

Brice jabbed the knife back into its sheath. "I'll go crazy if I don't do something."

"A little longer," Greta said to him. "Just until ..."

A few minutes later, her eyes grew cloudy. She shook with palsy. Her shirt was drenched, her head on fire. Time was running away like a ball of twine, unraveling and spilling in a mess of tangles. Johari's mind raced. There had to be a way. He wasn't thinking of Calista. Or even of Paul. He was thinking of Greta. And Brice.

Maybe the opposite of what Welty had said was also true: the nastier the person, the greater the good inside. Brice had discovered that part of himself. Johari wouldn't let him throw it away.

He tried to relax, knowing he couldn't force it. He timed his breathing with Greta's, if for no other reason than it distracted and lulled him.

The Magician card floated into his mind. He turned it away, tried to empty his mind, but it came back, tumbling down in slow motion, the figure showing on one side with its impish grin, the image of a rat on the other, though he did not recall if it had been there or not. The card melted away. He saw the kitchen he and Greta had argued in, the coffee spilling, the sound of a crying child. Then scratching from the cabinet, the rat, and the snowstorm of flour that had taken them to the Enchanter's world.

He wondered absently how the rat had gotten there.

In a flash, an idea came to him, just as Korounos's Lamp had shone inside the cave, revealing a path.

THIRTY-THREE

On the first floor, Johari shoved the last box from a closet over to Brice, who added it to boxes and odds and ends they had already removed.

"Is it there?" Brice asked, passing him an LED lantern from upstairs.

Johari squatted and set the light at his knees. He ran his fingers along a rectangular seam on the floor. "It is. Hand me the crowbar."

Brice passed him the crowbar. "Let's check it out. See what the foundation looks like."

"A rat got in somehow. It's scratching inside the walls of the study. It must have followed the pipes."

"And pipes lead to the sewer."

"And they need crawlspace access for repair."

Crowbar in hand, Johari pried up a three-by-four-foot wooden lid and pushed it aside. He dropped to the soft earth below. Brice passed down the lantern and then joined him. The foundation for the outer wall stood before them: massive squares of individual footing staggered around the tower's circumference and braced with narrower wall footing. A few feet away, a pipe from a bathtub adjoining the closet ran along the bottom side of the subfloor, turned, and led down to the narrower foundation.

Soon, they were excavating by the pipe, Brice wielding the pick, Johari the shovel. Though Paul's followers were little more than fifteen yards away, Johari wasn't concerned. Digging sounds would hardly carry to the first floor, let alone outside, where a rhythmic assault on the front door with a battering ram was keeping the Lightfighters occupied.

Johari hated leaving Greta alone, but his plan seemed viable enough to risk it. She promised she would defend the walls with her last breath, and he believed her. The symptoms had abated a bit. She could stand, her eyes had cleared, and she'd held her knife with a determined grip.

The sewer would be some distance away, which was fine. The plan was to tunnel alongside the drainpipe until they were under the bracing foundation, which, if Johari was right, would be no more than a yard down and a yard wide, unlike the massive squares, which surely sent columns thirty feet below into bedrock. What would happen when they tunneled out the other side was a wildcard. Bushes grew against the wall on this side of the tower. Johari hoped that guards prowling the perimeter were focusing on the parapet, that no one would notice when they broke through the surface. The sound of the battering ram was deafening. That would mask their escape.

If no one was walking by.

They dug quickly and silently, focusing all their energy on the task at hand, pausing only to listen to the crash of the battering ram against the steel door. So far, it held. But it urged them on.

An hour or so later, Brice said, "So, you got the girl." He spoke factually, without resentment.

"Nothing's ever certain with Greta. Go get her. I'll clear the last of this dirt."

The tunnel was done. All that was left was a poke to break through the surface dirt outside. Using the edge of his shovel, he raked earth to a mountain that had collected in the crawlspace, stopping only to mop sweat and grime from his forehead.

When Greta arrived, he asked how she felt.

"Still me," she replied, though the cloudiness was back in her eyes.

"Were you attacked?"

She had been, but a couple of ropes severed from grappling hooks stopped the attack cold.

Johari crawled into the tunnel. When he reached the end, he probed gently at an angle with the shovel. A slice of daylight pierced the tunnel. Little by little, he pushed dirt out and away, making no more sound than a bird scratching in the brush. As he'd hoped, the exit opened behind shrubs, not so thick that they grew against the wall, but a few feet beyond. He could see through the foliage to the perimeter path, and as he looked, a guard walked by and paused.

Johari held his breath. It was Kiel, the man who had captured them and taken them to Paul. He looked both ways, then gazed upward and studied the windows. With a grunt, he moved on.

With Kiel out of sight, Johari slid partway back beneath the tower, called softly for Greta, and then wormed his way from the tunnel to the bushes. When Greta joined him, they enlarged the opening to accommodate Brice, who handed up his pack and their weapons. Presently, the three of them were crouching behind the foliage. And not too soon. Two more guards came up the path. Like the first one, their attention was focused on the windows above.

When they were out of sight, Greta whispered, "Now?"

"Wait," Johari replied. "Let's see how often they patrol by."

Two more sets of guards passed, at one-minute intervals. During the next gap, Brice helped Greta across the path and into woods on the other side. Johari followed soon after. The area was deserted.

With the stealth of cats, they sneaked through the trees until they peeked into an alcove where Paul was directing his attack. The alcove was a small semicircular garden, surrounded by an evergreen hedge, which hardly looked green due to the fine coat of ash that forever sprinkled down on the city. Overgrown, the hedge had reverted to nature, though at some point, fire had cut an opening in several places, and an animal had trampled a narrow path through. Scattered around the garden stood an odd mix of statuary: busts of Roman statesmen and life-size statues. A boy fishing at the edge of a pond, now dried up. A lion pouncing on a zebra. Cherubim frolicking around a fountain. Triple-headed Cerberus guarding the gates of the underworld.

Paul sat on a stone bench, poised like a king. Calista knelt at his feet. He was running his fingers through her hair, his attention fixed intently on the tower. None of his followers were in the vicinity.

He sat in the shade of a statue of a man locked in a life-and-death struggle with a half-human monster. Paul's hood with the dog paws dangling on the sides and the snarling hound on the top made him an eerie twin to the monster.

With Johari and Greta following, Brice stepped through the opening in the hedge and trained his gun on Paul. "One sound, and I'll drill you."

A flicker of surprise registered on Paul's face and was extinguished.

Brice motioned with the gun. "Up. Slowly. Both of you. Then step forward."

Paul rose and extended his palms, like Jesus beckoning his flock. From the shadow of his hood, his crimson mad-dog eyes smoldered.

Unbidden, one of Johari's earliest memories surfaced. He was sitting by the edge of a pond, no older than three or four, and pigeons scurried toward him. At that age, they seemed monstrous and huge, and he was certain they would tear him with their beaks, which weren't beaks at all but giant sickles. He clutched Paul, who sat, unperturbed, beside him. Paul said, "Clap, and they go away." Paul clapped, and the pigeons backed off. Johari eyed them, not trusting them one bit. Each time they approached, Paul clapped. "See? Just clap."

Watching Paul now, he wished he could just clap to make the bad Paul go away and leave him with the one he had clutched on to.

If he had the power of sorcerers and wizards, Johari would conjure a spell, reverse the march of time, save Paul from the witches who had shredded his back in the House and sent him to the city that had warped and twisted his mind.

Now the only hope was the hypodermic in Johari's pocket. They'd debated who would administer the shots. Their only chance was to give them simultaneously, otherwise Paul's followers might be alerted. Since Brice needed to hold the gun, they decided Greta would have one needle, Johari the other. He had to hope neither Paul nor Calista would pass out, the one potential side effect according to

Welty. Carrying them through the city with scores of angry followers on their tail wouldn't be a picnic.

Paul started to speak, but Brice wagged the gun, scolding. "Not one peep," he said. "Walk to us. Slowly."

They rose, stepped forward, Paul a picture of calm, Calista's mouth twisted in a snarl. When they were within arm's reach, Brice stepped to one side, covering them with his gun.

"One false move and I'll take you out as quick as *pop, pop*," Brice said, aiming the gun first at Paul, then Calista. "He'll be first, sweetheart."

Calista scowled, showing she understood: sacrificing herself to save Paul wouldn't work.

Paul eyed Brice's scars. He held up one finger, indicating he wished to speak.

Brice trained the gun inches from his head. "Okay, but softly."

Paul said, "I will heal you, make you forget the scars and pain."

"Until you decide to tenderize me," Brice replied.

Paul turned his attention to Greta. Her breathing was ragged and labored. Her face glistened with sweat. Her eyes had dilated to black pools.

"Feel it," he said to her. "Give in to the heat. It calls. It surges inside of you. You want it. You want it now."

Fingers in his pocket, Johari slipped the cap off his hypo.

Paul turned to him. "And what of you, brother? Little boy wrenched from his mother. All the hurt, all the rage, I'll take it away."

Time to put a stop to this. All it took was one quick motion. But he and Greta had to strike at the same time. They had a prearranged code phrase he was to say to Paul.

Then it would be over. He would have his brother back. And Calista.

But Calista was staring at Greta oddly. Not on her face. On her neck.

Johari followed her gaze, dreading and knowing what he would see.

A rash painted Greta's neck, red as the red of a red-winged blackbird.

THIRTY-FOUR

Johari whipped the hypo from his pocket, whirled, and plunged it into Greta's arm. She sagged against him.

Calista screamed. Paul lurched back. Johari eased Greta to the ground. He fumbled in her pocket for the other needle. Her eyelids drooped, but she hadn't passed out.

Yet.

Brice put the gun to Paul's head.

"Grab Calista," Johari said.

"But he's your brother!" Brice replied.

"Do it."

Calista tried to spring away. Brice grabbed her with one arm, wrapping it around her neck, keeping the gun trained on Paul with the other. She twisted, kicked, and strained to sink her teeth into his restraining arm. He tightened his grip, cutting off air.

Paul edged away.

"Freeze," Brice snarled.

Cries of alarm came from the direction of the tower. The battering of the door had ceased. Footfalls were drumming toward the alcove.

Johari plunged the needle into Calista. She went limp. He turned, pulled Greta up. She leaned against him, one arm over his shoulder. He propelled her to the opening in the hedge.

Glancing over his shoulder, Johari saw Brice carrying Calista over his shoulder, fireman's style. With the gun, he waved for Paul to go before him.

Johari crashed through the hedge opening. A branch, broken and jagged, sliced his arm, setting it on fire. Greta's breath fell soft and ragged against his neck. She tried to run, but her legs wobbled, as if they'd turned to jelly. They careened down a slope. Snapping twigs from behind, and the command to move, assured him that Brice was prodding Paul as fast as he could.

Johari plunged into a dense copse of trees and stopped. A moment later, Brice entered with Paul. They tied him to a tree with one of the ropes Brice kept around his waist, and then gagged him with a strip of his mask.

Johari bent and whispered into Paul's ear, "I'll come back for you, get you out of here somehow." He hoped for a shadow of the old Paul, a softening in his eyes, a note of the old tenderness. None came.

With a heavy heart, he tore himself away. Then they were rushing down the hill. Greta ran on rubbery legs. Johari clutched her arm, praying she wouldn't pass out on him. With periodic stops, Brice might be able to carry Calista out of the city. Johari had no illusions about himself. He couldn't carry Greta more than a dozen yards.

They turned right and circled the hill rather than going straight down. In half a minute, Paul's followers would find and release him. Johari hoped they would go directly to the bottom of the hill, assuming the fugitives would make a beeline, wanting to put as much distance as possible between them.

Brice led—knowing the safest, most hidden routes—carrying a still unconscious Calista as if she were nothing but feathers. But for how long? Even Brice would tire.

They left the shelter of trees at the bottom of the hill, darted across a street, and entered the ruins of what might have been a clothing outlet. Behind one of the walls, out of view from the street, Brice eased Calista down, leaning her against a display pedestal.

"What now?" he asked.

Breathing hard, Greta sagged near a headless mannequin. "Across the bridge and back to the House."

"You really think your chances are better there?"

Your chances? Johari didn't like the sound of that.

Greta must not have liked it either. She looked at him levelly. "You're going with us."

Brice shook his head. "Not with this face."

"There's plastic surgery, as many as you need. Your father can afford it."

"I'm not convinced he'd pay a dime."

Greta stared at him, incredulous.

Brice said, "A million surgeries won't give me back my face. There will be scars, muscles and nerves that twist funny. They'll be a constant reminder to dear ol' *daddy* that I didn't make it out, that I failed. I can't live with that. Or the sneering triumph of my so-called friends."

"Forget them. We're your friends," Greta said. "That's why we came back for you."

Brice's eyes misted. He turned quickly away and picked up Calista. "We better get going. They'll be scouring the streets for us."

Greta rose. "I mean it. We came together. We leave together."

Brice didn't reply. Carrying Calista, he led them through a maze of toppled mannequins—picked clean of clothing—with cracked, chipped off noses and ears, and limbs that were broken off and scattered.

They took a stairwell that led to the basement. From there they accessed the sewer through a portion of a wall that had fallen away. Cold, damp, dark, rank with mold and decaying metal, this branch of the system seemed to press in on them. The brick walls, roof, and floor were crumbling, and a smothering foreboding overtook Johari that one of the explosions that periodically ripped the city would trap or bury them here.

Sometimes, Greta strode on her own power and seemed her old vibrant self. Sometimes, she leaned on Johari, as weak and ungainly as a newborn filly. At those times, she desperately needed to sit. No place dry presented itself, and he half-held half-propped her against a wall, while she trembled and strained to breathe. Then his mind raced. Why hadn't the antidote kicked in? Welty had said the effect would be immediate. Greta wasn't worse. But she wasn't better. And Calista hadn't revived yet.

Was the medicine old? Had it turned bad? He pushed the thought away, but it twined around his heart like a bramble.

Once, she seemed almost asleep against him. Nearly inaudible beneath the incessant drip of water from a rusty pipe, she murmured, "Would you come for me if I was lost ... trapped in a pit...? Would you come...?"

When she had spoken those same words in the kitchen, not so many hours before, she'd been strong and resolute.

Now it seemed she was sinking fast into that pit. It left him feeling hollow and haunted.

"In a heartbeat," he replied.

He folded her in his arms and rocked her. It reminded him how little life had allowed them to be together, how few kisses they had shared, and he wanted to clasp her to him all the more fiercely. But life intruded now like the cruel beast it was, and he released her. "She needs fresh air," he said. "We need to get her out of here."

Brice's mouth twisted in what remained of his smile, made stranger in the dim light. "The air's not exactly fresh up there."

"Better than here."

"Just a little farther," Brice replied. "I've got weapons stashed nearby."

"We've got knives galore."

"Greta needs a spear."

She stirred, looked around, and focused on Calista hanging limp over Brice's shoulder. "Why have we stopped? We need to keep going."

She tramped on. It seemed impossible that she could even stand, but something urged her on. It wasn't guts or determination, though she had those in spades. It was as if, in a deep recess of her being, something burned, spurring her forward with a red-hot metal poker.

The scrape and drum of little feet, echoing in the pipes above and feeding in from the sides, seemed to follow them. Brice glanced in the direction of the sounds with unsettled eyes.

When Johari asked him about it, Brice shrugged it off as normal, but with every murmur and scratch from the metal, his attention darted to the conduits and drains, and more than once, Johari thought he saw the glint of tiny eyes watching them.

The only bright spot was when Calista started to moan. When they emerged from the sewer and entered a basement, she opened her eyes.

Brice put her down gently and leaned her up against an old furnace. Her face was blank. Her brow tightened in confused wrinkles. Her eyes roamed and widened, as though she was in the grip of a terrible nightmare.

Then they locked on Brice. She recoiled. Her face crimsoned like a lobster plucked from a boiling pot, and she quickly stared at her shoes.

Brice turned away and reached for his mask, which he'd jammed under his belt.

Greta put a hand on his arm. "Wait."

Brice pulled away. "We've got to get going."

"Give us a moment."

She went to Calista, leaning against the furnace with her back to them. Curling an arm around Calista's shoulders, Greta drew her in, turning her until she was wrapped in Greta's arms. Inch by inch, as if life were returning to her by fits and starts, Calista folded her arms around her friend. The muscles in her arms tightened; one hand balled into a fist. It seemed she might start crying. What came instead was the soft, rhythmic knock of her fist on Greta's back, as though the hand said, *No! No! No!*

Brice stood a dozen feet off and turned away from them. "Time to go." Without waiting, he moved on.

Johari hurried after him, glancing back to make sure Greta and Calista followed.

"What was that?" Johari asked him.

"Just what it looked like."

"I have no idea."

"She couldn't stand to look at me."

"Maybe it was something else."

Brice turned on him. "What else is there?"

Johari took a reflexive step back. "Easy."

"Now you know," Brice said. "That's why I'm not going back with you."

He paused at the end of the basement. The floor had crumbled away, revealing a dark hole that he said led back to the sewer. Nearby, hidden behind a pile of bricks, he pulled out two spears. He handed one to Greta when she and Calista had caught up.

"Remember what I showed you," he said, his tone suggesting she'd better remember, or she was cooked.

Greta thrust and parried with the spear.

He nodded, satisfied. "The dogs'll smell us. We better get going." He pushed the second spear into Calista's hands and stepped toward the hole before she could reply. She seemed relieved.

Greta groaned. "More sewer?"

"Paul won't enter the sewer."

Calista, eyes averted from him, said, "Maybe there's a good reason for that."

At the sound of her voice, he turned and smiled, but seeing that she wouldn't look at him, he scowled and started down the hole.

This branch of the sewer was older, more decayed than the last one. They stepped along an edge of crumbling brick and mortar, as the center of the channel was thick with black sludge. In the lead, Brice was a pale figure, silhouetted in the viridescent light. As far ahead as he was, Calista straggled behind, looking down whenever Johari checked that she followed.

Walking beside him, Greta asked, "Why aren't they talking?"

"He thinks his face horrifies her."

"That's not it."

"She said?"

"No, she's mute again."

"Then how do you know?"

"I just do."

The scratch and scuttle of feet came from a pipe on his left. A moment later, more tapped and scraped from one on the right.

"Don't take this wrong, but she could still be loyal to Paul," Johari asked.

"She isn't."

"You just know?"

"Yes."

"One well-timed scream would bring Paul and his men right to us."

"She won't."

You better be right. Johari nodded toward Brice, who had paused at a Y in the system. "I'll talk to him."

Brice's head was cocked, listening.

"Trouble?" Johari asked, when he'd caught up.

Brice started walking again, picking up the pace. "There's always trouble."

"Calista isn't talking."

"She spoke in the basement and by the manhole."

"She isn't now."

"Not even to Greta?" The damaged muscles in Brice's face gave it a pained expression. The effect increased as he took in Calista, walking now beside Greta.

They all continued in silence. It seemed hundreds of

tiny feet echoed in the drainpipes they passed on either side. Brice glanced back frequently. Each time Calista looked away. At last, he said, "They're straggling. Tell them to catch up."

"I will. I want to talk to you first."

Brice looked at him askance. "We talked. I've decided."

Johari stopped, fixed his eyes on Brice. "I kept a fragment of the key."

Brice studied him. "Aside from being dumb—you're dead if they catch you with it—what good does it do you?"

"Blackmail. Your father *was* the one that got you the key, right? You'll get surgeries, all right, as many as you need. But, Brice, maybe your dad does care about you. Greta met with him before reentering the House. He knew the House sent people somewhere. He knew you were here and wanted her to bring you back."

"He wanted Welty."

"No. Greta didn't know about Welty."

"Doesn't matter. He wants me to be the poster boy of his empire. That's his only motive. Think what this face will do for that." Brice tipped his head, listening. Sounds from the pipes had stopped. "Thanks, but no thanks. There's nothing back there for me."

"Nothing here, either."

"Here, I can vent my rage at it all."

"Against sick creatures that don't know any better."

Brice stalked on, stopping from time to time to listen to the pipes, which had gone as mute as Calista. It gave Johari little comfort. Not only were there no scuttling and scratching sounds, there was no dripping, as if they had entered a part of the sewer even rats and spiders wouldn't enter. And it was darker. Even the spectral light that pervaded the system before would have been preferable to the impenetrable shadows that shrouded their path now.

On the upside, Brice found one of his stashes. He lit a torch. They drank fresh water from a plastic jar, as fresh as it came in the city, and he refilled his canteen. On the downside, Calista leaned against one of the damp walls and went into a fit of asthmatic coughing.

Greta wrapped an arm around her friend's shoulders. "Are you all right?"

When the coughing subsided, Calista nodded and glared at the walls, ceiling, and floor, like they were her worst enemy. Right now, they were.

On they went, past an oily slick, black and rank with decay; across a section almost too narrow to traverse, for the concrete had crumbled away on one side; into a metal pipe so rusted Johari's foot broke through the bottom. All the while, Brice was as mute as Calista, though he remained vigilant, peering into cracks and side channels, always listening.

At last, they came to a cloverleaf in the system. On the far wall of the left branch, a ladder led to a manhole cover. A few feet in on the right branch, the tunnels drank the trembling torchlight like black holes. Calista broke into spasmodic coughing that left her red.

"We should exit here," Johari said.

"No," Brice replied. "We need to get to the outskirts of the city. It's safer."

"Calista can't take much more of this."

Brice gazed at her, while she fell into a coughing fit that left her gasping. He pointed up. "That's the worst place for us to exit. Just a little more."

"Let Calista decide."

Calista waved them on.

"Are you sure?" Greta asked.

Calista was already following Brice, who led them into the right-hand tunnel. A dozen steps in, they stopped short. An abyss plunged before them, impossible to jump, impossible to climb around.

THIRTY-FIVE

"You haven't gone this way?" Johari asked Brice.

"I have. This is new. Probably from one of those explosions."

"Then it's the manhole."

"No, we retrace our steps and circumvent this spot."

Johari waved at the other passages of the cloverleaf. "What about one of these?"

"Nowhere you want to go."

They'd only gone a few paces when a sound from behind turned them back. Brice held up his torch, illuminating the tunnel and part way down the abyss. Hundreds of rats perched on crevices on the walls. More bubbled from the pit and lined up like an army at the edge. A shadow emerged from the inky depths. The size of a small dog, its red eyes burned, fixing on Brice. A tail looped and waved restlessly behind like a rope; a triangular face came to a point at the nose; and great flappy ears, ragged and chewed like a moth-eaten coat, protruded from its head.

Brice swung his slingshot and let a pellet fly at what could only be their king. It dodged easily.

And the rats attacked.

Whirling, Johari and his companions raced to the cloverleaf. The tunnel they'd come from was writhing with rats. So was the one on their left. The branch with the ladder seemed empty. They ran to it. A squealing gray flood surged toward them from behind.

"Quick," Brice cried. "Up the ladder."

Johari went first, lifted away the manhole, and climbed out. He reached back and helped out Calista, then Greta. Below, his back to the ladder, Brice was keeping a ring of rats at bay with a spear. They screeched like cars from hell laying rubber.

"Brice!" Johari hissed. "Get up here."

Brice skewered three of them, hurled them away like he was casting a fishing line, and then streaked up the ladder like a monkey. A dozen rats leaped after him. Two clung to his pant legs. He plucked them off and sent them flying.

Johari had no idea where he was or how to find the exit, but Brice glanced around and led them up a broad thoroughfare. The skeletons of buildings reared up on both sides, but no one lurked in the hollow and dead windows. Two blocks down, a mountain of rubble from a fallen building stopped them.

Brice scowled. "This shouldn't be here."

"One of the explosions we heard must've toppled it," Johari said. "Does Paul set them off?"

Brice's face twisted into a wry smile. "No. The City does that all on its own."

They retreated to an intersection and turned left. Halfway up, a cry rang out from one of the buildings. A man burst through the doorway of what may once have been a mom-and-pop grocery store but now looked like wreckage from a bombing. He came straight for Johari's party, his red-eyes burning, his tattered clothes flying like confetti. Five others followed—three women, two men. They ran on pencil legs with speed that belied their starvation. None of them wore Lightfighter's black flame.

The first man reached Greta in a few strides. She jabbed with her spear to back him off. He came on anyway with grasping fingers. For a heartbeat she hesitated, her eyes misting with tears, then thrust her spear into his thigh. The man dropped to the street, clutching his leg, blood spilling through his fingers, and looked up at her, bewildered.

Johari grabbed Greta's arm, and then they were dashing after Brice and Calista. Just before they turned the corner, Johari glanced back. The remaining five had fallen on the man, chunks of concrete raised above their heads. Johari turned quickly away. He'd seen enough of the city to know what would happen, and the horror of the place twisted in his stomach.

They zigzagged from street to street, making their way, Brice said, toward the suspension bridge. Lightning flickered above like an electrical short circuit. Johari never heard thunder.

Greta strode along resolutely, but her face had gone sickly white.

Brice glanced at her. "It was self-defense. You had to."

She glared at a point on the ash-covered pavement. "That doesn't make it any easier."

Somewhere a dog howled, a long note filled with desolation and despair. Brice tipped his head, listening, and quickened his steps. At the end of the block, he held up his hand and scanned both ways before leading them across. Two or three blocks away, a second dog answered the first. There was something in the cry Johari couldn't identify. It left him unsettled.

The buildings on both sides appeared empty, lifeless. Several leaned toward the street with such uncertainty, it seemed they would tumble with the slightest wind. A few were already in ruins, broken slabs of concrete that reared up sharply toward the oppressive gray above.

Another dog, closer, joined the first two in a discordant chorus. Farther off, others joined in.

Brice's eyes narrowed. "Would you kill a dog?" he asked Greta.

"Why?"

"Just answer."

She stared at that same point ahead. "I don't know … They're innocent creatures that don't know any better."

Brice took out his sling and loaded it with a pellet. "Listen to me. Strike their chests, not the head."

She glared at him. "Why?"

"Just do it."

Johari didn't know why, but he guessed: the dogs' skulls would protect them.

Brice took off running, his sling whistling. Yapping cut the air. Dogs rounded the corners ahead and behind and flew at them.

"Make for that building!" Brice cried, pointing to a store half a block up on the right. He raced toward the oncoming group, swinging his sling. One of the beasts fell with a yelp.

Then he was on them, whirling his sword. Snarling and snapping at his ankles, they dodged his weapon, yet the steel found a shoulder, drawing a piteous cry that was almost human. The remaining dogs retreated and fanned out to the sides, forming pincers. The rest of the pack was rushing up from behind.

"It's a trap!" Brice thumbed behind him when Johari, Greta, and Calista joined him. "Head for the store. Go slow.

One false move and they'll run us down. Johari, Greta, guard the left flank. Calista, we'll take the right."

Johari glanced behind him. The storefront windows were broken. The inside walls of the display enclosures were intact and appeared sturdy. The sign above—painted in yellow and sullied with ash—read Curtins's Hardware.

He and Greta backed at a snail's pace toward the store. Five dogs faced them, shoulders low, fangs bared, their growls rising like a revving engine. They came in slowly, eyes fixed on the weapons leveled at them—eyes enlarged from starvation, jaws grinning with such malevolence they no longer belonged to dogs but to demons, an impression heightened by their ghostly-white fur.

"Don't let them reach your neck," Brice said. "If they bring you down, you're done."

They edged toward the store. The dogs followed, creeping, stopping, tensing, readying to spring, perhaps waiting for one of them to run, then creeping on, the deep-throated snarling growing louder. Johari could feel the heat of their breath, could smell the foul carrion stink it carried.

It seemed an eternity, but at last Johari's party reached the front door. One by one, in slow motion, they slipped past the entrance. The last in, Brice shot the deadbolt from the inside.

Johari bent over, hands on his knees, trying to stop shaking. He sucked in lungfuls of air. It seemed strange to be out of breath without running a step, to feel so lightheaded the room almost spun. When he rose, Greta was sagging against the front counter. The only thing left there was dust. All the little containers that held small items for purchase were gone. So was the cash register. What would anyone do with that?

Calista backed slowly away from the door, eyeing it, as

though the dogs might eat their way through it. Her fingers tightened on her spear.

"That was close," Greta said, straightening.

Brice stood with his head cocked, listening, all the while scanning the empty aisles, as if enemies might lurk on the other side of one. "We're not out of it yet."

"Thank you for not killing them."

"Don't thank me yet. I still might. Come on, we don't have much time."

With a wave, he led them to a rear door. They looked out on a parking lot. Dismantled, blasted with fire, or both, a few cars were scattered across the pavement. Beyond was a broad boulevard. Three men with black flames painted on their backs trod like panthers down the far sidewalk.

"Damn, the fight brought them like sharks," Brice said. "Let's try our chances with the dogs."

But a pack of twenty-five hounds now formed a horse-shoe at the front door, cutting off escape. The only blessing was they couldn't enter through the broken storefront windows, though several were scratching and whining at the back wall of the display.

"The basement?" Johari suggested.

They looked for stairs leading to a lower level. Finding none, they concluded the building was erected on a slab foundation. Back at the rear exit, a knot of Paul's followers had formed on both ends of the block. One of them scanned the buildings on Johari's side of the street. Brice pushed everyone back and peeked out a slit in the door.

He turned to them at last.

"Well?" Johari asked.

Brice eyed Greta and Calista, gauging them. "Back to the sewer. There's a manhole on the street, the other side of the parking lot."

"There are a thousand rats gunning for you," Johari replied.

"It's the only way to the border. Hell, it's the only way out of this trap."

Greta said, "Calista can't breathe down there."

Calista pushed her way past them and spied out the door. "I'll manage."

Greta nodded and made for the door. Brice stopped her. Without explanation, he inspected their clothing, collar to cuff, front and back. When he got to Calista, their eyes met and searched a moment. Both glanced away.

"What're you looking for?" Johari asked.

"Blood," Brice replied.

"Why?"

"You know why."

Johari studied him. "Bats? That's crazy. They'll eat us alive. We're spattered with blood."

"Not if we cover it up. Give me a second. I saw a can of paint back there."

He returned with two cans, a mixing stick, and a one-inch brush. He held the cans up and grinned. "Pink or black?"

"If I'm going to die, it won't be in pink," Calista said, bringing a laugh from everyone.

Whatever doubts Johari had harbored about her loyalty evaporated. "Black's better anyway," he said. "We can paint a flame on our backs. They know Calista, but if we surround her, maybe they won't get a good look at her and will think we're another of their units."

"Won't work," Brice replied. "They know me."

It was true. Brice's height and muscular frame stood out. If there was anyone bigger in the city, Johari hadn't seen him.

He scrutinized Brice up and down. "They've never seen your face. That's in our favor. Lose some of your weapons. The obvious stuff."

"I won't give up the slingshot."

"Hide it. When we go out, hunch over, make yourself smaller."

Brice looked doubtful, but he began dabbing paint on each of them, searching for and covering the minutest specks of blood. Afterward, he painted the flames. Johari did the same for Brice, applying glistening black splotches.

To make the plan more convincing, Johari and Greta ripped their clothes until they were tattered and rubbed in potting soil they found in a corner. When they were done, it looked like they'd lived in the city for months. Though dwelling here could hardly be called living.

At the back entrance, Brice said, "If this doesn't work, race for the manhole."

They exited in a rough triangle formation, Johari in the lead, Calista between Greta and Brice. Johari scanned around him, like he was searching for prey. Three hundred feet off, Paul's followers still clustered at both ends of the block, where they could watch down the crossing street. Their heads swiveled in Johari's direction. He gave them a nonchalant salute and continued his trek through the parking lot, peering at cars like they might contain the fugitives.

Three of Paul's crew peeled away and started toward them. One of them was Kiel, and his eyes narrowed.

Just a little longer.

They didn't have a little longer. Kiel bellowed, pointed, began stampeding toward them. The rest of Paul's followers took up the cry. They charged, their footfalls echoing off the ruins.

Brice flew by, his slingshot a blur. A man next to Kiel crumpled to the ground.

As he raced after Brice, Greta and Calista beside him, Johari calculated the seconds before they'd reach the manhole. The parking lot was six lanes wide. The manhole was on their side of the street. That might help. Maybe.

Fifteen Lightfighters stormed down the street behind Kiel. Ten more rushed from the opposite end.

At the manhole, Brice bent over the disk and yanked. Johari arrived a moment later, didn't like the frown on Brice's face.

"What's wrong?" he asked.

"It's stuck."

THIRTY-SIX

Brice squatted. Johari whisked his sword from his belt and shoved the tip at the manhole cover's lift slot. Without speaking, they both knew their roles. Brice's strength was needed below.

The sword wouldn't penetrate the slot. Ash and dust from collapsed buildings mixed with constant drizzle had filled it and hardened like concrete.

Footfalls from behind.

"Hurry!" Brice cried.

Johari stabbed the other pick hole. "It won't go in."

"The seam!"

Drumming feet, louder, closer.

"They're almost here," Greta shouted.

Johari didn't waste a second to glance back. He jammed his sword into the seam and pushed down. The lid lifted slowly, painfully—almost groaned.

Brice crooked his fingers into the gap. The two groups coming toward them were near enough to see the red in their eyes, to see one man missing an ear.

In one smooth motion, Brice lifted and flung the cover

over with a clang. He whirled, grabbed Calista, urged her toward the hole.

She scurried down the ladder. Greta followed. Johari turned to face the mob with his sword.

Brice's sling sang. Loosing shots in both directions, he sent three attackers to the ground, clutching injuries to a hand or a shoulder. "Get the hell down the hole."

Johari didn't need any encouragement. He hurried into the cold air of the hole. At the bottom, he heard screams from the street. None sounded like Brice, who then was scurrying down the ladder. He leaped the last five feet and landed like a cat.

"Will they follow?" Greta cried.

"I doubt it."

"They could go down another manhole and cut us off," Johari said.

"They haven't yet," Brice replied.

Their trek underground was much as before: dark, damp, and oppressive. Calista slipped back into her shell, despite Greta's efforts to draw her out. The only sound she made was periodic coughing that left her doubled over. She did accept cloth Brice ripped from his mask, cleaned with water, and tied over her nose and mouth. It seemed to help.

If the sewer had been dark before, now it was as black as ink. Light from Brice's torch penetrated a dozen feet and was swallowed in the shadows.

The tunnel sloped down. The farther they went from the surface, the more it seemed to Johari he was being buried alive. More than once it appeared just that would happen when one of the deep-earth explosions sent down a rain of dirt and mortar.

At last, the way leveled out, and Brice signaled them to halt before the opening to a narrow passage.

"Tread quietly. Don't talk," he said.

Greta peered apprehensively into the velvety blackness. "Why?"

"Bats." He looked at Calista. "Try not to cough."

"We should take another route," Greta said.

"There is no other route."

"There has to be."

"Paul knows we're heading to the bridge. It's the only way out of the city. He'll throw a net around the surrounding streets." Brice pointed behind them. "A thousand rats are waiting back there."

"She can't control it; she's going to cough."

Johari laid a hand on Greta's shoulder. "Maybe not. She's been quiet since she put on the mask." He turned to Calista. "It's your call. Forward or back?"

"I'm never going back," Calista snarled. "If we don't make it out, it won't be because of me."

Reluctantly, Greta turned toward the opening.

"One more thing," Brice said. "No torch. A mineral in the rock throws out faint illumination. It'll have to be enough."

He stamped out the torch and led them in. The passage went six feet and came out in a cavern, or so Johari guessed it must be from the drop in temperature.

He sensed rather than saw Brice pause ahead. Minutes ticked by. Greta found Johari's hand. Hers felt clammy, and he gave it a reassuring squeeze. There was so much he wanted to tell her ... He wondered if he'd get the chance.

His eyes adjusted. In the dimness, bats cloaked the

ceiling as far as he could see, as if the stone had erupted in strange malignant tumors, and what seemed like walls stirred in the dusky gloom.

They continued on. All was silent except the occasional whisper of their feet on the path and the rustle of wings, which crackled like ancient papyrus.

Johari wondered if they'd blotted out all the blood. It took only one drop to make the bats go crazy. He'd only heard their frenzy when he was locked in the utility closet. It convinced him that, once aroused, they would be far worse than rats, dogs, or a horde of Paul's followers.

Time stretched. Had they been here minutes or hours? The possibility of hours sent a shiver through him. It meant they might never return to the House. What then? Living out their lives in the hellish nightmare of the city? It was unthinkable.

The thought gave him an almost uncontrollable urge to wrap his arms around Greta, to feel her touch, to remind him that he'd been loved with a love that was true. He saw that now. The fervor she'd brought to his defense in court was the same she brought to rescue a friend. Love like that, even for a moment, outweighed the darkness.

In the mineral light, the chamber was faint and ghostly. From time to time, he came upon a bat, big as a cat, hanging directly in his path. From time to time, one of them dropped from the ceiling or winged by, leaving a carrion wind in its wake.

It was by the smell, first, that he realized they'd left the cavern and the bats behind and were slanting upward. A minute later, they stood by a ladder leading to a manhole. The cover was missing. Gray light slashed down, cutting the darkness.

"We need a plan," Johari said, looking up at the hole.

Brice followed his gaze. "Paul will have the bridge guarded."

"Maybe not. If I were him, I'd stay hidden, wait till we're topside, then make my move."

"Makes sense. If one of us comes out and sees him, we can just scoot back down."

"Right, he knows that."

Brice went up the ladder like a cat. He poked his head above the surface. With a quick wave, he signaled the coast was clear and pulled from the hole. The others joined him.

A rusted four-sided guardrail squatted above the manhole to keep people from falling in. It was a sad note. Someone once cared about safety in this city. The street, a wide boulevard littered with the remains of a tumbled-down building, was deserted. Across from them, a short road leading to the bridge abutted the boulevard.

Staying low, they started sneaking across the rubble. A cry rang out. Half a dozen dogs bounded toward them from both ends of the street, leaping and scrabbling over ruins. Behind the dogs, men and women rose from the rubble, brandishing clubs.

Brice shouted, "To the bridge!"

They were already scrambling over bricks, mortar, and crumbled concrete. Shrilling, like a high-pitched siren, came from behind. Johari glanced back. Hundreds of rats were streaming from the wreckage and cracks in the street.

The dogs got there first. Experienced now, Johari's group fell into formation, swords and spears out. The lead dogs sprang. They flew at a forty-five degree angle, heads raised, paws curled, jaws wide, displaying teeth designed to tear flesh from bone.

Hot and cold prickled Johari's skin. The incoming snout, the glinting fangs, the individual strands of fur interspersed with raw patches of mange, came to him like snap-shots, moments in time.

The rest was a blur of lunging and gouging and snapping fangs. The scrape of their claws sent ash flying, turning them to pale specters, eyes burning like hot coals. The battle seemed to swim before his eyes, leaving vague impressions of Greta thrusting beside him; Brice protecting Calista, even as he fought two leaping for his throat; the yelp and squeal of hounds falling or limping in retreat; others rushing in to take their place, nostrils flared, grinning with the fervor of the hunt; the rasp and hiss of Johari's own breath. Sweat trickled down, blinding him.

Then it was over, a battle that seemed like minutes but had probably only been seconds. Blood dripped from their weapons, and the area before the manhole was littered with dogs swimming feebly in red puddles. The rest had scattered.

Johari bent over a fallen animal, its eyes vacant in death and a mortal wound gaping at its heart. To his surprise, the spear lodged there wasn't one of theirs. The opposing side had killed one of their own dogs.

His companions raced a dozen feet before they stopped and turned back to him.

"What are you doing?" Greta cried.

"Get going." Johari dragged the dog back to the manhole.

"Not without you."

"I'll be right behind." He took off his belt and fastened it around the dog's neck.

Understanding dawned in Greta's eyes. She turned and raced toward the bridge. Brice and Calista ran fleetly beside her.

The mob was closing in, black flames on their clothing

proclaiming who led them. Each had a dog, straining against a leash. The rats came on, cresting and pouring over pillar and block like water from a dam. It was anyone's guess which would reach him first, mob or rats.

Johari tied one end of the belt over one of the guardrails. Suspended, half hanging in the manhole, the dog's blood spilled down the ladder. As quickly as he could, he wiped blood from his hands and sword onto the dog's fur.

The mob was still scrambling over debris to get to him. But the rats came on, hunger in their screeching, close enough that Johari could see the glint in their eyes.

He took off. Most of the fallen wreckage was on either side of him, as though it had parted like the Red Sea. But not all. Twisted steel grew from concrete like macabre vines. A mangled car, a smashed baby carriage, a cracked doll, and the withered hand of a corpse reached out to him. Each seemed to carry a message: this is your fate, to be crushed, to have all that matters squeezed out until there's nothing left. Whether you're dead or alive, it's all the same to the City.

He reached his companions at the head of the bridge, where they waited for him. He glanced back. The rats were a whirlpool around the fallen dogs. The one suspended over the manhole was writhing with furry bodies. The rest of the rat horde surged on, but the mob seemed oblivious to the danger. They spread out in a semicircle, focusing on their human quarry, their eyes burning red with madness and hate.

Johari's band turned to dash across the bridge. A voice rang out above them. On both sides of the bridge, the suspension cables were anchored on two colossal towers. From a door in one of these, Paul stepped out.

He gazed down on them. "And the unrepentant shall

suffer my wrath and fall into the Abyss of Despair, where they shall burn for all eternity."

A new dog pack surged down one end of the boulevard. A second mob charged from the other end. Their flameless backs evidence they hadn't succumbed to Paul's spell.

He held out his arms. "Come to me, little sheep. No pain, no suffering shall befall you, only the balm of the shadows and everlasting peace."

Johari yelled, "Not today, brother."

Paul tilted his head, regarding him. With a slight motion of his hand, like he was brushing away a fly, he said, "Take them."

Johari's group sprinted onto the bridge. Paul's followers charged after them, the rumble of their feet like stampeding buffaloes. Screams came from behind. Johari didn't bother to glance back. It wasn't hard to imagine what was happening. Rats that couldn't feast on the fallen dogs had attacked Paul's followers.

Panting, a dozen strides later, a sound came that froze Johari's blood. The pack from the hardware store.

Now he did turn, in time to see them surge from a side street, thirty or forty of them. Barking must have alerted them to possible prey.

In the lead, sailing over the ruins as though he'd been bred to it, was the white giant Johari had encountered before. Bounding and flying over the blocks, it caught up with Johari. With a low growl, fangs flashing like daggers, it lunged. Johari braced for bone-crunching pain. Instead, the jaws locked on his pant cuff. He wrestled left and right, trying to shake free. Hunkering low, the dog backed away, dragging Johari back toward the City.

He swung his sword. The hound slipped the blow like a crafty boxer.

Brice, halfway across the bridge, Greta and Calista beside him, turned back. He urged them on with a push.

Calista yelled, "If you don't come, I don't come."

Greta stumbled.

"What's wrong?" Calista cried, latching on to her.

Greta swayed like a drunk.

Johari saw it all in a blink, down to the red clouding Greta's eyes.

The damn medicine. It has to be the damn medicine. Spoiled.

He swung, slashing the hound with his sword, over and over. He had to get to Greta, to get her out of the City. Maybe it was the air, the constant dust, or mold rising from the sewers, but something here was pulling her back, just as the dog was pulling him back, despite the ferocity of Johari's onslaught.

A dozen of Paul's people stormed onto the bridge. Another squadron appeared at the opposite end and pelted toward them, wielding shovels and pitchforks.

Greta collapsed against the bridge railing, seemed about to tumble over.

A new sound rose above the cries of the battling mobs, the savagely barking dogs, the screeching rats: beating wings.

A fluttering black cloud streamed from the manhole. Bats. Thousands of them. They spiraled upward, then descended on the mobs, dogs, and rats, wherever there was blood. Frightened, screaming, trying to escape, men and women stampeded in all directions, trampling fallen and injured comrades.

With a desperate stab, Johari sank his blade into the giant's shoulder. It wasn't a mortal blow, and the beast howled and let go of Johari's cuff.

He threw his bloody sword into the melee, then raced toward Greta, his heart in his throat. "Get rid of your weapons," he shouted. "Anything with blood on it."

Brice grabbed Calista's spear and tossed it into the squad coming from the other end of the bridge. A man fell, clutching his shoulder. Greta hung onto her spear, by reflex. Brice tore it away and sent it sailing. Kiel sank to his knees, the spear quivering in his thigh like a branch in the wind.

An ear-deafening explosion sounded below the City, the loudest all day, and close. The world went topsy-turvy. Buildings along the boulevard rocked and collapsed inward, sending up clouds of dust and debris. The street rolled in waves, knocking people off their feet.

The bridge reeled, twisted, swung. Johari spun careening to one of the rails. The bridge tipped. He clung to it for all he was worth and looked into the abyss below. The sick sound of straining, tearing metal cut the air. One of the suspension cables snapped. The bridge lurched, nearly shaking Johari from his hold, and the entire structure tipped at a frightening angle toward the City. He came up in a crouch, worked hand over hand on the rail toward his three companions.

Paul's voice rose above the melee: "Come, little sheep. Fear not, for you will find—"

Piteous shrieks from the battlefield and the rumble of falling bricks and girders obscured the rest.

Johari reached Greta and threw his arms around her. "Don't leave me," he cried, tears rolling freely down his cheeks.

She looked at him blankly. He clasped her tighter.

Barely audible in the chaos, a small voice breathed in his ear, "Never."

He pulled away. Her eyes were clearing.

"Can you walk?" he asked.

She nodded. He helped her up. Together they tottered up the bridge, Calista in their wake. By some miracle, most of the squad on this side had been shaken off. The few remaining were running off and into the valley.

The bridge groaned like a sick goat. Like a gunshot, another cable snapped and then whipped like a crazed rodeo rope.

That was all the prompting they needed. Johari grabbed one of Greta's arms, Brice took the other, and together they propelled her up the bridge. It tipped toward the City and the abyss, the angle growing every second. They were steps from land. The bridge shuddered, a cold, lonely thing caught in a blizzard.

The four companions leaped.

THIRTY-SEVEN

An explosion came from behind like the agonized bellows of a dying god. Johari turned back to the bridge. It was tearing apart, rending steel, girders and pipes and cables crashing into the abyss, sending up clouds of dust and debris. The only thing left standing were the towers, and these leaned obscenely.

A minute later, they were up the hill and standing before the six-foot-high, four-foot-wide opening to the House. The Lamp's light still shone, spilling feebly onto the ground where Johari stood, yet filling the doorway with brilliance. All beyond it was obscure.

Johari took Greta's hand. As they jumped through, Welty's words came back to him, "Careful. Unfinished business has a way of following you."

It better not, he thought. But who didn't have fears, disappointments, unfulfilled hopes, and wounds buried deep? Being human came with an endless supply of them.

The Lamp's golden haze enveloped him, seemed to wash away the grit and grime, the grief and misery of the City. Then they were through, landing in a clearing of ancient trees, like oaks but not oaks. Just ahead, within the circle of trees, a pond, cobalt blue and tranquil, shimmered in the first rays of the sun, peeking over the horizon.

Brice and Calista leaped through the opening holding hands. They landed in thick clover that carpeted the clearing.

Johari's legs buckled, as if all the nervous energy that had carried him through the City suddenly deserted him. Greta swayed, and they collapsed into each other's arms. He clasped her like a lifeline, his heart pounding, and they sank to the clover. A kind of shock gripped him, but as long as he could feel Greta, he was attached to something real after all the madness of the last hours.

A lone sparrow warbled in a nearby tree. Gradually, the shock abated, and Johari wondered at not jabbering away as he and Greta had when entering the City. But whatever had caused their coming-out-of-anesthesia-like banter before, returning was different. He hadn't a clue why, and with Dr. Welty dead, he would likely never know. He doubted it mattered. They were back, and the only thing to focus on now was getting out. From the moment they landed, according to Welty, their time in the House would begin ticking again, each according to how many hours, minutes, and seconds they had remaining the last time they were inside its walls. Brice and Calista had the most. Greta the least.

A splash from the pond drew his attention. Brice and Calista had taken off their clothes and plunged into the water, where they scrubbed and scrubbed themselves until their bodies were pink.

Brice climbed dripping onto some rocks and soaked in the warmth of the rising sun on the far side of the pool. Calista remained in the water, spending more time submerged than up for air. When she finally emerged, she took a spot beside Brice and hugged herself. They talked quietly.

Johari and Greta held on to each other, inhaling the perfume of tiny yellow flowers dotting the floor of the clearing, watching butterflies floating through bands of sunlight streaming through the trees.

A crow chased off the sparrow, taking its spot. He squawked, adding a dark note to the quietude.

Brice rose, pulled on his clothes, and began picking scarlet and red fruit that burdened the trees. He returned with an armful, and he and Calista tore into them like starving prisoners. For three weeks the two of them had eaten only stringy dog and sour rat meat. Or so Johari guessed. The jury was out as to what Paul was feeding his followers. Johari didn't want to know the answer to that, could barely consider the question.

Sated at last, Calista lay back in the sun. Brice collected more fruit and joined Johari and Greta.

"She remembers it all," he said, handing them fruit. "Everything before Lightfighter got her. Everything after."

"That was the illness," Greta said. "We love her no matter what she did."

"It wasn't my face at all. She was filled with shame."

Johari bit into an orange fruit. The sweet nectarine-like flavor soothed his parched throat. "Memories fade with time."

"No," Greta replied. "They're only hidden, quiet, and then they come out to haunt you." She looked about her sorrowfully. "I don't want to leave this place."

The crow squawked six times. With a chill, Johari realized this was the clock they'd heard tolling as bells every hour three weeks ago in the House; then yesterday as ringers tied around the necks of the sheep outside Muloch's tavern; then from Millie, the Enchanter's horse. And now the adamant cry of a crow.

He gazed eastward. The last fireworks of sunrise were waning. Night must have passed here while they were gone. Looking back at the opening to the City, he saw it fade until no sign remained it had ever been there, and the Enchanter's words came back to him: "But, child, you have only till morning. Then it closes forever."

He glanced at Greta. Her eyes were clear. Still ... "How are you feeling?"

She nuzzled closer. "Better. More like myself."

"We've got to go," he said, though he wanted to let the peace of the spot soak into him, wanted to keep feeling Greta breathing beside him in a way that seemed to make his heart stop.

She nodded toward the pool, where Calista had once again submerged herself. "Give her a little longer."

A little, and that's all, Johari thought. He took a bite of fruit and chewed it slowly, then took another. He couldn't fathom why the Lamp was here, rather than on the hill where they'd left it. Unless, like Welty said, the House, reading their desires, gave them the respite they needed.

A bubble floated up where Calista had gone down. The crow took off, rattling the leaves.

Greta gripped Johari's arm. "She hasn't come up."

He glanced at the pool, as smooth as glass now. "She's holding her breath."

Greta came to her feet. "It's been too long."

Johari rose and realized just how weary he was from the mad dash through the City, from two trials before Sparra Givvens, from two trips through the House. Greta ran to the water, Johari and Brice right behind her. When she reached the edge of the pool, Calista came sputtering up.

"Are you all right?" Greta cried.

"Just peachy," Calista replied, her old caustic tone back. "Are you here to gawk, or can I dress in private?"

Embarrassed, Johari turned away.

"Not you, handsome," Calista said to Brice softly, smiling now. Despite the invitation, he followed Johari across the clearing.

"She likes you," Johari said, handing him the Lamp.

"Don't read anything into it." Brice stowed the Lamp in his pack and shouldered it. "We went through a lot together."

When Calista was dressed, they followed a path and came quickly to the edge of the trees. Beyond, the volcanic plain of the Elders, with its black vents and crevices, stretched as far as the eye could see.

Calista shielded her eyes from the harsh sun. "That can't be the way home."

They retraced their steps and followed a trail going in the opposite direction. The trees thinned, and all too soon, they looked upon the same rugged terrain, barren but for steam or smoke rising from the fissures and hanging ghostly over the landscape.

Johari pointed ninety degrees. "Let's try that way."

But that way was more of the same, as was the remaining side. And each time they came to the perimeter, the edge of the trees seemed to come sooner.

Brice scowled. "The damn forest is shrinking."

"It can't be," Greta said.

"Let's test it," Johari said.

They walked in the direction they'd first taken, and it did seem the trees ended sooner.

"It's the House," Johari said. "Up to its old tricks."

Calista paled, gripped Brice's arm. "Don't let it take me. Not back there."

Brice wrapped his arm around her shoulders and drew her in. "Never."

Johari said, "Maybe it won't. When Greta and I came through the House the second time, it wasn't gunning for us. And we all left the City. Maybe that changes the rules."

Calista looked about doubtfully. "To what? Something better? Not on your life."

"Agreed," Brice said. "I don't trust this place as far as I can kick it. What now?"

"Look for a way out," Johari replied.

Brice nodded toward the land before them, which looked like a planet melted in a nuclear holocaust. "There's no exit out there. Just miles of that."

Johari dropped his chin into his palm, eyeing the terrain. "Welty said the House takes images from deep inside us. Something we need to face or deal with."

Calista darkened. "Haven't I dealt with enough?"

"Enough for a lifetime," Greta said. The blood seemed to have drained from her face, and she held Calista with her eyes. "But there's more. You know there is."

Calista looked back at the blackened world. "What does that have to do with this?"

"I don't know," Greta replied.

"It's moot." Johari pointed behind them. One by one, the trees were fading.

THIRTY-EIGHT

The crow took off from one of the few remaining trees and winged across the sweeping volcanic plain Greta had crossed to reach the mountains. Nearer, in the opposite direction, Johari saw the hill where he and the Enchanter had lit a bonfire and waited for her to return, and just beyond, the fog-shrouded pass to Korounos's world.

"Where now?" Calista asked.

Johari surveyed their surroundings. Toward the mountains, rents in the earth still split the land and periodically blasted steam, making that way more dangerous. And there was no way of knowing if the Elders would still be pacified. Yet the crow had flown in that direction. If Johari understood anything about the House, everything was significant.

He pointed toward the snowy mountains. "Follow the crow."

No one objected. They trudged down a low hill, now barren of trees, and began hiking across the plain. The ground was hardened lava that had once flowed in long rivers. The sun blasted, unforgiving. They avoided the gaping crevices. Nonetheless, sulfurous fumes soon had Calista coughing.

The hill behind faded from view. Except for the tramp of their feet and the occasional steam blast, silence pressed in on them, and the sameness of the land was oppressive. Greta hummed awhile, but soon stopped. No one spoke. It seemed like they were the sole occupants of a distant moon. A blanket of loneliness hung over the land, and Johari was glad for their companionship, for the companionship of true friends.

From time to time, they paused and drank water from a plastic bottle Brice kept in his backpack and had filled at the pond. He made them drink sparingly.

They began crossing what appeared to be an enormous crater. More fractures scored the surface like great open wounds. Johari thought he heard crying coming from one of the vents.

You could go crazy in a place like this, he thought. But then he heard it again, like the whimper of a small child, and another came from a crack a dozen feet away. Johari and Greta locked eyes.

"I heard that in the kitchen," she said. "Just before you came in."

"Me too. When I entered the House. What do you think it means?"

Her reply was little more than a murmur. "I don't know."

Frowning, Brice peered into one of the crevices. "This isn't a good place." He took a piece of his old mask from his pack and tied it over Calista's nose and mouth to protect her from the sulfurous fumes venting from the fissures.

On they tramped. The crying grew louder, and there were more, three, perhaps four of them, mewling desolately.

"It's going to drive me crazy. Any earplugs in that pack?" Calista asked. Brice ripped pieces of cloth, which she stuffed gratefully into her ears.

They came upon an upswelling of terrain, two great rivers of magma that had run side by side, creating a narrow alley in between. To avoid climbing they took the alley, no less scarred and fractured than the rest of the plain. A mile in, the alley entered a lava tube, dimly illuminated by frequent openings in the ceiling. The vents were more numerous here, the fumes a sick yellow brown. But the crying stopped, and the four of them stood in a cluster, no one wishing to move.

Without warning, Calista was sucked toward one of the vents, as though an invisible giant had latched onto her, lifted her up, and swept her toward a black opening at the bottom of the wall. She kicked violently to free herself. One of her shoes went flying.

Running, her friends reached for her. Greta was yanked toward another vent. Brice went flying toward a third. A force struck Johari like a tornado or the breach in a space-ship, sweeping all into the great vacuum of outer space. He flung out his arms. His wrists banged against rock surrounding a fourth vent. Pain screamed up his arms. Calista and Brice were gone, disappearing down two of the holes. Greta stretched out her hand to Johari. Then she hurtled into a fourth shaft.

The next instant, Johari was pulled into darkness, as if the sun, moon, and stars had suddenly snuffed out. Wind roared in his ears. Nausea and dizziness played tug-of-war between his stomach and his head. His mind grayed, as though the cells of his brain were flying apart.

Then nothing.

Trembling. What trembled? Legs ... shoulders ... a body. Cold. Cold feet—as if packed in snow—and freezing hands and frosty roughness against a face.

His face, for he realized he was a he.

Who?

Jo ...

Johari.

Fog clouding his mind evaporated. The image of a girl rushed in. Honey curls, lake-blue eyes that sparkled while they held you captive.

Greta!

His eyes flew open.

I've got to get back to Greta.

He struggled to rise. A hammer pounded inside his head, and he slumped back down.

Little by little, he pulled to his knees, waiting for his brain to stop swimming, and looked around. He'd passed out in a clump of dead weeds that sprang up wild and unruly and overran a backyard. A fence ran along one side, the posts sagging, the pickets weathered, peeling, and falling off in places. Brambles spread like an invading army from the opposite side of the yard and surrounded a beat-up mattress. Stuffing spilled from a huge rip; one of the springs was exposed. A birdbath rested on its side, surrounded by a tall growth of foxtails. A cement sculpture of birds flying down to the bowl had broken off and lay nearby.

He stood, swayed, hoping the throbbing in his head would lessen, and stumbled to an old-fashioned hand pump. On his knees, he tried pumping water over his head. The handle was rusted stuck.

Rising, he took in the rest of his surroundings. Shards of broken glass and pottery peppered a cement patio. He crossed the yard, stepping past a cracked rubber ball; a toy drum, the head broken through; and a three-year-old's striped T-shirt, torn at the belly. On the patio, on a picnic table, nestled in a basket lined with checkered blue-and-white cloth, he found the moldering remains of fried chicken, or so he guessed it had been. In another basket, biscuits sprouted a fulsome growth of green fur.

He turned away, took in a squat one-story stucco house with small dark windows beyond the patio, and realized with a rush of panic there was nothing else here, no opening, no cave, no fissure to return to the lava plain.

No way back to Greta.

His mind raced. Had she survived? Had the others? Were they safe?

He sank to the cement, slumped against the table legs, and clutched his arms, the coldness of the metal penetrating his shirt.

He scanned the yard again. There had to be a way back up. The pump had the only opening, but unless he could find a Drink Me bottle and shrink like Alice, he wasn't going that way.

The house was unexplored. He rose, and as he crossed the threshold of the back door, an idea struck him, and why hadn't he thought of it before?

Because your brain was practically sucked from your skull when you went down that shaft, he reminded himself.

This wasn't just a house. This yard, this bungalow, was part of *the* House. What had Welty said? The House was made to help people, not destroy them.

As long as there isn't someone else's shadow here, I'm safe. I can deal with my own shit.

He'd been doing that his whole life. Or had tried to.

Just past the entrance, he found a laundry room. The lid of the washer was up. A load of clothes marinated in muddy-brown water. He crossed into a hallway and entered a kitchen on his left; the linoleum groaned underfoot, suggesting decades of termite activity had weakened the subflooring. The refrigerator was empty; the cupboards were bare, their doors flung open. The tap didn't run; a spider crawled from the faucet.

No table, chairs, or china cabinet furnished the dining room, only a layer of dust blanketed a bruised hardwood floor that tilted down toward an outer wall.

The living room was empty but for a braided oval rug covered with stains. From an animal? The air inside was as frigid as it had been outside. He rubbed his hands and tried the dials on a wall heater. It didn't turn on.

A glance out the front door revealed another neglected yard. Past the picket fence, no houses lined a street because there was no street, only a gray blur, as though the house and its yards were an island floating in a void.

Rivulets of clammy sweat ran from his armpits. He dashed through the house, out the back door, across the yard, over the fence, through a huddle of old oaks, and came to a sudden stop. The trees ended abruptly. An endless blur stretched before him.

With a shudder, he returned to the house, the loneliness and isolation he'd been feeling tripled, casting a shadow over him that seemed to penetrate his bones.

The rear hallway formed one leg of an L, the other leg leading to what he could only assume were two bedrooms. The doors were closed. The sensation of heaviness, of something dark and forbidding, emanated from one of the bedrooms. He was certain whatever the House had plucked from his mind waited in one of those rooms.

It had waited all these years. It could wait a little longer.

He went back up the hall, opened a closet, found empty shelves, and then entered the bathroom. No water came from the sink faucet or tub. None filled the toilet. Back down the hall, he turned, paused, and a fresh flow of sweat trickled from his armpits.

Before, the House brought frightening things, creatures that pursued until you faced them or perished. Whatever lay beyond one of the shut bedroom doors didn't want to be found. He stepped to the first door, reached for the knob. It was icy beneath his fingers and locked. He moved on to the second door, opened it, and found the room as empty a shell as the rest of the house. Back at the first bedroom, he tried the knob again, jiggling it, leaning his shoulder against the door, in case it was stuck.

The sensation that he was unwanted increased. He felt it as clearly as if a sign hung on the door, saying, Keep Out!

If what Welty said was true—he had no reason to doubt the inventor of this place—that was the last thing he should do.

No light bled from the floor clearance. He guessed the bedroom beyond had no windows, no source for sunlight to stream in. Something was in that room, hiding in the dark, something that had to do with him. Or he wouldn't have been separated from the others and brought here.

He tried the door again, got the same result, and stepped back, considering. Inside doors were hollow, as he'd found out at age eleven when he'd rammed a desk through one, smashed the wood, and escaped a den lovely foster parents had locked him in. This house lacked a desk or chair to wield. He didn't need it. Three kicks near the knob smashed a hole. He reached through, disengaged the lock, and turned the handle.

The door swung open.

THIRTY-NINE

A horrible stench, like a toilet backed up for months, sent him reeling back. What he would have given for a piece of Brice's mask. Covering his nose with his arm, Johari stepped into the room. The inside was dim, but not so dim that he couldn't see human waste littering the floor and smeared like a child's first fingerpainting low on the walls. Otherwise, the room was barren, except for a small boy, about three years old, huddled and rocking in one corner. His arms and legs were sticks protruding from a ripped T-shirt and soiled short pants. His hair fell in matted tangles to his shoulders, giving him the appearance of a feral child wolves shunned rather than raised.

He fixed ferocious, burning eyes on Johari.

Johari approached slowly, palms out. "I won't hurt you."

The boy's lips pulled back in a snarl, displaying tiny teeth, and he growled.

Johari stopped. "Okay. No farther." He squatted, pondering what to do. He thought about Welty and the purpose of the House. If this were happening to him in a dream or a sequence of dreams, what would happen next? How would it evolve?

He didn't have a clue, except that he needed to deal with this boy in some way. Abandoned here, the child's circumstances were unthinkable. Maybe that was the key, to help him. But how? With what? This place offered nothing. No blankets, no clothes, no food, no water. No one to talk to. No one to nurture him.

Maybe that was the key. Johari could start with that. He looked for a clean spot to settle in. Finding none, he remained on his heels.

He thumbed in the direction of the backyard. "Might be more pleasant out there."

The boy glared at him.

Johari continued, "You must be hungry. Not much to eat around here but weeds."

A low vibration came from the boy's throat.

"Wish I had something to feed you. Damn cold in here. You could use a coat. I'd give you mine if I had one."

The threatening vibration rose.

This isn't getting anywhere. Time's ticking. I need to get back to Greta and the others and the hell out of the House.

Johari stood, held out his hand. "Who left you here?"

But he knew the answer: Sky Stormrunner and Loïc Hightower. His parents. All those years ago. To a world as loveless and unforgiving as this one. A great ripping ache welled up, as if all the tears and ruptures in the plain above found a home inside him, and tears pooled in his eyes.

The child pasted himself to the corner and shrank into a tight ball.

Johari wiped his eyes with his sleeve and took a step, just a small step. "I understand—"

Without warning, the boy sprang, right for Johari, who

stood his ground. He didn't think the boy could do any serious damage, though those teeth looked sharp and the unclipped nails were like talons. When the boy was almost on him, Johari reached to sweep him into his arms. The boy veered at the last minute and darted toward the door. Johari whirled, following.

Up the hall, through the dining room, into the kitchen, past the laundry room, the boy flew with preternatural speed, leaving Johari breathless as he followed out the back door and into the yard. The boy streaked into the trees. If not for the sound of snapping twigs, Johari would have lost him. He tracked through a haphazard course and came upon the boy trying to leap onto a tree like a monkey. Too small to reach the lower branches, he wheeled and bolted back into the house.

Inside, Johari considered closing and locking the doors but abandoned the idea. The kid was tall enough to unlock them. Besides, Johari never felt much love for caretakers who locked him up. And that was what was needed here, wasn't it? Love. Lots of it. And patience, which would take time, something he had precious little of.

He circled through the house. It wasn't hard to figure out where the kid had gone. All the cabinet doors in the kitchen had been open. Now, the cabinet under the sink was closed.

Johari said, "I wonder where he's hiding," like a father playing hide-and-seek with his son. He opened the dishwasher. "Not in here."

He crossed to the cupboards, looked up and down the shelves. "Not in the pantry."

He stepped to the refrigerator and opened the freezer, his fingers crossed that fried chicken, soup, or popsicles were stored there. All he found was a wave of mold assaulting him and quickly shut the door. "Or the fridge, either."

He sat by the sink cabinet and leaned against the nearest of the two doors. "Just can't find him anywhere. It's like he's disappeared. Wait! Maybe he's in here." He opened the first door, pretended to look all around the interior, though he saw the kid, knees up, balled in a corner beyond the pipes. "Yep, he's gone, just like—" He flicked all ten fingers. "Poof!"

He leaned back against the open door, keeping it from being closed again. "Too bad. I wanted to play with him. Tag, copycat. I guess hide-and-seek's his game, and he's won. Yep, he's the champ, the grandmaster of hiding."

In the shadows, it seemed the kid's eyes had lost some of their fire and had grown round with curiosity. Or maybe that was just wishful thinking. Johari could guess what his own eyes looked like: swollen and red from lack of sleep. His limbs felt like weights, his brain as clear as pea soup. He needed to get it back online or he was screwed. What he wouldn't give for about a gallon of that coffee Greta had brewed in the kitchen, black and strong enough to sprout hair on his feet.

Elbow on one knee, chin propped on one palm, he puzzled over what to do. He'd tried everything he could think of. The kid hadn't come out smiling and tumbling into his arms. From the look of things, he wouldn't any time soon. His thoughts strayed to Greta, Brice, and Calista. Maybe they'd fared better. They would linger, waiting, praying for him to come back. Then time would run down on them, forcing them to seek the exit. Greta would refuse, her eyes as fierce as the bird-girl's, the part of her that had given her bee venom. But Brice would get her out of there, even if he had to carry her kicking and screaming.

That would be fine. At least Johari would know she was safe.

His elbow slipped down his knee and ended at his front pant pocket, where he felt something. Remembering what he'd put there, an idea sparked. He reached in and removed the Good Times chocolate bar. It felt soft, half melted. He unwrapped it carefully, tore off a gooey square, and inhaled the aroma.

"Mmm, a Good Times. Nothing beats them."

His mouth watered for a bite, but he held out the piece for the child, whose lips parted, his eyes like saucers. He inched forward, his mouth so close to Johari's outstretched hand that he could feel the boy's breath. One instant, it seemed they would make a connection. The next instant the boy's jaws clamped on Johari's fingers. Hot bolts stabbed his hand. He screamed, dropping the square.

The boy released him and dove for the candy.

Johari wrenched his hand back and clasped it. It hurt like a son of a bitch, but he kept his eyes locked on the kid. Now that he had him cornered, he wasn't going to lose him.

He pressed the top of his hand with his fingers, waiting for the pain to subside.

The kid crammed the chocolate in his mouth. After he swallowed it, he licked his fingers, his eyes riveted on the rest of the candy bar, which lay in Johari's lap.

Johari stifled the urge to yell, "I would have given the friggin' rest of it!" He was half an inch from dragging the kid out and teaching him some of the corporal lessons he'd been taught. Had he ever bitten anyone? Yeah, he had. And this softened him.

He took a peek at his hand. Oozing blood, four punctures gouged the skin as if he'd been stabbed with a flathead screwdriver. Forget that now. He picked up the fallen candy, unwrapped two more squares, and held it out to the boy.

"It's yours, but no more teeth." He didn't know if the kid understood what he was saying, so he made a biting motion with his mouth and shook his head. "Okay?"

He put the candy on the unpainted boards near the boy, staying vigilant in case the kid decided a human hand was as tasty as chocolate. The boy took it up immediately and inhaled it in one gulp.

"Not like that, like this." Johari unwrapped two more squares. He broke off one, took a bite, and savored it, letting it melt in his mouth. "So you taste it."

He placed the other square near the boy's feet. They ate then, nibbling chocolate, dark and sweet. Anyone coming on them would think they were brothers, sharing a quiet moment after an exhausting afternoon of play. Johari let the kid eat most of the bar. By the time they got down to the last square, he took it from Johari's hand. He watched Johari as he ate, less wary now. When he'd sucked his fingers clean, he crawled out and studied Johari's pockets.

Johari chuckled. "Wish I had more. I have another idea. Come on."

With a wave to follow, he strode to the backyard, not glancing behind. Near the broken drum, he stooped and plucked the cracked rubber ball from its home in a nest of weeds. When he turned, the boy was standing ten feet away.

Using the unbitten hand—the wound in the other one was throbbing and oozing blood—Johari lobbed the ball a few feet up and plucked it from the air when it dropped. "I bet you never played catch. Come on." He waved the boy over. "It's more fun with two."

The boy hesitated, twisting at the tear in his shirt, but

then he took a tentative step closer, and another. Johari tossed him the ball. The boy missed, but he ran after the ball, picked it up, and threw it back to Johari.

It went wide, forcing Johari to retrieve it near the picket fence, but he sang out, "Good throw!"

He returned to the boy, who allowed him to stand closer, and after trading throws, even closer. They tossed the ball, low and high. They made a game of it, seeing how many times they could go without dropping it. Johari kept count. The rules came naturally, no words spoken, and the game evolved into how far apart they could go. When they tired of that, they played peekaboo. It seemed too young a game for a three-year-old, but the boy smiled for the first time and made him repeat it over and over again. Johari taught him hide-and-seek, and that got a laugh every time Johari found him, hiding behind a tree or a mountain of blackberry vines. Johari let him streak home to win.

The smoke from their breath faded as the day grew sunny. After what seemed like hours, though it was probably far less, they ended up lounging on the mattress, staring at ducks and puppies in the clouds. Johari told him about his life, how being shuffled from home to home for years was more than balanced by three weeks with Greta. He doubted the kid understood, but he seemed to like the sound of Johari's voice, and after a while, he slipped a tiny hand inside Johari's, sending a jolt, like static electricity, and then, wonderfully, warmth spread through Johari's body.

A short time later, the boy curled up and fell asleep. Johari took him in his arms, rolled back to the sky, and held him close. Prickles flowed into his chest. The sensation intensified, growing from an ache to a deep throbbing, as if anesthesia was wearing off that had masked a horrible wound.

With pain came images. Johari couldn't be sure whether they flowed from the boy or his own memories bubbling up. He saw himself and the boy in double exposure. He saw smiling faces. His mother and father? Their faces retreated with terrifying speed—too soon, too soon!— leaving him alone in a crowd. He, the boy, turned this way and that, searching among the indifferent faces. Where were they? What happened to them? Why did they leave him among these strangers? These giants who moved and undulated like a vast and turbulent sea, threatening to sweep him far from shore, away from everything safe and familiar, to be tossed by waves like driftwood and dashed against the rocks.

The crowd receded, leaving him and the boy alone. While the images cascaded down, he clutched the boy to his breast, among the foxtails in the backyard of the house, clasped him and sobbed.

He must be a hateful thing, a broken thing, unfit for anyone. Eyes closed, rivers pouring down his face, he hugged and hugged and hugged, drawing the boy in, holding him so tight it seemed he would pass through skin and muscle and lodge in a secret place inside him.

When he opened his eyes at last, he was clutching himself. Beside him, the boy sat up, yawned, and stretched. The picket fence was white and new. A lawn stretched from corner to corner, fresh and sweet with the scent of mowing. Tulips, irises, and great balls of blue and pink hydrangeas lined the house. Warm and golden as honey, light glowed beyond fluttering curtains in the windows, and cheerful smoke curled from a chimney, for now there was a chimney, and Johari knew it led to a fireplace and a warming fire.

A woman called from inside, her dulcet voice bubbling

with laughter, "Hurry in, sweetheart. Wash up. Dinner's ready."

The boy ran to the door. He turned. Looking back to Johari, he clasped his arms as if he were sending a hug. Johari returned the hug. The boy went inside, the screen door closing behind him.

Wind picked up, began roaring in Johari's ears. The house rolled away, the yard with it, as if carried by a swift tide.

The next thing he knew, he was whizzing through utter darkness.

FORTY

For a few ticks, Johari's stomach was back in the yard. His head grew fuzzy but quickly cleared. Wind carried him, rocketing him upward. He sensed, rather than saw, walls just beyond reach, and guessed he was back in the lightless vent that had sucked him from the lava tube. Air struck his face as if he sat in a convertible screaming down a highway.

No noxious fumes assaulted his nose. His heart thumped in his ears. He could have sworn a second heartbeat came from nearby, synchronized with his own and soothing. Darkness gave way to a warm and brightening red, as though he gazed out through a thin membrane.

Hope surged in him—he'd met the challenge. Despite a touch of sadness over leaving the child behind, he knew he carried the boy within him, as readily as if he had dreamed him. Yet as he zoomed along, the wind buffeting his face, his chest tightened. Something told him what he had gone through was just the beginning. He was a long way from the exit to the House. Welty's machine would keep testing him, throwing trial after trial at him, and if they'd survived, Brice, Calista, and Greta, too.

But right now, he was going back to Greta. He hoped. And that was all that mattered.

Light loomed ahead. The force propelling him eased, and he shot from the vent, almost gently, and hovered a moment before tumbling onto the floor of the lava tube.

Brice paced before the opening where Calista had disappeared. A child's baseball mitt was jammed onto three of his fingers. He clenched it with the other hand, staring at the shaft Calista had gone down, his face etched with worry. Calista and Greta were nowhere in sight. He whirled when he saw Johari and came running up to him.

Johari rose unsteadily to his feet. "Where are they? Have they returned?"

Holding Johari's arm, Brice kept him from toppling over. "No, but you're back. That's a good sign."

"How long have you been here?"

Brice stared intently at the vent Calista went through. "Thirty, forty minutes."

"You got out quickly."

Brice glanced at the mitt. "It wasn't hard."

"Something about dear old dad?"

"Who else?"

Johari nodded toward the vents. "Let's go after them."

Brice shook his head. "I tried. We're locked out."

"Let's try again."

They attempted to enter the opening Greta had gone through, then Calista's. Each time, they crashed into something as hard as a brick wall, though they saw nothing.

"Maybe we can break through with those." Johari pointed to rocks of hardened lava the size of grapefruits.

They struck the opening with all the strength they could muster. Brice's rock cracked and dropped in three pieces to the ground.

"It's no use," he said. "It's like the windows in the House, the first time."

Johari scanned the tube, searching for a tool, a clue, anything that would help. "There's got to be something."

"Wait and hope. That's about it."

Johari paced, panic rising with each passing minute. There had to be a way in. He couldn't accept, after all they'd been through, that Greta wouldn't make it out. She seemed the most together of all of them, the most balanced, the strongest. Yet all along, she hadn't been able to talk about something dark and painful in her past. The thought of it left a growing strangulation in Johari's throat.

A gust of wind rushed by. Her knuckles raw and bleeding, Calista crawled from the opening she'd gone down.

Johari hurried to her. Brice got there first. He knelt beside her and enfolded her in his arms. Snarling, she tried to shove him away, but he held on, and suddenly she collapsed against him, sobbing, her back heaving with terrible spasms, her face buried in his chest.

"It's okay," Brice soothed. "You made it out."

Calista shook her head, her hair, a matted rat's nest, swinging violently. "You don't understand. I saw Greta—"

Johari knelt beside them. "You saw her? Then she's coming out?"

The muscles in her throat throbbed. She tried to speak, but the words seemed to be stuck there. At last, voice strained, she said, "She's ... dead."

Johari rocked back. The world had suddenly gone crazy, was swaying and tilting. "No ..."

Calista turned grief-stricken eyes on him, giving him all the answer he needed.

He gripped her arm. "What happened?"

Brice locked on Johari's wrist and pulled it away. "Give her time."

Time? What did that mean anymore? If Greta was gone, time could march on without him and take the world with it.

He lurched to his feet and stumbled to the opening Greta had gone through. If he could only throw himself down the vent and join her. The lava tube seemed to dim, to contract, to consist only of him and the opening, which loomed before him, cold and indifferent.

He stood frozen there, the spirit to fight flowing out of him, dangerously close to empty. How much time passed, he couldn't say. Brice's hand on his shoulder roused him. "She can talk now."

Calista did, haltingly, swallowing back tears. The vent had taken her to a mine lit by weak bare electric bulbs hanging from wires strung along the ceiling. A child crying echoed off the walls. She followed the sound, going deeper into the tunnel along railroad tracks. It led to a limestone chamber with a pool in the center. One wall was made of glass. On the other side, like a mirror image, she saw an identical chamber with a pool and a mineshaft behind it. The pool on both sides went right up to the glass, allowing her to gaze into the depths. Along a promontory of rock like the one she stood on, she saw Greta waving to get her attention.

Calista ran to the glass, pressing her palms to it. Greta met her, touching the other side. They searched for a way around the barrier but found none. It was thick, impenetrable, and as soundproof as if the audio had been muted on a holo-vid. But Greta mouthed ... "Sweetie."

Calista choked back a sob.

"Take your time," Brice said, offering her water from his plastic bottle.

She drank gratefully and pushed on, her lip trembling.

The sound of crying intensified, demanding attention. It must have happened on Greta's side too, because she turned and peered about. Calista found no source for the sound until she looked down. At the bottom of the pool, a little girl was shackled with chains. Beyond the aquarium-like portion of the glass, where Calista could see into the depths, Greta's side also had a young girl clapped in irons. It didn't take a rocket scientist for both of them to figure out they were here to raise the girls to the surface and remove the chains.

Calista dived. Ten, twenty feet she went, slicing water, ignoring bone-chilling cold, until she reached the muddy bottom where the girl swayed and bobbed like a cork, her eyes unseeing, no bubbles escaping her lips.

Calista tried pulling the chains off, but they were a tangled mess. Her chest screamed for air. She kicked off the bottom, stroked for the surface, the dim lights on the ceiling blurred smudges through the murky gloom. She came up, sputtering and gasping, and stole a glance toward Greta's side but didn't see her. After gulping a breath, she returned to the bottom, tried lifting the girl, metal and all. All she could do was rock the still form with the thread-thin hair and the glassy eyes.

She surfaced, looking again for Greta—maybe she'd have an idea—saw her nowhere and dived again. This time she noticed a lock, snarled in coils of chain near the girl's heart. She searched the girl's pant pockets. She removed the shoes and looked in there. She checked the girl's slack fists and for a necklace the key might be hanging from. Finding nothing, almost out of breath, she streaked up for air and dived again. Running her fingers through the silt on the bottom only churned up mud. But a crazy idea seized her. She pried open the girl's mouth and found the key on her tongue. It fit the lock, and she pulled it off. It took several more dives to untangle the chains and throw them off, but at last she was able to raise the girl to the surface.

All through the account, Johari paced, hoping she'd get to the punch line, though he'd already heard it: Greta was at the bottom of the pool. And he was sinking fast. Soon he would be down there with her.

Still, a small part of him didn't believe it, wouldn't believe it, until Calista had told it all.

Why couldn't he have been closer when Greta was sucked into the mine? He could've latched onto her and refused to let her go.

Things didn't work that way. If the House wanted you, it took you, and no one else.

It wasn't hard to imagine the rest, and Calista confirmed it: Greta had gotten tangled in the chains; two loose ends seemed to have wrapped around her like octopus tentacles. She looked at Calista, they locked eyes, and Calista watched as the last bubbles streamed past her friend's lips and rose for the surface, fragile containers holding her last breath.

Burning lungs forced Calista upward. She swam to the pool's edge, pulled onto the rocky ledge, and streaked to the glass separating the pools and banged and banged, trying to shatter it. Maybe a battering ram would've worked, but all she had was muscle and bone, and she pounded until she collapsed, drawing streaks of red as she slid down the barrier, her hands swollen and bleeding.

Johari reeled and stumbled back. The rest of what had

been draining from him ebbed away, leaving him hollow. He began walking off, no longer felt his arms and legs.

Brice called to him, his voice distant and muffled, "Wait, where are you going?"

"Away."

"Where?"

"It doesn't matter."

Brice and Calista caught up with him and each took one of his arms, stopping him.

"We're running out of time," Brice said. "We've got to find the exit."

The sky was visible through one of the large holes at the top of the lava tube. High up, a vulture circled. He half-expected its call to drift down to him, pulsing and insistent, like the sheep bells. It didn't, but he felt the march of time, nonetheless. In a few hours, the House would take him. But Brice and Calista still had time.

"You go. I'm done." Johari nodded toward Brice's backpack. "You still have the Lamp?"

Brice swung the pack off and, pulling out the Lamp, tried to give it to him.

"You keep it," Johari said. "Maybe it will help you get out."

Brice tried to force the Lamp into Johari's hands, but Johari pushed it back, and as Brice returned it to his pack, some feeble spark inside Johari dimmed.

Calista's grip tightened on his arm. "She wouldn't want you to do this."

"Go. You two deserve a life. You have love and each other. Get out of here while you can. There's nothing out there for me. There never was. Except one girl who swayed when she danced and carried the scent of wildflowers."

Calista shook his arm. "You've got us. Friends forever."

"I do. The best in the world. But I'd be an empty shell out there, going through the motions." He pointed to the shaft Greta had been sucked into. "The last of my life ended down there. Go, find a way out of here. I'm done."

Without a wave, he stepped like a sleepwalker toward Korounos's Pass.

FORTY-ONE

A great distance away and behind him, Brice and Calista were calling, begging him to return. Their voices faded. He was on the hilltop where the Enchanter had laid out their tasks, for Greta to silence the Elders, for Johari to get to the Lamp. Before him was Korounos's Pass, veiled in mist.

He cared little how he got here so quickly, though a small part of him thought, *A trick of the House.* It was a vague thought, no more important than, *There's an ant on the road.*

The plain stretched away to his right, the occasional moan of the Elders rising up with columns of steam. He paid them little mind. They could take him if they wanted. He walked, aware his feet moved but not feeling them, as if he'd floated out of his body and watched himself with disinterest from a remote spot.

He cared about one thing: peace. Perhaps that's what guided his steps. He would find it ahead, through the pass and beyond. Time was irrelevant. Life was irrelevant. Peace ... only peace mattered.

He walked ... the fog in the pass swallowed him.

The trail brought him to Korounos's gray and weathered hut. No smoke curled from the chimney, no light shone through the windows. A lantern and a fire would be lit soon enough. Nets would be mended, fish cleaned. He bypassed the hut, continuing along the cliff edge, until he came to the stone steps. He followed them down and stopped where the two giant chairs had been. Now there was one. He felt no surprise, nor did he care. Only one chair was needed. It was still of Olympian proportions. He sat. The chair no longer dwarfed him. He filled its dimensions like it had been hewn for him.

He watched breakers form, die, and reform in the little cove below. Fog drifted in and enveloped him. As it cleared, Korounos stood on the steps nearby, holding his net and fish pail. He put them at Johari's feet. "You've come."

"I've come," Johari replied.

"You have the birds ... the sky ... the fish ... the sea."

"... I have them ..."

Korounos raised one hand. "Goodbye, Korounos."

"Goodbye, Korounos," Johari said.

"You need nothing."

"Nothing."

With his hand still raised, another billow of fog shrouded Korounos. When it passed, he was gone.

Waves rolled in, crashing on the rocks. The sun resided in its eternal place in the gray above.

The one-legged seagull landed nearby. Without thought, Johari reached in his pocket and found a piece of raw fish. The gull ate from his hand, a large hand, weathered, gnarled like roots, with gray sprigs of hair at the knuckles. The bird finished its meal and stabbed at its feathers with its beak, grooming. It lifted its head to cry but no sound came. Vaguely, Johari was aware it held a meaning. Something tugged at his mind.

Someone.

Who...?

It didn't matter.

He felt it again, as though someone called to him.

It didn't matter. Nothing mattered. He had the rocks. Salt air filled his lungs, bringing the scent of dry and decaying seaweed. Music of the waves filled his ears.

He gazed at the black-masked birds darting in and out of the cliff holes. He had the Lamp. It burned up there, eternal and safe, for no matter who found and took it, it was always there, he was certain.

He sat back.

He waited.

He watched.

He forgot.

He was still—melding into the stone—a formation of the cliff, an interesting shape. Nothing more.

Scrabbling on the stairs sounded out of place. He turned with ponderous slowness, as a statue might that has come to life. A giant leopard sat on one of the steps, growling. Johari turned back to the sea. The leopard leaped, landed beside him, thrust its head inches from his face, and growled.

"I have nothing for you," he said.

The leopard caught his sleeve in its teeth and tugged, pulling Johari from the chair.

"Go away."

The leopard held on and dragged him to the steps.

A thought floated into his mind, as flimsy as mist. *Someone sent you. Who?*

And then a memory, just as flimsy: someone saying, "Would you come for me if I was wounded and lost and trapped in the deepest pit? Would you come for me?"

And someone else said, "I'd dive into hell to find you."

Who?

Me.

Korounos.

No, Johari.

The leopard was backing away, dragging him up the stairs.

The sun flashed. No, it was still hidden behind clouds. Light, dazzling and white, flared in his mind. "Greta! You've come for Greta!"

If the leopard was here, there was a chance. He sprang onto the beast and wrapped his arms around its neck. A moment later, the cat rushed up the steps. In a few bounds it reached the pass. In a blink, the narrow split in the mountain was behind them, and they were flying across the plain, dodging blasts of steam. Giants, stumbling through the vapor, reached blindly for him, blood running from their eyes, their faces twisted, tormented, but the leopard sailed over them, and their terrible bellows fell behind.

Before Johari could catch his breath, he was in the lava tube. The leopard raced to the vent that had taken Greta and leaped. Johari braced for impact. Last time he'd crashed against an invisible barrier trying to reach her. But the leopard passed through, taking him along.

The tube was dark. Johari was vaguely aware of the walls whizzing by. He heard the scrape and scrabble of the beast's claws on the stone floor, and felt its muscle working and the wind in his face.

It leaped through an opening into a mineshaft. Weak, bare electric bulbs glowed a sickly yellow and hung from wires strung along the ceiling. A child crying echoed off the walls. The leopard raced on, faster it seemed. Johari sank his fingers into its fur to keep from flying off. They went deeper, following railroad tracks. The lights began flickering, threatening to go out.

A mournful cry came from the cat's throat. It streaked now, urgent, doubling its efforts. Johari held his breath. His heart rushed to his throat where it stuck, filled with dread.

Suddenly they were in a limestone chamber. A pool was in the center, the water midnight blue and placid. One wall was made of glass. On the other side was an identical chamber with a pool and mine tunnel behind it. The water went right to the glass.

Johari saw it all in a heartbeat. He leaped off the leopard and dived, his eyes glued to Greta on the bottom, tangled in chains shackling a small girl beside her. Neither moved. No bubbles escaped Greta's lips. Her eyes, gazing upward, were unseeing. As were the little girl's.

He stroked, tearing at the water, throwing it behind him as if Greta were buried beneath a mountain of earth. The cold cramped his muscles. The distance between them seemed unchanging. No matter what he did, he couldn't close the gap.

The lights blinked and went out. He swam blind, nothing to guide him but memory, nothing but the terrible dead-white image of her, planted in the mud. He hit bottom, felt for her, couldn't find her. He swung right and left. How many more seconds could he hold his breath? Ten? Twenty? He was about to lunge for the surface when the lights flickered back on.

It seemed impossible that he'd missed her. She was right

beside him, an arm's length away, bobbing in his turbulence. Her eyes shone dully like sapphires and were as blank as stones.

He found the key inside the little girl's mouth, sitting on her tongue, which was as hard as wood. The key fit the lock and turned. The lock sprang open. He pulled it away, his lungs burning now, thirsting for air. He ripped at the mess of chains, untangling them, pulling them away, though she seemed so buried in them it would be impossible to reach her. As he flung them aside, the ends seemed to loop and twist back, as though they'd sprung to life and threatened to retie.

He ignored them, following the links through the bends and turns of the knots. There was only one road. The rest led nowhere, the blind alleys of a maze. His fingers flew at the chain, knowing where to go, what to do, just as he'd known which path to take after he'd found the Lamp. Strand after strand came away.

A crushing weight sat on his lungs. In another moment they would betray him, inhaling water against his will.

The last loop fell away. He swept Greta under one arm, swimming for the surface with the other, kicking desperately, the instinct to breathe searing his chest like red-hot irons, the little girl somehow clasped in Greta's lifeless hands.

The surface seemed miles away. The water froze his muscles. He cursed the cold, his lack of sleep, his fatigue. He cursed Phillip March and Sparra Givvens. He cursed Jack Bernhard for tempting Greta. He cursed himself for not stopping her. He cursed the House.

It won. He could fight no more. One breath would fill his lungs. Drowning was painful, but his whole life had been pain. Thirty, sixty seconds, and it would be over. He'd be free, another statistic, another casualty of Bertrand Welty's invention.

Far above, the lights flickered like dying stars. Through the gloom, he could see the leopard perched at the edge of the pond, peering down at him. It threw up its head and a muffled roar reached Johari's ears.

The cat was still here. That meant something. He tried to turn off his mind, to ignore his body, to turn his attention wholly on the leopard, that big ferocious part of Greta that refused to die, that roared now, full and deep, refusing to let him give up.

His will was iron ...

Don't breathe—

Don't breathe—

Don't breathe—

... but his lungs were flesh. He gasped, drawing in water just as he broke the surface. Coughing, sputtering, he one-arm paddled to the bank, where he retched water. Still hacking, he pulled Greta and the child from the pool and up onto flat rock. He drew the girl from the lifeless arms holding them and put her beside him.

Greta first. Then the girl.

It felt hard and cruel, but she was just a phantom of the House.

What next? His mind reeled, the memory of Greta performing CPR on Brice a blur. All he could do was follow his instincts. She'd taken in water. He had to get it out. He tipped her to one side. Holding her below the ribs, he lifted her up. A frighteningly small amount of water poured from her throat. There had to be more, but it wouldn't cooperate and come out on its own.

What next? Compression? Breath? What order? He had no idea. But a voice inside told him she needed to breathe. The water was in there. It had to come out. He rolled her on to her back. He put his cheek near her mouth and nose, praying he would feel a whisper of air escape her lips. Finding none, he placed two fingers on her carotid artery. He waited ten agonizing seconds and felt nothing. He pinched her nose shut, took a deep breath, and pressed his mouth over hers. Two powerful exhalations expanded her chest. His own heart seemed to have stopped as he rechecked her pulse.

The leopard let out a howl, high and mournful, which was answered ten feet away. Bird-girl squatted there, beating her chest, head thrown back, ululating with a cry that echoed in the chambers of Johari's heart.

He sifted through images of what Greta had done to revive Brice. Now it came to him. With his hands on the center of her chest, he counted off compressions. How many should he do? Twenty? Twenty-five? After thirty, there was still no pulse. He gave her two more breaths and pushed on her chest, hard enough, it seemed, that he might break bones. The absence of snapping or cracking urged him to work at her feverishly, going between breaths and compressions, feeling his arms growing weary by the second, turning to lead weights with each cycle. At last, dizzy, out of breath, he fell back, exhausted. For some minutes—how many had it been since he'd started, ten, fifteen?—it felt as if he'd been pounding on a lifeless sack. He shook her now, tears cascading from his eyes, and cried her name over and over again, as if he could call her back.

The leopard growled, teeth bared. It fixed him with its eyes, crouched, and sprang. Johari flung aside. The cat sailed through the air like an arcing arrow. Not at him. At Greta.

His mind raced. Was this a final trick of the House, for

Greta to be consumed by this beast from within her? He knew that if he threw himself on her body—even in death it was precious to him—he would be mauled to death.

A light flashed again, not the dull bulbs above, but the one inside his head, and he saw things clearly. What happened next confirmed his hunch. The leopard dived, passing through her chest and disappearing inside her as it had the boulder after returning her from the mountain.

Johari held his breath. Five, ten, fifteen agonizing seconds passed. Then with a terrible convulsion, coughing violently, water and vomit spewed from Greta's mouth.

Johari was beside her in a moment, his arms around her. She sagged against him, shivering.

When she could stand, he helped her to the pond, where she rinsed her face and mouth and drank in a breath like it was the most precious thing in the world.

"The girl," she murmured, rising unsteadily to her feet. "What happened to the girl?"

The child was sitting up, but one look at her, and he deflated. Her eyes were vacant. Bird-girl squatted beside her, poking her with a finger, trying to get a reaction. Greta and Johari knelt next to them.

She waved a hand in front of the girl's eyes. "She's blind."

"I don't think so," he replied. He lifted one of the girl's arms and let it go. It remained in the air, still as a statue.

"Catatonic?"

"Probably."

"What do we do?"

Johari thought back to his encounter with the abandoned boy. "Hold her."

Greta gathered the girl in her arms and rocked her, leaving no doubt she would be a very different mother than her own. Though Greta caressed the girl's hair and spoke soothingly, the child remained as unresponsive as a doll.

Greta stared at him, her eyes pinched and bloodshot. They both knew what rode on this. If the child didn't come around, Greta wasn't getting out of the House. Worse, if she did manage to get out, she would limp through the rest of her life with this vacant mute inside her, weighing her down.

Greta glanced toward Calista's side of the pool. "She got out. What did she do?"

Johari wracked his brain, trying to recall if Calista had mentioned what she had done when she'd brought her girl to the surface. If Calista said anything about that, he couldn't remember it.

Greta's eyes bore into his. "She must have told you something."

"Just that she brought the girl out of the pool."

"Why is it different for me?"

"I don't know." But he did know. Same trauma, different people. Different road to healing.

The lights flickered, once, twice, seven times. It wasn't fear of them going out that made Johari stiffen. It was the electric buzzing that went with them. Down here in the mine, it must be the tolling of the bell.

FORTY-TWO

The lights faded and went out. In the blackness, Johari felt for Greta and put his arms around her shoulders. She still held the child, rocking her. He knew what she was doing was fruitless. If that was going to work, it would've.

An idea was forming in his mind. He could see the elements, floating like scattered puzzle pieces. How to put them together eluded him. The darkness aided him, though. It allowed him to look at the images without distraction. One by one they fell together. When the first piece fit, the others fell in place on their own. Another flash flared in his brain, like the ones he'd had since finding the Lamp. The electric bulbs flickered, died, then flickered back on.

Greta held the child, whose eyes were still vacant. Bird-girl squatted nearby, watching intently.

Johari nodded toward her. "She can do it."

He expected her to look up at him, sad, desperate, or both. He should have known better. What he saw was the woman who had stood up to Phillip March, not giving an inch, and faced Sparra Givvens with unwavering poise.

"I'm listening," she said.

"She's got the power. She can heal her."

"I have to do this."

"You did your part."

"No, I didn't release her from the chains."

"But you brought her up, clasped in your arms. She needs something else. Something fierce." He pointed to Bird-girl. "She's part of you. That's got to count."

Realization dawned in Greta's eyes. She brought the child to the wild creature squatting on the rock, who took the tiny thing and placed her gently on a flat portion of the shore. From the leather pouch tied at her waist, she took three smaller pouches and poured out the contents—yellow powder, black powder, and a root that looked oddly like a man—in small bowl-like depressions in the rock before her. At the pool, she drew water in her cupped hands, which she sprinkled onto the powders so they were well moistened. She sang in a low voice as she worked. The song seemed part of an incantation, just as shamans had done for countless millennia.

With her fingers she mixed the yellow pile until she had a smooth paint. She did the same with the black pile. Using her knife, she peeled the skin from the root and pounded the rest into a paste with the hilt. She painted half of the girl's face yellow, the other half black, and did the same on Greta's and Johari's faces. She placed a bit of the root under the child's tongue. She ate some herself and bade Johari and Greta to eat the rest. It tasted acidic and bitter.

Her chanting started again, low and rhythmic, and Johari thought he smelled the pungent scent of wild sage, such as his Oglala Sioux ancestors used in sweat-lodge ceremonies, an herb so strong it came out your pores for days afterward.

The wild cry of a hawk echoed far up the tunnel. Johari

turned in wonder to listen, for the bird seemed to be answering the chant. When his gaze returned to the child, she was sitting up, her eyes bright and peering at Greta. Greta reached for her, but Bird-girl, still chanting, knocked her hand away and took the child in her arms.

"Please," Greta said, "let me hold her."

The Bird-girl hugged the child closer, making a barrier of her arms.

"Please ..." Greta kissed two of her fingers and extended them. This time, she was allowed to touch the child's heart. The child's lips curled in the whisper of a smile.

The hawk called again, seemed closer, behind one of the rock walls. Answering with a fierce cry, Bird-girl ran toward the wall with the child in her arms and passed through the stone as if it wasn't there. And they were gone.

Greta looked after them. "She's safe now."

"She couldn't be in better hands," Johari replied. "Greta, we're down to the wire."

She looked about her, awakening to their circumstances. "How long?"

"Less than an hour."

She paled, gazing at the tunnel sloping upward. "It'll take half that to get out of the mine."

"We're not going that way." He pointed to the wall where the girl and child had disappeared. "We're following them."

"Tell me you see something, like when we were stuck in the attic and you found a way out."

"No, but it'll work. I've been getting hunches. None have been wrong."

She took his arm. "Lead on."

FORTY-THREE

The sensation of passing through rock was like going through the attic wall that time weeks ago. A few moments of expanding molecules, a sensation like being underwater, and they were through. One look around, and Johari knew they hadn't just crossed to a passage on the other side; they had traversed a great distance, for on the cave walls were the frescoes of the prophet, liberating his followers from a dark and dismal existence, just as he'd seen in the cave when he'd left Korounos's world with the Lamp. The same curious pattern framing each mural—a repeating pattern of broken pieces surrounding a star-like symbol—tugged at Johari's memory. He still couldn't place where he'd seen it, yet he was equally convinced it was the key to something important. He asked Greta whether she'd noticed them anywhere, but she hadn't.

They followed a corridor dimly lit by torches wavering at regular intervals. The House wasn't always inhospitable, he thought wryly. But the torches gave Johari a sinking feeling, as though they would snuff out any moment, he and Greta with them. Tunnels branched off, left and right. As in Korounos's cave, he guessed these offshoots were part of an intricate maze. Still, he paused before one, feeling a strong pull to follow it. He experienced no flash of light this time (they had increasingly been a brilliant violet, as though he were looking through the most lucid and transparent amethyst). Just an urge. He hesitated a moment, then went with his gut, turning down the narrow branch, Greta following in his wake. It twisted and turned upward so often he lost his sense of direction. In a few minutes, though, they exited into a wide chamber. A gentle stream ran through it, and Brice and Calista were drinking from its waters.

Calista looked up as Greta ran up to them. "Oh my god," Calista cried. "You're alive!" She practically leaped into Greta's arms.

Brice was grinning. "Okay, you got my attention, High-tower. How'd you revive her?"

"I had help. That's why we're wearing face paint," Johari said. "I'll tell you about it sometime. Right now, we've got to get out of here."

"I'll be really impressed if you know how," Brice replied. "We're lost."

Johari studied the chamber. There was a large exit on both ends, and smaller branches along the walls. "Which one did you come through?"

Brice pointed to a nearby offshoot. For no reason Johari could justify, other than a strong intuition, he said, "Then we go that way."

Brice looked at him a moment and handed him the Lamp. "You take it. It didn't do anything for me."

Before tying the Lamp in its sack to his belt, Johari cradled it a moment in his hands. A feeling of rightness flowed into him: a sense of relief that it was back with him.

And for a moment, the cave turned that warm comforting violet.

They stepped down the passage and took another offshoot. After a few hundred feet, they ran into a dead end.

Brice looked at him questioningly. "I thought you knew where to go."

"I thought I did."

"We can't afford mistakes."

"I know."

"No, you don't know." Brice hooked a thumb toward Calista. "If she goes back to the City, your brother will kill her."

"He'll kill all of us," Johari said. And if Paul didn't get them, dogs, rats, starvation, or madness would.

His confidence rattled, he led them back to the chamber, feeling like a blind man granted five minutes of sight, only to lose it again.

He took a moment to drink by the stream, to gather his wits. The last thirty-six hours had turned his brain to mush. If he got out of here, he was going to check back into the Lakeside Grande hotel, hang the Do Not Disturb sign on the door, and sleep for a week.

This time he held the Lamp aloft. While it brightened the chamber, it didn't reveal a shortcut through rock, much less reveal which path to take. He was back to his gut. The look on everyone's faces told him they had as much confidence in him as he did. Except Greta. She gazed at him expectantly, with unwavering trust. That felt good. Darn good. And restored some of his confidence.

He narrowed it down to two paths, side by side along one of the walls. There was nothing special about either of them. In fact, they were narrower than the others, suggesting either or both might quickly peter out into another dead end. He went to one, then the other, peering in, listening, sniffing, feeling the coolness of the walls. For a reason he couldn't explain, he pointed to the left-hand path.

Calista frowned. "Why this one?"

"Do you have a better idea?" he asked.

She studied him a long moment. "You got out of the House the first time, right?"

"Yeah, with Greta."

"Good enough for me." She put on a plucky smile, but her face, as pale as chalk, said otherwise.

He led on. The path twisted and narrowed. Before long, Johari was certain what would happen. He wasn't surprised when, after one more turn, the passage dead-ended in a small chamber. What did surprise him was the cache of weapons leaning against one wall: swords, knives, spears, halberds, battle-axes.

This time, Brice slapped him affectionately on the back. "Now we're talking. I lost everything but my slingshot when I went down that chute."

The weapons gave Johari a bad feeling. Their presence suggested they would be needed, and from the number and kinds, it would not be a skirmish.

Brice stuck a sword and a dagger in his belt, then hefted one of the spears.

"Do we need all that?" Greta eyed the weapons nervously.

"It doesn't hurt to be prepared," Brice replied, examining lead pellets, heaped in a large earthenware pot, he could use for his slingshot. "Better load up."

"Fine, but hurry." Greta snatched up a short spear and stood waiting impatiently by the exit.

Calista took a javelin and turned to Johari. "Do you have any idea where to go?"

"Yes," he said, sticking a light sword in his belt. "The passage next to this one, back where we met you." What he didn't say was that they needed to find these weapons before taking the other path, and when they began going down it, his apprehension grew, though nothing radically different popped out about this offshoot, which twisted and turned like the other one. Pictograms were drawn on the walls, and rune-like symbols Johari couldn't decipher. The passage widened and sloped upward, and soon they passed other branches, some narrow, some wider than the one they followed.

Each time, Calista asked, "You sure we don't take that one?"

"I'm sure." Because the first path had been right. They would need these weapons. And that wasn't good.

Her reply was to cough, which she continued to do intermittently. Brice tore off a piece of his sleeve and tied it over her mouth.

"I don't need it; I can hold it," she said, trying to pull it away.

"Leave it. You need your hands free," he replied. So Brice sensed it too. A coming storm.

A few minutes later, the air changed to cold, damp, and musty, an odor that seemed oddly familiar, as did the passage with its occasional offshoots. Primitive paintings and symbols no longer marked the walls.

"I feel like I've been here before," Johari said. "Not this exact place, but the layout, the sharp-angle turns and the timing of the offshoots." Something was missing, though. A sound.

Brice looked around, glowering. "Me too." Realization dawned on his face. "It's the sewer. In the City."

"It can't be." Calista gestured toward the walls. "No

bricks. No concrete." But she went ashen, no doubt wondering if they'd twisted back to the City somehow. It wasn't impossible. In the House three weeks ago, the four of them had seen staircases that led right back where they'd started. If they had looped back into the City, would Welty's antidote hold? Would she and Greta succumb quickly to the illness? Or would Paul get to them first?

Brice said, "I know every turn of that place."

"Then you better guide us," Johari replied.

"Where?"

"Up. Street level."

Brice nodded and took the lead, steering them down a branch Johari would've pondered about taking.

A minute later, the missing sound reverberated through the passage: the scratch and scramble of tiny feet. It came from behind, from cracks in the walls and the ceiling, from ahead.

Calista cursed. "We're trapped. We shouldn't have gone this way."

"It wouldn't have mattered," Johari replied. "They're everywhere in the sewer. They'd find us no matter which way we went."

"Shhh." Brice held up a silencing hand and listened. Hundreds, perhaps thousands of feet scrabbled from behind, accompanied by a chorus of hungry squeals. "They're coming for us."

"How long?" Johari asked.

"A minute. Maybe two."

"Can we get to the street first?"

"We can try." Brice ran, but not so fast that he outstripped the others. He pointed to Calista's javelin. "You know how to use that thing?"

"How hard can it be?" she replied. "You thrust or swing."

"Don't throw it."

Calista's eyes hardened. "Relax, I'm not going back to the City."

Brice nodded, but he appeared worried.

The passage exited into a chamber, a crossroads of four tunnels. Torches, set too high on the walls to reach or use as a weapon, provided illumination. A hundred feet ahead, along a wall where the tunnels intersected, stones protruded, forming a ladder. Johari held the Lamp aloft. It shone on a manhole cover on the ceiling above the ladder, promising a way out. It also revealed an army of squirming bodies lining the floor's perimeter and undulating like a stream about the openings of the other tunnels.

High up, deep in the shadow of a hole along one wall, sat something the size of a small dog. Its black eyes glinted like polished obsidian.

Brice launched a pellet at it with his sling. The rat, if that's what it was, retreated into the hole, and the pellet smacked harmlessly into rock. Then Brice was running toward the ladder, bellowing for them to follow. As one, the rats came, screeching like tires on pavement. One squeezed from a crevice in the ceiling and dropped toward Brice like a paratrooper.

"Look out!" Johari cried.

Brice batted it away, sending it flying. It thwacked into one of the walls, hung there a moment, flattened, legs spread wide, and slid down. Then Brice was a whirling madman, sweeping the floor with his blade, leaving a glimmering trail of crimson in his path. They surged in a wave on the floor. More poured from cracks along the walls.

"Form a square, facing out," Brice shouted.

Greta was at his back. Calista and Johari took positions at his sides. The rats paused in a circle around them. That gave Johari a moment to return the Lamp to its bag. He'd just finished tying it to his waist, when the circle began tightening, a lasso being slowly pulled closed. Like an eight-legged creature, the four friends inched toward the ladder, the rats in front giving ground. Johari pointed his sword at the mass of milling bodies, letting them know the frontline would feel his blade first.

Calista's eyes narrowed. "Did I tell you I hate rats?"

Greta angled her spear downward. "I used to take care of one at school. I loved it."

"Good, maybe you can pet them and tell them to go away."

"This is a nightmare," Greta replied.

"No, sweetie, it's the House."

They edged toward the ladder. Johari glanced at the hole in the wall. King Rat was back and glaring at them, its power cord of a tail twitching back and forth. Whether it was a signal or not, the tail stopped. The rats attacked. Four of them dropped from the ceiling.

Johari sent them flying, one after the other, with the flat of his sword. It felt balanced, just the right size for his hands. Good thing: most of the horde was below him. Bending over, sweeping the floor with his blade, he would have tired quickly with a heavier weapon. But swords, spears, and javelins seemed wrong. Why didn't the House bless them with scythes? Unless this wasn't the only trial they would face. As he swung right and left, trying to keep the rats away, the thought that another battle lay ahead grew in his mind.

The fight became a blur, allowing only a vague impression of Greta, striving with her spear; of Calista, beginning to wheeze behind him; and of Brice, grown larger somehow, poised like a knight of old, his eyes bold and burning bright. Beneath his flickering blade, the dead sank into a writhing pool of their comrades, who feasted on them.

A drop in the bucket, Johari thought, for the rest came on, as mindless and unrelenting as the tides.

They didn't seem like separate animals. They were one giant writhing monster with thousands of heads, a creature so vast, they were seeing only a small part of it. The rest twisted down the passages into the bowels of the earth, where it resided in the deepest, darkest, dankest space. The hundred feet to the ladder seemed endless; the ladder itself a mirage that could never be reached.

Swinging their weapons, Johari's band managed to keep some of them at bay. All too soon, rats began jumping from the floor and off the shoulders of their comrades. They latched onto thighs and arms, their teeth sinking into flesh, their claws tearing at clothing. Most were content to dine where they landed. A few scurried up to reach the face and eyeballs. Johari tore them away with his free hand, felt the tail of more than one whipping his ears and cheeks.

Blood from multiple bites ran down his arms. The wounds were superficial. It was the sheer volume of them that would take its toll. A glance at Brice revealed he had fared worse. His arms glistened red. Most of that might have been rat blood, but not the streams trickling from cuts on his face. A big enough army swirled around him that even he could be taken down, bite by bite.

The number leaping on him, the ferocity of the attack, suggested they were gunning for him, so much so that Johari wondered if this was payback for Brice's domination of them in the sewers. The notion seemed ridiculous. These were not the same rats. They were manifestations of the

House, torn from one of their minds. He doubted they came from Greta. Or Calista. It had to be Brice.

But then what? As Calista had said, you weren't going to make friends with them. They were ravenous, running on instinct, as was Brice by the fury in his eyes. The rats must have felt it. They drew back, hovered a moment, cresting like a wave, and then came with a rush. They swirled about the four companions, running up their legs, raining from the ceiling.

The temperature of the sewer seemed to have risen twenty degrees. Sweat dripped from Johari's brow and into his eyes. He no longer felt the bites. He was aware, numbly, that he wore a writhing pair of rat pants, a clothing that was spreading like a magical garb from a fairy tale up his torso. Brice was already wrapped in it. He fought on, his sword a whirling fan, spraying death wherever it landed, and the bodies piled up to his knees.

Greta cried, "We can't kill them all!"

Calista's reply was drowned out in the screech and squeal of the rats.

"We survived the City," Johari shouted. "We'll survive the House. Fight, fight with everything in you!"

They did, thrusting, slashing, stabbing, stamping, bones crunching underfoot, the scent of blood filling the air, the wind from Brice's blade singing in Johari's ears, for the big fellow had become a death machine, sending a hail of rats flying from him. They weren't just fighting for their own lives; they fought for each other. In that moment, a surge of love for his companions washed over Johari. They were bonded. They were a family. Knowing that, he redoubled his efforts.

The horde gave back. Brice stormed forward, a force of nature not to be denied, clearing the cave floor to the ladder.

"You first," Brice yelled to Johari, when they joined him. "Then the girls."

"You can't face them alone."

"Don't argue." Brice hoisted Johari up with one hand and thrust him onto the ladder, even as his sword defended with the other hand.

"They'll shred you."

"The manhole," Brice said. "Quick!"

Brice was right. Neither Greta nor Calista could lift the metal lid. Johari scurried up the ladder and pushed at the manhole, while Calista and Greta followed.

"Hurry," Calista cried. "Before they take him."

Johari slid the cover aside. He glanced down. Brice was crashing against the wall, crushing rats that had climbed up his back.

Johari pulled out of the sewer. With rats still hanging on his arms and legs, he extended a hand first to Calista, then to Greta, helping them out. Brice followed a moment later and slammed the cover in place. The remaining rats, separated from the horde below, gave up the fight. They dropped off and scurried away.

Johari leaned on his knees, catching his breath. When he rose, Calista was tending to Brice, blotting away blood with the piece of sleeve he'd given her. Rats had not only bitten him, they'd clawed, shredding his clothes and making a mess of the exposed flesh. Johari, Greta, and Calista had bites on their arms and necks, but nothing like what Brice had suffered.

An echo turned Johari's attention to his surroundings. He'd expected the street level of the City. Here it all was, the streets, the ruins, the fragments of stone, brick, and concrete. What he didn't expect was what came with it. Just as the tunnels below had taken on the layout of the sewer, this place was also the cavern where he'd faced a ball of fire, drinking in the flames, and where, as a boy of ten that first time in the House, he'd seen his brother torn to pieces by witches. The City and the cavern were like a double exposure. The columns of the cavern were the fallen buildings of the City. The cavern chamber was the central park where he'd first seen the mob; the tunnels the witches had streamed from were the streets leading to the central square.

And he knew what was coming for them with terrifying speed.

FORTY-FOUR

The dogs. The pack was still in the tunnel, but started howling like banshees, evidence they'd caught the scent.

"Tell me *now* this isn't the City," Calista said as the four of them ran.

"If we don't get out of here," Johari replied, "it will be." Because the House would send them there fast enough.

The hounds streamed from the tunnel, jaws grinning, forepaws eating up ground. A hundred yards separated them from Johari's group.

"Where to?" Brice asked.

Johari had no idea. Not only did he have no violet flashes, he searched inside for that thrilling feeling in his gut when he just *knew*. He got nothing. It had completely deserted him.

A clamor of voices made him glance back. A mob rushed from the tunnel the dogs had come from. They seemed to fly like the wind, wielding clubs and pipes, their ragged clothes whipping behind. One tripped and fell, revealing a black flame painted on his back. Johari didn't have to see it to know which mob this was. At the apex of the throng, dog paws swinging from his hood, was Paul.

Calista, wheezing but keeping up gamely, said, "And that's not Lightfighter?"

Johari wondered the same thing. Had his brother found a way to slip through the doorway between the City and the House? Bent on vengeance, had he brought rats, dogs, and followers with him? It didn't seem possible. Only the four of them had made it over the bridge. And that had collapsed.

"If it's him," Calista said, "he'll roast me alive. He's not beyond it."

Brice, running beside them, thrust the air with his sword. "I'll plant this in his heart first."

Greta flashed a worried glance at Johari.

He saw it plain as day, the sword cleaving a face, not the rabid megalomaniac of the City, the beautiful kind loving face, the one bright light in a childhood filled with neglect: Paul. A sick feeling clawed inside Johari's stomach. He struggled a moment—aware that Calista stared fixedly at him, then, "It's not Paul," he said to Brice. "It's the House. Do what you have to."

Half starved, the dogs' skin was parchment thin, their rib and shoulder bones protruded, their spines coiled and stretched like springs, and they'd cut the distance to forty feet.

Johari's mind raced, searching for an escape route, a plan, anything that offered a chance. He saw now that the similarity to the City was no greater than a stage set. The ruins had no doors. There was no inside to the crumbling buildings where they might lose their pursuers. They could dart into one of the tunnels, but then what? What lurked in the shadows, waiting to pounce? More dogs? More red-eyed devils? Fighting was a last option. They were woefully outnumbered. It seemed all they could do was flee and hope they didn't run into a dead end.

The dogs closed the gap to thirty feet.

Drumming echoed from a tunnel to Johari's left. It drew closer, near enough that vibrations ran all the way up his legs, made his teeth rattle, and a clammy sheen of sweat made his shirt cling to his back.

Greta's eyes narrowed at the sound. Her grip on the spear tightened. Even the dogs seemed to slow and looked uncertainly at the opening to the tunnel. It looked no different than the others. Roughly shaped like arches, they were dark passages. But the one echoing with thunder flickered with light. A moment later, mane flying, Millie shot from the tunnel, hauling the wagon. The Enchanter sat on the driver's seat, holding the reins in one hand. In his other hand, he held his rattle, flames leaping from the top like a roman candle.

Bouncing and rattling, he streaked toward them. "Jump on!" he shouted when he neared them.

He slowed the wagon enough for them to run beside it, then jammed the rattle in a holder and dropped the reins. Leaning over, he seized one of Greta's hands—she clutched her spear in the other—and hauled her onto the step.

The wagon pitched sharply as a wheel jounced over a rock. Greta swayed. Johari's heart leaped into his mouth. But she held on to the Enchanter, steadied herself, scooted along the footrest, and dropped to the seat beside him.

The grate and scrape of the dogs drew near. But Johari focused on the wagon. He didn't like that step one bit. Brice must have felt the same. Arms outstretched, he followed Calista closely, prepared to catch her if she fell as she was drawn up gripping her javelin in one hand. She teetered, seemed she would slip through the Enchanter's fingers, but righting herself, soon slid in between him and Greta.

Brice leaped onto the side, grabbing the handles of the double window covers, and then swung to the roof with the grace of a gymnast.

To make space for Johari, Greta had slid along the floor-board to the far left of the wagon and then perched on the step. The dogs were close enough that Johari could see foam gleaming on their canines. The stench of their breath struck his nose.

The Enchanter snatched up his rattle. Johari grabbed his free hand, surprised at the strength he found there. As he jumped aboard and sat, the Enchanter threw the rattle. It tumbled through the air, flames shooting. The handle pierced the ground like a spear. The vibration from the impact ran up the haft, rattling the rattle. The world revolved a hundred eighty degrees. Johari clutched the seat. His stomach flew to the ceiling. They should be falling in a rain of dogs, wagon, and horse, but gravity stayed in the direction of their bodies. The world changed with the turn to the basement of the House, a vast limitless basement.

And simultaneously the crossroads. Just as the cavern was also the sewer or the streets of the City in double exposure.

Millie raced full tilt, the bouncing wagon sending up clouds of dust. Paul, his followers, and the dogs were gone.

Someone else chased them on horseback, leaning, whip-ping his ride, hat pulled low, claret scar etched into his cheek.

No. Not him. Not now!

FORTY-FIVE

It was Muloch, the killer who had stolen the Enchanter's shells, the cutthroat Johari had plied with drink in the tavern.

Despite the rocking of the wagon, Johari stood and watched with dismay at the unfolding tableau behind him. Riding furiously, his arm bandaged and crimson where Johari had stabbed him, Muloch notched an arrow and drew back the bowstring, aiming at Greta.

"Duck!" Johari pulled her toward him.

An arrow struck the step where she'd been standing, spurring her to scramble onto the footrest and grip the lip of the seat to keep from flying off.

Muloch was already pulling back another arrow, this time aiming at Brice, who was firing his slingshot. The pellet whizzed by Muloch's head. Muloch's arrow thudded an inch from Brice's knee.

"You can't stay there!" Johari held his hand out to Brice.

Brice launched another shot. "There isn't room."

"Get inside the wagon."

"Not while it's moving."

He was right. Leaning over the side, opening the window, and going through headfirst would be a miracle with the wagon bouncing and rocking full throttle. Worse, Brice would be defenseless.

"He's a sitting duck," Johari exclaimed.

The Enchanter urged Millie with a snap of the reins. "I know."

"Why did you bring us here?"

Another arrow smacked the wagon, drawing an oath from Brice.

The Enchanter hung his head like a scolded schoolboy. "I didn't, child. It be bad business. Very bad unfinished business."

Johari didn't think so. Muloch didn't belong to the four of them. He was a wildcard, a roaming shadow left by an earlier visitor to the House. Hell, for all Johari knew, the killer came from Sparra Givvens.

"Do something," he yelled. "Pull one of your tricks."

The Enchanter brightened. He handed the reins to Johari, then laid one hand over Johari's forearm and gave it an encouraging squeeze, the way a parent would. "I be going. But not to worry, child, the magic be inside you now, whispering in your heart."

A wild plan was hatching in Johari's mind. And he had a pretty good idea the Enchanter knew what it was. If he was right, the Enchanter was part of him the way Bird-girl was part of Greta. "Wait. Give more. You know what I want."

"I know ..." The Enchanter's eyes twinkled. He leaned and whispered in Johari's ear.

"It'll work?"

The Enchanter threw back his head and laughed, making the little moon tokens hanging from his hat swing and flash. "It will. Good luck, Johari Hightower. You have the Lamp. You be a powerful sorcerer now."

He grabbed his bag of shells, mumbled a few words in a strange tongue, and swung the open sack out in an arc. Shells streamed out, hundreds, thousands, far more than could ever fit in the bag, spinning and as golden as coins. They fell to the ground where they evaporated. Vapor rose in a thick cloud. Just before visibility reached zero, the Enchanter disappeared.

And Johari saw his chance.

FORTY-SIX

The steps leading from the basement to the kitchen of the House were just ahead. Johari raced Millie in that direction. In a few words, he told Greta his plan as she dropped to the seat beside him.

"It's crazy!" she cried.

"It's our only chance." Johari shook the reins, urging Millie on. It *was* crazy. But the Enchanter had given him magic. He had to believe it would work.

She clutched his sleeve. "I won't leave you."

"You have to."

She turned eyes so mournful and piteous on him he almost caved. But they were well-nigh the stairs. On the roof, looming behind her, Brice grasped her shoulders, making it clear he would carry her to the kitchen if he had to. She pushed him away, threw her arms around Johari, and crushed her lips to his. For a thrilling moment it seemed she'd poured her soul into his.

Johari slowed the wagon as much as he dared so everyone could leap off. As they dashed up the steps, he sent Millie flying.

He drove blind, trusting her instincts to avoid obstacles. The basement here was filled with mountains of boxes, rusty tools, old books. The fog began to clear. An old-fashioned washer came into view. It lay on its side, the wooden rollers cracked. An old mattress leaned at a low angle against one of the wooden pillars. As before, the layout mirrored the countryside they'd first trundled through with the Enchanter. The wooden pillars were trees. The mounds of junk were boulders. All in double exposure with the basement. But those rocks looked solid enough.

Johari had no time to reflect on the meaning of this. The thunder of hooves came from behind. He glanced back. Muloch rode alongside the wagon. His eyes, sharp as knife-points, fixed on Johari. His horse slowed, dropping back. Johari heard a thump. Muloch must've jumped onto the wagon.

Good, he thought. *This will work even better.*

Boots drummed across the top of the wagon. Johari rose. Muloch loomed above him, sword raised.

"Pretty Millie!" Johari cried.

Millie twisted left and sat. The holdbacks, traces, and shafts hitching her to the wagon disappeared. But not before her action swung it around.

Johari leaped. He landed on the mattress, cradling the Lamp at his side. The wagon leaned on two wheels, skidded with a shriek, and crashed into one of the boulders.

He sprang up and bolted for the stairs. He glanced back when he reached them. Muloch was staggering up from a pile of shattered wood and wagon pieces. He drilled Johari with his eyes and started limping toward him, his sword swinging with each step. Johari dashed up the stairs. When he reached the kitchen, he slammed the door shut.

His friends waited nearby.

Greta rushed toward him. "Oh my god! Are you all right!"

"Fine. Muloch's coming! Grab something. Block the door."

He angled a kitchen chair beneath the doorknob, and then they leaned the small kitchen table and the other chair over that. He wished there were more; he could still see part of the doorknob and most of the door above.

Two sounds followed, one after the other. The first came from the kitchen cabinet. No mistaking it: the scratch and scuttle of tiny feet; the hungry squeal of little mouths. And the dozens of bites on Johari's arms and legs, forgotten in the heat of the last minutes, began to burn and bleed.

Before he could react, another sound came. The basement door rattled. A moment later, Muloch's sword thrust through the wood above the doorknob.

"Quick," Johari said. "The back door!"

They rushed to the mudroom and tried the door leading to the back porch. It was locked. Brice rammed into it like an offensive tackle. It was sealed, as impenetrable as the vent Greta had been sucked into in the lava tube.

Another blow struck the basement door.

"Now what?" Calista cried.

"The front door!" Johari urged them into the kitchen. The cabinets were swelling, distorting like funhouse mirrors. One of the doors burst open. Boxes of cereal tumbled out. Cans of soup, beans, and vegetables rolled from shelves, teeming with rats. They jumped to the counter and leaped to the floor.

Greta stormed forward with her spear, her eyes flashing, leopard wild. She sent dozens of rats flying.

Calista was just as determined. With each thrust of her javelin, she shouted, "I'm not. Going. Back. To the City!"

After their first journey to those dog- and mob-infested ruins, it was all too clear how quickly Greta might succumb to illness if she returned there. Johari would die before he let that happen. Gripping his sword, he batted away attackers like they were tennis balls. Brice was with him, forming a rear guard, swinging his blade with deadly accuracy.

They found the entry to the dining room as locked as the back door. The only way to the front entrance was through the pantry. Just before they entered it, two blows struck the basement door in quick succession. Johari glanced back. Muloch's sword had knocked the table down. His dark and wrathful face was visible through holes he'd opened in the wood.

No time to worry about that. The pantry posed a bigger problem. Shelves lining the walls from floor to ceiling were crawling with screeching gray bodies. They launched, their little arms and legs spread like skydivers. A wave of rats surged in on the floor from the kitchen. Johari's group would be covered in seconds. But fighting in close quarters was to their advantage and kept most of the rats from the kitchen trapped behind the front lines. No need to go deep inside the pantry. A turn to the right, three quick steps, and they were in the dining room.

The top of the long foyer leading to the front entrance was to their left. Twenty-five feet to freedom.

If they could open it. And he had a strong hunch they could. The Enchanter had taken them toward the kitchen stairs. Not away from it. He wanted them to go up.

Johari grabbed Greta's hand. Together they ran, closing the gap. Get to the sunshine and the strawberry fields beyond, and the rats and Muloch would disappear. Her hand was hot and sweaty, but it fit like it had been made for his.

They were two steps from the front door. Her hand wrenched away. Johari couldn't fathom what he was seeing. Her arm outstretched to him, she seemed to be rushing away like she was on a bullet train. Back the way they'd come.

He tried to run after her but was flying just as fast in the opposite direction, while Brice and Calista were hurtling apart toward opposite foyer walls.

Then it hit him. The House was stretching into a plain. And another double exposure. The walls were boulders. On the right, from gaps between the giant rocks, the dog pack streamed. On the left, where the entrance to the second-floor staircase should've been, Paul's mob came charging.

Johari raced, trying to close the gap between him and Greta. The distance grew with each step. This wasn't getting him anywhere. He had to make it all stop. But how? Givvens had disabled the fail-safes.

Before he could think further, he slammed into something hard. He crumpled to the ground, head spinning. A seagull squawked, one, two, three times, faint but persistent.

Woozy, wobbling like a floored boxer, he rose, certain of one thing. The bird was calling the final countdown, not for him, nor for Brice and Calista.

For Greta. She'd entered the House first, almost twenty-four hours ago.

The expanding plain had hurtled him into the front door. Holding his breath, he tried the knob. It wouldn't turn.

There had to be another step. One more thing to do. His eyes locked on the strange symbol carved on the door. It still made no sense.

In double exposure, Korounos appeared beyond the door, the cliff and the gray sky of his world behind him. He reached out to Johari. "Come, Korounos ... To the sea, the rocks, the birds."

The pull was magnetic. It would all be over. No more hurt, no more betrayals. Just peace, sweet and endless. He understood now what would happen. The House would send Greta, Brice, and Calista to the City. He would spend eternity as the lord of nets and lonely coastline.

He glanced back. The battle raged behind him. Brice was covered head to foot with rats. He swung right and left, trying to pull them off. Their leader sat like a small dog on a nearby rock, a gray god towering over his horde. Its eyes burned, pinpointed on Brice. It leaped. Struggling, Brice went down, buried beneath an avalanche of rats.

The pack had Calista pinned to a rock wall. One of the dogs was leaping, its jaws open, its teeth inches from her throat.

Muloch reared behind Greta, his arm locked around her, his sword at her throat.

Korounos was calling.

The gull, circling in the cloud-clad sky, bawled.

Four seconds—

Three—

A voice spoke—not Korounos, the Enchanter!—the one who whispered in his heart: "It's the magic that releases us."

Violet burst across Johari's vision, brighter than the sun, and quickly cleared. And it all fell into place.

The symbol on the door—

The symbol on the wainscoting—

The symbol on the frescoes in Korounos's cave depicting a man and his people finding a way from darkness to light—

The symbol was not a star drawing pieces toward it. It was thrusting them apart. He had the power with him, awesome and unstoppable, as indomitable as a mountain before a breath of wind, as unceasing as the rhythms of the ocean.

The Lamp!

He ripped it from the bag at his belt.

The seagull cried twice. One precious second. All that remained.

Johari reared back, pivoting. Then he slammed the Lamp with all his strength into the symbol on the door. A riot of color burst from the Lamp and rained down like fragments of the sun. No time to dodge them—two drops fell into his eyes, burning, searing like hot oil. In a blur, he saw the House shake, the walls crack, plaster and dust falling, the door exploding to flinders.

He rushed out.

FORTY-SEVEN

Johari found himself on his hands and knees. New shoots of grass, cool and dew laden, wet his fingers and seeped through his pants.

It must've rained last night, he thought.

Air—sweet, fresh, and heavy with the scent of ripe strawberries—caressed his face. A song sparrow caroled close by. He tore out blades of grass and pressed them against his eyes, longing to cool them. When at last he looked about him, the world was recognizable but out of focus, like a blurry photograph.

A deafening roar from behind turned him back to the House. The walls were swaying, crumbling inward. The conical towers were falling. Smoke and dust billowed, obscuring the porch.

Greta!

He lurched to his feet. He stumbled toward the rising cloud where the House had been. He collapsed to the ground, his legs jelly beneath him. He clawed at the grass, straining to rise.

Ghostly, someone staggered through the smoke. No,

there were two of them. It was Brice, tottering down what was left of the porch stairs, carrying Calista in his arms, her hands clasped around his neck. At the bottom, he sank to his knees and put her down, gently. They both turned, looking back at the House.

The House trembled, as if trying to hold itself together. The chimney still stood, and some of the outer walls. As the smoke cleared, the second-floor steps appeared, leading nowhere.

Johari forced himself up. He reeled. He fell. He rose. He tilted. He dragged one foot after the other, two weak soldiers putting up a last fight, and collapsed beside Brice and Calista.

"Is she alive?" he gasped. "Did you see her?"

They hadn't.

The House shook violently, as though an earthquake rolled the foundation. It was gearing up for something. Johari could feel it. He rose, stumbled forward.

Brice locked on to him. "It's too late."

Johari tore away. He stumbled onward, moving slow, too slow. With a deep rumble, something exploded. A hot blast knocked him from his feet.

Dazed, numb, helpless to move, he looked up. The remaining walls fell, one by one. Flames shot up, hot and red behind columns of smoke. Ten, twenty seconds ticked by, each endless and empty.

He was fading, the world with him. Just before he lost consciousness, he saw her as in a dream, running through crimson smoke with the fleet stride of a leopard.

FORTY-EIGHT

The pungent aroma of liniment filled Johari's nose, prodding him awake. Something thick covered his eyes. His fingers found bandages, then touched the sheet, the light blanket pulled to his chest, and the pillow propping up his head. He sensed someone nearby.

"Who's there?"

Warm fingers slipped into his, fitting inside his perfectly, and then another hand folded over his.

His whole body relaxed. "Greta." Her name was sweet on his lips. He held her hand tight. "You survived. I thought I dreamed it."

"I told you," she said with a laugh as musical as a stream, "we all get out."

"Then Brice and Calista? I didn't imagine that either?"

"They're in the next room."

"Then we're out? This isn't another trick?" He began to sit up, tense.

She pressed him gently back. "We're out."

"Good … that's good." He sank into the pillow. "How long have I been asleep?"

She laughed again. "Sixteen hours."

That made sense. He'd been up almost forty-eight. Still, it sounded like a lot and he gave a little whistle. "I could sleep another sixteen." He put his other hand over hers and clasped it. "It feels good to hold you."

"Scoot over." She climbed into bed bedside him and nestled her head beneath his chin. It fit there, the way their hands fit. She'd washed the stench of the City from her hair; it was as soft as down. Her scent, more alluring than any perfume, mixed with the odor of the liniment, reminding him of the bandages.

"My eyes ... Are they all right?"

"The doctor thinks so," she murmured, yawned. "We'll know ... when he takes them off."

"You've been here, awake the whole time."

"I think I dozed ..." She snuggled closer and her breathing fell into the light stirrings of sleep. His rhythm matched hers. Soon he joined her.

Johari sat up in the bed. Brice and Calista had joined them. The doctor was due any minute to remove the eye bandages.

"Explain this again," he said to Brice. "We're in a military compound?"

"Yes," Brice replied.

"Run by your father, kept secret from the government."

"Kept secret from me," Brice said dryly.

"And we're here why?"

"You brought down the House, sport. Sparra Givvens won't be happy."

No, and Phillip March wouldn't be either. The way

Brice explained it, at this point, no one knew Johari was responsible. But blame had a way of finding him, even if he was innocent.

He'd been kidnapped from his bed, thrown into a cell, and hours away from passing through the gray door across the prison corridor, never to return. Courtesy of March, no doubt. March, who right now would be scouring the country looking for him, itching to pin the "bombing" of the House on him. Though each city had a House, all of them were considered sacred. No slap on the wrist for destroying Grafton's.

The door to the room opened, letting in distant conversation, and then closed.

"So I'm a prisoner here?" Johari asked.

A new voice said, "You're here for your safety."

Johari recognized it at once. The man he'd met in the hotel room. Brice's father—Jack Bernhard.

Johari said, "No thanks. I'm allergic to being cooped up. As soon as these bandages are off, I'm out of here."

"That would not be wise," Bernhard said. "Your face is plastered all over the media."

Johari's jaw tightened. "I thought they didn't have a suspect."

Bernhard continued. "They don't. Not officially. You're being advertised as a missing person. There's a hefty reward for information leading to your recovery."

"Fine, I'll walk into a police station. Found. End of problem."

"That would also not be wise. I pulled you from prison once. Twice may not be a charm."

He was right, of course. March didn't need official channels. If he could make Johari disappear once, he could do it again.

Bernhard said, "Patience, my friend. And rest. When the time is right, we'll figure a way."

Johari slumped back on the pillow. "Sorry I didn't bring you Welty."

"You tried. Here's the doctor. Let's see about your eyes."

Johari had thought little about them. He'd been relishing his time with Greta. After they'd awakened, they'd talked quietly. Mostly, though, they'd just held on to each other, jealously stealing time, which had been at a premium since they'd met. Now that the doctor was here, the possibility loomed that Johari might be blind.

The doctor introduced himself—a name Johari promptly forgot in his worry about his condition—and then asked, "How are you feeling? Any pain?"

"No."

The bandages started coming off.

"Any sensations of light?"

He'd been seeing flashes like he'd had in the House. He didn't think that qualified. Otherwise, everything was dark, but two thick pads covered his eyelids, and the bandages were wrapped pretty thick.

He reached out. "Greta, where's Greta?"

Fingers slipped into his. "Right here."

"Will you love me if I'm not a mummy?" he asked.

She chuckled. "I don't know. It was growing on me."

The last of the bandages fell away.

"I'm just going to remove the tape holding the dressing," the doctor said. "The surrounding skin is burned. It might hurt a little. Are you ready?"

Johari nodded. The pads came away. A cool breeze from an open window caressed his face. It felt good, like his skin could finally breathe.

"Open your eyes," the doctor said. "Go slow."

Johari did.

"Can you see anything?"

Everything was a blur. He saw four forms, one close, bending toward him. That would be the doctor. A smaller one, standing on the far side of the bed, would be Calista. The two out-of-focus giants would be Brice and Jack Bernhard. Sitting next to Johari, squeezing his hand, so close he could feel her breath, had to be Greta. He wondered numbly what it would be like to never look on her again.

Her hand trembled in his. She was waiting to hear. They all were.

He turned back to the giant closest to Calista. "That yacht's waiting, Brice."

Greta gasped.

"Nice try," Brice replied. His voice came from the other large smudge. "Can you see anything?"

"You're pretty, in a fuzzy sort of way."

"Works for me."

Greta asked the doctor, "Will it improve?"

The doctor bent close and shone a light into Johari's eyes. "It's good he's seeing something. Hopefully, with time ... Things do get better."

Things did. Greta thought he needed stronger medicine than the eyedrops he received twice a day. She took him outside, leading him along paths and through the trees. For once, little needed to be said. She was here. That's all that mattered.

Vision was a relative thing. He saw blue. He saw green. Sky was sky; trees were trees; fields were golden from summer. Some things didn't need to be in focus. You just felt them.

She told him that from the outside, Jack Bernhard's compound was a sprawling ranch—horse corrals, a grove of apple and plum trees, a meadow where deer grazed, a garden near the house. The barracks, weapons, and training facility were underground. He wouldn't say what all this was for, but it didn't take a genius to figure out the man was either expecting a war or planning to make one. He'd as much as told Johari that the world according to Sparra Givvens was bad for business, and Jack Bernhard, if nothing else, wanted profits.

The billionaire was clear about Brice, though. He promised as many surgeries as were needed. Brice had the first one there on the ranch. He wasn't impressed. As far as he was concerned, his father wasn't motivated by love. Brice's sister wasn't considered a suitable candidate to run the empire when dear old dad kicked the bucket. So Brice was it—though he confided confidentially to Johari and Greta that he wasn't sure he would step into the role—and the face of the company needed a face.

It took a lot more to convince Jack to get a message to Cody Gilbert. Johari argued his attorney was bound by confidentiality. Besides, if Johari wasn't a prisoner here, he could just walk out if he wanted to. He could understand the agony Greta's dad would be going through, and Cody could get a message to him.

A glacier would slide more in a year than Jack Bernhard. In the end, it was Greta who pulled out the trump card. She revealed she'd copied most of Welty's computer files. She would turn them over if Jack agreed to let them contact a few people.

Jack caved, promising to deliver the following note to

Cody: "We're all right. Need to stay low awhile. Let Dannie and Dean Orngold know, but no one breathe a word. Destroy this note. Watch your back. March has a long reach. Yours, Johari and Greta."

With a platoon of soldiers around him, Bernhard could've forced the files from Greta, but if nothing else, he had business ethics. A contract was a contract. Johari and Greta had done their part, risking their lives in the House. It came as no surprise, then, that Johari was rewarded with the rest of the file about his parents. He tossed it aside.

"Don't you want me to read it to you?" Greta asked.

"No," he replied. "I don't want to think another second about any of that stuff."

"Then we won't."

She led him outside, down the paths, through the trees. Yellow was yellow. Dappled sunlight was dappled sunlight. They lay down in a glade. All was quiet save for birds singing in the boughs and a soft breeze rustling the leaves. She leaned close. Her hair brushed his cheek and ran across his eyes.

He took her in his arms. "God, you feel good. You aren't planning to leave?"

"Never."

"No more adventures?"

"Everything I want is here."

But there was another adventure, and no way of ducking it. Paul was still in the City. When the time was right, they would return for him, Johari's eyes allowing.

For now, there was nothing but the thrill of her lips on his and the crushed leaves of autumn beneath them.

AUTHOR'S NOTE

Did you enjoy this book? It would mean the world to me if you took two minutes to share your thoughts about it in a review on the site you purchased it from. Or send me send me an email with your honest feedback.

Your input helps me provide the best quality books and helps other readers like you discover great reads.

Thanks!

A. R. Silverberry

Email: contact@arsilverberry.com

Review Link US Amazon: https://www.amazon.com/review/create-review?&asin=B0F2CT9FS5

Review Link Everywhere Else: https://books2read.com/u/4jxovv

Silverberry Website Link: www.arsilverberry.com/contacty

AVAILABLE NOW!

SHADOW WORLD

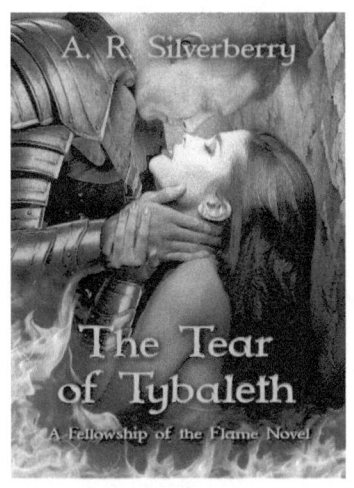

The Tear of Tybaleth

The Fellowship of the Flame Book 1

THE FATE OF A KINGDOM

HANGS ON THE EDGE OF HER BLADE ...

The Treasure of Trenton

The Fellowship of the Flame Book 2

DARK ENCHANTMENT HIDES A SECRET ...

Also By A. R. Silverberry

The Fellowship of the Flame, A Prequel Novella

Cerberus, Tales of Magic and Malice

Wyndano's Cloak

The Stream

ABOUT THE AUTHOR

Adler wouldn't do—I needed the right handle to go where I was going. Silverberry unlocked the magic door. Now I quest through the limitless realms of the imagination, here, official scribe to bold knights and treacherous kings, there, intrepid recorder of the future and the far reaches of outer space. Wherever I land, I promise to hold nothing back.

If you'd like to know about all things in the Silverberry-verse, signup for my newsletter at the link below. You'll receive a free copy of my short story collection, *Cerberus, Tales of Magic and Malice*!

Newsletter Signup!
https://www.arsilverberry.com/contact

ABOUT TREE TUNNEL PRESS

Tree Tunnel Press is an award-winning publisher of fiction and nonfiction, including *I Love Birds, An Enchanting Coloring Book,* featuring twelve beautiful hand-drawn illustrations of birds. We create products that entertain, encourage, and inspire. Requests for rights or permissions should be directed to: Tree Tunnel Press, P.O. Box 733 Capitola, CA 95010

Visit our website, www.treetunnelpress.com, to purchase books and for more information.